OFF KEY

WHISPERING KEY
BOOK 3

MAY ARCHER

Cover Art: Cate Ashwood Designs
Cover Photo: Wander Aguiar
Editing: One Love Editing
Beta Reading: Leslie Copeland, Molly Maddox, Lucy Lennox, Neve Wilder, Chelsea Bell
Proofreading: Victoria Rothenberg, Lori Parks

All the good bits are theirs, and any mistakes are my own!

PROLOGUE
JAY

Eleven years ago

"Twenty bucks says I can swim over to the rocks at the Point faster than you."

Rafe Goodman—all six foot something of him splayed out facedown on a beach towel so tiny it left most of his legs in the sand—turned his head toward me. A big hank of damp brown hair fell across his forehead as he lifted one eyelid only halfway, like the sunshine and salt air had stolen the energy he'd need to open his eyes fully. "Twenty? Did you take lessons overnight or something? 'Cause I *just* won ten dollars off you yesterday swimming that exact same distance."

"That was a one-off." I waved a hand. "You can't win 'em all. The law of averages says so. Also, yesterday we raced in the morning. Now it's afternoon."

He grinned up at me, his teeth a stunning flash of white against his golden skin, and propped himself up on one elbow so he could run his fingers idly over the strings of the guitar cradled in my lap. "You swim faster in the afternoon, is that it? Like the inverse of the early bird getting the worm? You're an afternoon bird..."

"No." I shuddered. "Do not compare me to one of those horror movie rejects."

Rafe pushed his lips together and nodded solemnly. "My bad."

Rafe knew—was maybe the only one who knew—about The Terrifying Seagull Incident from six summers ago, when I'd spilled a bag of chips on the dock outside the Goodmen Outfitters Tours office in the center of Whispering Key. The way I remembered the story, I'd barely processed dropping the bag before an entire phalanx of winged creatures dive-bombed me, cawing and shrieking. It had been as terrifying as anything Alfred Hitchcock ever dreamed up... and the fuckers had taken my Cool Ranch Doritos, too, which had been more annoying than traumatizing, but still.

Rafe flipped onto his back and stacked his hands behind his head, supremely unconcerned that his legs were covered with sand or that his broad, tanned chest gleamed in the sunshine. His gaze held mine. "Forget the money," he said softly. "If I win, I want a song."

Oof. The guy made me feel warm all over when he looked at me like that. Made me think thoughts and dream dreams... and write songs that were all about him.

Chill out, Jay.

I clutched the neck of my old guitar and made myself stare up and down the empty beach until I was able to swallow down all those sappy feelings. I had already thought things through and decided not to tell a soul about my sexuality, including Rafe. I couldn't be out and do all the things I wanted to do with my life.

"*Pssht*. You hear me play all the time! That's not a payment for a bet. Shit, sometimes I think my dad would pay me to stop playing entirely."

"Because your dad is incompetent with anything that doesn't have a dollar sign in front of it… whereas *my* family can't deal with anything that *does* have a dollar sign in front of it. Families, Rollins. Pick your poison," Rafe drawled.

I huffed out a laugh. He wasn't wrong. Rafe's mom liked to say the Goodmans were "rich in ways that didn't involve money." And it was also true that I talked to my dad as little as possible and never about anything that mattered. Neither of these situations was ideal. But though I knew better than to ever say it out loud, if I had to pick a poison, I'd pick Rafe's.

I mean, yeah, he was in college on a scholarship, rather than having his parents pay tuition like mine did. And yes, Rafe had worked five shifts a week at their family's tour boat business all summer, basically for free. And yeah, the Goodmans lived in a small house on Whispering Key rather than having a three-floor showplace in Rock Gulch, Alabama, *plus* a summer cottage on the Key, like my dad and my stepmom, Belinda. And it was also true that Rafe was pretty much expected to come home after college and keep working for Goodmen Outfitters Tours.

But when Rafe had come out as bisexual in high school and his brothers had come out as gay, too, everyone on Whispering Key had taken the news without a blink. Rafe's mom had gotten a pride flag somewhere, and his dad had constructed a flagpole to hang it from the front porch for her, and that was that. His parents wanted him around, and they accepted him as he was.

Me, on the other hand? I didn't have a place where I fit, except during these summers with Rafe. I'd figured out years ago that the only thing I was good at was playing music, which was handy since it was a thing I loved, but my dad refused to accept it. He wanted some alternate-me he'd envisioned when I was born, the son he'd christened for his grandpa Jay and his grandpa Don, who'd become a legacy member of the Rock Gulch Country Club. And once a semester, like clockwork, he called to tell me what a disappointment I was and not to expect financial support from him if I didn't give up my silly dreams.

Ironically, my dad's doubts made me a hundred billion percent more determined to make those "silly dreams" happen, no matter what I had to sacrifice... including the possibility of having a relationship.

I mean, it wasn't like I was fighting off potential relationships anyway, you know? The world was full of hot guys, but I'd only ever wanted *one*... one who'd never shown any indication he was attracted to me in the slightest. And as I looked down at that man, I had to remind myself to pretend I wasn't soaking in every detail of his face, his body, his *presence*, because the last thing I wanted to do was make our friendship awkward.

"Hey." Rafe nudged my knee with the palm of his hand, and his fingers brushed my thigh—a total accident, but so fucking thrilling I committed it to memory. "What's wrong?"

"Oh... just thinking. You know, sometimes I feel like you're the only one who believes in me and my music."

"No way," Rafe immediately denied. "Everyone who hears your stuff loves it. You know how much *I* love it. Even my dad thinks you're incredibly talented, and I'm not sure he's really liked anyone since Duran Duran. Plus, I happen to know your sister thinks you're amazing."

I felt my face go warm, basking in his approval.

"Aimee's biased," I argued. "She loves me, and she's loyal. She'd think I was great no matter what."

Since our mom had died back when Aimee was a preschooler and I was all of seven, I'd tried to look out for her. I wanted to shield her from Dad's lack of attention and Belinda's quest to turn her into a mini church lady. She was a pretty cool kid for her age.

"Doesn't mean she's wrong," Rafe said mildly. "But it's cute the way you two protect each other."

I rolled my eyes. "Cute. *Pfft*. You're the same way with your brothers! I mean, maybe not Beale, since he's bigger than you..."

"Shut it." Rafe shoved my leg again playfully. He didn't enjoy being reminded about how his *little* brother had shot up above him in height. "Besides, it's not the same at all. You feel like you have to protect Aimee, probably because she's a pretty girl, and then she feels like *she* has to protect *you* from spending too much time protecting *her*. Cute, like I said."

Part of me wanted to take exception to this, because I wasn't sure how he thought Aimee protected *me*, but my mind was like an old-fashioned record player, stuck on Aimee being "a pretty girl."

I knew Rafe didn't mean anything by it. *Obviously*. I mean, she was seventeen, and Rafe and I were almost twenty. And I was 99 percent sure he saw her as a sister, the same way I thought of his brothers. But also...

"You think Aim's pretty?" I asked super casually.

"Hmm? Oh, yeah. Very. She's got those big, green Rollins eyes and that streaky blonde hair." He reached up and yanked at a piece of my hair in demonstration, which made my stomach flip.

I felt my dick stir in my shorts and pulled away from his touch before I could get any more caught up in the moment than I already was.

"Any beer left?" Rafe asked, tipping his face to the sky sleepily.

I set my guitar carefully back in its case and checked the little cooler next to my towel. "Two." I handed one over and kept the other for myself.

"Perfect." Rafe clinked the neck of his bottle against mine and took a deep drink. I very much did *not* notice the way his throat worked as he swallowed.

"I'm gonna miss this in a few weeks," he said wistfully. "When does your semester start again?"

He asked this in a hopeful little voice, like maybe the dates would have changed suddenly or like August might decide to stretch into September this year.

I understood this. I wished someone would miraculously insert a few more weeks into summer, too.

"Two weeks," I told him. Two more weeks of him and me. Two more weeks to soak in his smiles, and his genuine affection, and the understanding I always found in his eyes. Two more weeks to sustain me until this time next year.

It wouldn't be enough, though. It never was. The more time I spent with him, the more I wanted.

There'd been a moment last March when I'd thought about skipping my family vacation to the Key this year. Maybe getting one of those internships my dad kept hammering me about instead, since business skills might come in handy for me later, or even spending summer break playing in bars near campus. I'd wondered if I went a whole summer without seeing Rafe whether these feelings would die off and I'd be satisfied being friends.

But that thought had only lasted about four seconds before I'd dismissed it completely. It would be like trying to survive without oxygen all summer; I simply wasn't capable of it.

I sucked down more beer, then cleared my throat. *Get back on track, Rollins.* "So, back to my wager... I'll play you whatever song you want if you win. And if I win, I get my ten dollars from yesterday back."

"Yeah, about that," Rafe began sadly. "I may have paid Gage in advance to leave us alone for the next two weeks."

I spluttered. "Ten bucks? That's all it took?"

"He's thirteen." Rafe grinned again. "He doesn't understand how capitalism works yet."

"You know, it's okay if he comes along sometimes," I reminded him. "I like Gage."

"I like him, too. But… I like it best when it's just the two of us doing stuff." Rafe shrugged.

I swallowed hard. When Rafe said things like that, even though I knew he didn't mean it the way I wished he did, I melted like tar in the hot sun, all sticky-gross and useless.

"Speaking of us doing stuff," Rafe continued, totally unaware that my brain had gone gooey, "Perseid meteor shower tonight."

"Yeah, I know. You made me write it on my calendar. And I don't even use a calendar."

"'Course you do. It's how you remember my birthday."

I bit my tongue against the need to inform him that I knew his birthday by heart and probably always would. "So, I take it we're coming back out here tonight?"

"'Course. It's our place." Rafe lay back in the sand and smiled, his expression bright and open. "And this is our thing. You and me, stargazing. Even if you can't ever remember the names of any of them and you make me point them out over and over," he teased.

I shrugged sheepishly. "What can I say, man? My memory is for shit."

In truth, I remembered every constellation he'd ever shown me. But when Rafe pointed them out, he pressed his chest against my shoulder, and when he told me their names, his warm breath tickled my ear and his stubbled cheek almost touched mine. I felt like whoever came up with the saying about ignorance being bliss must've experienced something similar.

The fact was, *stargazing* wasn't my thing, Rafe was. If he'd wanted to try walking on hot coals or swimming with sharks, I'd probably have said yes, so sitting in the dark watching the stars was an absolute no-brainer.

And the best part was, I was pretty sure Rafe felt the same way about me. One of the greatest truths of my life was that Rafe Goodman liked me better than anyone else on the planet outside of his family. Sometimes when I got down or nervous, that knowledge carried me.

"Jay, if you could have anything in the world, what would it be?" Rafe asked suddenly.

I was so unprepared for the question, so caught up in the sticky-tar of my emotions, that my brain stalled.

I want us to spend the autumn together. Every autumn together.

I want our magic not to end when the summer does.

I want to write songs about you and play them for people who love them.

I want to be so big and make so much money, people will respect my choices.

But most of all, I want you to want me.

I want you to love me.

And then I want you to wait for me...

Until I'm free to love you back.

"Uh. More beer?" I croaked. "Maybe Doritos?"

"I meant in terms of your *life*, Rollins." Rafe sounded both amused and disapproving. "Think big picture."

"Oh. That."

"Never mind. I already know."

"Do you?" I highly doubted it.

"You want a Grammy or ten, and a giant sold-out show. Legions of screaming fans. Hot girls."

Just as I suspected. It was crazy how a person could know me so well in most ways and be so wildly off base in others.

"You got it," I agreed. "Iron Pipes or bust, baby!" Rafe clinked our beer bottles together again.

"Seriously, though," I said slowly, "if I could have anything, it'd be one of those big ol' mansions up on the hill on the other side of the island, where Grandma Goodman's house is. That's what I'm going to do once I've made it big. That way we can keep having our summers together."

Rafe snorted. "No way. When you've made it big, you'll be able to afford a big mansion in *California*. Or Europe. Or on your own private island. Places you have to *fly* to get to, which means I'm not gonna be there," he said with a self-deprecating smile. "Meanwhile, I'm gonna be telling the same old ghost stories on my dad's tour boat until I'm a ghost myself." He sucked down the last of his beer.

Sometimes when he talked about the future, he sounded so bleak. I wanted to tell him it didn't have to be that way, that we had the power to make the future look like whatever we wanted it to... but I knew better. Rafe and I *both* had to make sacrifices to have the things we wanted most. And for him, that was making sure his family was taken care of, despite his dad's crazy get-rich-quick schemes.

"You're wrong. No place else will ever be home to me like this island is," I vowed staunchly. "Whispering Key is the most beautiful place on earth."

Rafe's grin was back, just like that. "Yeah? How many places have you been, world traveler?"

"Lots! Dad and Belinda took us to Mexico once over Christmas, and I went on a school trip to Greece, and we all flew out to California to visit my dad's sister two years ago. But I don't have to see the whole earth to know where I wanna be. My best friend lives here." I elbowed him lightly. "I'd never not wanna be where you are, dude."

I put my hand out to shove at his shoulder. His skin was hot from the sun, and I slid my thumb over it surreptitiously, another tiny touch to store away.

Rafe's muscles bunched and flexed beneath my hand as he stood up, and then he turned and held out a hand to me. "Come on. I want a song before sunset, so it's time for me to whup your ass."

"Wait! We didn't decide what I get if I win!"

"If you win..." He pursed his lips. "You get to play me *two* songs," he decided. Then he took off down the length of the beach, tossing a smirky little smile over his shoulder.

"Fuck you!" I tossed my unfinished beer down on the sand next to our towels and followed him as he sprinted headlong through the summer sunshine directly into the waves, both of us laughing our heads off.

I had no clue what the future held. I knew after college there'd be music, no matter what my dad said. I knew there'd be touring, which I didn't love, and fans, which might be fun. I knew it would take a long time, and I knew if I kept at it, there'd be money—enough to convince even a skeptic like my dad.

But most important of all, I knew Rafe would be by my side.

My teammate. My constant. My rock. My North Star, guiding me home.

My love.

Always.

And he was.

Until the day he fell in love with my sister.

And all the love between us turned to hate.

1

RAFE

"Well now, Rafe, I'll tell you the truth," Littlejohn Jennings began, his guilty squirming making his chair springs squeak. "I didn't really *perceive* the situation as bribery at the time."

I resisted the urge to roll my eyes. Just outside the Whispering Key Rec Center's second-story window, the turquoise Gulf waters sparkled and beckoned. Beyond that lay an entire world I'd hardly seen in three decades of living, with endless opportunities to explore. And now that my brothers and I had found a treasure one of our ancestors had hidden on the Key, I had the resources to enjoy myself to the fullest.

So what was I doing?

Chaperoning a meeting of the Extravaganza Committee. As one does.

Or at least, as one did if that person was a direct descendant of one of the founders of the island and also the son of the current mayor of the island—a man who'd birthed a half-assed brainchild last spring called "The Whispering Key

Labor Day Extravaganza" and then promptly drafted *me* to coordinate it.

I took my responsibilities seriously... which was more than I could say for my dad.

Or a certain other guitar-carrying sellout I used to consider my best friend.

I scratched at the stubble on my jaw and reminded myself that I didn't think about *that person* anymore. Just recalling his name conjured all sorts of memories, good and bad— and the good ones were even more annoying than the bad ones because they reminded me how stupid I'd been.

"You're saying Caroline Mitchell only agreeing to date you if you got her brother a food truck in the Whispering Key Extravaganza didn't raise a single red flag in your mind, Littlejohn?" I asked.

"Weeeeell. It mebbe gave me a moment's pause," he allowed. "But then... Caroline smiles awful pretty, you know? *And* she mentioned her brother gave her enough free appetizer coupons for the whole Extravaganza Committee." Littlejohn grabbed a bright pink coupon from the stack in the center of the long table and handed it to me proudly. "So I said to myself, 'Littlejohn, Caroline's brother can't be a bad guy if he's willing to give all your friends free food!' And anyway, Dale 'n me just got done watching *The Crown*, didn't we, Dale? And I figured if all them kings and queens of Europe could bring their honeyboos a little whajamacallit to sweeten the pot—"

"Dowry," Dale Jennings piped up from halfway down the table.

"Yeah, that! So why not me and Caroline, you know?"

A dynastic marriage with a dowry of loaded nachos was not the weirdest setup for a Whispering Key love story I'd ever heard. Literally not even the weirdest this month.

I stuffed the coupon in my pocket.

"I only told her I'd bring the request to the meeting along with the coupons, and let us all vote our consciences," Littlejohn said earnestly.

"Well, my conscience says I love me some Mitchell's conch fritters!" Lorenna McKetcham, spry despite being approximately as old as the glaciers that formed the island an eon ago, leaped out of her chair, grabbed a stack of coupons, and stuffed them down the front of her blouse where not a single soul on the committee would ever be tempted to retrieve them. "Hot dang!"

My dad—Rafe Goodman, Senior, also known as Big Rafe—leaned back in his chair at the head of the table, pursed his lips, and tapped his fingertips together, like he was Don Corleone rather than the mayor of a tiny Gulf Coast island. "I'm pretty sure that's still technically accepting a bribe, Littlejohn," he began cautiously.

Predictably, though, his gaze kept zinging right back to the pink coupons like magnets to iron filings. Sure, we'd just cashed in on a treasure, but free appetizers were free appetizers.

"*But* I'm thinking it's my job as mayor to support local businesses, isn't it?" He tilted his head and smiled beatifically. "Plus, Lorenna makes a damn good point about those fritters. I say the more the merrier! Let's welcome Mitchell's

Fine Family Dining to the Extravaganza family!" He grabbed his own generous stack of coupons and lifted his chin in my direction. "You go ahead and add a spot for another food truck at the Extravaganza, then, Rafe."

I fought the urge to roll my eyes. "Of course, Mr. Mayor." I mock saluted. "Your wish, my command."

On paper, I was the head of the Extravaganza Committee, but everyone at the table knew what that really meant. My dad loved delegating responsibility. Delegating *control*, though? Not so much. He hated being told "no" more than anything.

"Just so you're aware, though, Mr. Mayor," I continued, "we're already eight trucks over the 'absolutely unbreakable ten-truck limit' you agreed to in the spring, and if the more gets any merrier, we'll be parking trucks out in the Gulf." I smiled serenely.

Dad scowled. Being called out for his utter lack of common sense was the thing he hated *second* most. Which was why I tried to do it as often as I could.

"Now." I rapped my knuckles on the table. "Ms. Jonquil, Ms. Lorenna, how are we coming on decorations?" I asked, turning to the older ladies across from me with a polite smile like a dedicated committee head. "We're just about a week out, so it's time for us to make some final choices."

This was one of many, *many* Extravaganza-related situations where I could have gotten things done all by myself with no muss and no fuss, but apparently, a good committee head was required to do things *by committee*, which was why Dad had delegated arguably the most important event-planning job of all—the decorations—to a pair of octogenarians, at least one of whom couldn't work the internet.

Jonquil Pepper darted a look at Lorenna and cleared her throat. "Well, we're of two minds on the subject," she began. "You might say our theming ideas... diverge slightly? We sure could use some decision-making help."

One more week, I reminded myself, fighting against impatience. There was one full week until the Extravaganza, and then I promised myself that my life was going to change. My last official responsibility around here would be fulfilled, and I could... I could...

God, how pathetic was it that I had no clue what I wanted to do with my life? I'd spent thirty years taking care of my family, trying to make sure our tour boat business stayed afloat, attempting (mostly unsuccessfully) to rein my dad in. Now that we'd found the treasure, my brothers and my cousin Fenn were set financially. Since Beale and Fenn had boyfriends, and Gage was about to start his last year of college, and my *dad* was engaged to his secretary, Gloria, I knew they were all happy, too. And it was finally time for me to think about me and what I wanted.

Which absolutely did *not* make me think of off-key singing rock star wannabes I used to have a crush on.

My troublemaking cousin, Fenn, nudged me with his elbow and leaned far enough into my space to whisper, "Since when is Littlejohn back on the dating market?"

Like I monitored the dating lives of all Whispering Keysters? "Shhh. I'm listening."

But Fenn did not, in fact, shush. "Thought he was dating someone else we didn't like. Veruca? Violet? Victoria?"

Fenn's boyfriend, Mason, elbowed him lightly in the ribs from his other side. "Victoria's *my* ex-girlfriend," he whisper-hissed.

Fenn shot him a teasing smile. "You sure?"

One side of Mason's mouth quirked up. "It's getting harder to remember, but yeah."

They exchanged a look so full of love and amusement, I felt a little pang of something in my stomach. A little ache for something I'd almost had.

I ignored it.

"Pay attention," I commanded under my breath. Jonquil had already finished speaking, and I hadn't heard a *word*.

"LJ was dating *Veronica*," my brother Beale whispered to Fenn over my head.

"Mmm, and you're *so* right, we didn't like her one bit," Beale's boyfriend, Toby, leaned around him to add. "We're reserving judgment on Caroline, though."

Toby had only been a permanent resident of the Key for a couple of weeks, but it felt like much longer, maybe because he already knew more island gossip than I'd ever known.

And I liked the man, I really did, because he made Beale incredibly, magnificently, believe-in-a-benevolent-Universe happy.

But also, it was incredibly difficult to be around him sometimes because every time I looked at him, I remembered the tabloid photos that had made him flee New York to hide out on Whispering Key a few weeks back—photos of him supposedly hooking up with a certain friendship-forsaking musician I'd once thought I was in love with.

And even though Toby had explained how the pictures of him and Ja—*that person*—had been staged, and I believed Toby one hundred percent when he said he'd been pushed into *that person*'s lap and hadn't actually been going down on anyone in the middle of a crowded club, the image had seared itself into my brain and made it difficult to keep certain people out of my mind where they couldn't get to me.

I had a big, thick wall around my heart where Jay Rollins was concerned. But the fucker kept sneaking in somehow anyway.

"And *then* I'm thinking *rockets*!" Lorenna exclaimed.

I shook my head, concerned I'd heard wrong... and even more concerned that I hadn't. Rockets? Where were we getting rockets on short notice? What had I missed?

"Quiet," I hissed at Toby and Beale. "Pay attention." But then, because I didn't want Toby to think I didn't like him just because I tried to avoid looking at him, I added, "Please."

"Look at you and your new vocabulary!" Fenn marveled. "Today it's *please*, tomorrow it might be *thank you*! The Rafe I know and tolerate is a bitter little ball of righteous indignation who wouldn't be caught dead telling his dad 'your wish, my command.' So, tell me honestly as your favorite cousin: have you undergone a personality transplant, or did you finally get laid?"

Neither. I hadn't been laid in... Jesus wept. A really fucking long time.

And I was absolutely not sharing that information with Fenn or anyone.

"I've adopted a new attitude toward life, Reardon," I lied. "It's called wisdom and maturity. You might try it."

"Meh. Sounds lame."

I smiled smugly. "Also," I said, moving my lips as little as possible, "I planned for twenty trucks and told Dad ten, so he has two more trucks before I actually have to rethink my plan."

"Delightful," Toby breathed.

"Smart," Mason said softly.

I nodded, accepting both compliments. "Now hush, *all* of you, so I can listen."

But instead of taking my own advice, I stared out at the sliver of water I could see through the window and thought about what Fenn had said.

I was *not* bitter. I wasn't. Bitter people were people who weren't reconciled to their lives, and I was. I accepted the way things were.

I accepted that my dad was impulsive, and charming, overly enthusiastic about all the wrong things.

I accepted that my marriage to Aimee Rollins had been a mistake, even if I'd done it to help her out and my intentions had been good.

And I accepted that *certain people*, people I'd once considered a fixture in my life, had decided to remove themselves entirely from my orbit entirely once their career finally started taking off... even though I didn't understand *why* any better than I had back when it happened.

"Jay! Jesus, it's good to hear your voice! You're fucking hard to get hold of these days! Where have you—?"

"Hey, um. Sorry to interrupt, but now's not a great time. I've got rehearsals. Second tour's starting up in a couple months, and—"

"Wait, a second tour? Wow. Didn't you just finish your first tour? And when were you gonna share this info with your best friend?"

"Well..."

"I got why you couldn't make it to the wedding, Jay, but I thought you were gonna try to come out to the Key over the summer—"

"Oh, right. I guess I did sorta spitball that for a minute early last spring, didn't I? But it's not gonna work out. Way too busy. Gotta strike while the iron is hot, Debbie says! Debbie's my—"

"I know who Debbie is."

"Ah. Right. Well. Um. First single's out, and the rest of the album is dropping soon and... you know how it goes."

"I don't, actually... But maybe you can make it out for a visit next month, if it's before the second tour starts? I was thinking of having a birthday party for Aimee, and you always said you wanted to see the island in the fall, remember? It'd really mean a lot to her and to—"

"No! Nope. I... I can't. Sorry. I'll send her something, though, for sure. Look, I—"

"What about Thanksgiving? Or Christmas? Or basically anytime, ever?"

A sigh. "I've got dates scheduled through the end of the year. And my producer's throwing a Thanksgiving thing in the city I kinda have to attend. I mean, I'll try to get down there, but I just hate to promise and then cancel. I'll let you know. I'll get one of Debbie's people to send you a copy of my schedule when it's final."

"You'll have Debbie's people let me know? Are you fucking serious?"

"What do you want from me, Rafael?" Impatient now.

"Did I do something to piss you off? You don't call. You don't text. You don't come out here. Aimee says you don't communicate with her either. And I just don't get it. I love you. You're my best friend. My... my... brother-in-law—"

"Look, Rafe, I have to go. I..." A hesitation. "Give my love to Aimee, okay? I'll call when I can."

Yeah, no, Fenn was wrong. I wasn't *bitter.* I was hurt.

Still.

And it was pretty freakin' ironic that Aimee, my legally wedded wife, had up and walked out of my life sixteen months ago with zero explanation and no contact since, not even to update me on her health, and *that* I'd mostly gotten over. But Ja... *certain other people*? The scars they left were permanent.

"Rafael?" My dad's voice, dripping with sarcasm, interrupted my thoughts. "Sorry to interrupt your daydreaming with our pesky meeting, son, but the ladies need you to officially choose between their two proposals for decorations since it's *your job*." He gave Harvey Culpepper, the committee's most dedicated rule-follower, a sideways look. "Fortunately, Jonquil's plan is the only correct choice here."

I blinked. *Shit*. Jonquil Pepper and Lorenna McKetcham stared at me expectantly, and Fenn's teasing smile suggested they'd been trying to get my attention for a while.

My face went hot. "I wasn't daydreaming. I was, ah… visualizing the decorations they described. Particularly yours, Ms. McKetcham," I lied. "Mesmerizing."

Toby snickered behind his hand.

"I always knew you were a visionary, Rafe!" Lorenna said eagerly. "You like my idea for the hats? The balloon tower? The favors?"

Balloon tower? What?

"Oh, uh… sure. Yeah. It's just… the balloon tower is a lot for a simple man like me to take in all at once."

Toby snickered. "Precious, fifteen feet would be a lot for *any* man to take in, and I've had more practice than most."

Mason gave a startled snort-laugh, which made Fenn laugh, too. Beale blushed. My dad shot Toby a look that said he, for one, was *not* amused, then folded his arms over his chest and *hmphed*. "Could we be adults, please, gentlemen? This is official Key business."

Harvey nodded firmly.

What the hell had I missed?

"Er, Ms. McKetcham, maybe you could just go over the… the

highlights of your theme again? Just so it really penetrates, you know?" I tapped my temple.

Toby made a choking noise, but when I turned to look at him in concern, he waved a hand. "No, no. Sorry. Don't mind me. Mayor Goodman's right. We're adults. By all means, get... penetrated."

Beale's shoulders shook. Mason made a wheezing noise like a cat with a furball.

Dad scowled. "Rafael, I don't believe we need to hear any more about—"

"Dicks!" Lorenna said happily. "Cocks, peckers, schlongs. From giant ones—" Lorenna threw her arms wide "—to tiny ones." She held up her thumb and first finger like she was measuring off an inch. "And we'll throw in some vaginas, too, for those who are into that sort of thing." She leaned right and patted Harvey's hand. "Whispering Key prides itself on being inclusive, after all."

Harvey nodded, then frowned.

I shook my head to clear it. "You mean... you mean...?" I had no idea how to finish that statement, since I had no idea what Lorenna *could* mean.

"I *mean* Safer Sex and Body Positivity." When it was clear I wasn't following, she added, "Did you not hear a word I said a couple minutes ago, honey? Did thinking of the giant penises rot your brain?" She gave me a sympathetic smile. "It's okay. Happens to the best of us."

Fenn gave a whimper, like the force of restraining his laughter was physically painful.

"I'm thinking condom favors. Penis jousting! Not with real penises," she reassured Harvey, who did not seem reassured. "Inflatable ones. And the whole festival would be clothing optional. It would increase tourism like *heck*! We'd get all kinds of publicity. Plus, my Maddie helped me price it all out on the internet, and even with a lifelike fifteen-foot balloon-tower phallus, we'd be well within budget!"

I stared at her, blinking slowly. "A *lifelike* fifteen-foot..."

"I told my granddaughter, there's no need to overspend. Cheap dicks work just as well as expensive ones," Lorenna told Harvey, as Maddie McKetcham nodded in agreement. "That's a life lesson there."

Harvey nodded again, like he wasn't sure whether he wanted her to be his new best friend or to stay far away from him. This was pretty on-brand for Lorenna McKetcham.

"This whole discussion is ridiculous!" My dad sat forward in his chair. "I *told* Lorenna this is a family-friendly festival. The goal is to increase tourism and do some fundraising for the island, *not* to cause a stir for the sake of it. Under no circumstances will Rafe even entertain this so-called option."

"And I say, what's more family-friendly than safer sex and body positivity?" Lorenna demanded. "Open your *mind*, Mr. Mayor."

"Rafael, tell her no one brings their children to a festival with giant, inflatable penises!" Dad said, exasperated.

"Rafe, tell your father that's only because nobody's thought of it yet!" Lorenna insisted.

As much as I hated to agree with my dad on principle, he was totally right. Still, I hesitated. "Ms. Pepper, now maybe you could repeat the idea *you* were working on?"

Jonquil Pepper, my old kindergarten teacher, sat forward, glancing at Lorenna warily. "Well. Um. It wasn't nearly as exciting. I was thinking... stars?"

Dad nodded approvingly.

"Stars," I repeated, relieved. "Right, okay. So, like..."

"Um, star garlands strung back and forth across the street like a big canopy? And a star-shaped archway you'd pass under to get to the parking lot where all the food trucks will be? And maybe one of those booths that prints out the star chart from the day you were born or got married? And star T-shirts for all the volunteers that show what the skies over Whispering Key will look like the weekend of the festival? We should still have time to make them up, if we can get a design done fast."

"Rafael could help you out with that," Dad volunteered. "He was all about stargazing when he was a youngster, weren't you, Rafe?"

I nodded reluctantly. "Not so much anymore, though. I've forgotten all of it," I lied.

"Ah. We'll figure something out. I was also thinking twinkle lights on all the food trucks that would turn on when the sun went down? And lights on the trees? And foil stars suspended over the dance floor over by the gazebo?" Jonquil looked exponentially more confident as she warmed to her topic.

"Wow." That idea really *was* mesmerizing. I could imagine the lights swaying in the warm breeze off the water. It was beautiful. Perfect, really. "What else?"

"Well," she said excitedly, "we'll also need a big ol' banner behind the stage where Jayd Rollins will be playing his concert on the last evening of the festival, of course! Something with the album cover for *Constellations* on it, since that's where I got the idea for the stars—"

I inhaled sharply as his name hit my stomach like a rock—*Jayd*. Stupid, affected stage name. He would *never* be Jayd to me. *Ever*—and I turned to Lorenna with a smile. "On second thought, tell me more about the dicks."

"Rafael!" Dad narrowed his eyes at me. "Jayd's concert is the keystone of the whole Extravaganza. It makes sense to—"

"Oooh, that's gonna be a hard no." I folded my arms over my chest. "There is no way that we are theming our decorations after the name of that sellout's overproduced, meaningless, bubblegum album. The label chose that name, you know. Jay couldn't find the Big Dipper if you drew him a map. And furthermore, half the lyrics of those songs don't make sense. *'Drowning in the light of the truth of you and me; I'm forever locked tight, 'cause you hold the key'*?? Total bullshit. It's like he was left unsupervised with a bottle of grain alcohol and a rhyming dictionary."

"You hate it that much... but also listened to it enough times to recite the lyrics from memory?" Toby tilted his head to one side. "Hmm."

I changed my mind. I really did *not* like that guy.

"Look," I told my dad, "I didn't say anything when you invited my *former* friend to perform a concert here without considering my feelings—"

"Ehhh. Is that accurate, though?" Fenn demanded. "'Cause I feel like you said some things."

"Lots of things," Beale the traitor agreed.

"—but I draw the line at this," I concluded.

"Jayd is the reason most folks will be attending, which is good enough reason to theme the decorations after him," my dad said reasonably.

"You know what? I concur." I smiled with no humor. "Which means we'll go with Lorenna's idea, since a giant dick really captures who Jay is as a person."

"Oh, Lord," Dale Jennings muttered. "Here we go."

Dad shook his head at me like I was the ridiculous one. "You have got to get over your petty squabbles, Rafe. It's been years since that mess with Aimee."

Years? *No.*

Yes, it had been over three years since Jay had gotten too famous to remember who his friends were, that was true... assuming our friendship had ever been real for him to begin with.

But had only been sixteen months since the last time I saw him. Sixteen months since Aimee had left me a note informing me that our marriage was over. Sixteen months since I'd followed her to Tampa, where Jay was staying after a show. Sixteen months since I'd gone to his hotel suite and demanded to talk to her... and he'd told me off at the door with words that had destroyed the last dregs of our friendship.

Fuck.

Remembering how I'd smashed my hand into his jaw in retaliation should have been more satisfying than it was, but honest to God, I just wished I'd hit him harder.

Hard enough to forget the look of his face in the sunlight, his hands on his guitar, the freckles on his shoulders, and the countless hours I'd spent reminding my teenaged self that Jay was *straight* and therefore didn't want me.

Hard enough that I'd be able to walk on our beach, or look up at our sky at night, or have his stupid songs come on the radio, without feeling shitty and bereft, like I'd lost a part of myself I'd never recover.

Hard enough that he'd have known to stay away from the Key permanently.

"It's not a petty squabble," I told my dad for maybe the fiftieth time since he'd announced this concert in the spring. "I just don't like him. I don't trust him. When he started getting famous, he stopped giving a shit about anyone on the Key—including his own sister for a while there. He didn't even make it to our wedding." Small as it had been. And I'd really, really needed him there. "What makes you think he'll actually show up for this?"

"Because Jayd gave me his word he'd be here—"

I snorted. His word? Like *that* meant anything.

"—and even though he's dealing with his own personal tragedies right now—"

"Personal tragedies? He got caught at a gay bar by the paparazzi and had a couple embarrassing pictures printed," I scoffed. "Don't make it sound like his family went down on the *Titanic*."

"Hey," Toby objected softly, a little frown between his eyebrows and his customary smile missing from his face. "It *was* kind of a big deal, you know."

My gut twisted guiltily. Toby was right. The media frenzy that followed the paparazzi pictures had upended Toby's life and caused problems with his job, too, when all he'd done was stand in the wrong place at the wrong time. That *was* a big deal.

For him.

But for Jay?

"Jay wanted to be famous," I reminded him. "This is the price he's gotta pay."

"The price of having entire Instagram accounts devoted to posting every fan selfie he ever took so the public can speculate on his sexuality? Of becoming a gay icon to people on Twitter before he's even confirmed or denied the rumors? Rafe, precious..." Toby shook his head disapprovingly. "You came out as bisexual when you were a teenager, right? On your own terms? Those hellbeast paparazzi took something from Jayd that he can't get back."

I ground my teeth together against the logic of those words.

"As I was saying... Even though he's dealing with these tragedies," my dad repeated, his dark eyes daring me to interrupt again, "he's still making beautiful music. He's a hero."

"And that 'Pretty Girl' song of his! Get dust in my eye every time it comes on the radio," Littlejohn interjected, sniffling a little.

"I heard he wrote it about Olivia Merry, that actress from the *Scarlet and the Moon* movies. They dated last year," Maddie said with a happy sigh. Then she frowned. "Wait, do you think they're still together? I haven't seen any pictures of them since the tabloid story came out! *Omigod*, how awful would it be to have to keep playing a love song you wrote for someone you weren't with anymore? Jayd's, like, so brave." She clapped a hand to her chest and sniffled slightly.

Ugh. Gross.

"I have the utmost confidence that Jayd will not let us down," my dad concluded.

"If you're so confident of that, why'd you send your youngest son like a sacrificial lamb to go and collect him from Colorado?" I folded my arms over my chest.

"I didn't sacrifice Gage, he volunteered. Your brother knows how important this concert is, and he's always had a li'l case of hero worship for our Jayd, too," Dad said fondly. He tilted his head and stared at me. "Plus, unlike *some* people, Gage can fly in an airplane without throwing a hissy fit, which is why I didn't consider sending *you*."

"Not to mention only one of 'em woulda made it home," Dale Jennings grumbled to no one in particular.

Accurate.

"Hey!" I jabbed an accusatory finger down the table at my father. "You know exactly why I'm afraid of flying! It's a very *logical* fear, okay? That therapist I used to see said I'd get over it in my own time."

Actually, she'd said she couldn't help me get over my fear until I really *wanted* to get over my fear. Same difference, really.

I took a deep breath and tried to get myself back under control. "Ms. Lorenna, Ms. Jonquil, I'm gonna think on these ideas some more and come to a decision in a day or so. Thank you both for your hard work."

Jonquil preened under the praise, but Lorenna pursed her lips. "Just to say, you might want to put a deposit on the giant phallus. Dicks that big go quick, and we don't have time to mess around."

I nodded solemnly. "I'll take that under advisement. In the meantime, just in case our guest of honor doesn't show, I took that wish list of fill-in acts you guys came up with last meeting"—I took a worn sheet of notebook paper from my pocket and slapped it on the table—"and made some phone calls to book a backup—"

"He's *going* to show," Dad insisted.

"Sure he will. Where'd you say Jay and Gage were the last time Gage called?" I asked.

Dad's jaw worked. "Wyoming. Still."

"Uh-huh. A state *northwest* of Colorado, when Whispering Key is southeast. And they haven't told you why they're there, have they? Or why Jay was even in Colorado to begin with? I thought the latest statement from his agent said he'd cancelled his tour dates for 'exhaustion.' Is Colorado where tired people go? Can exhausted people be trusted to play Extravaganza concerts?"

"I have a pretty good idea why they're in Wyoming," Dad blustered. He stuck out his chin. "And Gage says Jayd is in good spirits. They could be here any minute now. It's all going to be *fine.*"

Fifty-something years old, and my dad sounded like a little kid trying desperately to believe in Santa. So sad.

"Sure, Dad. But just in case, I booked that Jimmy Buffet tribute band from over in Fruitville."

"Aw, hells yes!" Littlejohn's eyes lit up. "You mean Quincy Berger and the Cheez-Bergers in Paradise, right? Nicely done!"

At least someone appreciated my contributions.

Dad groaned. "You realize Jayd Rollins would be playing big venues and festivals if he hadn't canceled his tour dates this summer? And that his first tour a couple years ago sold out? And his second one also? And he has a *gold* album?"

"So?" I demanded.

That first tour had consisted of venues smaller than this conference room, where maybe three people could squeeze in together if none of them had any concept of personal space or fire laws.

Not that I'd googled the venues, of course.

Not *all* of them anyway.

The second tour had been more high-profile and had even

gotten written up by various bloggers and entertainment reporters, but still. I refused to be impressed.

"*And,* Jayd Rollins is Whispering Key's pride and joy," Dad continued.

"Okay, now that's just crazy talk." I clenched my jaw.

As any hyperventilating teenage fanboy or -girl with access to Wikipedia could tell you, Jay Don Rollins had been born and raised in Rock Gulch, Alabama, nowhere near here. The son of a bitch had only summered on the Key as a teenager, that was all, in a little cottage his stepmother's grandmother had owned. And sure, my brothers and I had basically adopted Jay and his sister during those summers, since there were hardly any other teens on the island, but that didn't make Jay a local, no matter what anyone said.

Especially since Jay hadn't been back in *years.*

Despite all the promises he'd made once upon a time.

"Ergo, you're cracked in the noggin if you think ticket holders are going to be satisfied by you substituting the Cheez-Bergers in Paradise for a recording artist of Jayd's caliber," Dad concluded. "Who else was on your list?"

"Funny you should ask." I unfolded the notebook paper and skimmed the contents. "Whoever suggested One Direction, I'm sorry, but they're not likely to get back together for this—"

"Damn." Dale Jennings sighed. "Knew it was a long shot."

"And Perry Como died about twenty years ago, so that proved tricky—"

Lorenna McKetcham gasped and looked around at the assembled committee. "Never say so! The man was so young!"

"Shockingly, Shawn Mendes wouldn't return my calls—"

"Figures," Maddie said glumly. She added as an aside to her grandmother, "He never returns mine either."

"And Taylor Swift's people said she only does benefit concerts for kid or animal charities," I concluded.

Toby clasped a hand to his chest but nodded in acceptance. "I'm sad but unsurprised. She's a modern-day *saint*," he choked out. "Like *Folklore* wasn't enough of a gift to the world."

Beale patted his shoulder sympathetically.

"And Ari Friedrich, my own personal choice, is playing Iron Pipes that weekend. *Whomp, whomp.* So, as it happens," I continued, "there was exactly one act on the list the committee put together that *was* available to do a private concert on Labor Day weekend. Hence, the Cheez-Bergers."

Dad grimaced. "Rafe, I gave you this job because I trusted you to do it—"

"And I will. Look around you! I *am.*"

He shook his head dubiously, and I fought down a wave of anger. In my entire life, I'd never let him down when it counted. I wouldn't let him down this time either.

"Oh, son. You'd better hope like heck Jayd shows up," he said sourly. "And do whatever you've gotta do to keep him happy."

I pushed my chair back from the table and stood, forgetting for a second that the chair would keep on rolling. It hit the wall behind me with a dramatic crash that made Mason widen his eyes and say, "Oh, shit! Fenn, is that—?" while Toby went wide-eyed and gaped like a fish... which was fine because at least he was quiet.

"Listen, I know you all think Jayd Rollins is gonna come in and save the day. I get it—he seems so charming, right? He's got that handsome face and that charming smile that make you think you know him. I did, too, once. But he's not a guy who sticks around when things get inconvenient. He's allergic to responsibility. The sooner you get that, the less disappointed you'll be."

I sure wished I'd figured it out sooner.

"Rafe," Beale said urgently. "Shut up."

I ignored him. This was not my fault. I was doing fine not thinking about *certain people*, but now he was being pushed in front of my face. And it turned out maybe I couldn't be wise and mature about everything. At least not about this *one* thing.

"Jay Rollins doesn't keep promises," I went on, hoping at least *one* of them would get it. "He walks away from people he claims to love—"

"Rafael," Dad said in a panicked voice, slapping a hand on the table. "Shut it!"

But I shook my head. I wouldn't be silenced, not about this. I was speaking the truth.

"He has his own agenda and always has! He doesn't care about *you*. He sure as hell doesn't care about *me*." I stood up straighter, lifted my chin, and informed Littlejohn, "And 'Pretty Girl' couldn't be more overproduced and soulless if it came with an '80s synthesizer track and its own Macarena-type *line dance*."

"Aw, jeez," Littlejohn said, his eyes darting past me to the door like he was plotting his escape.

Dad buried his head in his hands and moaned a little.

Even Ms. McKetcham clutched the place where her pearls would be, if she were the pearl-wearing type, which was a little excessive, as far as I was concerned. I was entitled to my opinion, after all.

"I only hope he *does* show up so I can say the same damn thing to his face," I added with a firm nod.

"Is that so?"

Jayd's voice, which had already been deep and raspy back when he was fifteen and had only gotten rougher over the years, registered in my brain before his words did. Like Pavlov's pathetic dog, the sound made my lips start to tip up in a smile before I caught it and forced myself to turn around instead.

Shit. *Shit*. He was here.

Jayd Rollins was actually *here*.

And for all my bold talk, I was wildly unprepared for the reality of him.

I got a momentary impression of Jayd's long, blond-streaked hair, his rangy body—nearly as tall as me but not nearly as wide—dressed in heavy jeans and boots that by rights would kill a man in the Florida summer sunshine. His dark green eyes—bloodshot, like he'd had too much worry and too little sleep—blazed hot enough to incinerate me where I stood.

"Thank you, Rafe," he said. "I'd *almost* started to question myself."

Jayd's voice had always had this kind of magical quality to it. Stupid DJs went on and on about the resonance of his voice, the texture that made every word he said sound like it contained entire symphonies. But to me, it had always felt like every word he spoke was part of a dream—one that kept me hanging on, waiting to see what he'd say next.

Even though I didn't trust him, even though I didn't *want* to listen, even though I wanted to hate his guts, I stood rooted to the spot.

"Question yourself about what? Your song being an insult to music?" My voice was also deep, but totally unmagical, like the croak of a bullfrog with anxiety. "Fine. I forgive you."

"Nah. About whether I should live out this little fantasy I'd had about our reunion." Jay smiled an angelic smile, a smile I hadn't seen in way too long and was mortified to find I'd *missed*, as he strolled closer to me.

"You fantasized about our reunion?"

"Oh, yeah," he whispered.

Then he punched me in the stomach so hard I doubled over.

2

JAY

Six days earlier

"Hey, hey! You've reached Aimee, and I'm either out bungee jumping or home taking a nap, so leave a message and have a brilliant day!"

My sister's voicemail. *Again.*

I looked out the window of the Denver studio I'd been bankrolling for my sister, stared at the snowy Front Range in the distance, and low-key wanted to cry.

Aimee was sure as heck not home taking a nap, I could tell you that much. I'd flown into town a few days ago to surprise her—and yes, to get the hell away from New York and the fallout of the "Jayd is Gay!" tabloid pictures that still haunted me there—and she hadn't been home at all yet.

Then again, I was pretty sure this apartment wasn't her home.

In fact, if the rental company hadn't sent me a spare key when I signed the lease for her sixteen months ago, I might have thought I was in the wrong place entirely, because looking around the apartment with its lumpy futon, empty closets, and inches of dust, it was obvious no one had been living here for a while. Months, maybe.

Aimee had moved out... and hadn't told me.

What the hell had happened to her? And, maybe more importantly, what had happened to *us*?

The two Rollins kids, always looking out for one another, always each other's greatest champions... Not so much anymore. And I was pretty sure it was all my fault.

"Hey. Jay again." I clutched the phone tightly. "Just wanted to let you know I'm still here. In Denver. I'm back at your... the apartment. And I know you hate it when I'm overprotective and all up in your business, but Aim, *where are you*?"

I sat down heavily on the futon. "Look, I get that you're upset at me, okay? I don't blame you. I... have not been the best brother recently." Or even a half-decent brother. "I know we haven't talked much lately, except right after that tabloid article came out." I winced. "And I know how much it hurt you to find out I was gay from BlazeNewz. It's been hard for us to connect the past few months, what with your job, and me on tour and traveling all the time—"

Excuses and lies. Lies and excuses. I was sick of it.

"I haven't *made* time the way I should have," I said truthfully. "And there are reasons for that, and they're probably terrible reasons, but I'd really like to talk to you about them. Be honest with you about them. Maybe get us back on track to where we used to be, but better? I've messed up so many things, like..."

Like being a jealous fuckup who couldn't handle Rafe choosing you, which was why I never made it to your wedding or went back to the Key to visit.

Like focusing on my career all these years and disappearing from your life, just like Dad, so now I've got a big pile of money and hardly anyone I can trust.

Like being such a petty bastard that I agreed to play this concert on Whispering Key over Labor Day weekend, just so I could show Rafe Goodman how happy and successful I am without him, and conveniently overlooked the fact that I'd have to be around Rafe freakin' Goodman for the entire weekend.

Like going out to a gay bar a few weeks ago because I was lonely, when I knew better than to think there was anywhere I could be anonymous anymore, especially in the city.

I closed my eyes and blew out a breath. "Well, there are too many things to count, really. But I love you. That's the most important thing. And I really hope you'll call me—"

The recording cut off with a long, shrill *beep*.

"—back," I whispered into the empty room. "*Fuck*."

I threw myself down on the futon and groaned up at the ceiling. The metal frame beneath me creaked ominously, but honestly, if the whole thing collapsed, that would probably be an improvement.

A metaphor for my life, I thought gloomily.

My phone rang in my hand, and I answered it immediately. "Aimee?"

"Jayd! *Finally*." That cultured, perpetually impatient voice did *not* belong to my sister but to my agent. "You've been ducking my calls again."

Yes, I had. For five days and counting, damn it, and now my streak was at an end. I scrunched up my face. "Nonsense! I love talking with you, Debbie! I would *never* duck your calls. I'm actually out of town. Family business—"

"No doubt," she said, in a bland voice that conveyed nothing but doubt. "Listen, the people at *Good Morning USA* called again. I'm thinking a very tasteful interview—it's morning television, you know? There'll be none of those salacious questions you don't want—and then we can get started rescheduling the tour dates—"

"No."

She *tsked* me. "Jayd. This is not a court of law, honey. There is no pleading the fifth. You have a highly public career—"

"I know."

"Well, then, *act* like you know," she snapped. "You want the public to buy your albums and attend your concerts, right? You wanted to be famous? Now you are. And with that comes curiosity."

Except I wasn't well-known. None of them knew the real me at all. And I'd never realized how isolating it could be to have people "know" you without knowing you until it had happened to me.

It was the kind of thing I couldn't talk about without sounding like a giant whiner—go cry into your piles of money, why don't you, Jayd?—and I hated that. But it was also *true*, and I hated that more.

"They all want a piece of me, and I get that. But they can't have *this* piece, Debbie. Not this one."

"Jayd," Debbie said, more patiently this time. "Listen to me. I know that you're upset over the picture in the tabloids. I know it's embarrassing. And I know it's even worse because the whole thing was a setup, and the photographer pushed that guy into your lap. But this is not the end of your life. It's not even the end of your career! You being gay is not the story here. You *hiding* being gay is the story. And if you stop, if you give them a sound bite, then they'll stop hounding you. Trust me."

"Will they? Can you guarantee that?" I laughed without humor. "Can you promise they won't be writing crap tomorrow linking me to Chris Evans instead of Olivia Merry? Or trying to dig up stuff from my past to figure out what all my lyrics were *really* about? No," I answered myself before she could. "You can't. And there are some things I just don't want people speculating about."

"Jayd—"

"Debbie, I said no."

Her sigh was so gusty, I was pretty sure I could feel the breeze from half a continent away. "The record company isn't going to like this. It's going to make it very difficult for them to publicize the next album. Speaking of which... Do you have an update I can offer them?"

"Sure. Yeah. Things are going really well. I have half the album done. The other half is, you know, coming along nicely. In its own time."

This was a euphemism for "I have half an album in the can, and I hate every single note of every song. Nursery rhymes are more complex than the shit I've been dredging up. Oh, and I haven't even attempted to write a song in weeks, because every time I open my mouth, I make a noise like an Edvard Munch painting."

I was pretty sure Debbie read this truth between the lines, because she sighed again. "Jayd Rollins, you are one of the most talented musicians I've ever worked with. You have serious songwriting ability, and your voice is heavenly. Soon enough, you'll be able to write your own ticket. Headlining arenas, collaborations people would kill for. I even heard rumors about you getting invited to Iron Pipes this year. But you have to learn to play the game, honey. You have to control the narrative and not let it control you."

I rolled my eyes. "I was *almost* convinced you were sincere until you got to Iron Pipes. That was just a touch too far."

My platform wasn't nearly big enough for an invitation to the biggest music festival of the summer. *Constellations* was my only album, and after the tabloid photos had gone up, I'd canceled all my remaining tour dates for the summer due to what Debbie's people were calling "exhaustion," which was not a total lie and was also not the kind of thing Iron Pipes' organizers wanted to bring into the fold.

"I'm being serious!"

"Okay."

She snorted. "Honest to God. Sometimes it shocks me that you wrote this lovely album about sunshine and simple love, when deep down, you're a giant jaded cynic."

I didn't use to be. I used to believe in love emphatically. I used to believe it could happen to me. And then I'd gotten a phone call three years ago.

"Aim, I can't hear you! I'm about to go onstage. Can I call you—?"

"I said, Rafe and I are getting married!" Her excited laughter filtered through the phone line and sucked all the air out of the little bar in Pittsburgh. "The day after tomorrow! You need to come to Whispering Key ASAP."

"But, wait. Rafe? You mean my *R—? I mean." My lungs forgot how to perform their primary function. My eyes hyperfocused on the safety posters in the bar's backroom. "I just talked to Rafe this morning." He'd teased me. I'd laughed. I'd told him Debbie wanted me to do my very first tour, a nationwide tour of tiny venues, but if I said yes, I wouldn't make it to the Key all summer, so I was thinking to push back and get a couple of free weeks at least. I needed to see him at least that much. "He... he never mentioned it... you... it. H-how is that... possible?"*

"Surprise! I guess these things just happen! Love is unpredictable like that. But gosh, he's just the nicest, most wonderful guy, Jay. How could anyone help but love him?"

I wasn't sure. I certainly hadn't been able to help it.

I still couldn't, despite all the hurt we'd dished out to each other since then.

"Jayded. It's right in my name," I told Debbie now, and she laughed. She'd been the one who came up with Jayd as my stage name three years ago, since it was "sexy and different," an upgrade from plain old Jay. I had been more than ready for that upgrade.

Now there was hardly anyone on the planet who didn't call me Jayd, even people I'd known for years. People assumed I preferred it, I guess... and mostly I *did*. Jay Rollins was a roiling mass of insecurity, overthinking, and bad decisions. Jayd, on the other hand, was a badass who hung out with Grammy winners. Which would you rather put in your Contacts list?

"Alright, here's what we're going to do," she said. "I'm sending a car for you at twelve. We'll have lunch at *Maman*. Give the tabloids proof of life—"

"Debbie, I'm not in the city."

She paused. "Wait, really?"

"Really. I'm visiting my sister. Sort of? It's a long story. And then I have a... a thing I promised to do for an old friend after that." I was *not* telling her it was a concert, otherwise she'd show up and accost me in person.

"And then you'll be home?"

I hesitated. *Home* was a funny word, wasn't it? I supposed my apartment in the city—which was pretty modest by rock star standards, since I was too much my father's son to ever throw money around—was the place where I got my mail. Did that make it home? Even if I'd spent less than ten weeks a year there since I'd bought it? Even if Aimee had never been there or my friend Oak either?

I supposed it was closer than anything else I'd found. Home was for sure not in Rock Gulch—I hadn't been back in years. And I didn't have a home anywhere else either... even if there was one particular place I secretly yearned for.

Or maybe a particular person you yearn for, a voice in my head taunted before I shut it down. *A person you'd like to have back in your life.*

It was bad enough that I'd been in love with Rafe Goodman since I was fifteen years old. Bad enough that I'd found out firsthand that spending summers without him didn't dim my feelings for him one iota. And *beyond* bad enough that my entire career had been built on songs I'd written about him—songs I sang, night after night, like squeezing a bruise, which meant my broken heart would likely never heal.

I was *not* going to start thinking dumbass thoughts about having him in my life again. No fucking way.

"I'm not really sure what I'm doing after that," I hedged. "It depends on a lot of things. I'd like to prioritize my family for a while—"

"Oooh. We could talk about that in the interview—"

Jeez. "Goodbye, Debbie," I said wryly.

"Uh-huh. Next time I call, you'd better answer," she warned before signing off.

I clasped the phone to my chest and sighed.

What the hell was I supposed to do with myself now? For so long, I'd been focused on taking the next step, and the step after that, I honestly wasn't sure what to do anymore. I was utterly rudderless for the first time since I was ten and I'd told my dad I wanted to be a musician.

When I closed my eyes, I saw Aimee the way she'd been the last time I saw her, the day she left Rafe. I'd been playing a couple of dates in Tampa at the time and trying to decide whether I could find a way to see her without going down to Whispering Key myself—I hadn't been back to the island in years at that point, because I couldn't look at Rafe and see my *brother-in-law* instead of the guy I'd fantasized about fucking on his dad's tour boat—when suddenly she'd turned up at my hotel.

She'd looked so tired, her face pinched with anxiety and stress, as she'd breathlessly explained that she'd married Rafe for all the wrong reasons and that she didn't want to see him again.

And what had I done? Had I offered to talk her through it? Get them counseling to save their marriage?

Fuck no. I'd felt sorry for her, but I'd also felt like some great cosmic error had finally been set right. I'd ordered us a bottle of tequila and promised to give her whatever she needed to move on. Money to relocate, money for a lawyer, money to cover her bills so she wouldn't have to worry about finances.

Money, money, money.

Looking back, I hadn't been there for her emotionally. Not even a little. I'd been selfish and immature.

And when Rafe had come looking for Aimee at my hotel suite a few hours later while she was napping, had I listened to his side of the story? Had I tried to help them reconcile?

Once again, that was a big fat no. Instead, I'd had the powerful urge to soak in his handsome face and broad shoulders, to throw my arms around him and beg him to want me instead.

And I'd been so fucking horrified by my own thoughts that I'd lashed out.

It's your fault Aimee looks so miserable.

I thought I could trust you to take care of her.

You obviously don't know how to give her what she needs.

She's none of your business anymore.

She's better off without you. We both are.

No lie, it had felt *good* in that moment to say those things, even the ones that weren't true. I'd told myself the pain on Rafe's face as he'd absorbed my words had been payback for the betrayal I'd felt when I'd found out my best friend had been harboring romantic feelings for my sister and hadn't bothered to mention them to me until the day he proposed to her.

I'd told myself that Rafe's right hook to my jaw was the punctuation at the end of our relationship.

It hadn't worked like that, obviously. I'd felt like shit almost immediately, because when Rafe hurt, I hurt, and I didn't know how to stop that from happening.

I still looked for Rafe's damn face in every crowd I played for. And I hated him for that nearly as much as I loved him.

My phone rang, and I scrambled for it eagerly, sitting halfway up in the bed. "Aim?"

"Guess again."

I deflated slightly as I recognized my friend Oak's deep voice.

Oak had been the security detail Debbie had insisted on during that first tour three years ago, when *Jayd* had been barely more than a figment of her imagination and I'd played at any venue that would have me.

Back then, in the aftermath of Aimee and Rafe's wedding, when I'd swan dived into a puddle of self-pity and wallowed in it, the only thing I'd needed protection from was myself, and I could barely afford to comp the man's drinks, let alone pay him a decent salary. But Oak hadn't needed the money. He'd stepped up as a friend, even though I'd had nothing to offer him, and I loved him for it.

Now he was still on the very, very short list of people I trusted implicitly, especially when it came to anything security related. I'd gotten used to a life where anyone who claimed to care about me had an ulterior motive, but the only time Oak held out a hand was when he tried to help me up.

"Did you find Aimee?" I demanded, getting to the point immediately.

I'd forgotten Oak was allergic to *the point.*

"Do you need me to repeat my lecture about checking your caller ID before answering the phone?" Oak rumbled. "Because you'd think, as a person who very recently got his ass outed by the damn paparazzi, you'd have slightly more situational awareness. I could've been anyone from the media, man. Hell, I could have been your agent. The wild turkeys that try to attack my mom's lawn ornaments have more sense than you."

I sighed, sank back down against the mattress, and

unwrapped one of the five hundred honey candies I always carried on my person.

"I knew you weren't Debbie because she already called. I'm refusing to do interviews about the tabloid story, and I'm feeling like it's a matter of time until she drops me."

"Aren't you a little ray of sunshine?"

I snorted. "I try."

"Try harder," he advised. "Things are gonna look up, Jay! Watch and see. This time next week, you won't even remember what you were so sad about."

"You think?" I demanded. "Really? You think I won't remember that my sister moved out of the apartment I'm renting her without telling me, or that I was outed by tabloid assholes, or that my career was hanging by its fingernails since I can't write a fucking song to save my soul?"

"Sure! You'll get invited to Iron Pipes," Oak said with the confidence of someone who had no idea how the music industry worked. "Then, Debbie'll suddenly recall you're her bestest and most favorite client, and she might actually show an emotion for the first time since Botox was invented. You'll get inspired to write again—it'll be great."

"You're adorable. Iron Pipes is next weekend, and I've already got a show scheduled. Besides, if they didn't invite me before the tabloid stuff, they're not gonna do it now." No matter what Debbie said.

Because I was *not* making a public statement about being gay, nor would I lie and claim I wasn't, and that was final.

"So can we get to the part where you tell me what you learned about Aimee yet?"

"Jeez. Right down to business, huh? No 'Hey, Oak, what's going on in your life? Let's chat about *your* feelings.'"

I remained silent, and Oak finally caved. "Okay, okay. I found her. Obviously."

"Holy shit." I sat up straight. "Why didn't you *lead* with that, man? Jesus Christ. Where is she? *How* is she?"

"Your lack of faith in me is troubling. And from what I can see, she's fine—"

"Fine?" No. If she were fine, she'd be here, or she'd have told me where she was. I was sure of it. "Where is she? I need to talk to her."

"Jay." Oak hesitated. "If a person is sad or bored and wants to leave her old life behind, she should be allowed to do that, even if she's your beloved baby sister. That's one of my hard limits."

"But she wouldn't," I argued, conveniently ignoring all the evidence that she *had*. "Or if she did, it's only because she's upset at me, and I need to find her so I can apologize. Please, Oak."

He sighed. "Okay, I'll tell you this much, since I got this info from combing through her Instagram account, which means it's practically public knowledge: she's been spending a lot of time in Larindosa, Wyoming."

"Wyoming," I repeated dumbly. "What the heck could she be doing there?"

"Drinking tea at a place called the Billy Goat Cafe? She's been posting pics of tea and scones a couple times a week for months, and when I checked the accounts she was following, I spotted a cafe that offers a ten percent discount to their Insta followers. The decor in her pics matches the decor in their promo pics, *et voilà*."

I took a deep breath and let it out slowly, nearly dizzy with relief that she was safe… and not in Florida. When Oak had started getting all squirrelly, I'd imagined a nightmare scenario where Aimee and Rafe reconciled and were more in love than ever… though I didn't know why that seemed worse than her living a secret life in Wyoming.

Yes, you do, that voice in the back of my brain taunted again. *You know exactly why.*

That voice sounded a lot like Rafe's dry, sexy, teasing voice, and my stomach clenched nervously.

I cleared my throat. "This is incredibly helpful, Oak. I really owe you one. Send me the address so I can go find her, okay?"

Oak hesitated. "I could fly out there and we could go together."

"Nah. What for?"

Another hesitation. "Because you don't have to do hard things alone?"

"I won't be alone."

"No?" Oak sounded surprised but pleased, and I understood why. I didn't have a lot of friends these days—or, okay, *any* friends aside from Oak.

I mean, I had collaborators and mentors and people I hung out with from time to time, obvs. Guys I'd hooked up with. Cari and Cheryl and Max, the musicians who toured with me. Ari Friedrich, who'd worked with me on a couple of his songs. Debbie and her staff. There was always someone around if I wanted there to be. But most of those people were with me because I paid them, either directly or indirectly.

And the few times I tried to convince myself that it was still possible for me to relate to people on a different level—like, for example, the night when I'd heard that my album had gone gold and I'd decided to venture out of my apartment and get lost in a crowd, soak up some good energy, and people watch—it ended poorly, like with a photographer throwing an innocent bystander to the floor so it looked like I was getting head in the middle of a crowded club.

I rolled my eyes at Oak, though he couldn't see me. "Yeah, don't get so excited. I'm not over here making new friends. I don't need them."

"Shoulda figured. You know—"

"Not everyone is an asshole who's out for himself? Yeah, yeah. So you keep saying, but the world keeps proving you wrong. Anyway, you remember a couple weeks ago I told you I was gonna play a concert in Florida on this little island called—"

"Whispering Key! The land of teenage dreams—and I mean that very much in the Katy Perry sense." He hummed a few bars. "The place where you first fell in love with—"

"Yes!" I interrupted snippily. "Yes, thank you. I recall." I huffed out a breath. "And I do not remember ever telling you about… that."

"Oh, but you did," he said cheerfully. "In glorious detail. Maybe the second or third night of that first tour, someplace in Connecticut. Tequila makes you loquacious. And apparently forgetful."

Loquacious. Great. Just what every man wanted to hear.

"Wait, how forgetful?" I asked, slightly panicked. "You and I never…"

"You and me? Shit, no. I like 'em a whole lot twinkier than you and way less sassy. Also, just to say, if we'd ever messed around, you'd've remembered. I'm basically unforgettable."

"And so *modest*," I marveled. "Anyway. I decided I'll drive down to Florida instead of flying, to stay off the media's radar as much as possible—"

"Good call. You're lucky you even made it to Colorado without attracting attention."

"—and the mayor sent his son out to ride with me."

Oak was silent for a moment. "Okay, please tell me when you say the mayor's son you don't mean your former brother-in-law. Because—"

"No," I cut him off before he could remind me of all the reasons why being around Rafe would be a disaster. "No, I mean Gage, the youngest brother. He's a good kid. I won't tell him I'm going to see Aimee, 'cause it's none of his business, but—"

"My dude," Oak interrupted disapprovingly, "you're keeping so many secrets from so many people, you've gotta be clenched tighter than a virgin's ass on Fleet Week. Someday you're gonna realize how much easier your life will be if you just start living openly."

No fucking way. When you gave people an inch, they took twenty-six miles.

"Thank you, Aunt Hagatha. I'll remind you of this someday. Will you send me the address for the cafe?"

Oak sighed. "I'll text you. But after you find your sister and see that she's okay... then what?"

"Then the concert on Whispering Key." I tried to keep the dread out of my voice, but I was pretty sure I'd failed.

"Okay, but *after* the concert?" he pressed. "What do you want to do?"

Jay, if you could have anything in the world, what would it be?

"I don't know, Oak. I'll cross that bridge when I come to it, I guess."

"Dear Diary," Gage Goodman grumbled from the passenger's seat of the sedan I'd rented in Denver for our drive to Larindosa. "It's the fifth day of my captivity. Food supplies are dwindling. I feel the life force draining from my pores."

I pulled my gaze away from the purple awning of the Billy Goat Cafe and glanced at the anthropomorphic bottomless pit wearing clunky boots and a bright green T-shirt that read "Hedgehogs: Why don't they just share the hedge?"

"If food supplies are running low, it's because you ate them all, kiddo." I gave a speaking glance at the bag of fast-food wrappers and empty cans littering the floor of the car.

Gage rolled his dark head against the headrest so he could look at me over his sunglasses. His eyes were dark and full of snark, just like his brother's.

"I boredom eat, okay? It's what I do. Just like you're addicted to those damn honey drops of yours. 'Go to Colorado, Gage,' they said. 'Road trip with the rock star,' they said. I was prepared for parties, Jayd. Trashing hotel rooms, running from the paps and their cameras—"

"Jesus." My lips twitched.

"Maybe hitting up a gay bar or two, since you're, like, super gay now." Gage lifted one dark eyebrow. "Instead, I get here and find out this guy I remember being really cool is more boring than fucking *Beale*. Beale, at least, has a hot boyfriend. Heck, you're more boring than *Rafe!*"

"Nonsense." I scowled.

"Evidence: we've spent the last four nights eating takeout burgers and watching basic cable at a mid-priced hotel in suburban Wyoming with America's slowest Wi-Fi and such shit locks on the doors that you insist on packing our stuff every day and putting it in the trunk." He jerked a thumb toward the back of the car.

"Because my guitar isn't just a guitar! Vega is a prewar Martin, which makes her a work of—"

"Let me take a second to tell you just how weird I find it that you named your guitar. Because it's very fucking weird." He paused like he was observing a moment of silence.

"It's actually quite comm—"

"*Then*, you drive us to the middle of this old-fashioned street, which looks like something out of a Hallmark movie or the opening credits of a slasher film, and you stare creepily at people, which suggests that *we* are going to be the slashers—"

"What?" I sputtered. "No! That's not—"

"But at least *that* would be exciting. Instead, we just *sit*, like Dale Jennings outside the Gas n' Sundry back home, watching other people—people who have purpose in their lives—pass us by." He turned to me suddenly. "Is this some kind of social experiment? Is that what we're doing here? Where are the cameras?"

I cuffed him lightly on the side of the head. "There are no cameras! We're people watching. It's fun! It's—"

"Do *not* treat me like I'm still thirteen and oblivious, Jayd. It's hurtful... *kiddo*."

"I'm not. I'm..." I trailed off. "You know, I remember you being a lot more easygoing than this."

"You remember me being a teenager with a crush on you," he muttered. "That ship sailed. Then it sank."

I blinked at him, then blinked some more. "You? Me? I... But... you're so... young." And not the right brother, I definitely did not add.

Gage rolled his eyes, and his lips split in a grin. "I'm twenty-three, dumbass. But don't stress. If I wasn't over you before, I'm sure as hell over you now. Rafe can have you."

"Rafe?" I demanded, my heart beating fast. "No. What? No. We are… we *were* friends. Brothers-in-law," I choked out.

"Right." He smiled wider. *Toothier.* "So, about this cafe. What time is Aimee supposed to show?"

I was so flustered, I didn't think. "Ten o'clock is her usual time, according to her Instagram posts, but she hasn't come in days, and I'm starting to wonder if Oak's information is… Wait! *Wait.* What makes you think Aimee has anything to do with my errand?"

Gage waved a hand dismissively. "FYI, your phone password is concerning on a number of levels, and guessability is the least of those."

My face went hot, and my fingers went cold. "You hacked my password?"

"Hack is such an ugly word. I've waited days for you to tell me what's going on, and you didn't, so I took matters into my own hands while you ran into the diner this morning and read your texts. Did you know that social engineering is by far the greatest threat to cybersecurity?"

"I… you…" I shook my head. "No."

"No? You mean you *didn't* intentionally set my brother's birthday as your phone passcode?" Gage blinked innocently. "What a strange coincidence. Who's Oak?"

"Just a friend." I closed my eyes and shook my head some more, trying very hard to pretend this wasn't happening, but the way my face went hot suggested that it *was*. "That's not… My passcode's been that way for *years*, and I…"

Gage gave me a pitying look. "Look, I might legit die of boredom if I'm stuck here another night." He leaned toward me confidingly. "I was meant for adventure, you know? So let me handle this."

He jumped out, crossed the street, and pulled open the cafe door before I'd managed to lock the car and jam a baseball hat on my head. When I caught up to him, he was already showing his phone screen to the blue-haired teenager at the counter.

"Oh, sure," the woman said. "Aimee! She's a chai latte, extra honey."

Gage smiled broadly and leaned a hip against the counter. "Ah, Megan, you're a lifesaver. I was totally spaced when I was talking to her earlier. Couldn't remember what she said to get, couldn't remember the address where I'm supposed to go to meet her." He grimaced. "At least now I only have to call her to repeat *one* thing."

"Brothers." Megan rolled her eyes good-naturedly, grabbing a paper cup to start making the drink. "I have three." She winked at Gage. "Aimee's at St. Vincent's. Two lights down, make a right, and it's on your left. Can't miss it."

"St. Vincent's?" I repeated. "What's that?"

"The hospital?" Megan frowned, like she hadn't noticed I was there. Then she did a double take and stared at me.

Damn it.

"Ignore my friend. He's really forgetful," Gage said.

Megan smiled again and handed over the drink. "M'kay.

Well, tell your sister I hope everything went well, and she should come see us when she gets out."

Gets out?

Gage and I both froze for a moment. He recovered long before I did. "Thanks a bunch, Megan. You have a great day."

He followed me out onto the sun-baked pavement. "Breathe, Jayd."

But I couldn't. "Get out? Like, she's hospitalized? For what?"

"Dude, I don't know. Maybe she fell down. Maybe she's getting a nose job."

I stared at him. "She's not getting a nose job."

"We don't know that. We'll just drive down and ask politely—"

"Oh, we'll ask, alright," I said hotly as guilt ate at my insides.

Three days I'd spent sitting around in Denver. Four here in Wyoming. And all that time Aimee had been *hurt*? Ill? Needing me?

Fuck.

"Get in the car, Gage."

I couldn't remember actually driving to the clinic, but when we pulled up outside, Gage rushed around to stop me when I would have charged into the lobby.

"This is a medical facility. They're legally not allowed to tell you much about her condition, remember? HIPAA laws and whatnot?"

I stepped around him. "I'm gonna ask to visit my sister, that's all."

But Gage was right. I was losing my mind from a combination of fear and frustration, and that would help nothing. I forced a smile and summoned every scrap of charm I possessed as I talked to the white-haired lady at the reception desk.

But Shirleen, after taking an excruciating three full minutes to type Aimee's name into the computer, was unmoved by my charm. "Sorry, honey. She's on an NOV for anyone not already on her approved visitor list, and there's no Jay on the list." She tapped the screen with the end of her pen.

"An NOV?"

"No Outside Visitors."

"How weird!" I shook my head in feigned bafflement. "I'm pretty sure it must've been an oversight. Could you call her and check?"

Shirleen tilted her head. "No can do, I'm afraid. Not when she's on an NOV. Have *you* tried calling her? She's in a step-down unit, not in ICU anymore, so she'll have her cell as long as she's feeling up to it."

Not. In. ICU. Anymore.

Words to strike terror in a person's heart.

I set my jaw. "Right. Good idea. I'll just... call her." I stepped away before I could do something really inadvisable, like sprinting around Shirley and yelling Aimee's name as I ran up and down every hall in the facility.

Meanwhile, Gage stepped up. "I'm sorry, Shirleen, but we're both so worried. We didn't even know Aimee was here until today," he explained. "I'm guessing she's trying not to worry us."

"Yeah, if that was her plan, it's not working," I muttered.

Gage shot me a quelling look. "I wonder if you could tell us who *is* on your NOE list, ma'am?"

"NOV," Shirleen corrected kindly.

"Ah. Of course. I'm so silly. NOV."

Shirleen patted his hand gently, in hard-core mothering mode over "silly" Gage who seemed so out of his depth.

"Maybe we'll just have whichever friend or family member *is* on the list come by and check on her." Gage lifted a hand to his forehead and gave her a tremulous smile. "It would go a long way to relieving our anxiety."

"Well, I suppose *that* wouldn't hurt anything." Still, Shirleen looked left and right like she wanted to make sure there was no one else around before tapping another couple of keys on her computer—which took so long an entire marching band could have filed through the lobby. I clenched my teeth hard enough to crack a molar.

"Here we go. Hmm. Just her medical team on the list, I'm afraid," Shirleen said sadly. "And her emergency contact, of course. Someone named Rafael Goodman?"

Rafael. Goodman.

I sucked in a breath as betrayal burned sharply through me, evaporating all the purposelessness I'd been feeling for days.

My sister—the sister Rafe knew I'd do anything for—was in the hospital, in *ICU* for the love of fuck, and he hadn't told me? Screw all my sappy feelings, all my silly hopes and my foolish regrets. I was going to *kill him*.

I pushed blindly out of the clinic and covered the ground to the parking lot in long, furious strides.

"Christ, Jayd, slow your ass down!" Gage called from behind me. "I think you should talk to Rafe—"

"Fuck yeah, I'm going to talk to him," I said as I yanked the car door open. "In person, so he can't lie or evade me. We're going to Whispering Key *now*."

3

RAFE

"Tell me what's going on with my sister." Jay leaned into my space and spoke in a voice so low none of the other Extravaganza Committee members could hear.

"With Aimee?" I shook my head. "How the fuck would I know? Is she okay?" Was it her heart?

Jay's nostrils flared. "I am so done with secrets and lies."

I didn't know what he was talking about, and I didn't care, because *I* was done with Jay Rollins treating me like I was dirt under his feet he couldn't wait to shake off.

And considering I was still hunched over and wheezing slightly from the force of his punch—though I'd be damned if I showed it—I wasn't inclined to say a word at all or do anything but stare at the man in front of me. The man staring at me with fury in his eyes.

My best friend.

My *former* best friend.

Damn it.

"Jesus Christ." Gage grabbed Jay from behind and hauled him back. "We talked about this, Jayd. We agreed you were gonna be chill."

"*You* agreed," Jay muttered. But he took a deep breath and calmed down slightly.

"Let go of him," I told Gage. Even though my brother thought he was helping me out, seeing his arms locked around Jay's chest bothered me for reasons I didn't want to admit. "If Jay Don doesn't like hearing me speak the truth about his music," I taunted, "he's welcome to hit me again, but I only owed him that *one* punch."

Jay's green eyes flashed dangerously... and fuck if that didn't make my stomach flip all the way over, which in turn made me scowl. I'd figured the silver lining of our friendship imploding was that I wouldn't feel this instant *want* just from being in the same room with him, but I'd been wrong.

"Good Lord, this is more exciting than them Turkish wrestling videos on the YouTubes," Lorenna breathed. "Don't stop your fisticuffs on our account, boys! Maddie, where's my camera? Does anyone have any oil?"

Jay's gaze darted to the side, like he was just then remembering we had an audience, then just as quickly came back to me.

"Heya, Jayd!" Lorenna added belatedly. "Welcome home, honey."

"Rafael." My dad got up from his seat, two minutes too late to actually help anything, which figured, and came around the table. "What in the Sam Hill is going on?"

"Exactly what I'd like to know," Jay gritted out. "I need to speak to Rafe. *Privately*."

"You couldn't've kept your mouth shut, eh?" Dad shot me a withering glance. "Like *you* know the first thing about over-produced albums."

"Hey! I know one when I hear it! And this is not my fault! I was just standing here, and *he* hit *me*." I was aware that I sounded like a little kid, and that only made me angrier. Especially since Dad was already giving Jay his brightest smile.

"Jayd, son, welcome home!"

This was *not* his home.

"You must be exhausted. I'm sure Rafe's real sorry for all the mean-spirited things he's said. Why don't you let Gage take you over to the Five Star so you can freshen up—"

"*No*." Jay exhaled a bit and forced a smile. "I mean, no, *sir*. I'd rather not go to the motel just yet. But thank you. Right now, I need Rafe."

I inhaled sharply at those words. Jay didn't need me. He didn't even want me in his life, and he hadn't for a while. But looking at him now, up close and personal? Seeing his familiar face and hearing his voice say my name? It made me ache for the closeness we'd once shared.

For the friendship he'd walked away from.

"I'm busy, and I think we've said everything we had to say to each other." I moved to retake my seat.

Dad blocked my path. "Ha ha! Nonsense, son! If Jayd wants to talk, you'll talk." His eyes flared with warning, and the implied *"Don't let me down, Rafael"* came through loud and clear. "After all, there's no higher calling for the head of the Extravaganza Committee than keeping our musical guest of honor happy. Is there?"

Jay's eyes locked on mine as he replied smugly, "I certainly can't think of any."

Fucker.

"Fine, then. Let's get this over with. Gage," I said without looking away from Jay, "while I'm chatting with our *guest of honor*, I'm deputizing you to be acting head of the Extravaganza Committee. Choose dicks at every opportunity, you hear me?"

"Uh. I always do," Gage agreed blandly, but he cast a worried look between me and Jay.

"Shit, so *this* is wisdom and maturity?" Fenn asked with faux innocence. "Mase, does this mean I've been mature for decades and haven't known it?"

"No, babe." Mason patted his arm gently. "Definitely not."

"Hey, Rafe? Since Jayd's here, does this mean you're canceling the Cheez-Bergers in Paradise as a fill-in act?" Littlejohn demanded.

"With Jay's track record?" I smiled grimly. "Absolutely not."

Jay gritted his teeth.

I gestured him out the door, pettily pleased that this meant he needed to turn first, which meant he also had to break our stare first.

This was the sort of person I became when Jay was around: overwhelmingly irritated and childish.

We clomped down the wide staircase side by side, and the heavy tread of Jay's boots mimicked the heavy beat of my heart. I tried—and failed—not to notice how the air between us crackled or that Jay smelled faintly sweet, like honey and citrus.

I frowned. I did *not* want to notice what he smelled like, damn it.

I'd spent way too many years comparing every potential romantic partner to Jayd fucking Rollins and having them all come up short. One woman might have green eyes, a guy might have a killer smile, occasionally someone would have his sense of humor. No one else had his voice, though, and no one else had ever looked at me like he knew me and liked me better than anybody either.

And no one else had ever fooled me as completely as Jay had because I'd never let them get close enough to try.

Jay pushed open the rec center door, and we stepped into a wall of heat and sunshine.

For the first couple of seconds, the warmth and humidity felt amazing after the chill of the air-conditioning. But like all good shit, that feeling was fleeting, and I quickly had to pull my sunglasses out of my pocket before the brightness seared my retinas.

I folded my arms and planted my feet. "Okay, that's far enough. What's this about?"

"It's about Aimee. Why is she—"

"*Ai, Dios! Jay! Jay, is that you? Mijo, como estas?*" Lety Irvine yelled from the front door of the Concha, waving broadly.

Jay waved back hesitantly.

I groaned. There was no such thing as privacy in this town, and as much as I didn't want to have this conversation with Jay, I *really* didn't want to have it in front of everyone. I dug my keys out of my pocket and headed left down the sidewalk, toward my truck. "Come on."

"Uh, hello?" Jay gestured right, toward an Escalade with Florida tags that probably cost him more in daily rental fees than I'd earned in a month doing boat tours for my family business. "My car's here."

"My truck is *there*." I pointed to the gleaming silver beauty.

"Your truck doesn't have my guitar and all my shit in it, and I'm not leaving my possessions parked on the street, waiting to get stolen." He bleeped his locks open. "I'm driving."

"Stolen? In the hotbed of crime known as downtown Whispering Key?" I set my hands on my hips. "You haven't the first fucking idea where you're going. *I'm* driving."

Jay folded his arms over his chest. "We really gonna whip our dicks out over this, Rafael? I'm pretty sure mine's bigger."

Those words, spoken in that goddamn magic voice of his, stopped me in my tracks, and the image they conjured had me eyeing the front of his jeans the way my dad had eyed the fucking appetizer coupons earlier. Hot and cold electric shivers ran down my thighs, and my dick plumped behind my jeans.

Goddamn it. I flat-out *refused* to still be attracted to this guy. I'd pushed down this attraction for *years* while we were teenagers, and I could do it now, too.

That's because you thought he was straight then.

But I didn't *know* that he was gay now either. Not for sure. Tabloid stories weren't facts. And even if he was gayer than six sparkly rainbows, it didn't matter. Because now that I knew his true colors, I didn't want a damn thing to do with him or—I licked my lips and glanced down again, before resolutely looking away—*his dick.*

I'd spent three years building a giant titanium-and-concrete wall around my heart where he was concerned, too high to scale and too wide to go around. It was not going to crumble.

Not today.

"I'm confident you're wrong." I tried to sound bored, but my voice almost cracked and betrayed me, damn it. "And the last time I rode in a car with you, you almost killed us."

Jay rolled his eyes. "Gimme a break. I was a teenager then! That possum came out of nowhere, and I had to swerve to avoid him—"

"You were almost twenty-four, and that possum was meandering along, minding his business, while you were singing 'Wild' at the top of your lungs and *emoting* all over the place."

"Fuck you, no one can sing Troye Sivan without emoting!"

"Yeah, but *you* could never emote with your eyes open. You know, like some people can't walk and chew gum?"

Jay laughed, and the sound seemed to startle him as much as it did me. "Shit." He ran a hand over his face tiredly, and *just that fast*, I felt the first tiny crack appear in my giant unbreakable, insurmountable wall.

Fuck. They didn't build walls like they used to anymore, huh?

This did not bode well for me.

"We're wasting time, and your committee's gonna come after us. Can you stop pretending I'm plotting a murder-kidnap spree and just get in my damn car?"

Since I couldn't think of a good reason not to, I did... and regretted it almost immediately, because the honey scent of him became more concentrated and harder to ignore the second he'd climbed in, too.

You hate him, I reminded myself. *He abandoned you when he got famous. He abandoned Aimee, too, for years. You cannot trust him.*

But when Jay rubbed his palms against the thighs of his jeans, my eyes followed the motion, noting just how thick his muscles there were, and just how nervous he looked, and—

Shit. I was such an idiot. Such a horny, sex-deprived, perpetually lovesick idiot.

Note to self: no more riding in cars with Jay Rollins. Ever.

Fortunately, I expected this would be the last time I ever had the chance.

"I'm sorry for hitting you."

"What?" I blinked over at him because Jay was not one to apologize, ever, and this was the last thing I'd expected to hear from him.

Jay sat hunched over the steering wheel with his fingertips pressed to his eyes, but he sat up straight when he sensed me looking at him.

"You heard me." His green eyes were intent, determined. "I said, I'm sorry for hitting you. Unlike *some* people, I'm not violent unless provoked."

"Well, neither am I." I scowled, thinking about how I'd hit him in Tampa. "Unless *seriously* provoked."

Jay rolled his eyes and put the car in drive... then slammed it back into park. "Wait. Where am I going?"

"My house," I said immediately.

"Your house? Heck no." Jay shook his head. "You realize that's literally the first place everyone is gonna turn up, telling us they just happened to be in the neighborhood, right? Taffy's gonna bring her turtle pie, and Lety will have *chuchitos*, and Littlejohn will whip up that casserole he makes out of canned spaghetti and spray cheese, and the Stallions are gonna get beer, and the next thing you know, Ms. McKetcham's naked on your front lawn doing keg stands. Not exactly conducive to you answering my questions."

I gritted my teeth. It irked me that Jay had thought of that. That he knew this island and the people on it. That he fit here.

This was not his home. It never was. I once thought it could have been, but he'd made his choices.

"Well, I don't know where else—" I shifted in my seat and heard a distinctive crinkle. I pulled the bright pink appetizer coupon from my pocket. "Actually, I do. Turn around. Head back over to Cooter Key."

Jay nodded once and pulled out in a wide arc, nearly clipping Lorenna's ancient Buick parked across the street. His face flushed, and he shot me a look before I could say anything. "Shut up. I'm a perfectly competent driver. I'm just not used to driving this particular car, that's all."

"Sure." I tucked my tongue firmly into my cheek before I spoke. "You're used to driving a tank where you just *roll over* all the other cars on the road, is that it?"

"Fuck you. *No.*" He pressed his lips together like he was either trying not to smile or trying not to haul off and hit me again. Either way, it was sexier than it had any right to be.

I was angry, damn it.

"It's been a while since I owned a car. Not much use for one in the city, and I haven't been to Alabama in years." He smirked a little. "Probably won't be invited back anytime soon either, now that Belinda's church lady friends have seen the headlines."

The pang of sympathy I felt was instinctive and annoying. Jay's family was all about appearances, and even though I'd always thought his dad was an ass, the idea of not being welcome couldn't be pleasant.

I opened my mouth to say something half-decent but what popped out was, "*Is* it true?"

The second I spoke the words, I wanted to take them back. I had no right to ask anyone that question, even if we were the very best of friends… and Jay and I weren't even close to being that anymore.

Jay's jaw tightened, and his hands clenched around the steering wheel. I waited for him to deny it, but instead, he said, "Shut up. We're here so you can answer *my* questions. For example—"

"Holy shit, it *is*," I blurted.

Somehow, I hadn't fully believed it. Maybe I hadn't wanted to.

I mean, he'd never talked about guys when we were growing up, only an endless parade of women. We'd shared everything back then—he'd been one of the first people I'd come out to when I realized I was bi—but he'd never suggested he was anything but heterosexual. Maybe he hadn't known yet.

He shot me a sideways look. "You can stop looking at me like a bug under a microscope anytime now."

"Sorry. Shit, sorry." I ran both hands through my hair and tried to temper my anger into something supportive. I had a lot of genuine issues with Jay, but this obviously wasn't one. "For what it's worth, a lot of guys don't realize they're bi until later in life. Take Fenn's boyfriend, Mason, for example. Or… Do you know the singer Ari Friedrich? He's fucking phenomenal, and *he* just came out as bi last—"

"It's not new, Rafe," Jay said dryly. "And I'm not bi."

"Oh." I was back to staring at him again. I knew every line of that face as well as I knew my own, even after years of not seeing it. The little freckle behind his ear, the notch in his right eyebrow, the way the ends of his hair curled up when he got sweaty. But I clearly hadn't known him as well as I thought I had.

Hearing him say those words was like scratching an old wound. With every look and every smile we'd exchanged during our summers together, I'd had to remind myself, "*He loves you as much as he can, Rafe. He can't love you back the way you want him to.*" Except he *could* have. He just hadn't.

Ouch.

And the fact that he'd kept all that to himself was a painful reminder that I'd been way more invested in our friendship than he ever had... which was why he'd walked away from it.

"Where'm I goin'?" Jay demanded when the rental car's tires hit the bridge to Cooter Key. He held back his hair with one long-fingered hand, and the muscles in his arms flexed.

"Mitchell's. Half a mile up," I said gruffly, disgusted with myself for wanting the guy, even still. "Take a left and it's on your right."

He pulled into the parking lot of Mitchell's Fine Family Dining and found the lone remaining spot in the shade. He contemplated the restaurant in the rearview mirror. "How likely am I to be recognized in there? I've got a baseball hat, but it can only do so much."

I wasn't the person to ask. I'd recognize Jay Rollins in the dark on instinct alone, even though that was a skill I'd pay someone to take away.

But since the parking lot was half-full, and word of Jayd Rollins crashing the Extravaganza Committee meeting was probably burning up the phone lines on Whispering Key, I had to think I wasn't the only one who'd spot him.

"Pretty likely that people will be looking for us. It's too hot for most folks to sit outside, though. Grab one of those picnic tables." I tilted my head. "I'll order at the outside window."

I didn't wait for Jay to agree or even ask what he wanted, and it wasn't until I was carrying a plastic tray loaded with cups of beer and plates of delicious fried food to a table shaded by a huge umbrella that I realized he probably didn't eat conch fritters anymore. His leanly muscled body suggested he ate a diet of organic grass and filtered fairy tears.

Oh, well. More for me.

The afternoon sun really was brutally hot, but the breeze made the temperature almost bearable... for someone used to it, anyway. Jay's face was already flushed, and his hair curled damply around the bottom of his cap as he engaged in a stare-down with a small flock of seagulls attacking some abandoned french fries nearby.

Unwillingly, I remembered Jay's phobia of birds, especially seagulls.

"They're descended from dinosaurs," he used to say in a fearful whisper. *"Don't let the feathers fool you."*

I dropped the tray in the center of the table with a clatter. Jay reached for one of the beers and downed a third of it without comment while I was still busy contorting my long legs into the bench seat.

"Any other invasive questions about my sexuality you'd like

to ask before we get to business?" he demanded the second my ass touched the wood.

I took a fritter from a plastic basket, dipped it in the spicy sauce, and answered frankly, "Tons." I popped the whole fritter in my mouth and nearly groaned at the taste.

Littlejohn was right; Caroline's brother couldn't be *all* bad if he could make fritters like this.

Jay stared at my mouth as I chewed for a full ten seconds, then looked away in disgust.

"Too bad, 'cause it's none of your damn business. It's my turn to get information." He lifted his hat and dragged a hand through his hair impatiently. "Tell me what's going on with Aimee. And I mean the *whole* story."

"You're barking up the wrong tree, Jay Don. I haven't talked to her in sixteen months."

"Bullshit."

My eyes locked on his. "No," I said slowly. "Not a single phone call, text, or Christmas card. Dead radio silence since the day she left." And yeah, I was just a trifle bitter about that. "When a Rollins is done with you, they're done. *You* should know that. You practically invented the rule."

Jay's cheeks flushed. "This isn't about you and me, Rafael. It's about Aimee. About her *health*."

"What about her health?" My pulse skipped a beat, just like it had back in the conference room. "Is she okay?"

I was angry at Aimee for leaving the way she did, and hurt as fuck that she hadn't stayed in touch, but I loved her like a sister anyway. I figured I always would.

"You tell me." Jay's eyes flashed combatively.

"You keep saying shit like that." I spread my hands. "I don't know what part of 'I haven't talked to her in sixteen months' is not getting through to you."

He leaned forward and hissed, "The part where my sister made you her freakin' emergency medical contact! Why the hell would she do that when you claim you haven't talked to her in over a year!"

I blinked at him and paused with a mouthful of fritter. "*I'm* her emergency contact? Me? Why not you?"

Jay folded his arms over his chest. "Excellent question. For that matter, why would my sister be getting treatment at a hospital in Wyoming in the first place? Why didn't she tell me she was sick *or* put me on her approved visitor list?"

He watched me closely, like he truly believed I knew the answer. Like he was positive I knew more about Aimee's condition than he did.

Until that moment, though, I hadn't known I did. Not anymore.

Aimee had been diagnosed with a chronic heart condition a few years back, after years and years of misdiagnoses.

She hadn't wanted to tell anyone. Not her family, not my family, not anyone on Whispering Key. For sure not Jay, who would have dropped his recording contract, his tour, his career, and all his musical talent in the trash to stand guard over her. I'd agreed to keep her secret, even from my best friend, and we'd handled things the old-fashioned way, with a lovely little marriage of convenience that got her on my health insurance.

But even when she was on the proper medication, she still dealt with chronic fatigue, breathlessness, and debilitating headaches that made it hard for her to hold down any job, let alone the kind that came with health insurance—and she *needed* health insurance, or at least someone to pay her medical bills.

Besides which, her symptoms weren't exactly subtle. You couldn't be around her for long and not know she was sick. She'd only kept it hidden when she lived on the island by keeping to herself, especially on her bad days. The way she panted with any kind of exertion wasn't exactly subtle.

How could Jay not know?

"I appreciate that you think I'm omniscient, Jay Don," I said carefully, my heart rate kicking up a notch, "but I can't read Aimee's mind. I never could." And wasn't that the fucking truth? Her decision-making rationales had always been a mystery to me. Like the time she decided to try some quack experimental treatment our insurance wouldn't even consider, or the way she'd up and left the island, leaving me nothing but a note and blocking my number.

"Did you tell her not to tell me?"

I laughed out loud. "How can I say this more clearly? We don't *talk*, Jay. Jesus, maybe she didn't tell you what's going on because she thought you'd run off half-cocked, throwing punches and accusing people of shit? Maybe she kept quiet because she hates when you're overprotective?"

"I've never been *over*protective. I was just-the-right-amount protective. And I haven't even been *that*. Not recently." He straightened in his seat. "Which is why you're going to tell me what's going on right now, so I can do what I should have been doing all along," he said firmly.

"Oh, am I?"

In truth, I couldn't imagine what the fuck Aimee was thinking not coming clean to Jay about all this.

But also, her story wasn't mine to tell.

Especially not to her freakin' *brother*, who swung into town like a rock-star wrecking ball, demanding information like I was a member of his entourage contractually obligated to give him information. Hells to the no.

I'd get more information from him, and then I'd check on Aimee *myself*.

"I figured since you were the person Aimee turned to when she wanted to leave the Key, you'd be around her all the time."

"Not exactly." Jay grabbed a napkin and began tearing it into strips. "She didn't want to live with me in New York. I'm never home anyway. She decided on Denver, so I got her a place there. And we... I... I was busy. I didn't call as often as I should. She didn't either."

"That's why you were in Denver last week, when Gage flew out to babysit you, all heart-eyes and hero worship," I snarked. "Aw."

"There are no heart eyes. Not anymore, anyway. And you'd better not tease him about it," Jay said severely. "Jesus, didn't you ever have a misguided crush on someone when you were young and stupid?"

I snorted. "You have no idea. Worst mistake of my life." And I flat-out refused to repeat it.

Jay scowled and tore the napkin strips into smaller strips. Precise halves of halves of halves. "Besides, Gage wasn't *babysitting*. He was keeping me company while I tried to find her."

"To *find* her?" I demanded in rising concern. "She's not just sick, she's *missing*? Jesus, Jay Don."

"I found her eventually! Thanks to my friend Oak." He set his teeth and admitted, "She's not living in the Colorado apartment anymore. She moved without telling me. I tracked her to St. Vincent's Hospital, where she's apparently a patient, but I can't get any more information. Which brings me to *you*."

Lucky me.

"You're still claiming you and Aimee haven't been in contact?" Jay asked again, a little desperately this time, like he really *needed* to believe that I had all the answers for him.

Alas, no.

But this much, at least, I could answer honestly. "Other than through lawyers, signing uncontested divorce papers, Aimee and I have not been in contact." I dug my wallet out of my pocket and removed a folded-up piece of paper I'd kept there for over a year. "This was the last communication I had with her. Go on." I nudged the paper across the table, avoiding the tray. "Read it."

He unfolded the paper, still eyeing me mistrustfully, then glanced down.

"*Rafe*," he read aloud.

I wanted to tell him he didn't need to read it to me, since I had the damn thing memorized—I took it out and read it every time I found myself thinking about either of the Rollinses as a reminder not to be weak ever again, which meant it got read pathetically often—but I wouldn't give him the satisfaction of knowing it bothered me.

"*You have no idea how hard this is to write. You've been an amazing friend. I don't know what I would have done without all of your love and support these last couple years. But I can't keep living halfway like this, alive but not fully living.*" Jay cleared his throat "*There's beauty and pain and wonder in the world that neither of us are experiencing, and that's all my fault. We both deserve better.*"

He looked up at me like he wanted me to explain it all, but *nope*. Not going there.

"What can I say?" I shrugged. "Your sister loves overdramatic letters the way you love overproduced tracks."

He gave me a narrow-eyed look and resumed reading. "*I know it's your nature to be responsible for every-damn-thing, and to never admit defeat, which is why I have to leave like this. If I gave you a chance to talk me out of it, you would. If I didn't burn the bridge, I'd find myself crawling back over it. We need a clean break, and someday when we're back in each other's lives again, you'll admit I was right to do this. I'm seriously looking forward to that.*"

He looked up at me again.

Again, I shrugged. "Not sure when that magical day is supposed to come. Hasn't happened yet."

"Marrying you was the best idea I ever had—" Jay paused, and his nostrils flared. *"—but leaving is the second best. You'll see. Thanks for everything. Love always, Aimee."*

Jay let go of the paper, and it fluttered to the tabletop. I refolded it tidily and put it back in my wallet, where it would sit as long as my poor, gross heart still ached for the idiot sitting across from me.

Sadly, I didn't think I'd get to toss it anytime soon.

"I haven't heard from her since," I told him. "Now, why don't you tell me more about what you learned. What was the name of that hospital again?" I tried to act all fake-casual, like I wasn't planning on hunting her down and making sure she was okay.

Jay shook his head once. "No. You're still answering *my* questions."

Didn't it figure? Always Jay's way, always on *his* fucking terms.

"What was she missing out on?" he demanded.

Love? Sex? A real marriage?

"Hard to say exactly," I semi-lied. "I think she felt stuck on the island. She didn't always appreciate the, uh... *quirkiness* of the Keysters the way y—" I cleared my throat. "The way some people do."

Jay frowned. "Nuh-uh. Everyone's so kind. She loved it here."

"No, *you* did. Folks on the Key are all up in your business, and that bugged Aimee." Mostly because it made it incredibly hard to keep her secret. I wasn't sure how we'd managed it. "Also, you might've noticed the bridge to the mainland still isn't fixed? It's not exactly an easy commute to anything off Key. And, you know money was never particularly plentiful for us Goodmans. Not until we dug up that treasure a while back."

I chewed another fritter meditatively.

All of that was true, but in general, I'd thought Aimee was… fine. If not happy, then happy-ish.

As happy as a woman with a chronic heart condition and a guy in a marriage of convenience with the sister of the man he was in love with could possibly be.

Huh. Okay, maybe it shouldn't have come as such a surprise when she left.

"She never told me she was unhappy directly," I informed Jay. "If she had, I would have done what I could to fix it. I had no clue she was planning to leave until I opened her bedroom door to check on her one morning and found that letter and figured out she'd had Littlejohn drive her to Tampa to see you."

With nothing else to go on, I'd assumed she'd decided Jay's career was established enough that she could be honest with him. That he'd take care of her.

I sighed. One of these days, I was going to stop assuming I knew what the Rollinses were thinking.

Just like one of these days, I was going to stop assuming that the Rollinses were capable of caring about me the way I cared about them.

I sat back in my seat and focused my gaze on the tree fronds swaying in the breeze beyond his head so I didn't have to look at him. If I kept trucking down Pity Party Lane, I was pretty sure I'd end up sobbing into my fritters, whining out loud about how both Rollinses had left me without a backward glance and wondering what about me made me so damn *leave-able* by the people I loved.

And after *that*, I'd pray for spontaneous combustion, because the last scraps of my ego couldn't handle being that vulnerable in front of Jay Rollins. Even contemplating it made me want to vomit.

I cursed the day my dad had gotten the brilliant idea to invite Jay to the fucking Extravaganza, I really did. He had no freakin' idea how much torture he'd signed me up for.

"Her bedroom door."

My gaze met his impatiently. "Huh?"

"You said you opened *her* door." Jay lifted an eyebrow like he was Sherlock Holmes and he'd just found a clue. "And you went to *check* on her in the morning? You weren't with her in the room?"

I snorted. "Uh, no. Obviously. I mean, it's not like we—" *were sleeping together*, I was about to say.

Except *duh*. Jay thought we'd been in love, so of course he'd assumed we'd slept together, even if the idea of ever touching Aimee in that way gave me the heebie-jeebies.

"Tell me this, Rafe." Jay watched me closely, his eyes tight. "Did you ever love her at all?"

I opened my mouth and shut it again with a shake of my head. "I'm not getting into this with you."

"Because when we were in Tampa... Fuck. She was pale as a ghost. She looked like she hadn't slept in years. And I just... I don't get how you could be that cruel. That's not the Rafe that I knew."

Seriously? He'd explained away the symptoms of Aimee's illness as... as *heartbreak*? From the end of our nonexistent love affair? No wonder he'd been so confrontational back in Tampa, charging in to overprotect, as he always did.

The clusterfuckery was so thick I could hardly breathe.

Goddamn it, Aimee.

But she wasn't the only one to blame for all the secrecy; I'd been right there, too, agreeing with her. And Jay wasn't the only one who'd tried to ride in like a fucking white knight and save the day either. That was on me, too.

And sadly, it looked like I hadn't learned my lesson, because here I was, about to mount up again.

"I loved Aimee a lot. It just... didn't work out, I guess. But I'm very concerned about her health. So, now it's your turn. Tell me again what you know, and then you can fly back off and rejoin your regularly scheduled rock star life, already in progress."

Jay ignored this jibe. "She's at St. Vincent's in Larindosa, Wyoming."

"Great. I'll make some calls. And I'll let you know that she's okay, I promise."

I mean, it was the nice thing to do. After all, *I* wasn't the asshole at this table.

"You can't call," he mumbled, tracing the edge of the plastic food tray with his finger.

"Uh. Pretty sure I can. That's what being an emergency contact means."

"Yes, well." Jay cleared his throat, and his eyes flitted around, from the table, to the roof of the restaurant, to the road, to the seagulls. "Look, they wouldn't give me information this morning in person, and all I could find out on the website was that they were a holistic treatment center that offers everything from yoga retreats to surgery, which was not helpful! So it's... somewhat possible that I called the hospital this afternoon to get more information while pretending to be Rafael Goodman."

"*Somewhat possible*?"

He winced. "By which I mean definite. And when I called, the *idiots* over there wanted me to verify my identity by giving them my birthday, which is to say *your* birthday, and when I did, they told me I was wrong. Repeatedly."

"What a surprise."

"It *was* a surprise, because I definitely had it right! I mean, it's the freaking pass—" He flushed. "Er. It's a date I used to know in the *past*, and as you know, I have an extremely good memory." He made an impatient gesture with his hand. "Anyway. I maybe got a little agitated, which is entirely understandable given the circumstances, and um... maybe possibly, by which I also mean definitely, made a somewhat rude comment about going over there to teach the receptionist how to type correctly." He frowned. "It's sort of a blur."

"You did *what*?"

"Yes, okay! It wasn't my finest moment! But the long and short of it is, your name is on some kind of terror watch list —or whatever the hospital equivalent of that is—so they're not giving out any information on her condition unless Rafael Goodman shows up in person with identification or submits a notarized affidavit or something."

I peered at him for three entire beats with my mouth hanging open before I exploded. "Are you kidding me?" I scrubbed my hands through my hair. "Is that even legal?"

"Which part?" Green eyes peeked out from beneath thick eyelashes. "The part where they want ID, or the part where I pretended to be you? 'Cause the illegality of the second thing means I can't really call them out on the possible-illegality of the first."

I tilted my head all the way back and groaned up at the umbrella. "Jesus Christ, you've fucked this up."

"Me? *No.*" His nostrils flared. "No, no, no. This situation was *already* fucked-up, ever since my sister decided to keep something this important from me. And it's further fucked-up because you know more than you're saying, and *you're* keeping me in the dark, too."

"Pfft. You have no idea what you're talking about."

He leaned in over the table again. "Do you know, when you lie your nose twitches like a teeny, tiny bunny rabbit." He reached out, lightning fast, and *booped* the tip of my nose with his finger.

I clapped a hand to my face. "Fuck you! It does not."

He smiled smugly. "'*No way, Mom! Me and Jay weren't drinking out on the beach.*' Twitch. '*Sorry, Gagey, Dad says you can't come out on the Zodiac with us. He needs you to work the tour.*' Twitch, twitch. '*No, Jay, I don't have a crush on anyone.*' Twitch, twitch, fucking *twitch.*"

Oh my God, I hated him in that moment. *Hated.* How dare the man notice shit like that and not care about me? How dare he know me so well and just walk away? I clenched my hands into tight fists beneath the table.

"Now." Jay drew a deep breath. "I admit I may have used slightly unorthodox means in an attempt to get information—"

"Slightly unorthodox? Jay Don, you wouldn't recognize integrity if it walked right up and started sucking your dick."

He gasped. "You *hypocrite.* Like you wouldn't have done the same thing if it were Beale in that hospital? Or Gage? Or Fenn? Or your dad?"

"I wouldn't have had to," I growled, "because *my* family doesn't keep things from me."

This was blatantly untrue, as evidenced by Beale's entire relationship with Toby and basically every ridiculous decision my father ever made, including but not limited to inviting my archnemesis to play a concert on the Key, but in that moment, I wasn't concerned with accuracy. I wanted to hurt him. And I did.

Jay's green eyes flared with pain, and he sucked in a short breath... and my triumph tasted like ashes because—*fuck me sideways*—when Jay hurt, I hurt, too.

I held up a hand before he could clap back. "Sorry. I'm sorry. That was… shitty and uncalled for." I swiped the back of my hand over my sweaty forehead. "We just bring out the worst in each other."

"We didn't use to," Jay said softly.

"We didn't use to do a lot of things," I countered. We'd gone from being people who told each other everything to being people who couldn't tell each other *anything*. I squeezed my eyes closed. "Look, this whole thing is so complicated now. What do you expect me to do? Trot off to Wyoming and bring her a Get Well balloon? I'm in charge of the Extravaganza. I promised my dad."

"Then un-promise him! Rafe, this is *serious*. I have no idea what's wrong with her. You don't wanna deal with Aimee? Fine! Just come to Wyoming with me, get me past the dragons at the desk, and leave it to me."

I ran my tongue over my top teeth, pondering this. It was tempting, not gonna lie. The more time I spent with Jay Rollins, the less time I wanted to spend with Jay Rollins. The man was dangerous to my mental health. And if he was on the case, then Aimee would be well cared for, and I'd be out of their drama for good—

"Come on, Rafe," Jay insisted. "You owe me that much."

Uh. What?

I peered at him across the table, then tilted my head and peered at him some more, like maybe he'd become less of an entitled jerk if I shifted my perspective.

But no. Nope. Same entitled jerk no matter which way I looked at him.

I didn't owe Jay Rollins any-damn-thing.

"Come on! Rafe, you said you love her, right? You carry her breakup letter like a lucky charm?"

I huffed out a laugh. That was one interpretation.

"So, we get on the next flight, maybe even tonight, and you could be home in twenty-four hours. I'll pay for *everything*," he wheedled, leaning toward me with his elbows on the table. "First class!"

First. Class. Did he think I gave the first *shit* about that? Had he *ever* really known me?

A shaft of sunlight spilled through a hole in the umbrella overhead and made Jay's imploring eyes glow greener. It had always been Jay, and never Aimee, that I couldn't look away from.

Looking at him in that moment, I could see that he was scared and unsure beneath all the bravado, and though I wanted to hate him for what he'd done to our friendship, hate was a hard emotion to hold on to.

Self-preservation, though, was something I could get behind.

"Please, Rafe." Jay summoned a half-smile. "You and me? Partners in crime again? Saving the world from arrogant receptionists and all manner of birds? You know you wanna say yes."

I took in a calming breath and tried really fucking hard not to notice the scent of honey or how it was more appealing than any of the food on the table.

"The answer is *no*."

4

JAY

I blinked at Rafe Goodman—my first crush, the guy I'd held up as my ideal for an embarrassing number of years—trying to make sense of the last syllable he'd uttered.

"No? You mean... no, we can't fly out tonight?" I smiled winningly, like maybe this was all a joke. "That's fine. We can go tomorrow. I haven't even checked the flight schedule, so..."

He stood up from the table. "No, I mean I'm not going anywhere with you."

Shit. This was about the "first class" thing, wasn't it? I'd known I sounded like a pretentious dork the second it was out of my mouth. Rafe wasn't Debbie.

"*You're* free to go whenever you'd like, obviously," Rafe continued. "In fact, I hope you do! Go now and just... keep right on going." He made a sweeping motion. "Don't look back."

"Rafe, think about this," I demanded, standing up also. "You're ducking out on your ex-wife when she needs you? Where's responsible, problem-solving Rafe Goodman, huh? Where's the guy who just bitched to the whole Extravaganza Committee that *I* wasn't a person who stuck around when things got inconvenient? You're telling me *you* can't be inconvenienced now?"

Shit. I hadn't intended to let on that I'd overheard that, because I didn't want him to know how much it had bothered me. But then again, I hadn't *intended* a lot of things with Rafe, and they'd ended up happening anyway.

Rafe's expression shut down totally, the fire in his eyes going cold. "Remember that unlike certain people who only have to please themselves, I have responsibilities to my family, to Goodmen Outfitters Tours, and to the people of the island who are counting on me to run the Extravaganza. Important... responsible... responsibilities." He nodded firmly. "I won't abandon them just because *you* fucked up."

How very dare he! My lips parted in outrage. I couldn't remember the last time anyone had utterly dismissed me like that, and it drove me a little crazy.

Okay, a *lot* crazy.

"Are you *trying* to make me angry?" I demanded, setting my hands on my hips.

"Aw. Poor Jay." He rocked back on the balls of his feet and pouted with mock sympathy. "No, let me explain. You see, what's happening here is that, unlike your rock star entourage, I'm not automatically saying yes to you. That's because, *also* unlike your rock star entourage, making you happy is not my job."

My rock star entourage? I wanted to ask him where he thought they might be hiding. In my luggage, possibly?

"This is not about *me*, asshole. And it's not about *you* and your bullshit priorities. If you're mad at me—and Jesus, what right do you have to be mad at *me*?—but if you are, then *fine*. I'll somehow find the strength to go on." I rolled my eyes. "I wouldn't be here if *Aimee* didn't need you, or if there were any other solution short of getting a court order." Which I'd already had my attorney start checking into, but which was a long shot unless I could prove Aimee wasn't capable of making decisions for herself. "Aimee's more important than you having your panties in a twist. And she's more important than my pride, too, so what will it take here? I already apologized for hitting you. I'll apologize for everything I said in Tampa, too. I apologize for the time I stole your Gators shirt—"

He gasped. "I fucking *knew* it was you!"

"Of course it was me! There were only two of us on that camping trip."

"You *said* you thought maybe a manatee ate it."

"And you knew I was lying." I shrugged. "So now what? Should I beg? Get down on my knees?"

Rafe's eyes blazed, like the very idea horrified him. "Fuck no. Why would I want you to beg? I don't want a single damn thing to do with you, Jay Don. And you can mock my responsibilities all day, but I don't run away when it suits me." He lifted an eyebrow. "I'm not a Rollins."

I sucked in a breath and glared. That was a direct hit, right in the vulnerable spot of my heart that worried I was a shit brother who'd let my sister down, but I wouldn't let him see it.

"No," I breathed. "You're just an *ass*."

Rafe's expression turned grim, but he nodded once. "When I have to be." He folded his arms over his chest. "Seems like we don't have anything left to say to each other."

On the contrary. I had many, *many* choice words to say to him, but I pushed them down, recognizing the mulish set of his jaw for what it was.

He'd worn that expression when Jeremy Mickell had told him there was no way he could hold his breath underwater for five whole minutes. He'd worn it when I'd told him my dad wasn't sure I'd be able to make it as a musician and he'd insisted I would. It was an expression that dared the world to defy him, and seeing it now, I realized this was the first time he'd ever used it against me. Always in the past, it had been me and Rafe against the world. It made me wonder if the Rafe I'd known—the Rafe I'd *thought* I'd known—had been a figment of my imagination.

This shouldn't have come as such a shock. After all, I hadn't known he and Aimee were more than friends until they'd gotten *engaged*. Clearly, I'd never known him as well as I thought I had.

Ugh.

"Well. This certainly has been fun." I pushed up, too, making sure I stood every bit as tall as he did. "Glad we had this chance to catch up and see that we have literally nothing in common anymore, if we ever did, and that all my memories of you being a decent human were some kind of hallucination. Hopefully Aimee's not *dying* or whatever."

I mean, she probably *wasn't* dying. Shirleen at the front desk had said Aimee wasn't in intensive care and that she'd probably be able to return my call soon.

But probably wasn't good enough.

I turned and stalked toward the car with rage and hurt churning in my gut, leaving Rafe to deal with the trash. I started the engine, turned the air conditioner on full blast, backed out of my spot, and waited for Rafe to jog over.

The second he reached for the door handle, I rolled forward slightly. He stepped forward and reached again, and this time I engaged the locks.

To his credit, it took him less than a second to figure out what was happening here.

"Ah. I'm not doing what you want, so you're ditching me?" He folded his arms over his chest. "How incredibly mature of you, Jay."

"You see—" I smiled tightly. "—after thinking about it, I'm just not sure if this car is big enough to carry you, me, my invisible rock star entourage, and the weight of your enormous, responsible responsibilities. Besides, I think the walk might be good for you. The fresh air might help you sleep tonight, since I'm not sure how you'll manage otherwise."

At least, the Rafe I knew would've had trouble sleeping. *This* conscienceless, selfish prick, though? The one who basically admitted he'd been sleeping apart from my sister and wouldn't inconvenience himself by going to make sure she was okay? Who the fuck knew.

"I think you're not used to people saying no to you anymore," Rafe countered, taking a step back. "Fine. Enjoy your temper tantrum."

Temper tantrum?

Figured the jerkface would manage to take away even the small amount of petty pleasure I'd get from leaving him stranded.

Rafe slid his hands into his two back pockets, making his white T-shirt pull tight across his broad, muscular chest... which was so fucking sexy it nearly left me breathless, even though I was angry enough to low-key visualize running him over.

"You know what else?" Since this was probably the last time I'd ever lay eyes on the man, and it was important that he should know. "'Pretty Girl' is maybe the best song I've ever written, and it's not my fault you're a cretin who's so biased against my music that you haven't listened to the lyrics or tried to understand the subtleties in the melody. Also, I regret writing every fucking word of that song, and never more so than at this exact moment."

"Uh." His face screwed up in confusion, like he wasn't sure whether I was insulting him or myself. I wasn't either. "Okay?"

"I feel incredibly inspired to go write another song now, though," I continued. "A song of vengeance called 'Rafe Goodman, Junior, of Whispering Key, Florida, is a Self-Centered Shithead.' It's not a pithy title, but I figure this way ignorant listeners like yourself won't break your tiny brains figuring out who I'm writing about and why. I envision the lyric track will be three minutes of me screaming into a microphone in frustration. And to symbolize your selfishness, the melody will be one lone note plucked over and over on an out-of-tune ukulele until your ears want to bleed. I'll send you a copy."

"Can't wait." His dark eyes narrowed in challenge. "You *did* promise to write a song for me, once upon a time. And you're obviously no Ari Friedrich or whatever, but it might be fun to hear what an amateur can do. What rhymes with 'Rafe is a delight'?"

I shook my head, torn between pity and killing rage. *Amateur?* I was "*no Ari Friedrich*"? Really? Also, the fact that Rafe could listen to my album and not understand what it was really about...

Gah. Like it wasn't hard enough playing those songs night after night, when everything I'd written about felt like a dream of another life.

"I'm going with 'Rafe's a necrotizing boil on the ass of friendship,'" I informed him. "And I'm gonna make sure it's so overproduced, the '80s are going to call and ask for their synthesizers back. Bye, Rafe. Have a nice life."

I pulled out of the parking lot and purposely turned left, heading further away from Whispering Key. I was so fucking angry, the last thing I wanted was to run into Big Rafe, or anyone in the Goodman family, or anyone who'd ever known any of them. Instead, I pulled over in a coffee shop parking lot maybe a quarter mile down the road, pulled out my phone, and immediately began searching for flights back to Wyoming that night.

Of course there were none, because fuck my life anyway.

But that was fine. Fine! Even if I could get to Larindosa immediately via teleportation, I couldn't do anything to help my sister until I'd gotten that court order or until she called me back. So, I texted my attorney and Oak to update them on the situation, texted Aimee (in case my three hundred voice messages had been misdelivered), and booked a flight for the next morning. Then I found a hotel right on the Gulf that promised "ice-cold air-conditioning" and "noise-proof rooms"—I assumed their clientele ran to serial killers and musicians—and checked into a room for the night.

A few minutes later, I was sitting on my balcony, watching the waves roll in and trying to force myself to relax.

Fortunately, it wasn't that hard while I was staring at the water. There was something about the hypnotic sound and movement of the tides that fed my soul and always had. I remembered Mary Goodman, Rafe's mom, saying that staring out at the water helped her keep things in perspective.

"No matter how big a mess I might've gotten myself into, honey, the Gulf is big enough to wash it clean so I can try to do better."

Looking at it reminded me that no matter how many people knew my name or my music, I was still just a collection of atoms. A grain of sand on the beach, just like everyone else. What mattered were the things that connected us. That made us a force strong enough to hold back the water.

Like music.

Like love.

Like bone-deep rage-lust that made you wanna simultaneously kiss your former friend until he melted into a puddle and shake him until his teeth fell out.

I propped my feet on the balcony railing and stared out at the setting sun, wondering why the hell it was that Rafe Goodman got to me like no one else in the world ever had. The statistical probability of Florida breaking off and floating away into the ocean was higher than the chances of us ever being anything to each other again… so why was *he* the guy I kept coming back to and comparing to every other guy I slept with?

"We bring out the worst in each other," Rafe had said. And *fuck*, he was so, so right, because here I was feeling jealous of my sister—my *hospitalized* sister—because Rafe keeping her secrets felt like him choosing her instead of me all over again.

But he was so, so wrong, too, because nothing in my life had been in harmony from the day I cut him out. No matter how murderous he made me, no matter how we scratched and bled each other, when I was with him, something in my soul sighed and whispered, "Ah, *there* you are!" And I was pretty sure it always would.

We were engaged in a lifelong game of Fuck, Marry, Kill, where he was my first and only answer in every single category.

I froze. Then I jumped up from my chair and ran back into my room. My suitcase lay untouched on the floor, but I grabbed my guitar and dragged it outside along with my beaten-up notebook and a ballpoint pen from the desk.

By the time the sun set a few hours later, I was plucking out the melody of a song and fitting it to some lyrics that started out as a giant fuck-you... and had maybe ended as something else entirely.

How could you be the answer to every question?

The secret in my confession,

Give me comfort with your aggression,

After all this time,

How is it still you?

They weren't great lyrics. Heck, I wasn't even sure they were *passable* lyrics, but after months of zero inspiration, months of feeling like I'd never *want* to write another line of a song again, even that abysmal offering felt like a victory worth savoring.

Figured that Rafe was the catalyst for that, too, didn't it? He might be an asshole, but there'd never been a time that he didn't make me *feel*, and now was no exception.

The stars were high in the sky by the time I put my guitar down, and my eyes found Lyra by instinct. One of the first constellations I'd ever learned to recognize.

"That collection of stars right above us reminds me of you. See that tilted rectangle shape? That's Lyra, and the bright star on the end there is Vega."

"Which?" I narrowed my eyes, trying to see what Rafe saw. "The ones that look like a bent coat hanger?"

Rafe snorted and turned toward me on the blanket, his face so close I could feel his breath on my cheek.

"It supposedly looks like Orpheus's magic lyre. It created magic music that made people feel joy and sadness and hate and love.

All kinds of shit, just like you do. When his wife died, Orpheus played his harp and convinced Hades to bring her back to life, as long as he had faith and walked out of the underworld without looking back for her."

"Huh. He looked back, didn't he?"

"Obvs." Rafe rolled onto his back again, but his laughter on the warm night breeze surrounded me. "The happily ever afters never get turned into constellations."

I sighed.

But when I crawled into bed that night, despite feeling like I was trying to swim upstream on my own, I felt more hopeful than I'd felt since the day those damn paparazzi pictures got posted.

The air near Whispering Key was magic.

I woke up the next morning before my alarm, showered, and made it to the airport with hours to kill before my flight. The air outside was already dripping with humidity, which was great for my vocal cords but kinda miserable for the rest of me.

I turned in my rental car, hefted my bag and my guitar on my shoulders, jammed my baseball hat down over my eyes, and started a deep, intellectual debate with Oak via text as I entered the elevator that went something like:

OAK

I can see the headlines now. Why's Jayd
flying into Denver? Is he meeting a BOY
there? Is it the BOY from the PICTURES?

You're basically asking the paparazzi to crawl up your ass if you fly commercial right now.

ME

I'll ignore them.

OAK

Sure you will. You're so good at ignoring people who ask insensitive questions.

ME

I am!

OAK

You stick your nose in the air, and pull out the freezy-eyes, and try to turn them to ice on the spot.

ME

I do what I have to. Gotta go grab breakfast now, Mom. Text you when I land.

The elevator doors started to close when someone yelled, "Hey, hold the door?"

Instinctively, I reached out a hand to prop it open, and a really extraordinary number of children—all of different sizes yet somehow wearing the same color shirts, like the world's shortest basketball team—streamed in, followed by a couple of parental units toting a baby carriage and a luggage cart.

"Say good morning to the nice man, children!" the mother-type person singsonged... and like something out of a creepy nightmare, her many spawn opened their mouths simultaneously and chorused, "Good morning, sir!"

I repressed a shudder.

The second the doors closed, an overpowering perfume smell seared my nostrils, and I coughed a little.

One of the shorter spawn blinked up at me with wide eyes. "Baby Jebediah puked in the car. Scrambled eggs."

"Ambrose!" the mother chided. "The nice man doesn't need to hear this." To me, she mouthed, "Sorry."

I smiled wanly.

Baby Jebediah began to cry.

"Augusta spilled Mommy's whole perfume bottle down the front of her, trying to cover up the smell," the tiny informant whispered. "The rental car man said it smelled like a whorehouse. What's a whorehouse?"

The mother gave me a panicked look.

Please don't let them be going to Denver, I begged the Universe. *I'll do a good deed, I promise.*

The doors mercifully opened, and I lifted my guitar over my head to protect it from the stampede of mini marauders who made a run for the baggage drop-off. Then I stepped off also, sighing in relief from my close call with extremely bad luck...

And in the second I took to catch my breath, I spotted *him* standing head and shoulders above the crowd on the far side of the check-in desk.

Rafe Motherfucking Goodman, at Sarasota Bradenton International Airport, rolling a little suitcase like he was jetting off for the weekend? What the actual fuck? Where did Mr. I-Don't-Traipse-at-Your-Convenience think he was going?

Gone was his laid-back beach-vibe outfit from the day before. Instead, he wore fitted jeans and heavy boots similar to my own, along with a vintage Eagles T-shirt that molded to his body like a second skin and left zero doubt exactly how many muscles he was packing.

Fortunately for me, everything above the neck spoiled the effect, because the man looked objectively awful, like he'd been rode hard and put away wet... or like he'd stuck around for a few more beers after I'd left him at Mitchell's. His dark hair was a tousled mess, and his unshaven face had a pale, greenish cast to it, like he might pull a Jebediah at any moment.

I did *not* feel bad for him, let the record show.

If Mr. Responsibility couldn't help me help Aimee, but he could head out of town on a trip, I was *not* going to suggest my foolproof hangover cure of a breakfast biscuit and wrist acupressure, damn it.

As I watched, he darted a glance at the line for the check-in machine, covered his mouth with his hand, and made a break for the men's room. I narrowed my eyes and stalked after him, ready to say all the angry things I'd tried to hold back the previous afternoon.

By the time I made my way through the crowd to the bathroom, though, Rafe had already ducked into a stall and was very audibly losing his breakfast.

I hesitated.

I mean, it wasn't exactly sporting to run over and chew him out through the door while he was heaving. There were limits to how petty I could be. *I* wasn't the jerky jerkface of the two of us.

So instead, I ducked into a stall myself and pulled out my phone to check my messages.

There was nothing from the attorney—not that I'd expected anything at this hour of the morning—but Oak had written back.

> OAK
>
> Please, please be chill if you get spotted, Jay. Even if fans and reporters say ignorant shit to you. Remember, being an asshole to other people makes them want to be an asshole to you.

I smirked and typed out *Polite is my middle name.*

Before I could hit Send, though, a toilet flushed down the line. I stuffed my phone in my pocket and watched through the crack in the door as Rafe braced his hands on the countertop by the sink and regarded himself in the mirror. A few strands of hair clung to his sweat-damp forehead, and the overhead lights made him look haggard, like death warmed over.

"That's enough," he hiss-whispered at his own reflection. "No more puking. It's going to be a very safe, turbulence-free, three-hour flight. You can do anything for three hours, Goodman. You've run races in *summer* that lasted longer than three hours. Hell, you've listened to Lorenna McKetcham talk about her sexual conquests for longer than three hours. Millions of people fly all over the world every damn day, and cars are more likely to crash than planes. So you're gonna cowboy up, right here and now, and do what needs to be done..." He blew out a breath and narrowed his eyes. "This isn't about you. It's about Aimee."

Oh.

Oh.

My chest squeezed tight, and a couple of very important realizations occurred to me simultaneously.

First, Rafe Goodman wasn't going on vacation; he was at the airport to do the very thing I'd asked him to do—to go see Aimee—except without me, damn it.

And second, the man wasn't hungover. He was having a motherfucking panic attack because he hated flying and had ever since one of the planes carrying his class to Miami for his senior trip had crashed in a thunderstorm... which was really something my self-righteous ass should have remembered while I was going off on him the day before.

In fact, I was pretty sure me forgetting something that serious about a guy who'd been my best friend *did* make me the jerky jerkface of the two of us.

Goddamn it.

The story had made the national news at the time—one teenager had died, two others were badly injured—and I remembered it was one of the few times I'd been really glad my stepmother was the world's biggest gossip, because at least Belinda had been willing to get on the phone and call the Goodmans to find out more information while Aimee and I had been paralyzed with fear. Rafe had been physically fine, but emotionally it had taken a huge toll. Big Rafe and Mary Goodman had driven down to Miami in the aftermath to collect Rafe and bring him home, and that whole summer, he hadn't even liked being in a car when anyone else was driving. As far as I knew, he hadn't stepped on a plane since.

The fact that he was about to try, for Aimee's sake, said a lot about his feelings for her and about who he was. A good man. A man who'd been hurt when Aimee left him.

And maybe it was no surprise that Rafe hadn't trusted me with Aimee's secrets, given that the only emotions I'd shown him in the last few years were bitterness, outrage, mistrust, and avoidance.

Fuck.

Oak's words came back to me: *Remember, being an asshole to other people makes them want to be an asshole to you.*

I blew out a breath and watched Rafe splash water on his face, then pat himself dry with a paper towel. The many gorgeous muscles in his back bunched and flexed as he gripped the sink with white knuckles, still determined to take care of things, even when anyone else would have consoled themselves that they'd done the most they could and gone home.

But who was taking care of Rafe? Who'd looked out for him since Aimee left?

It's not your job, that's for sure, Rollins, I reminded myself.

Rafe straightened suddenly and stared at himself in panic. "Nuh-uh. Don't do it," he told himself. "Don't you do it, Goodman... Ah, shit." He ran for the bathroom stall again.

I rubbed at my forehead as a truly terrible idea sprang into my brain fully formed, and even as I cursed myself for my own stupidity, I knew I was gonna go through with it.

I erased my half-written text to Oak and instead typed, *Hey, what if I told you there was an alternate way for me to get back to Wyoming with no paparazzi, if you just did me one teeny, tiny little favor?*

OAK

I'm in.

5

RAFE

"Mr. Goodman? Rafael Goodman, Junior?" the deep voice on the phone said.

"Speaking." I held the phone with one hand and dragged my suitcase toward security with the other. It was a sign of how messed up my head was that I'd hesitated a full two rings before answering the call, even though the Caller ID said Sarasota Police Department. I felt like my brain couldn't handle even one more molecule of stress without cracking entirely.

I'd already vomited more times this morning than I had in the past ten years, *including* the time I'd eaten some questionable potato salad at Remy Burke's barbecue, and I hadn't drawn an actual deep breath since it had hit me, while waiting for Beale to come and pick me up at Mitchell's restaurant yesterday, that flying out to check on Aimee in Wyoming meant not just abandoning all of my responsibilities to the Extravaganza Committee, which was enough to make me low-key panicky, but that I would have to *fly* in a fucking *airplane* to Wyoming.

Worst of all, I'd barely slept a wink all night, thinking about Jay's flashing eyes when I'd refused him, and how damn sexy he was when he was angry, and how truly inappropriate it was for me to get hard over either of those things.

"Sir," the caller said, "I'm afraid there's been a massive sewage leak in your neighborhood."

Yep. There it went. My brain, split right in two like a coconut.

I stopped in the middle of the crowd of people streaming toward the TSA checkpoint, leading a couple of people to make rude noises as they were forced to go around me.

"Sewage?" I repeated blankly. "My neighborhood?"

"Yepper. And it's a *bad* one, too." The guy sounded somewhere between gleeful and appalled. "Worst I've ever seen. Your front yard's lookin' to become a swamp."

"That's impossible," I said with a confidence I didn't quite feel. "I was home maybe an hour ago, and everything was fine. You've made a mistake, Mr.... Wait, who are you?"

"Officer Oakmont Rainesent, Badge Number 0223001," he rattled off. "Your home located at 343 Marbella Court on Whispering Key?"

My stomach cramped, though I knew for sure it was empty. "Yeah."

"Mmm. 'Fraid there's been no mistake, sir. The sewage is eight inches deep and risin' fast. We removed your lawn ornament before it sank—lovely gnome, by the way. Very realistic—but I'm not sure how much we can do for the rest of the place, 'specially since we haven't located the precise location of the leak. Seems like it might be coming from under the house. We've got a couple inspectors on the scene, but it's lookin' like—"

"Boys, we gotta knock 'em down!" a voice in the background yelled. "Everything from 343 to 347's gotta go."

"Ah, dang. I was afraid of that," the officer said sadly. "Sir, your house is gonna have to be destroyed, for the health and safety of everyone on Whispering Key."

"*What*?" I yelled so loudly the sound ricocheted off the walls of the terminal, and more than one security guard tossed me a suspicious look. "No way!"

Not my beautiful house where I was finally living *alone* now that all my family all had newly renovated houses of their own.

"Easiest thing is gonna be for you to just give me your permission over the phone," the officer went on, like he wasn't talking utter nonsense. "That'll save us a lot of trouble—"

"Hell no. Under no circumstances."

The officer's sigh didn't disguise the *beep-beep-beeping* sound of heavy construction equipment backing up. "I was afraid you were gonna be difficult about it. Alright, then, sir, how long will it take for you to get to the location and see the damage for yourself?"

"I... I..." I looked around the airport blankly. Ordinarily, I was the person people looked to for answers. This morning, I had none.

I cast a single look over my shoulder at the terminal, then turned around and headed for the exit.

"Thirty minutes? Maybe forty? I'm at the airport in Sarasota. But my father can be there in ten. He's the mayor of Whispering Key, and he can act as my representative."

Dad would go, even though *deeply displeased* did not begin to describe his feelings about my decision to leave town six days before the Extravaganza and deputize Gage and Beale to handle things on my behalf.

"Excellent! Is he also a legal owner of the property, sir?"

I hesitated. "No, but—"

"Ah. Well, then, regrettably, I'm afraid I won't be able to speak to him about this situation." I heard papers shuffling in the background. "For what it's worth, we've already gotten teardown permission from the Brickell Estate at 347 Marbella and a Ms. Jodeen Farmer at 345, so you're the lone holdout."

What the—?

"Ms. Farmer gave you permission to tear down her house?" I demanded. "I don't believe it. You must've coerced the poor woman."

Jodeen was ninety if she was a day and hard of hearing to boot. If she'd inadvertently given permission to tear down her house... Sweet Jesus.

I walked faster.

"I take offense at that," the officer insisted. "But I understand you must be under strain, so I'll let it go for now. Now, sir, if you'll stop being contrary and listen to reason, I'm sure you'll understand—"

"What I understand is that you'd better not touch a single blade of grass on *anyone*'s property before I get there!" I fumed, dragging my suitcase past the check-in desk. "Understand?"

"Lord a'mercy, we got us a geyser!" a voice in the background yelled. "The end-times are upon us!"

A geyser?

"Mr. Goodman, I need you to get here as soon as possible. This has become an emergency situation."

"I understand. I'll get a cab—"

There was a squelching, static sound, like the officer was covering the phone, and his voice was muffled as he yelled, "Tell Jerry we need to bring in the boats! Evacuate, evacuate! *Move, move, move!*" To me, he added, "Cab won't be fast enough. We've got an officer in an unmarked vehicle detailed to the airport. He'll meet you out front in thirty seconds and get you here in half the time. He'll be in a white van outside door number three."

"Yeah, fine," I agreed in a growl as my feet hit the sidewalk out front. "Remember, not a single blade of grass!"

I dragged my suitcase out the sliding doors and found a white passenger van with all its windows open parked at the curb. I hesitated, but the side door slid open and a guy in a baseball hat called me by name. "Rafael Goodman? Officer Rainesent sent me. Hustle it up. You can stow your stuff back here."

I hefted my little suitcase into the cargo area and quickly hopped into the passenger's seat.

"Belt," the driver barked even before my door was closed. And then while I was still distracted buckling the damn thing, he pulled out into traffic.

"Fastest route to my place at this hour will be 75 South." I straightened and scooped both hands through my hair. "Tamiami Trail's gonna be backed up for hours yet—"

The driver snorted. "Figures you'd tell a police officer the fastest way to get to your house. Rafe Goodman, control freak of America."

I blinked in confusion for exactly one second before turning my head to find gold-record-selling liar and all-around troublemaker Jay fucking Rollins, smirking at me in profile.

He turned his head toward me, and the smirk became a grin. "Gotcha."

How was it possible for a human to feel both shocked and furious and simultaneously, bizarrely settled just from staring at another person's face?

I didn't understand it at all, and therefore, I didn't *like* it at all.

"What the fuck is going on here?" I demanded.

Jay handed me a greasy, paper-wrapped sandwich. "Breakfast biscuit? Helps a nervous stomach, I promise."

"Hey there, Mr. Goodman!" a disembodied voice asked over the van's speakers. "Rafe. Can I call you Rafe? I feel like we're already friends."

I closed my eyes and shook my head. "Officer Oak... Raine-sent, was it?"

"Er... you can just call me Oak. Rain Scent is the flavor of the candle my sister left burning on my desk," he corrected a little bit sheepishly, "since she says my office smells like a locker room. Nice to meet you."

"Wish I could say the same." I ground my molars together and unwrapped the biscuit. It *did* smell kinda good.

"I happen to have some excellent news for you!" Oak said cheerfully. "Your house is not, to the best of my knowledge, actually sinking into a cesspool of sewage! Congratulations! I, for one, think we should all take a minute to appreciate that happy circumstance, don't you? A man never appreciates what he has until shit's more than half a foot high and rising, am I right?"

"You're hilarious," I bit out. "Jay Don, if making me late for my flight is your way of... Honestly, I have no clue what you're attempting to achieve here, but I promise you, it's not working. I thought when we said goodbye yesterday that was more or less forever."

"Yeah, well, you can't get rid of me that easily." Jay followed signs for the highway—exactly the route I'd told him not to take, which totally figured. "Look, I was planning to fly back to Wyoming today, and when I got to the airport, I saw you." He darted a sideways glance at me. "From a distance."

"You saw me in the airport." Lovely. I wondered if that was before or after I'd tossed my cookies. I folded my arms over my chest, only slightly mortified.

"You looked... nervous," he decided, which was as good a euphemism for shit-scared as I'd ever heard. "And that's when I remembered, about the, um..." He cleared his throat and said with genuine sympathy, "The crash, and how you were always afraid of flying after that."

If there was a worse thing than having your mortal enemy know your weakness, it was having your mortal enemy *pity you* for your weakness.

"I was handling it just fine," I gritted out, taking a giant bite of biscuit.

A little smile fluttered around Jay's lips. "I know. You always do, right? But I figured you probably weren't *handling it* for anything less than a really good cause, which meant you were doing it for Aimee. Which meant you never intended to abandon her, which I should have known, deep down. And all that being the case, it's possibly possible that I was a bit of a shithead yesterday, demanding that you come help me when you have a very real phobia." He paused and darted another glance at me. "I mean, I wasn't as much of a shithead as *you* were, obviously, for not telling me you were going in the first place."

I rolled my eyes. There was the Jay I'd been expecting. "Possibly possible, huh?"

"Yes. Anyway, I knew if I went up to you at the airport and tried to maybe apologize, at best you'd just brush me off, and at worst you'd chew me out and we'd get caught on tape by the paparazzi, and they'd speculate about who you were, and how long we'd been fucking, and which of us bottomed." He snorted. "Like you'd bottom."

I blinked, and my stomach swooped like I was riding a roller coaster as I imagined him hovering over me, grinning down at me. I would so bottom for Jay Rollins…

Fuck. *Not* helpful, Goodman. My head already felt oxygen-starved. The last thing I needed was to divert any blood south.

Fortunately, Jay didn't expect a reply. He went on, "So I called my friend Oak to help me figure out how to stop you from getting on a plane, 'cause I knew otherwise you'd force yourself to do it for Aimee's sake." Those green eyes skewered me to the seat. "I needed your help. I still do. But I don't want you to make yourself sick over it."

I swallowed hard, still riding an emotional roller coaster, and my voice came out all raspy. "Let me understand. You thought the best way to apologize was to insult me, after getting your friend to impersonate a police officer, which is highly illegal," I croaked out. "You have strange friends."

"It's theoretically illegal," Jay allowed. "But it'd be your word against Oak's. And you're not the type to call the cops anyway."

I mean, no, I wouldn't. But I didn't like how easily he dismissed the idea that I *could*. I didn't want to believe that Jay knew what sort of person I was anymore. Just like I didn't know him.

I shifted lower in my seat and let my head fall against the headrest. "You're risking a lot on an assumption."

"Doesn't matter. I'm babysitting my twelve-year-old nephew, so I have an ironclad alibi right now. Isn't that right, Jack-Jack?" Oak called.

"Sure," a bored voice said. "As long as I get the twenty bucks you promised and tacos every week for the rest of vacation. Otherwise, I'm turning state's evidence."

"Atta boy," Oak approved.

My eyes narrowed at the speaker on the dashboard. Who the heck *were* these people?

Jay sighed. "You know, Oak, it occurs to me that you were willing to spoof the police department's phone number and impersonate an officer, but you won't get any of your cyber-security people to hack a single clinic computer to get my name on a visitor's list…"

"Every man's gotta draw his own line about what's acceptable behavior, Jay. I value a person's right to privacy. Yours, mine, *and* your sister's." Oak's voice was mild, but there was a little undercurrent of rebuke, and seriously, who *was* this guy who called Jay *Jay* instead of Jayd and didn't take his shit?

I didn't like it. It made me want to immediately dismiss everything he said, even though I totally agreed with him.

"If you could erase that line and redraw it about a foot in my direction, it'd save me a world of trouble," Jay said wryly. He shot me a look. "Rafe'd probably be pretty grateful, too."

"Sorry?" Oak made a hissing static noise. "The connection must be bad, Jay. I think I missed the part where you said, *'Thank you, Oakmont, for doing me this service at great personal risk. I treasure our friendship.'*"

"I do. And if I didn't already love you, Oak," Jay said with a sincerity that made me grit my teeth, "I would now."

Love?

Jay sped up and took the on-ramp for the highway.

The highway *northbound.*

"Hey, you're going the wrong way." My voice was barely audible over the roar of air suddenly rushing through the open windows of the van, so I reached over to smack his arm lightly. "Whispering Key is south."

"Yeah, about that…" Jay yelled back. He glanced at me nervously. "We're not actually heading south."

"And, on that note, Jack and I are out," Oak said warmly. "And I'd like to state for the record that we did not hear a single word about Jay committing any felony kidnappings, nosiree."

Kidnapping? I looked from Jay to the highway through the windshield, then back at Jay as the pieces fell into place. Ah, *fuck me.*

"I think your line of acceptable behavior is drawn in crayon, Mr. Rain Scent!" I yelled, and I could almost swear I heard him chuckle before he cut the connection.

"Take me home," I told Jay loudly.

Jay ignored me, and I was 99 percent sure it was deliberate. "As I was saying," he shouted over the rushing air, "I realized back at the airport that you were getting on a plane to Wyoming to go see Aimee, and that changed everything."

I tried to read his lips, but I still could only make out the gist of what he was saying… and me focusing on his lips was a dangerous thing. "Roll up the windows."

Jay shook his head stubbornly. "Admit it."

I leaned over the low console in the center of the van so I could yell in his ear, which was also dangerous, since it meant I was breathing in the honey-citrus scent of him. "Doesn't matter if I'm going to see her. We're not doing this together, Jay." We couldn't if I wanted to protect Aimee's secrets and, what seemed like a more pressing concern at that moment, my *sanity*.

"It matters," he shouted back. "Because if you're going to save my sister, even after everything that happened between you two, it means you're still the guy I knew, deep down. A good person. My best friend."

Ugh. My stomach must've still been weak from earlier because hearing that made it roll over. I couldn't deny how relieved I was not to have to get on a plane or how nice it felt that Jay's motivation had been, at least partly, to look out for me. Not drive-to-Wyoming nice, but still.

"And that being the case, it's maybe possible that I didn't start things off on the right foot yesterday. I was pissed off, and hurt, and worried. I got... aggressive." Jay pushed impatiently at his overlong blond-brown hair, which the wind kept snapping across his face.

His *maybe possiblys* were *so* not cute.

"And maybe that makes it hard for you to trust me or want to help me. So, okay. I thought... what better way for us to get to know each other again, to trust each other again, than on a road trip where it's just you and me alone in a van for thirty hours? Plus, this way, you don't have to fly, and I get to stay under the radar and not let the media know where I am." He gave me a tentative smile. "And I'll even let you pick the music when you're driving... which will be, like, twenty percent of the time."

I shook my head.

"Fine, twenty-five. And you don't gush about Ari fucking Friedrich. Final offer."

My stomach burned with something like panic when I didn't *do* panic. Hadn't it been just yesterday that I'd vowed never to be in a car with him again? And now he wanted me to be alone in a van with him for days, with absolutely nothing to do but stare at the angle of his jaw and the way his lashes fell against his cheek and the way his thick thigh muscles flexed in his jeans, and wonder how they could be so familiar even after all this time?

Thirty *hours*, steeping in that gorgeous, sweet smell of him and trying not to get a contact high, or listening to him doing something as mundane as ordering drive-thru off the dollar menu in that fucking voice of his and trying not to get hard?

Two thousand miles of me remembering on an endless loop all the things I used to like about him—his sweet, slow-burn smile, his quick laugh, his weird sense of humor, his curiosity about the world, his random acts of unrecipro-cated kindness, the way he tapped out a tune on whatever happened to be in his hand like he was keeping time to a rhythm only he could hear—when what I should be remembering was how he'd cut me out of his life for years when he started getting even a teensy bit famous.

It sounded like acute psychological torture. The kind guar-anteed to break me. I wasn't sure what would happen to either of us when I broke.

"This sounds like the worst idea anyone's ever had," I said truthfully.

"Ugh. *Fine.* You drive a hard bargain. Thirty percent of the time. The Ari rule remains, but I won't even complain if you put on that EDM shit you used to like that made me feel like my ears were buzzing."

"Jay." I stared at his profile, his sharp jaw and strong nose, and shook my head once more. At this point, I felt like a bobblehead that moved from side to side rather than up and down. "Listen to me. *No.* Besides, what would your... *Oak...* say? About the two of us traveling alone together?"

"Oak helped me come up with this idea!" Jay shouted. "We can get there in three days. And maybe you and I can, you know, try to be friendly again."

Since my current feelings for him vacillated between fury and longing, this seemed unlikely.

"You thought the best way to resurrect our friendship and make me think you were *less* of a shithead was to get your boyfriend—friend, whatever he is—to help you kidnap me in an unmarked van, *then* insult me, then force me to accompany you to Wyoming?"

"He's my *friend*, not that it's any of your business—"

He was right. It *shouldn't* have been any of my business. So why did it feel like it was?

"—and it's not kidnapping if you agree."

I set my teeth. "But I don't."

"You what?"

"I *don't*." I pulled at the lever to make the passenger's window slide up. "God. Why do you want us to have to scream this conversation across the—" I broke off with a cough as my eyes began to water and the scent of a hundred dead flowers pummeled my nose. "Holy shit. Did someone's grandma die in here?" I pulled the collar of my T-shirt up over my face.

"Not by my hand. Pretty sure that's eau de baby puke overlaid with Shalimar? See, when I saw you in the bathroom and went back to the rental desk, this completely unhelpful woman told me my Escalade had already been rented out again. This was the only car left in the lot, and I didn't have time for them to steam clean the upholstery, so... Here we are."

Yeah. Here we fucking were. With him being nice to me, smiling that bright smile. *Fuck.*

"So yesterday when you forced me in your car and assured me you *weren't* planning a murder-kidnap spree," I yelled, "you were lying?"

"I told you, kidnapping is a wild exaggeration of what's happening here. And I haven't murdered anyone. Yet."

"Don't be so sure. The fumes might get me."

He shot me a look. "Take shallow breaths."

Dear God. No one should make me feel so good while being so absurd. That supposedly insurmountable wall around my heart was made of LEGOs, damn it. Thin plastic, full of cracks.

"The circumstances aren't ideal at all," he went on. "But we can still find a silver lining. Make something good come of it. I mean, it's gotta mean something that our road trip mobile smells like a hundred Belindas in high heels and dresses packed into the Rock Gulch, Alabama, Twenty-Third Church of the Redeemer on a Sunday morning, right? That's the scent of righteousness."

"It's choking me," I gurgled.

He took a wrapped candy out of his pocket and held it over the console. "Honey drop?"

So I could start to smell like him? So I could *help* him assault my senses? But when I coughed again, I grabbed the candy in desperation as I rolled the window open a bit again.

This trip was literally doomed.

"I order them specially from this organic place in Tennessee," Jay went on, filling the silence like he thought it might stop me from arguing with him. "I'm kind of addicted to them. At first it was because I'd been playing a lot in smoky bars and I'd heard somewhere that they'd help my voice, but then it was just because I liked the taste. They remind me of your mom and how she'd make us honey tea on rainy afternoons. You know, I tried for a whole winter to figure out what kind of tea she used that tasted so good and always made me feel better? When I finally got to ask her the next summer, she said there was no tea at all, just a jar of orange and lemon slices covered in honey. Remember, Rafe?"

I stared at him, transfixed, letting the power of his voice wash over me. Even when he was chattering about nothing, listening to him speak was more soothing than all the honey in the world. *Dangerously* soothing.

This trip to Wyoming was *not* supposed be about repairing our friendship, damn it, because that was impossible. It was about seeing through my obligation to Aimee.

Yet the temptation was incredible.

"I remember," I admitted grudgingly. "She'd keep mason jars of it around all the time just for you." I rubbed a hand over my face and tried again. "Jay…"

"You look tired," he interrupted. "Did you sleep at all?" His eyes flashed toward me again, filled with concern. But was it concern about me or concern that I wouldn't go along with his plan?

"Not much," I admitted.

"Because you were worried about flying."

"Partly."

"And worried about Aimee."

"That too."

Jay nodded once. "Because you *are* responsible, and you *do* care. I knew it. Just rest, Rafe. Trust me to drive for a little while, alright? Let me do this. Everything else can wait."

I sighed. Could it, though, when the other thing I'd been worrying about was sitting right next to me?

He was everything I'd ever wanted and was *also* the man who'd walked away from our friendship. I couldn't trust him for shit.

Before I could argue further, though, Jay turned up the radio on some Top 40 station and started humming along in his deep, lovely voice. It felt like a private concert—the kind people all over the world would kill to experience—sitting up close and personal with *the* Jayd Rollins, seeing him bite his lip and tuck his hair behind his ear, watching his long-fingered hands tap out a percussion solo on the steering wheel with a kind of effortless, graceful talent that I'd never admit to his face that he possessed.

There were really, *really* good reasons why I shouldn't want any of this—the attraction, the doomed attempt at getting friendly again, the strolling down a thorny, rocky memory lane.

But I wasn't thinking of any of them as I gave a jaw-cracking yawn and let my eyes drift shut.

"I can't believe summer's almost over." Jay's voice was as soft and lazy as the gentle swells that rocked our raft where it was docked in a little cove.

Neither could I. Mere days until Jay left again for nine whole months, back to his school and his friends, back to his real life. It was weird how fast the summers flew by and how long the winter dragged on without my favorite person around. I hated thinking about it.

"Someday, I'm gonna write a song about this summer. About you. It's gonna be my breakout song. I'm gonna play it at Iron Pipes someday."

I turned my chin toward him without opening my eyes. "Oh yeah? You're gonna write a song about getting sunburnt, drinking cheap beer, swimming naked, and hiding from my annoying kid brother?" The alcohol had made me sleepy, and sunshine made colored fractals explode on the inside of my closed lids. "You think that'll score you an invite to Iron Pipes?"

Jay laughed, and like always, my eyes forced themselves open so I could catch a glimpse of it, 'cause seeing my best friend happy made my own chest go tight with happiness. "Something like that. You'll have to wait and see." His eyes opened too, and his green gaze was curiously intense. "I hope you'll like it."

"'Course I'll like it. It's yours, asshole."

"Hmm." His thumb drummed lightly on his breastbone, like he was counting out a beat to that imaginary song.

Then he rolled toward me and pressed his lips firmly to mine.

My eyes shot open, and I sucked in a breath through my nose like I was resurfacing after a deep dive. The clock on the dash said I'd been asleep for almost five hours, which didn't seem possible, but the crick in my neck said it was.

Jay had two hands on the wheel as he sang along to the radio, his deep, throaty voice harmonizing effortlessly with Ari Friedrich's slightly higher, sweeter sound on the track "Trust," and *fuck*. Just like that, I was officially hard and fucking annoyed about it.

Popping *afternoon* wood was not supposed to be a thing for guys my age—or for guys of any age who were trapped in a car with the man who'd broken their heart—but between Jay's gorgeous voice and that kiss, I was all turned around.

The kiss had been a dream. *Completely*. I had never acted on my attraction to Jay. In fact, I'd tried as hard as I could not to even acknowledge it to myself so I wouldn't start wanting something I couldn't have.

Looking back, knowing what I now knew, I couldn't help but feel like we'd been a hairsbreadth away from something and

I hadn't even realized it. What would have happened, back then, if I'd just leaned over and put my hands on him and…

"Well, hey. Welcome back to the land of the living." Jay shot me a teasing grin as I knuckled my eyes. His deep voice sent tingles into places that I very definitely didn't want tingling at that moment.

I clenched my hands into fists. "Pull over."

"Sure, but can it wait a few minutes? I just got gas an hour ago. We're good for—"

"No. Pull over," I said again. "I need to piss."

I needed to get out of the car. *Immediately.* Away from that dreammaker voice and the intoxicatingly sweet smell of him.

Jay sighed. "Alright, alright. Yeesh. Next rest area in three miles."

"Fine."

He got into the right lane just as the song on the radio changed and the opening chords of "Pretty Girl" filled the car.

This is what they call irony, kids.

Because *this* was Jay's *actual* breakout song. A song which hadn't been about our summer, but apparently about the first girl he'd fallen in love with. Award-winning actress Olivia Merry, maybe, if Maddie McKetcham was to be believed.

Jay reached for the knob to turn the volume up, but I

knocked his hand out of the way and changed the station to some super-staticky news station instead.

"Hey!" Jay protested as he took the exit for the rest area and pulled into a parking spot near a decidedly sketchy-looking squat brick building. "Driver picks the music."

"Perfect, 'cause I'm driving when I get back, and we're listening to talk radio. Getting caught up on world events instead of listening to pop drivel." I unbuckled my seat belt and made a come-hither motion with my hand. "Gimme the key."

"What? The van key? No way. It's *my* rental van—"

"You mean your *kidnap* van."

"Ah, Jesus, are we back to this? Napping makes somebody a crankypants, hmm?" He mock pouted his lips, which naturally gave me all sorts of *other* thoughts about his mouth and the uses I could put it to.

Fuck again.

I gritted my teeth. "Having you abandon me at Mitchell's yesterday was bad enough. I would rather not be abandoned at a truck stop in the middle of..." I looked around. "Where are we?"

"Just south of Macon."

"In the middle of Georgia." I laid out my palm and made a *gimme* motion with my fingers.

Jay rolled his eyes and dug the key out of his pocket. "You're insane, you know that? It's a push-button ignition. You don't even need the key."

"I know."

He clutched the key in his palm. "I'm not going to leave you."

"You've turned over a new leaf since yesterday?" I laughed shortly. "Dude, leaving's all you ever do. But sure, let's say I believe you. If you're not leaving, it doesn't matter if I have the key, right?"

Jay's eyes were stormy. He held out the key but didn't let go of it. "Tell me right this minute that we're going to Wyoming together in this van. That we're partners."

"Heck no." I scowled. "I'm not falling for your Stockholm syndrome bullshit. We're not partners."

His face fell, and I told myself I didn't care.

"But... fine. Yes," I allowed. "We've come this far, so we'll go to Wyoming together. I will make sure Aimee is okay, and I will let you know that she is. No more, no less. And then we will be out of each other's lives forever. Okay?"

"For now." Jay let go of the key, and his whole face lit up.

I told myself I didn't care about that either.

But later that night, after I'd gotten us adjoining rooms at a motel just outside Chattanooga and done everything I could to distract myself—texting my family to let them know where I was (Gage had seemed annoyingly unsurprised that Jay had virtually kidnapped me), turning the air conditioner up as high as it would go so the white noise might drown out the sound of Jay strumming his guitar next door, chowing down an unsatisfying vending machine dinner, and jumping in the shower to scrub off the lingering stench of perfume—I still couldn't stop my mind from going exactly where I hadn't wanted it to go.

Back to that damn dream.

I stood under the hot water, stretching my crimped neck muscles, and my hand trailed down my stomach without conscious thought to wrap around my cock.

It had been a while—a long while—since I'd let myself think of anyone in particular when I jerked off. Mostly, these days, I took care of myself quickly and efficiently, and it was about as exciting as brushing my teeth. But after the longest day in the history of the world, all my barriers were down, and I was tired of fighting the pull. So there, in the privacy of that steam-filled shower, I closed my eyes and let myself think about Jay.

His green eyes glinting fire at me when he'd barged into the Extravaganza meeting.

His melodic voice singing along with the radio. Saying, *"Remember, Rafe?"*

That smile.

That fucking dream, which was so real I could almost feel the heat of the sun on me.

I reached for the tiny bottle of conditioner on the shower ledge and dumped some out into my hand. It was supposed to be cucumber scented, I was pretty sure, but all I could smell was honey and Jay. I slicked my hand up and down my length, slowly at first, the way I imagined Jay might have done it back in the raft all those years ago, with hesitation giving way to eagerness.

I used to study his hands constantly when he thought I wasn't looking, and I knew the shape and texture of them. The wide palms and long fingers, calloused from his guitar playing. The short nails and blunt fingertips. I imagined how they'd feel gliding along my shaft, toying with my balls, sliding over my taint to toy with my ass. I wanted those hands on me nearly as bad as I wanted his mouth on mine, which was to say more than I'd ever let myself want anything in my life.

I imagined him saying things, too. Shit that was way too sappy to ever come out of his mouth in real life—like how he'd wanted me forever, and he'd been waiting for me, and he loved me—but that somehow almost felt real because that dreammaker voice made things real.

My stomach cramped and my balls tightened as I moved my hand faster and faster. I imagined him going to his knees for me, right there in the shower. Green eyes looking up at me, lashes stuck together with water. His tongue darting out of his full lips to tongue my slit before he stretched his mouth around me and sucked me down into that priceless throat.

I'd never let myself get this far, back in the day. I'd never gone beyond imagining a kiss. A touch. Shit, just a *look* that said he wanted me like I wanted him. That had been enough of a fantasy. And I'd known that if I let myself go further, had let myself imagine the two of us fucking this way, I'd never have been content with friendship.

Now, though, we weren't friends—even if he was sincere about wanting that, I didn't know how it was possible with so much *hurt* between us—so there was nothing to stop me from imagining the perfection of him groaning around me, being aroused by my arousal. And maybe if I could jack Jay

Rollins out of my system, I'd be able to get to Wyoming and home again without losing my mind.

Fuck.

My hand moved faster and faster, and I nearly lost my balance at the insane pleasure of it. Jay watching me. Jay teasing me. Jay *wanting* me.

My knees went weak, and when I threw out a hand to catch myself, my palm hit the wet tiles with a loud *slap*. I imagined Jay next door, hearing that and knowing I was jacking off for him... then I came so hard my vision went white, and my shout reverberated off the walls of the tiny bathroom.

Holy mother of masturbation. I couldn't remember coming that hard in... Jesus. Ever? Pretty sure it was ever.

I rinsed myself off quickly, since the water had started to run cool, and threw myself down on the bed with a grunt before I'd even fully dried off.

Surprisingly enough, jizzing my spleen had not made me feel any more in control of this situation. I had twelve texts from Whispering Key, ten of which were from the Extravaganza Committee's group chat wondering where Jay was, and whether he preferred panko or regular bread crumbs on his chicken casserole, and whether he'd make an appearance for open mic night at Fisher's Wreck, the Key's new bar. The other two texts were from Gage.

GAGE

An impromptu road trip less than a week before the Extravaganza you've spent months helping Dad plan????? This is a whole new side of Responsible Rafe Goodman. Me gusta.

Then, a few minutes later, he'd sent:

GAGE

BTW, if you need a fun way to pass the time, play "Guess my phone password." Always enlightening. <laugh emoji< <heart emoji> <upside down smiley emoji>

I scowled and turned off the phone without replying.

I was confident he was mocking me somehow, but I wasn't sure how. I'd had the same phone password for a year or so —my birthday, because I was clearly super security conscious—but I was almost positive Gage didn't know it.

For the record, I did *not* feel good about being off Key this close to the Extravaganza. I knew how many people were counting on me, I knew my reputation was on the line, and I also knew my dad wouldn't hesitate to throw me under the bus if things didn't go right... especially if the "not right" meant losing his big-name entertainer.

But the mortifying truth was, when I thought of Jay sleeping mere inches away on the other side of the wall, closer than he'd been any other night in way too many years, I found it hard to care about any of those things. And for the first time in a while, I fell asleep the second I closed my eyes.

6

JAY

The sun had barely risen, and the air was still clammy-damp when Rafe met me on the concrete sidewalk by the van in the morning, carrying his suitcase in one hand like it weighed nothing.

He was wearing another outfit like the one yesterday—tight jeans, tighter T-shirt, and boots—and his hips rolled as he walked. The self-assured swagger was so damn attractive, I couldn't look away even as he got closer.

Fortunately for me, the jerk was too busy thumbing a text to notice me standing there. Who was he texting? A girlfriend? Or a boyfriend? Wait, how did I not know if Rafe was seeing anyone?

JesusChristFuckingA, maybe possibly because it's none of your damn business if he's seeing anyone, Rollins?

As always, though, Rafe was the *only* thing I noticed. And adding insult to injury, he looked rested and refreshed, which so was incredibly unfair when I was so dang tired I could fall asleep standing. I felt my bitchy mood dip toward ultra-super-bitchy.

I crossed my arms over the front of my sweatshirt. "Nice of you to join me. *Finally*. I knocked on your door more than ten minutes ago. I didn't remember you being such a prima donna."

Rafe glanced up from his phone—*finally*—and looked mildly surprised to see me there, the fucker. "I'm sorry, did we have a specific departure time, Jay Don? I wasn't given a copy of the kidnap itinerary, so I was unaware."

Grr.

I was the cute and snarky one of the two of us. The sunshine to his grumpy. It had always been that way... until yesterday. And I did not approve of this change in the natural order of things.

"Drop it with the kidnapping bullshit. *You've* got the key to the van, which is why *I'm* out here waiting with my stuff even though I could potentially be recognized at any moment."

Rafe turned in a circle to inspect the precisely zero other people and cars in the parking lot. He lifted an eyebrow.

I flushed.

"I apologize for making a national treasure such as yourself beat back the crowds single-handedly for a whole ten minutes while I showered." Rafe looked me up and down, from my shorts and flip-flops to my Jayd Rollins *Constellations* Tour sweatshirt. "But if you don't wanna be recognized, maybe don't wear your name on your clothing while you're *kidnapping people*? Just a thought."

My face got hotter. Like I hadn't thought of that?

"I'll have you know, my merch is comfortable and high quality! Not to mention, I had a few other things on my mind while I was packing." I narrowed my eyes defensively. "And it's *chilly*. And *furthermore*, if this *were* a kidnapping, it'd be a fuck of a lot more efficient than this, okay? Like, you'd be tied up, for one thing. And probably gagged."

Rafe lifted an eyebrow. "Kinky."

"Ugh. Not like *that*." And getting kinky with Rafe was the *last* thing I needed to be thinking about. "You have the maturity of a twelve-year-old."

"I do seem to be regressing," Rafe agreed. His lips quirked up. "Boy, a full night's sleep makes someone a crankypants," he remarked, throwing back my words from yesterday.

I huffed out a breath. My problem was, I had *not* had a full night's sleep.

You know how they say no good deed goes unpunished? Well, if I'd stopped to think about the punishment for sorta-but-not-actually mercy-kidnapping Rafe—which I hadn't—I would have told you that spending three sexually frustrated days in the car with a man who actively disliked me was punishment enough, especially since Rafe even managed to *sleep* in a way that made my blood hum, with this concentrated frown between his eyebrows like he was vigilant and responsible even in sleep.

I mean, my attempts to fill the awkward silences yesterday afternoon with friendly chatter, only to have him say, "You want me to talk, Jay? Let's discuss all the things I hate about 'Pretty Girl.' For example, what's with the overlaid harmony on the chorus?" was bad enough to make me seriously rethink ever doing a good deed again, so surely the Universe could see I'd learned my lesson, yes?

No.

No, no, no.

The real punishment had come last night, after we'd checked into the Tissue-Paper-Walls Motel. I'd lain on my exceptionally squeaky mattress, idly strumming my guitar, worrying about my sister and thinking about reworking the bridge in the song I was temporarily calling "Fuck, Kill, Marry," when I'd heard the shower go on next door. Suddenly, my traitorous brain had conjured up an image from almost half a lifetime ago, reminding me *exactly* what Rafe had looked like with water glistening on the honey-gold skin of his shoulders while he smiled at me like I'd personally made his sky blue, because *fuck my life.*

And though I'd valiantly tried to block this out and focus on my song, I'd heard something—it was a hand, I just *knew* it was a hand—hit the wall in the shower so hard my headboard shook, and the images that jumped into my mind were something out of my dirtiest fantasies.

Was Rafe Goodman jerking off just inches away from my bed?

The hoarse shout of pleasure-pain a few seconds later confirmed that *fuck yes, he had been.* And best-worst of all? I would've sworn he shouted *my* name as he came.

I mean, he didn't.

Rationally, I knew he couldn't have.

But the tantalizing possibility of it was enough to have me weaving together a fantasy where I was in that shower, too, pushing Rafe to his knees—like the paparazzi photo that had upended my life, but *real*—while my rock-hard dick and I had been trapped on a mattress that squeaked loud enough to raise the dead every time I breathed too deeply.

Fucking *torture.*

And realizing I had a hard-on for the guy who carried around a folded-up letter from my sister while she was in the *hospital*?

Torture of a whole other kind.

"Hello? Earth to Jay? Can you hear me?" Rafe stood by the sliding door of the van, holding out his hand in a gimme motion.

"Huh?" I rubbed a hand over my eyes.

"Would you like to put your luggage in the van, Your Highness? Or were you planning to just stand there all day? You're the one with the schedule."

He'd already loaded his rolling suitcase and my bag, so I handed over my guitar case. "Be careful with this, okay? Vega's the most precious thing I own."

"Vega?" Rafe repeated, stowing it behind the passenger's seat. "As in..."

Shit. I did not want to open that can of worms.

"I said Vega*s*," I informed him. "With an *s*. You know, as in *Las* Vegas? As in... as in, what happens there stays there? Ha ha. Boy, could I tell you stories!"

Shut up, Jay.

"M'kay." Rafe slammed the door shut like he didn't give a shit either way. "Have you eaten?"

I shook my head. "I was waiting for you. Because I'm thoughtful. And also because I have a highly advanced metabolism that needs to be fed real food at regular intervals. No more fast-food vending machine junk. We're eating *there*." I pointed to the squat brick-and-glass diner on the other side of the parking lot. The sign over the door read "Tommie's," but the middle letters had faded nearly beyond recognition—unless you'd been standing on the pavement for ten minutes with nothing better to do than puzzle them out.

Rafe lifted an eyebrow. "We're feeding your advanced metabolism at a greasy spoon called Toes?"

"Tommie's! And it looks... very down-to-earth. Charming."

Rafe made a skeptical face but turned toward the restaurant anyway. "Was that a euphemism for dirty back in Alabama?"

I jabbed an elbow into his side as we walked. "No. Also, gimme your phone number while I think of it," I said, extracting my own from my pocket. "That way I won't have to come pound on your door tomorrow morning."

Rafe lifted an eyebrow and rattled off a number I'd memorized a decade ago. "Same number I've always had."

"Oh." I frowned. "Really?" It was strange to think I could have called him all this time. Except, of course, I couldn't have. Not after he'd fallen for Aimee. "I, uh, changed mine. A couple times."

"Not a surprise," Rafe said mildly. "You've changed a lot of things over the years."

"Nuh-uh." I frowned. Had I? Did he really think so? Because to me it felt way too easy to slip back into the way things had been before. "*Some* stuff's changed, maybe. The phone number wasn't really a choice, though."

"No?"

"Nah. A few years back, right after I went on my first tour, my stepmother gave my number to one of her friends, who then gave it to her college-aged daughter, who gave it to all *her* friends." I rolled my eyes. "Cue her entire sorority sexting me on a daily basis. It was like fighting a freakin' hydra—for every unsolicited boob pic I blocked, I'd get two more."

"Wow. I, uh… I'm not sure what I'm supposed to say here." Rafe rubbed a hand over his jaw. "On the one hand, unsolicited. But on the other… free boobs."

I snorted. "Yeah, well, in case you haven't figured it out, I have about as much interest in seeing boobs as you do in, I dunno, listening to accordion music, so—"

"Someone's gonna be shocked when I break out my Weird Al polka collection."

I snorted again. "Okay, you're right, bold of me to assume. But even if I were into girls, I didn't *know* any of them, you know? They'd never met me. And it wasn't like they felt some connection to my music either, because I wasn't getting any radio play then." I shook my head. "It had nothing to do with me. Not really."

Shut up, Jay. You sound like the whiniest whiner.

Rafe grunted. "That is pretty shitty," he allowed. "So you had your people change your number?"

"My people," I repeated wryly. "Like the entourage you think sits around making me happy all day, maybe picking out all the green M&Ms from my candy dish before I throw a hissy fit? No. I was on my dad's phone plan at the time, and my dad laughed his ass off that I was getting *free boobs*." I shot Rafe a sideways glance, and he grunted. "So I got myself a new number. Then I had to do it again two weeks ago, after the... you know."

"The paparazzi pictures."

I nodded. "Because I don't want unsolicited dick pics either." I shot Rafe a quick text of a van emoji. "There. Now you're one of, like, four people who has my newest phone number."

Rafe glanced down at the text, and a smile twitched at the corner of his lips, which made my stomach tighten pleasantly. Making Rafe smile had always felt like such a huge accomplishment.

He gave me another sideways look. "I'm honored."

"As you should be. Only the best for my kidnap victims." I grinned.

Oh, damn. Was I flirting with him? *Seeeeriously, Jay, shut up.*

Rafe pulled open the glass door to the diner, and the smells of bacon and coffee made my stomach grumble.

A thirty-something blonde in an old-fashioned pink waitress dress and apron bustled over. "Mornin', y'all. Nice to see you. Welcome to Tommie's."

My jaw dropped before I set my teeth with a click. Entitled? *Ridiculous.* I did plenty of nice things for people. *Plenty.* I donated money to a dozen charities! And Rafe was six and a half feet of hypocrisy, because *he* wasn't trying to give *me* the benefit of the doubt, was he?

When we reached the table, Rafe gave Shelly a brilliant smile while I slid into the booth seat. I pretended to be very occupied with my phone to give me an excuse to duck my head... but Shelly didn't so much as glance in my direction.

Rafe did, though. His laughing eyes caught mine as he slid into the opposite seat, mocking me for my shit attitude, and then he freakin' *fluttered his eyelashes* at Shelly, clearly enjoying himself hugely. I was glad one of us was.

"Thanks so much, Shelly," he said.

"Sure thing, handsome." She flashed Rafe her dimples, which *were* objectively cute. If you were into that sort of thing. And apparently Rafe was. "Coffee?"

"Oh yeah."

"And do you know what you'd like to eat? Or would you like to see the menu?" Shelly leaned her hand on the table and cheated her body toward Rafe, which made the question seem incredibly dirty. "I could make some... recommendations?"

I wrinkled my nose. Could she be any more obvious? If this place had those comment cards, I was totes giving Shelly low marks for professionalism, despite her dimples.

"I appreciate the offer," Rafe said fervently, "but I know exactly what I want. Waffles with blueberry syrup—"

"And crispy bacon," I singsonged along with him before rolling my eyes. "You really *haven't* changed."

Rafe's gaze flicked to me in surprise.

"Still eating inferior breakfast food," I sighed sadly.

He rolled his eyes.

"I'm so, *so* sorry, honey, but our waffle maker's broken!" Shelly appeared horrified by her inability to provide Rafe—and his big broad shoulders—with their breakfast of choice. "We got pancakes, though. And pancakes are even better than waffles."

Rafe's gaze swung to me again, and I didn't even try to un-smug-ify my smile. Shelly had unwittingly parachuted herself into a breakfast food battle that had been raging for nigh unto fifteen years, and she'd joined *my* side.

The side of truth and justice.

"Pancakes aren't better..." Rafe looked up at her soulfully. "But if *you* recommend them, Shelly, I'm sure they're wonderful."

"Blueberry topping, too, honey?" Shelly asked, blushing furiously. "Or maybe apple? Or mix it up with banana or praline? Or—"

"Blueberry sounds great. Thank you."

"Sure thing. I'll put that right in for you this *second*." She scurried away from the table.

"Excuse me?" I called. "Could I order also?"

Rafe snickered.

"Oh. Oops." Shelly blinked. "Ha! Forgot you were there for a second. What can I getcha?"

"An omelette, please. Spinach and cheese."

"Sure. Toast? Pancakes?"

"I'll have pan—"

"White toast it is," she agreed. "Be right back." She tossed Rafe a wink.

"Coffee, too?" I called, but she didn't seem like she heard.

I narrowed my eyes at Rafe, who wasn't making any effort to hide his laughter anymore. "What was that?"

"What was what? Me ordering breakfast?" His innocent look was absolutely unattractive.

I shuddered. "I need another shower after watching you two. 'What flavor topping would you like, handsome? Blueberry? Banana? *Shelly*?'" I mocked in a low voice.

"I was trying to divert her attention from your famous self, Jay Don. Since you *said* that's what you wanted. But I'm getting the distinct impression that you like being the center of attention."

"Uh, *no*, I really don't." Or not *Shelly's* attention anyway. And wasn't that a lowering realization? "I'm simply marveling at how weak your flirtation game is."

"Of course it is." Rafe raised one eyebrow. "And you think yours is superior?"

"Infinitely."

"Right. Still a competitive bastard, I see." Rafe licked his lips and smiled a slow smile. "By all means, then, feel free to show me how it's done."

"I *would*. I totally would. And it would be a shock-and-awe campaign the likes of which you've never seen—" Rafe's laughter made my stomach spin again. "—but unlike some people, I don't want to set expectations I don't plan to fulfill." I gave him an arch look.

"I think you're lying. I think you're not used to having to work to get attention anymore." Rafe leaned toward me over the table. "I think it all comes a little too easily to you."

I blinked at him. "You think it's been easy for me?"

"Aside from the boob pics and the tabloids outing you? Yeah, kinda." He shrugged. "I remember it was tough for you in the beginning, getting labels to listen to you and stuff. But now that you've hit it big? Everyone throws themselves at you, and—"

"You know what it's like when you hit it big?" I whisper-hissed, leaning over the table. "You find yourself in your apartment, hearing that your album has gone gold, and you realize you don't know who to celebrate with. So you decide to take your ass to a club, to get lost in a crowd. Except you're an idiot who didn't realize that having a gold album would mean people suddenly *cared* what you were doing or with whom, or that you could wind up in some photographer's money shot. Hitting it big is being one shitty song or bout of writer's block away from being a joke. A one-hit wonder. Hitting it big is hustling every day and..." I broke off and blew out a breath. "And if you ever dare to complain about any tiny part of it, people remind you how spoiled you are, and…" I broke off with a head shake and sat up straighter in my seat. "Whatever. Fine. Flirtation challenge accepted.

I was low-key horrified by how much I'd admitted, but I also had to bite my tongue to keep from telling him more. About how lonely it was, having handlers and managers and not friends. About how it had felt when I'd thought my only choices were making a giant statement about my personal life or living in constant fear of exposure. About the fear of being one underperforming album, one hot new replacement act, or *yeah*, one tabloid scandal, from being yesterday's news.

Rafe didn't care about any of that, I reminded myself.

He frowned. "I didn't challenge you. And I never said you were spoiled either. I only said—"

Shelly came back with the food at that exact moment. She practically tossed my omelette on the table, with so much force the plate spun for half a second. Meanwhile, she set what must surely have been three orders of pancakes, three pigs' worth of bacon, and a *jug* of blueberry topping in front of Rafe.

Rafe smiled in thanks and picked up his fork… but Shelly did not leave. Instead, she leaned both elbows on the edge of the table, which was *seriously* inappropriate. Then she hunched over with her ass in the air and her chest resting perilously close to the jug of blueberry topping, which had to be some kind of health code violation.

I looked around for a damn comment card.

"Go on and tuck right in," she told Rafe eagerly. "I can't wait to see what you think."

Rafe's gaze darted from Shelly's face, to her chest, to me, and then to his pancakes.

"Uh..." he began, and he was so predictable, I could practically *see* the thoughts flashing through his mind as he replayed my words from earlier.

Was he leading her on and giving her expectations? The proximity of her mammary glands to his food suggested *yes*.

And *was* I thinking about his earlier *free boobs* comment and judging him harshly for staring at what Shelly was offering? Also yes.

I grinned evilly. He was so easy sometimes.

"Go on, *handsome*," I said, deliberately making my voice even huskier than usual. "You look hungry. You should eat up."

Rafe's eyes flashed to mine, and his forehead suspiciously creased at my sudden concern.

Meanwhile, I took a big bite of my omelette, popped it in my mouth, chewed for half a second, and groaned orgasmically, leaning my head back against the red pleather booth and doing my very best imitation of that scene in *When Harry Met Sally*.

"Oh my *Godddd*. This is the best thing I've put in my mouth since..." I pushed my lips together like I'd accidentally said too much, darted a glance from Shelly to Rafe, licked my lips, and lifted an eyebrow meaningfully at him. "Well. You know."

Rafe's mouth dropped open slightly as he stared at me.

I held his gaze for a beat, then cut off another bite of eggs and held out my fork. "You wanna try some, *handsome*?"

Rafe's eyes flared, and he swallowed hard.

"Try the pancakes first," Shelly insisted, trying to recapture Rafe's attention. "I think the cook puts, like, lemon or something in the blueberry topping. It's amazing."

"Mmm. And this guy loves a good topping," I husked huskily, like the old diner was a love palace and I was Barry freakin' White. I deliberately slid my sandal between Rafe's boots, hooked my heel behind his ankle, and whispered, "Don't you?"

Rafe cleared his throat. "Sometimes I do," he agreed, his voice so deep I shivered.

The heat in his eyes was unmistakable, and I wasn't sure if this meant I'd won our little flirting contest thing or I'd lost spectacularly, because my poor cock—which was still on a hair trigger from the night before that had not been appeased by a quick jerk in the shower this morning—started plumping behind my zipper.

Shelly sighed and straightened, removing her chest from the condiment area. "Y'all let me know if you need me, I guess," she said glumly.

"Sure will," I returned brightly.

When she was gone, Rafe kicked me under the table. "What the hell was *that*?" he whispered.

"What was what?" I took another bite of my omelette and looked at him guilelessly. "Me owning your ass at flirtation?"

He ran his tongue over the top of his teeth like he wasn't sure if he was amused or pissed off, which was really a running theme for us, at least these days.

"Thought one of your goals with this whole—" He waved a hand.

"Say kidnapping one more time, Rafael. I dare you."

"—road trip," he said innocently, "was to stay under the radar. Do you *want* to start rumors about you and me?"

"No! God, no." I scowled. "Jesus. Me with my brother-in-law? Like me being gay wasn't enough of a story?"

"Former."

"Huh?" I glanced up from my omelette.

"Former brother-in-law."

"Yeah. Technically, I guess," I muttered, thinking about the stupid letter from Aimee he kept in his wallet. I was pretty sure people didn't generally do that for their *former* spouses. "Don't think the media would care much about the former-ness. But it doesn't matter. Shelly doesn't know who I am, like you said, so we're fine. In fact, we're *better* than fine, because now we know who's the better flirt. I mean, flirting with the waitress is rookie shit. Flirting with a guy who hates your guts, on the other hand..."

Rafe shook his head and dug into his pancakes. I stretched out my fork and sliced into the other side of the stack.

Rafe jabbed my finger with his fork. "Hey! Manners."

"Since your girlfriend forgot my pancakes, I figure you should share." I shoved the bite in my mouth, and it was so good, I couldn't help chasing the last bits of blueberry juice off the fork with my tongue.

Rafe stared at the fork in my hand and swallowed hard, and I'd have paid big money to know what he was thinking of.

Or maybe it was better I didn't know.

I shifted my omelette to the middle of the table. "You're welcome to have some of mine."

He rolled his eyes but dug in anyway. "So, earlier this morning, I plotted out the trip for today," he said a moment later, pulling up a Google map on his phone. "I figure we can stop for the night around Kansas City. That's a little more than ten hours from here. We can take it in two-and-a-half-hour driving blocks and switch off a little past Nashville—"

I swallowed another bite of pancakes and stared at him as I licked the fork. "You plotted out the trip."

"Yeah. I mean, I'm open to suggestions, but—"

"This morning."

"That's what I said. I've been up since five. I did some planning, snuck in a quick workout, and I was ready to jump in the shower when you knocked."

Jesus. Why was that so damn attractive? I knew it was partly because he was so freakin' capable and responsible, and that had always been attractive. But part of it was because, despite what he thought, I *hadn't* had an entourage to rely on over the years, or anyone really. I'd had Debbie, and Oak, and some other people on Debbie's team, but they were there to take care of Jayd... not Jay.

I knew Rafe wasn't really taking care of me either. This trip was about my sister, and I was just the guy with the van, but it still felt nice.

My gaze tracked over Rafe's dark hair and the little creases at the corners of his eyes. The way his T-shirt clung to the defined muscles of his arms. The way his big hand clutched his fork.

The sad truth was, he was as attractive to me as he'd ever been. And every bit as out of reach.

"This is the part where you call me the world's biggest control freak," Rafe said, making a gimme motion with his hand. "Go ahead. I'm braced."

"It's no fun insulting you when you're expecting it." I stood up from the table, hoping he wouldn't notice how quickly my mood had tanked. "I'm gonna take a walk. Too restless to eat."

Rafe frowned like he wanted to say something, but when he opened his mouth, all that came out was "You want the keys?" He held them out to me.

"Yes. Always." I shoved them into the front pocket of my sweatshirt. "I'll be out front."

I walked back to the front desk, where Shelly stood texting something into her cell phone. *Shit.* I didn't want to have to deal with Rafe's offended groupie.

But when she looked up at me, she seemed curious and had none of the bad attitude I'd expected.

"Can I pay the check, please?"

"M'kay." She set down her phone and activated the old cash register with a thump. "So how long have you and the cutie... you know?"

I shook my head blankly.

"Been involved," she elaborated.

"What? Oh! No. That was a joke. We're old friends. Sort of." I glanced back at the table where Rafe had his dark head bent over his phone, possibly calculating how many tanks of gas we'd need based on the cargo weight of the van and the wind speed and direction between here and Kansas City. It should not have made my stomach go all warm and melty. "He's not interested in me that way."

She snorted. "Fine, then. Keep your secrets if you like." She hit a few keys. "But I wasn't born yesterday, and those sparks I felt dancing around y'all were *not* friendship."

"They weren't?"

She snorted. "Sixteen forty-five."

I handed over my credit card and tried to figure out how to make her elaborate, though maybe it was better if she didn't.

"Here's some free advice, honey." She handed over my card and the receipt to sign. "If you're not hitting that, it's not for lack of interest on his part."

"It's not?" I looked back at Rafe again, and this time I found him looking at me, so I quickly looked away.

"Ain't no such thing as a one-sided spark," Shelly assured me.

I added on an enormous tip and thanked her, then walked back out into the sunshine.

The morning chill had burned off, so I threw my sweatshirt in the back seat, grabbed my baseball hat, and spent a few minutes sitting against the front bumper of the van, since the inside still smelled like a department store perfume counter in hell.

This whole trip was about *Aimee*, I reminded myself for the umpteenth time. Not me reviving an old crush or even an old friendship. I needed Rafe to get me into the hospital, and I maybe needed to convince him to convince Aimee to tell me what the fuck was going on. Getting involved with him in any way would only backfire.

And even after I got to see my sister, I had a billion other issues to deal with, like what to do with my career. The overly friendly voicemail Debbie had left last night asking me to call her had either meant she planned to drop me as a client or wanted to beg me *again* to do some kind of come-out interview for the media, neither of which I wanted.

Trouble was, for the first time since I was ten, I didn't know precisely what I *did* want.

The bell over the door to the diner jangled so loud I heard it across the parking lot, but I kept my eyes closed and tried to prepare myself.

Rafe was either going to say something snarky about me flirting with him, or he'd lecture me about being nicer, or he'd remind me how spoiled I was. And I vowed to myself that no matter how sexy he looked with his one quirked-up eyebrow and that little smile that played around his lips, I would react with nothing but polite amusement. We were *not* friends. He didn't want to be friends. And neither did—

"Here," Rafe said in a gruff voice, and I opened my eyes to find him standing right beside me. He shoved a plastic bag at me, and I took it without thinking.

Without another word, he opened the driver's door and pushed the button to start the car. I blinked and got in the passenger's seat.

"What's this?" I demanded.

Rafe busied himself with his seat belt and didn't meet my eyes. "Pancakes. Blueberry. And I got her to put some blueberry topping in a cup in there, too."

I stared at him like he was speaking pig Latin. I mean, he might as well have been. "You... bought me pancakes."

"Has the lack of adoring fans in the vicinity affected your comprehension? Yes. Pancakes. For you. Yum yum. Sustenance." He sounded crankier than usual.

"Why?"

"Because..." He rolled down the window and shifted the van into reverse with his big hands and still didn't look my way. "You seemed to like them well enough when you were stealing mine. And you hardly ate any of your own breakfast. And your highly functioning metabolism requires real food at regular intervals." He swallowed. "But if you don't want them—"

"I want them!" I insisted, holding the container with two hands like he might try to take it by force and throw it out the window.

"Good." He pulled out of the parking lot and headed for the highway.

A long minute—and maybe half an order of pancakes—later, he spoke again. "You said, back there, that it was a challenge to flirt with a guy who hated your guts."

I frowned, licking blueberry juice from my fork just like I'd done in the diner. The blueberry shit was really good.

"Well, I don't. Hate your guts, I mean. And I don't think you're spoiled. And I... I should not have said what I did about you having it easy."

He looked at me finally, like he wanted to see if I was paying attention. Like there was a way in hell I could *not* pay attention to him.

"I don't trust you," he continued quickly. "At *all*. You destroyed that trust when you walked away from our friendship years ago—and don't tell me you didn't because you *did*. Also, you drive me insane, because you don't take no for a damn answer, which is why I'm in this van, which is one hundred percent a kidnap van, even if I'm driving. But... I don't hate you. I told myself I did, but I could never quite get there. And that seemed like something you should know."

He turned up the radio, signaling that the conversation was over, and I clutched my plastic fork tightly, thinking maybe, *maybe* we could be friends after all.

7

RAFE

We absolutely could *not* be friends.

"I told you, Gage, we are not doing festival decorations based on *Constellations*," I insisted, bracing my foot on the dash in what I hoped was a casual way and not an "oh my God, Jay, if you got us any closer to that moving truck, we would be *in* the truck" sort of way, which required a supreme act of will. "Not happening."

"I'm sitting right here," Jay muttered from the driver's seat. "In case anyone's forgotten."

I definitely had not forgotten.

And not just because my life had been in jeopardy thirty unique times in thirty minutes.

Gage's sigh filled the car through the speakers. "Rafe, dude, be reasonable. Jayd's playing the concert. There'll be all sorts of merchandise there *anyway*—"

"Which is more than enough. Surely there's *some* theme someone can come up with that's not dicks or stars. Don't people have other suggestions that are island related? Like... like... seashells? Or scrimshaw?"

Legit anything that would not put Jay Rollins in my face and force me to think about him more than I already was.

"*Scrimshaw.* Now that's the kinda crazy genius I expect from you," Gage enthused. "Perhaps you can lead us in a rousing sea shanty chorus, as well."

I set my jaw. "Still better than *Conste*-fucking-*llations.*"

"Hey! Still here." Jay waved a hand in front of my face and raised his voice. "Still *right* here."

Yes. Yes, I was aware that he was there. I'd been way, way, way too aware of him being *right the heck there* ever since he'd looked at me back in the diner, held his fork in his calloused, long-fingered hand, and licked blueberry juice off it.

If that was not a crime in the state of Tennessee, it damn well should have been.

Since then, he'd compounded his sins by eating the takeout pancakes in a way that made me think of blow jobs and sucking on honey drops in a way that made me want to kiss him, which was so distracting I could almost forget what a truly terrible driver he was.

But not quite.

I'd debated instituting a no-licking and sucking rule, but I felt like that would probably say more about me than Jay's forking habits. And to be honest, I'd been hyperaware of him long before cutlery had gotten involved. Since yesterday in the van...

Heck, since two days ago, when he'd stood near me on the street in Whispering Key and I'd realized that the wobble in my gut wasn't *just* anger but some new anger-lust hybrid... Or, fine, since I was fifteen because even before I'd recognized my attraction to Jay, I'd known he was one of the most important people in my life and there wasn't much I wouldn't do for him.

"Listen, I'll be home in a few days," I reminded my brother. "Let's table this for now, and later we can—"

"No. Nope! We are not waiting until the day before the concert to pick the damn decorations. I plan to spend the Extravaganza drunk off my ass, *not* hustling up and down a ladder to hang a thousand foil stars when you finally come to your senses."

"Then come up with a new theme! Because I refuse to have the Extravaganza associated with—"

"I'm *literally sitting right here!*" Jay shouted before I could finish my sentence. "God."

"Sorry, Jayd," Gage said. "For what it's worth, I respect the stars."

"Not your fault," Jay gritted out. "I know exactly which Goodman doesn't want to be associated with me."

I huffed out a breath. That was not the problem I was having. That was the polar opposite of the problem I was having.

I was trying to remind myself of all the lessons I'd learned the first time Jay broke me, but it was hard to wrap myself in a dark cloak of hurt when Jay kept smiling at me and spreading sunshine around, damn it.

I didn't want my heart to soften toward him, but how the hell could I help it when he talked about getting a gold record—having the world in love with his music—and having to go out to a club so he could find people to celebrate with?

Did he even know how lonely he sounded?

"Rafe," Gage said slyly. "Have you played that game I suggested? You really should. And thank me later."

I scowled. I was not in the mood for games.

After Gage hung up, Jay darted a glance at me. "I thought you didn't hate me," he said, his voice so flat and monotone that guilt clawed at me.

"I don't. This isn't about you," I sort of lied. "Not everything is about *you*." Except that these days, for me, it sure felt like it was.

"You could tell me what's going on with Aimee," he said in that same neutral voice. "If she's really sick, too sick to act on her own, my lawyers will find me a way in to see her. You don't have to see this through if it's fucking you up that badly."

I thought about that, about just telling Jay the whole thing and washing my hands of it. It made sense, really. He was already too invested for Aimee to hold on to her secrets, and he'd never let her down. I could be home by tomorrow, back to my usual responsibilities, and my comfortable island existence, and my daydreams of an exciting future.

"Nope," I said firmly. "Not happening."

Jay sighed and fell silent for a minute.

"So this decoration thing isn't about me having a huge scandal attached to my name?" he demanded abruptly, like this had been weighing on his mind. "And you wanting to keep that away from the Key?"

I turned in my seat to face him. "Fuck, no. That never crossed my mind."

Jay accelerated. "So it's about the shit you said at the meeting the other day. That you think I'm allergic to responsibility—"

I sighed. Deep down, I'd known that was a stretch even while I was saying it. Yelling it. Whichever.

"Not... exactly. No. You've always taken care of Aimee. And your career." I hurried on before he could question what I thought he *hadn't* taken care of and realize I was mostly talking about *me*. "I shouldn't have said that."

"So then... it's my album? *Constellations*?"

I ground my teeth together.

"Because Rafe, I've got to tell you, if you're critiquing the tiny piece of my heart I put out in the world and saying you hate it, you might as well be saying you hate me. The album *is* me. I mean, it's not the entirety of me, obviously, but it's..."

"It's *not* you," I muttered. "That's the problem."

Jay swerved into the passing lane again, nearly sideswiping a Corvette that dared to be going only twenty over the speed limit. "What the hell does that mean?"

I grabbed the strap over the door. "Could you maybe slow down?"

"Could you maybe answer the question? Or is this another super secret you can't share with me?"

"Yesterday, you told me you didn't want to hear my thoughts on the album," I reminded him, possibly taking my life in my hands.

"I don't want to hear your thoughts on it being *overproduced*, which, by the way, doesn't mean what I think you think it means. This is not an issue of you saying, 'Had you considered less percussion on "Variable Skies," Jay?' because I could discuss that. I could. This is you having a giant visceral reaction to my entire record—"

He braked hard and pulled around a flatbed trailer hauling a load of plywood. In the cargo area, one of the suitcases *thunked* against the side of the van.

"It doesn't sound like you!" I finally blurted, more concerned about surviving the trip than policing my mouth. "Not the you that I know... or *knew*. None of the songs are songs I ever heard, and they're all about people I've never met and places I've never been... They're about the Jay you became after you left the Key, I guess, which is fine. Which is great. Which is... just... just... *stellar* for you. Obviously. I'm glad you've changed and grown. But *I* am the same guy I was. The same guy I've always been. Boring, small-town Rafe. And it bugs me, okay? It's a me thing, not a you thing. Are you happy now? How about if I drive for a bit?"

"You already drove. Don't make it seem like I'm a bad driver. I'm perfectly capable—you're just a control freak." Jay slowed down. A minuscule amount. "And you're wrong, you know."

"Okay," I agreed, still clinging to the strap. "Sure. I'm wrong. That's fine."

He sighed. "It's like you decided that I changed, and you started interpreting everything through that lens. But maybe I haven't changed as much as you think." He gave me a long look. "Maybe you're looking at me wrong, so you're looking at the album wrong."

"And maybe *you* shouldn't be looking at *me* at *all*. Eyes on the road," I snapped.

I really did not need to be having deep, feelsy discussions with Jay Rollins, who'd be back on the road before the last phallus balloon left Whispering Key after the Extravaganza.

"What did Gage mean about playing a game?"

I sighed. "He's being a shithead and suggesting ways for us to pass the time. Don't worry about it."

"We could always turn the music back on to pass the time," Jay said sullenly. "Not sure why we had to turn it off."

"Because I wanted to play Ari Friedrich's *Trust* album and—"

"You listened to the entire thing on repeat. Twice!" Jay exploded. "There are other good songs in the world."

"True. But I like his."

"I think you like pissing me off."

Also true. "Nonsense."

"You know," Jay said with fake casualness, "Ari Friedrich and I wrote songs together once. He said he loved 'Pretty Girl,' and I helped him write 'Incidental Cruelty'—"

"Sure you did."

"I *did*!"

"Okay."

"He credited me! It's on the internet! I really— Ohmygod, you are the most provoking human," Jay groaned, smacking a hand against his thigh. "I can't tell if you're giving me shit or if you actually think I'd lie about it."

"Aww. Poor Jay. Does my nose not twitch when I give you shit?"

"No—"

"Hmm. So maybe you don't know me as well as—"

"When you give me shit," the fucker went on, "you get these little crinkles in the corners of your eyes." He pointed to the spot on his own face. "But I figured if I turned to look at you, you'd be all 'Oooh, Jay, you're such a bad driver. *Meow meow meow.*'"

"Meow meow meow?"

"When you bitch about my driving, you sound like Sigmund, Belinda's flatulent, grumpy-ass Maine coon."

My lips parted in shock. "That... might be the most comprehensive insult anyone has ever given me."

"I like to be thoro— Hey, what's that?"

"What?"

"*That.*" He nudged his chin toward a neon pink-and-white billboard on the side of the highway ringed with enormous flickering lightbulbs. "I can't make out the words. The flashing lights are blinding me."

"It says 'Visit Missouri's Famous Hole Inn the Wall Pleasure Emporium and Corn Museum.'"

"You have to see it for yourself."

"Oh, no. Pretty sure I do *not*—"

"No, the next sign." Jay tilted his chin again, and I glanced out my window to find a whole row of billboards just like the first, strung the whole length of a field.

"Adult Entertainment!" I read. "Live music! Fun for the whole family!" Then, perhaps most mystifying of all, "Corncob crafts that will delight and astound you!" I shook my head. "What astounds me is how they think corncob crafts have anything to do with adult entertainment or *pleasure.*"

"Guess it depends on what they're making out of corncobs, hmm?" Jay wiggled his eyebrows.

"Huh?"

"Aww. Don't strain yourself." He snorted and reached over to pat my hand. "It'll all make sense when you're older, honey." He paused. "Or maybe possibly bottom-ier."

Maybe possibly?

Bottom-ier?

I stared at him for half a second before I managed to croak, "Okay, so can we talk about this?"

"Talk about...corncobs?" Jay frowned. "I don't actually have

a corncob dildo, Rafe, but if you're looking for a recommen-
dation, Oak probably—"

"Not that! Talk about... *this!*" I waved my hand in a circle to
indicate his whole being, the very air around him. "The fact
that you're gay. That you're making corncob jokes."

He snickered. "That's, like, a new level on the Kinsey scale. It
goes from 'mostly straight' right up to 'gay enough to understand corncob jokes.'"

I looked at him steadily for a minute, and he relented with a
sigh.

"What is there to say? I'm gay. I've known I was gay since I
was... I dunno, fourteen? I just never came out, not to
anyone, until a few years ago."

"You know people would have supported you, right? *I* would
have—"

"Yeah, I know. I *do* know. But... my family wasn't like yours,
with Beale and Gage being gay, and your parents being cool
with it when you came out, so coming out felt like a big
huge deal to me. Maybe even more than it did for you?" He
shrugged. "And... okay, real talk. From the time I decided I
wanted a career in music, I had my dad quoting me stats on
how few people ever make it in the industry and telling me I
should get a business degree instead, and I... I didn't really
believe I could come out until I got famous. I felt like if I
cracked open the closet door, if I told *anyone*, I'd start to
want things I couldn't afford to want. So I decided to be
patient. I figured..." He darted a look at me. "Well. It doesn't
matter anymore what I figured. Suffice it to say, when I *did*
get famous... I figured out pretty quick that didn't make

coming out any easier. In fact, it brings a whole other set of problems."

"So you dated women instead? Like Olivia Merry?"

"No. That was…" He shook his head. "That was a whole other thing. I didn't actually date anyone until three years ago when I was on my first tour." He cleared his throat. "Or something like that."

Right around the time I was marrying Aimee, I realized with a sour feeling in my stomach. Well, at least one of us was getting some action that summer.

"You used to tell stories, when we were out on the boat—"

"About girls I thought were pretty back in high school?" He smiled ruefully. "Yeah, well. I did think they were pretty."

I shook my head. It wasn't fair for me to be upset, but…

"We were friends. I cared about you. And you knew I was queer. You could have told *me*, even if you couldn't tell anyone else. I wouldn't have told anyone."

He laughed. "Rafe. You were the last person I'd tell."

"What? Why?"

"Because…" He shot me a look, then bit his lip and focused on the road. "You just were." He shrugged.

I nodded slowly. "Well. If you need help with anything now that you're out…" I shut my mouth quickly and cleared my throat. What was I about to offer right there? Advice? Instruction? Moral support for the next couple of days?

Jay grinned like he could read my mind. "I'm actually pretty sure I've had more experience with guys than you have, but thanks."

I rolled my eyes. "I mean. You're cute and all, but I doubt you've had *more* experiences since you didn't get started until three years ago. But you're welcome."

Jay did that thing where he stretched his jaw from side to side, which seemed to be what he did when he got annoyed. No lie, it was starting to give me a little thrill every time he did it. "Once I broke the seal, I made up for lost time." He cut his eyes to me. "So it's not only possible, it's almost definitely fact. Remember, I wasn't dividing my energies sleeping with women."

"Please. I haven't slept with a woman in yea... Um." I broke off with a little gurgling noise, remembering who I was talking to and all he didn't know. "When I was in college, I once had three partners in a single night, one right after the other. So. Pretty freakin' experienced."

He wrinkled his nose. "Is that supposed to impress me? I've had three partners at once."

"You have?" I cocked my head. "Really?"

His cheekbones flushed. "Okay, *two* partners. Three of us total. And yes, really. It was after a show. I... I went back to their hotel room."

"Was this in Vegas?" I demanded, remembering his words from earlier about the stories he could tell.

The idea of him with a pair of guys was undeniably hot. It also seemed seriously fucking dangerous, for *anyone* but especially for him.

None of your business, Goodman.

"What? No," Jay said, confused. "Peoria. FYI, Iowans are amazing lovers."

"Peoria is in Illinois."

His mouth opened and shut like a fish. "*Whatever.* We weren't talking about *geography* at the time, if you catch my drift." He cut his eyes to me again and added unnecessarily, "Because we were busy having *sex*. Bountiful, sweat-ful sex."

I rolled my eyes, pushing back an acute stab of highly inappropriate lust and even weirder and more inappropriate jealousy. "Yes. Thank you. Got that." I made a face. "*Sweat-ful.* Tell me again what a brilliant wordsmith you are?"

"You don't have to be all pissy," he said in a smug voice that suggested he was enjoying my discomfort, "just because I've packed more sexual adventure into a few years than you have in a lifetime."

"I'm not pissy! I don't *get* pissy," I lied. Pissily. I uncrossed my arms, which had somehow crossed themselves over my chest. "And I don't think we've established that you have. In fact, I was just now remembering one of my own, ah... adventures." I hesitated, my mind completely blank.

"Oh yeah?" Jay challenged. "Adventures involving multiple partners?"

"No! Involving... involving... monster trucks." I winced.

Of all my sex-related memories to dredge up, I'd picked the most embarrassing one.

His jaw dropped open. "You had sex in a monster truck?"

"I... No. Not exactly. Hey, should we stop for lunch soon? I'm hungry, and your metabolism—"

Jay would not be sidetracked. "My metabolism's fine because I just ate my weight in pancakes a couple hours ago. And when you say *not exactly*, does that mean you *sort of* had sex in a monster truck?"

"I..." I cleared my throat and muttered, "I had sex in the bed of a pickup truck outside a monster truck rally."

His jaw dropped. "You did not."

"I did." I felt my face go hot. "Isn't it time to switch drivers?"

"We are never switching drivers again unless you tell me that entire story."

"Because you want the details of me having sex with some guy back when I was twenty-four?" I asked, like I wasn't equally desperate to hear about every part of his life that I'd missed.

"No, I want to know because you obviously don't want to tell me, which means it's a good story. I'm imagining a beer gut and an I Heart Tractors shirt..."

I rolled my eyes. "Not quite. His name was Vinnie. He, uh, sang the national anthem before the trucks came out?" I bit my lip at the memory. "He had all this messy, dark hair, and he wore a sleeveless shirt with huge cutouts all the way down to his waist to show off the tattoos on his flank. He wore the tightest jeans I'd ever seen," I said wistfully. "They were a *bitch* to get on and off, but at the time I really appreciated that he displayed how much product was in the package right up front."

Jay made a choking noise.

"Plus, he sang with his eyes squeezed shut, like thinking about those stars and stripes caused him actual pain—" I demonstrated. "*Hngh.* Hot as fuck."

Jay spluttered with laughter. "And yet you mocked me for looking like a jackass when I emoted over Troye Sivan!"

"I never mocked you." I cut my eyes to him, then away. "And I definitely didn't think you looked like a jackass." I cleared my throat and straightened in my seat. "Anyway, at least Vinnie wasn't trying to drive at the time."

Jay was silent, thoughtful maybe, and I cursed myself for running my damn mouth.

Finally, he said, "So, I'm not seeing why this story was so embarrassing—"

"I never said it was. You assumed."

"—unless Vinnie was, like, singing the national anthem *while* he fucked you—"

"No! He didn't *fuck* me! We were in a parking lot. Jesus."

"—or one of you started randomly crying in the middle of the act—"

"No! Fuck, no."

"—or one of you called the other by the wrong name."

Jay laughed.

I did not.

"Oh my fuck!" he gasped, so delighted he accelerated until we were hurtling past other cars. "What did he call you?"

My face went hot. "Done with this convo now. Watch the damn road."

But Jay's eyes widened further, like just by looking at the fists clenched on my legs he could hear all the words I didn't say. "Wait, it was *you*? *You* called *him* by the wrong name?"

I stared fixedly out the window. "Pull over. I need a rest stop."

Jay bounced up and down, which was fucking terrifying considering how shitty his driving ability was when his ass was firmly in his seat. "I cannot believe you did that!" he crowed. "Oh my God, no wonder you didn't want to tell me!"

"It's gonna downpour any second." I gestured at the low clouds on the horizon. "If you don't keep your eyes on the damn—"

"What'd you call him?" Jay's voice, that deep, dreamy voice, was laced with laughter. "Come on, tell me! Did you call him your ex's name? Or, no, wait, you said you were twenty-four? You didn't have a boyfriend back then, did you? So did you call Vinnie by the name of your fantasy fuck? *Oh, Eddie Redmayne!* Or no, wait again. You said he was a singer, right?"

"No. Not really. Kind of. We didn't exchange life stories. Jay, drop it," I pleaded. "Just... let's... maybe there's a podcast we could—"

"Nope. Now this is a puzzle I need to solve! Lemme think of musicians you liked." He tapped his lips. "You had that thing for Jared Leto from Thirty Seconds to Mars—"

"Jesus." I ran a hand over my face. "The gas gauge is at less than a quarter tank, you know. There's a rest stop in five miles, and—"

"Yeah, yeah. We'll stop. But first... Who's the lead singer of Nickelback again? 'Cause you always claimed you didn't like them, but I wonder now if you were protesting too—"

"Chad Kroeger is not my fantasy fuck!" I scowled. "And you need to stop with this. Trust me."

Jay laughed again, and it was exquisitely terrible because I was conditioned to love that laughter, to glory in it, but meanwhile, I was flailing.

Lie. Just lie! You called him Johnny Cash. You called him Kurt Cobain. You called him Meat Loaf. Anything!

But I couldn't make my mouth move, and anyway, something about this moment felt inevitable, like we weren't just hurtling down the highway, we were hurtling toward a reckoning.

"Okay, so not Chad. And I'm guessing it's not Jared, 'cause that would be too easy. And your precious Ari didn't even have an album out then. So who did you listen to who had messy hair and got all emote-y when he sang? I don't remember you being a huge fan of anyone else back then, except m—"

In my peripheral vision, he ran a hand through his own thick, overlong hair and froze.

"I mean..." He laughed again, shakily this time, and his hand flexed on the steering wheel. His eyes darted to my face, but I couldn't make myself turn my head. "I mean..."

"Gas station," I croaked, pointing out the exit. "Eyes on the road, *please*."

"Yeah." Jay's voice was thin. Thready. "Yeah, okay."

8

———

JAY

I leaned against the side of the van while the gas pump worked its magic and watched as the wind blew a crushed can across the ground all the way from the pumps to the parking lot.

I felt a lot of kinship with that can.

Every cell in my body was on high alert, like the pre-storm electricity that charged the air around me was inside me, too, stirring things up. It felt like something monumental—possibly monumentally *unpleasant*, given my track record—was about to happen, but like that freakin' can, I had no control over any of it.

Rafe had called some guy by my name while fucking.

Fact.

I mean, okay, not a fact-fact, since he hadn't totally admitted it. But considering the way he'd frozen solid and refused to look at me while anxiety poured off him thick enough to drown out even the perfume smell in the van, the truth was apparent.

And almost just as shocking was the fact that he hadn't denied it.

I mean, if I were in Rafe's wrong-name-shouting shoes, I'd have lied my ass off about it. "Oh, Jay, the only reason I did that was because you and Monster Truck Vinnie wore the same stupid cologne and have the same weird, long skeleton fingers! Otherwise, I'd *never* have thought of my best friend during sexytimes!"

But Rafe hadn't said anything like that, and I couldn't think why... unless he'd had the same more-than-friendly feelings toward me that I'd had toward him.

My dick didn't give a shit about the whys. It had very positive, very proprietary feelings about Rafe railing some guy and yelling my name, period, and urged me to kiss the shit out of Rafe and damn the consequences.

My brain, on the other hand, was skip-skip-skipping like a record player, pondering what might have happened if I'd come out as a teenager, and whether Rafe might still find me attractive after all this time... and what I'd do if he did.

Suffice it to say, thanks to this mental traffic jam, I hadn't been able to think of a single word to say to Rafe, and I still couldn't. We'd driven into the rest area like we were sitting on a grenade, afraid to make any sudden movements or even breathe too deeply, and when Rafe had disappeared into the building muttering something about "restroom" and "snack" and "Gage" and "food trucks," I'd been glad.

"Nice whip," a voice beside me said.

"Huh?" I whirled around to find a man wearing a black beanie and a hair metal T-shirt pulled snugly over his beer gut patting the hood of the van appreciatively.

"This here's a 3500 model, isn't it? Looks real sturdy." He leaned down to peer at the tires, and his long sandy hair nearly touched the ground before he peered up at me. "Triple treads?"

I opened my mouth to say something dismissive so the guy would go away before he recognized me, but then I heard Rafe's voice in my head, reminding me that I used to be more open with people and that not everyone was gonna sell me out.

And while my first instinct was to roll my eyes at *anything* Rafe said, especially when he talked in that tone of voice, maybe he had a tiny point about me thinking the worst of people.

It also helped that this guy was clearly more starstruck by the van than by me.

"Seems like it," I agreed, as though I assessed tire tread counts all the time. "It's not mine, though. I'm just renting it for a few days."

"Ah." The man nodded, and little creases formed at the side of his eyes as he smiled. "Must be nice to live the dream for a little while, huh?"

The dream? I looked at the serviceable white passenger van with its dark tinted windows and the run-down gas station in the middle of nowhere. Well... different people had different dreams, I supposed.

I gave him a half-smile. "Kinda, yeah."

"I'm Chet, by the way. Chet Hatcher." His smile turned sheepish as he extended a hand covered in silver rings for me to shake. "And before you ask, yes, I'm *that* Chet Hatcher."

"Oh." I blinked. "Sorry, I don't..."

"Of Chet and the Newsmen? Voted Cass County Fair's band of the year for four out of the last five years?"

I shook my head and fought not to ask what had happened the fifth year. "Sorry. Still not ringing a bell."

"Not much of a music fan, then?"

"No, no, I am," I assured him. "I'm just not from around here."

His eyes lit up. "Yeah? Where ya from?"

"Florida," I answered without thinking. *Fuck.* I was such an idiot. "I mean... I mean, I came from Florida just now." I waved a hand in that general direction. "I'm from outside of Huntsville, originally, and then New York."

"A travelin' man like me, eh?" He nudged my arm with his elbow companionably, then stuck his thumbs through the belt loops of his worn jeans. "Well, in a couple years you'll have heard of the Newsmen, 'cause we're gonna be *big*. And you'll get to tell folks you met me, once upon a time."

"I definitely will," I said solemnly.

A couple of years back, that had been me, so confident fame was around the corner and every stranger was a potential fan who just hadn't heard me yet. Chet seemed a bit older than me—maybe forty or so—and I wondered, if I hadn't gotten my record contract, whether I'd have been offering my music for free at gas stations when I was his age.

Probably. I'd been *that* determined to make things happen for me and for Aimee.

Now here I was living Chet's actual dream—not the van, but Debbie, and a gold record, and tour dates, and songs getting national airplay—and I was in danger of losing it all because I didn't want to make my private life public. It seemed like an inconsequential hill to die on, considering all I'd given up already… but how much more of myself was I willing to give?

Chet grinned. "Remind me to getcha a CD from my trunk in a minute. It'll blow your mind."

I blinked back to awareness. "Oh. Uh… cool. Thanks."

"Listen, I've got a favor to ask," Chet began, and I froze. Did he recognize me? Did he want me to listen to his album because he thought (incorrectly) that I could somehow help him get a recording contract, or—

"Do you have some spare change? I'd get it back to you somehow," he added quickly. "Promise."

"Oh." I blinked, then patted my pockets and scooped out the few coins I carried. "I don't carry much cash, but if you need some lunch, or something, I could…" I nodded toward the brick building.

"Nah nah nah." Chet waved me off. "I got plenty of food. It's just that my car broke down." He pointed toward an old Chevy hatchback parked off to the side of the parking lot with its hood up. Its gray body was sprinkled all over with rust freckles, and its rear side window appeared to be fashioned entirely from lime-green duct tape, which added an intriguing pop of color. "And my lady's waitin' on me back home."

"Your lady?"

"Chrissea Drake. That's Chrissea with an s-e-a. Special, just like she is." He rocked back and forth on the balls of his feet proudly, making his wallet chain swing. "She's the prettiest girl in Dry Hump."

"In... *pardon*?" The word came out in my stepmother's church-lady voice, which was slightly horrifying.

"Dry Hump, Missouri. Way over on the western side of the state," he explained. "And at least I *think* she's still my lady. Today's our six-month anniversary, see? And Dotty went 'n gave up the ghost this morning, so I told her I might not be home in time, and she hung up on me."

"Dotty did?"

"No, Chrissea." He looked askance at me. "Dotty's the car."

"Right, right."

"I tried calling Chrissea back a hundred times at least, but every time she hangs up." He scuffed the toe of his boot against the asphalt and grumbled, "And now my cell's as dead as Dotty, and I had no change for the pay phone."

I winced sympathetically.

"She's not an easy woman, my Chrissea," he said proudly. "That's why I love her." Then he sighed. "But she's gonna cost me a fortune in quarters."

"That's tough," I agreed. "But maybe—" My phone rang in my pocket, and I took it out, half expecting it to be Rafe saying he'd come down with a rare disease somewhere between the restroom and the soda fountain and he'd need to cancel the second half of our road trip...

But it was *not*.

"Oh my God! Sorry, Chet, I've gotta take this," I said excitedly. "It's my sister."

He grinned and lifted a hand in goodbye, and I hit Accept as he started to walk away. "Aimee! Aim, are you there?"

After a second's pause, my sister's voice came over the line. "Yeah. Hey. It's me."

Her voice was scratchy-rough like she had a cold, but so familiar that I felt my throat go tight. I hadn't fully realized how worried I'd been until that moment.

"Are you okay?"

"Yes. I'm fine. I—"

"Aimee, you're not fine. You're in the hospital—"

"Jay, stop interrupting! I *am* in the hospital, you're right. I had a surgical procedure, and I'm recovering, and it's... slow. But I'm telling you I'm fine because I am. Okay? Better than I've been in a while."

I swallowed. "Yeah. Yes. Okay. Surgery for what?"

Aimee hesitated. "I owe you *so* many explanations, Jay. But this is a long freakin' story, and I'm so, so tired. I'm not up to it right now. I just called because I got your five billion messages, and I didn't want you to worry any more. Okay? I'm here, I'm good. I love you."

"Okay." I clutched the phone more tightly. "Yeah. We'll talk about it when we get there."

"When you... get here?"

"Yeah, we should be there tomorrow or the next day. I wanted to be with you. To make sure you knew you weren't alone in dealing with... whatever's going on."

"Wait, who's *we*?"

"Rafe? I uh... contacted him—" Punched him. Same diff. "—when I heard you were sick, so we're driving up there from Florida right now."

"Rafe." She paused uncertainly. "Do you mean... Young Rafe?"

I frowned. That was a really odd way to refer to her ex-husband and the guy she'd put down as her emergency contact, wasn't it? But then again, she was in the hospital and probably out of it. No wonder she was confused.

I clutched the phone tighter. "Yes. Yeah. Young Rafe."

"You're *together*?" She gave a raspy gasp. "Sweet baby Jesus, it's a miracle! You worked things out and you're friends again! You stopped avoiding him!"

"What? No! We haven't worked anything out. There's nothing to work out." I scowled. Sure, he'd called my name when he was fucking another guy, and I'd been hard all night after fantasizing about him taking a perfectly innocent shower, and I supposed he'd bought me pancakes to make sure I didn't die of malnutrition, but none of that meant we were friends. "We're just two guys who grew apart after he *hit* me and *insulted* me, and even though he *keeps* insulting me, he somehow believes *he's* the injured party, so we're engaged in a cold war standoff while hurtling down the highway in a rented van, and we're only together because we both love you. Also," I added, "I haven't *avoided* him. Don't be insane."

"Oh, Jay," she croaked. "You avoided him for years because you hated knowing you weren't as important to him as I was, after he and I got married. You admitted it to me, back in Tampa. Under the influence of tequila."

"I... I..." I stammered helplessly, feeling my anger and righteousness deflate like a balloon. Damn fucking tequila.

There was a commotion in the background, and a female voice said, "Dr. Clemmons said five minutes on the phone, Ms. Rollins."

"Just five more seconds, April. Pinky promise," Aimee vowed. To me, she said quickly, "Look, I've done a *lot* of thinking about you and Rafe over the last year since our breakup. A *lot*. Especially the last couple weeks after the tabloid thing, and... Well, like I said, I have a lot of explaining to do. And apologizing. And I know it's not my place to interfere, but..." She broke off with a slight cough. "*Ugh*. Anyway, I'm pretty sure Rafe thinks you stopped calling him years ago because you were too busy living like a rock star. So. Use that information as you see fit."

"Wait, *what*?" That was the most nonsensical... "He was marrying *you*, Aim. He probably barely even noticed that—"

"His best friend stopped returning his calls?" she asked ruefully. "And forgot his birthday? And didn't come to his wedding? Yeah, right. You're not an idiot, Jay, but I'm pretty sure you've acted like one where Rafe was concerned."

"Nonsense." I swallowed. "I *never* forgot his birthday."

"Okay. But you never bothered to text him happy birthday either, so what was he supposed to think?"

"I... hadn't thought he'd care much at all."

But even as I said the words, I realized how ridiculous they sounded. Even if he'd been in love with Aimee, he hadn't suddenly forgotten my existence from one day to the next. My stupid jealousy had made it feel like a zero-sum game... but it hadn't been.

"If you love me, promise me you won't waste this one golden opportunity to make things right. Lay your cards on the table, Jay. Tell him how you feel. It would make me feel way less guilty."

"Guilty? What could you have to be guilty for?"

She sighed. "For all the things we're gonna talk about when you get here?"

"You're infuriating."

"Back atcha. 'Cause here's another piece of crucial info it seems like you haven't figured out yet: it should always have been you with Rafe. And I swear I didn't realize it until now, but if I were a betting woman, I'd say he wished it had been even then."

My heart literally skipped beats—one, *skip,* two, *skip, skip*—and my head whirled like the wind whipping through the trees beyond the parking lot. I clenched my free hand into a fist so my nails dug into my palms, but even the pain couldn't convince me I wasn't dreaming.

"Uh. No. That's not... accurate," I blurted desperately. She hadn't seen the way Rafe carefully folded her letter. The way he'd dropped everything to go to Wyoming *on a plane* for her. "He loves you. You loved him."

"Still do, but... not romantically," she said weakly. "Ask him."

"Ask him? Ask him what? Jesus, Aim. I asked him to tell me what was wrong with you and he wouldn't tell me a damn thing because he'd made a promise to you. He made it seem like I was asking him to divulge state secrets. And you want me to ask him if he's in love with his ex-wife?" I laughed, a short, desperate little sound.

"Exactly. Ask him exactly that." Her voice was fading. "Tell him I said to tell you everything. That the secrets are over. And tell him I said to stop being an idiot and remember *why* he made that promise to me in the first place."

I sucked in a shaky breath. "But I—"

"Well, well," another voice—a teasing, *male* voice—said on Aimee's end. "Looks like April was right. You're supposed to be resting, babe."

Babe?

"I'm laying in bed. Can't get more restful, Doc." Aimee's thready voice carried a fond, flirtatious tone I'd never heard her use in her life... not even when talking to Rafe. "And I'm speaking to Jay."

"Finally," the man said.

"Aimee? Who's that?" I demanded. "What's going on?"

"Jay, I've gotta go. I'll see you when you get here, okay? Talk to Rafe," Aimee whispered. "Love you."

"But—"

She disconnected… and the heavens opened.

I stared at the far side of the portico, where Chet was hanging up the pay phone dejectedly. Fat droplets of rain speckled the back of his shirt and the ground around him. Chrissea clearly wasn't relenting, and Chet looked a little lost.

I totally understood that.

I stared down at the phone in my hand and took a deep breath. My fingers trembled. I'd wanted Rafe Goodman forever, and I'd gotten used to the idea that I couldn't have him. The idea that he ever might have felt the same way about me was… was….

I had no word for it. It scared me to death. It made me angry. It made me feel stupid. It made me feel… hopeful.

I pressed my fingers into my eyes. It was like the Universe was saying, *Hey, Jay! There's a chance everything you ever wanted could maybe happen!* And there I was, shaking like a leaf.

"Hey. Y'okay?"

I glanced up, my vision blurry for half a second, and found Rafe strolling toward me with a coffee cup in his hand. On either side of the portico, rain sluiced down like a curtain, slapping the ground, making it feel like we were cut off from the whole world, but Rafe glanced around in all directions anyway, like he wanted to find the source of my distress and maybe beat it up.

Sadly, the source of my distress was *me.*

"Yeah. I'm... yes. Fine."

"Okay." He lifted an eyebrow like he wanted to question me, then shrugged awkwardly like he'd thought better of it. "Anyway. I got you a coffee. Black, three sugars, since milk's bad for your throat. And I got you Doritos, Cool Ranch, obviously, and a Diet Coke, too—" Rafe shook the bag that dangled from his wrist, and his eyes didn't quite meet mine. "—since I remembered you used to mainline them before your metabolism got all fancy. This way we won't have to stop until Kansas City, which... why are you looking at me like that?"

Because I've gotten all twisted up today, and I'm overthinking every-damn-thing. My sister. My music career. You.

Because I loved you so damn much before I told myself I hated you, Rafael. And I regret that I never told you.

Because I'm pretty sure I still love you. And I don't want to blow this second chance.

Because I know it's ridiculous to think I love you when I don't know the person you are now and you don't know me—especially since you fucking lied to me, and you're still not telling me the whole truth—but I'm almost positive I do because I feel it in my bones, the same way I know I've written something good and true.

Because I miss you trusting me, and I keep thinking of what Oak said, about how if I'm not an asshole to other people, they won't be an asshole to me.

Because you said my name while you fucked him. And you didn't lie about it when you could have.

Because maybe I need to trust you. Maybe I need to apologize for my part in this stupid misunderstanding and see where that leaves us.

Because I'm fucking terrified.

"Because I need to pee?" I cleared my throat and gestured toward the building. "So can you?" I waved toward the pump, which had long ago stopped pumping. "Then we can." I nodded toward the highway. "Okey doke."

I didn't wait to see if he could interpret my gibberish but scurried inside. I washed my hands in the bathroom sink and splashed my face with ice-cold water, trying to control the flush on my cheeks. Then I looked at myself in the mirror, sorta like Rafe had at the airport, except I wasn't trying to give myself a pep talk. No, what I needed was a Come to Jesus.

What the *hell* was I doing?

Was I actually contemplating the possibility of... of... *anything* with Rafe Goodman? Good God.

Even if he'd wanted me in the past, there was no sign that he did anymore! Besides which, I had a career to salvage somehow, and an apartment in New York, and a phone call from my agent to return. Not to mention, I had a sister who was *sick*, who'd been keeping secrets from me, and whose doctor called her *babe*.

I needed to focus on the right things. The *important* things.

Maybe the second chance here was just a chance to walk away calmly. With no animosity.

I nodded firmly to myself, decision made. I wasn't going to say anything to Rafe about Aimee's revelations, or about my feelings.

We would keep on as we had been. Quasi-friends. Trip-mates.

I popped a honey drop in my mouth and took a deep breath.

I found Rafe and Chet squatting down by the front passenger's-side tire of the van. Chet gestured animatedly, no doubt pointing out the many benefits of triple treads, and Rafe nodded along, seeming totally absorbed, but the second I got close, Rafe's entire attention swung to me, and his eyes raked me from head to toe like he needed to reassure himself I hadn't been mauled by lions in the five minutes I'd been gone.

That was all it took to make my heartbeat go all syncopated and my resolve crumble to dust. One. Freakin'. Look.

There was no way I could get back in that car with Rafe Goodman. Nope. I'd look at him, and he'd ask me what was wrong, and then... I'd tell him. I'd just vomit it all over him in a way no amount of perfume could cover.

God. I legit didn't know what would happen then. I wasn't sure I could handle the consequences, no matter which way things went.

"Hey, friend! Gotcha that CD!" Chet straightened as I got closer and held out a plastic jewel case, the kind I hadn't seen in a hot minute. "Don't listen to it without supervision." He winked and mimed an explosion in his brain.

I smiled half-heartedly. Little did Chet know, I'd already experienced a brain explosion this afternoon without even listening to... I glanced down at the CD in my hand.

"*Cosmic Star Patterns*?" I read the words off a cover that looked very, *very* much like the cover of *Constellations*, but not quite. "This is your album?"

Rafe looked over my shoulder and covered his laugh with a cough. "How unique," he enthused.

"Eh. It's mostly covers this time." Chet shrugged modestly. "The Newsmen trying to show our vocal range, you know?"

I forced a smile. "I'm sure it's delightful."

"It was nice meeting you, Chet," Rafe said, "but we've got a ways to go yet today, so... Best of luck to you getting home, I guess?"

A wildly *perfect* idea occurred to me. "You know... we're heading west."

"Good job," Rafe approved. "I knew if you practiced you'd be able to learn your directions. Soon, we'll work on those ABCs, and there'll be no stopping you."

Smart-ass.

"Chet also needs to go west." I lifted an eyebrow. "Right, Chet?"

"Yep. Just about an hour south of Kansas City. Dry Hump," he explained to Rafe.

But Rafe was too busy staring at me to react. "That's a heck of a coincidence, alright," Rafe said in a hard voice. "But one thing has nothing to do with—"

"But it could." I smiled brilliantly. "It *could*. And you know, Rafe, you really should be nicer to people. Stop being so suspicious and inclined to make snap decisions."

Rafe's mouth opened, but no sound came out.

"It's okay! I forgive you." I patted his shoulder gently. "Not everyone can have my relentlessly positive, sunshiny disposition."

Rafe began to protest, but I cut him off by turning to Chet. "How would you like a ride as far as Kansas City, Chet?"

Chet gasped. "Ya mean it?"

"Sure. We'd be happy to." I elbowed Rafe. "Wouldn't we?"

Rafe's reply was an audible grinding of teeth, but that didn't seem to dull Chet's enthusiasm at all.

He looked back and forth from the two of us to the van. "Oh ho! Road trip! Lemme grab my stuff!"

"Are you out of your goddamn mind?" Rafe said through clenched teeth as Chet ran through the deluge to his rust box. "What happened to 'low profile' and 'avoid the media,' Jay Don? What happened to being in a hurry? What happened to—?"

"Chet doesn't recognize me at all, and I didn't give him my name," I said reasonably. "Besides, what happened to 'Be nicer, Jay'? What happened to 'You used to be such a decent human, and now you *suck* because you're too afraid people will recognize you'?"

Rafe's nostrils flared. "You keep putting words in my mouth! I never said that, and you need to stop making crazy-ass assumptions. I said you should give people the benefit of the doubt. I did *not* say we should pick up random strangers at truck stops and offer to chauffeur them to their destinations." He leaned into my personal space, and his handsome face turned a spectacular shade of red. "I didn't mean we should turn your kidnap van into a potential *murder* van!"

Except I knew I'd done the right thing, because Rafe was now way too annoyed to remember what we'd been talking about before, let alone feel awkward about it.

Finally, this day was looking up.

I smiled sweetly. "So I take it that means you don't want to drive?"

9

RAFE

"This is *not* funny," I said, stalking around to the driver's door, because at least with me behind the wheel, it was still only a *potential* murder van and not a guaranteed-vehicular-manslaughter van.

"I didn't say it was funny." Jay climbed in his door and shut it smartly. "I said we were being nice."

He smelled like honey and oranges again, and I gritted my teeth. This trip could not be over fast enough.

I was so flustered—by his proximity, by what I'd admitted to, the whole shebang—that I spent half a minute patting my pockets for the damn keys before remembering Jay had them and that the engine started with a simple push button anyway.

I blew out a breath. "We are going to have *so* many words later on about what being nice means."

Jay clenched his candy between his teeth and sucked in a way that should have been obnoxious and not remotely sexy but somehow managed to be both. "Orrr, we can revel in the good karma points I earned us both. You're welcome."

"Karma's not going to mean shit if we don't survive the trip," I grumbled... but I drove the van out to the parking lot anyway, to save poor Chet a second run through the rain.

"Are you telling me Chet looks homicidal?" Jay lifted a hand toward the guy who'd dived so deeply into his trunk, he was only visible from the knees down. "Did he tell you the story about his Chrissea?"

"No. And I didn't want him to," I added when Jay opened his mouth to expound on the subject. "Also, I have no idea what a homicidal person looks like. I doubt they wear signs that say 'FYI, I'm homicidal.'"

"If you want to see homicidal, maybe look in the mirror right now." He folded his arms over his chest. "And the story about his girlfriend was extremely moving."

"Yeah? Well, Jeffrey Dahmer had a moving cover story, also." I pulled up behind Chet's car, popped the gear shift into park, and glared at Jay. "And the only person I'm inclined to murder right now is *you*, which I'm pretty sure would be considered self-defense when I tell them about the kidnapping."

"Hush." Jay pushed my arm. "Chet'll hear you."

I wasn't sure which part of that he didn't want Chet to overhear, but I was so relieved that Jay was acting normal again —giving me shit and grinning at me like he'd decided to overlook the whole sketchy I-fantasized-about-my-best-friend-while-fucking-someone-else thing—that for once I *did* hush. Temporarily.

Chet slid the side panel of the van open and threw in a pair of giant black trash bags and another, smaller grocery bag before climbing in himself.

"Shew!" He stuck both hands in his long hair and shook them, sending water droplets flying around the van. "It is damper than a fish at a wet T-shirt contest out there!"

"And now in here, too." I side-eyed Jay in a way that made it clear I blamed *him* for the musty odor that now overlaid the perfume in the van.

Chet snorted like I'd made a joke. "I sure do appreciate this favor... uh... what were your names again, boys?"

"J... Jerry," Jay said with a tight smile. "And it's no problem."

In the rearview mirror, Chet's gaze met mine. "And you?"

"Tom," I lied smoothly as I pulled out of the rest area and onto the highway.

From the corner of my eye, I saw Jay roll his eyes at me like *I* was the one responsible for this foolish scenario. *Not even.*

I cleared my throat. "So, Chet, you're a musician? That's cool." I glanced down at Jay's lap and the CD he was still holding. "Tell me all about it. Do you write your own music? Are you anything like Ari Friedrich? 'Cause that dude's talented as fuck."

Jay's eyes rolled back further.

"You know, I *do* write my own stuff from time to time. But this go 'round, I covered some tunes from Jayd Rollins. He's a, um... close, personal friend of mine? So, like, I knew he wouldn't mind."

"You're friends with Jayd Rollins?" Jay twisted in his seat. "Really?"

"Yep! You a fan of his?" Chet asked.

Jay faced forward again. "Depends on the day," he said darkly.

"Who's Jayd Rollins?" I demanded. "Sounds pretentious."

I ignored Jay's glare.

"Who's Jayd Rollins?" Chet demanded. "Tom, my man, you're missing out. He's only, like, one of the most talented singer-songwriters on the planet. Blows Ari Friedrich out of the water."

Jay looked slightly mollified by this, and my lips twitched. "Impossible," I proclaimed. "Ari Friedrich paints glorious pictures with his words. Plus, he's hot."

"No, no, for real. And Jayd's good-looking, too!" He wrinkled his nose. "Kinda short, though."

"Short." Jay looked down at his own long legs. "Really?"

"No one looks the same in magazines as they do in real life, Jerry," Chet explained patiently.

"Ah. I suppose not."

"Though he does have soulful eyes and rock-hard abs. Not like us schlubs, eh?" He slapped Jay lightly on the shoulder.

"Mmm. Definitely not," Jay agreed, surreptitiously laying a hand on his stomach like he was checking the firmness.

Christ, he was adorable.

"Huh. Would I have heard any of the Jayd guy's music?" I asked.

"Pfft. For sure. He's all over the radio. You know, lots of people have actually compared his sound to mine. Not that I think Jayd copied me or anything," Chet said modestly. He paused. "That I know of."

I rubbed a hand over my mouth to smooth out my smile. "Well, I'm sold. Why don't you pop Chet's CD in the player there, Jerry? I'd love to hear this."

Jay's jaw did that side-to-side thing, which could not be healthy for his molars, but I knew he was fighting amuse-ment, too... or at least he was until the CD started playing and Chet's cover of "Unmade" came out the speakers, because that was decidedly *un*-funny.

"Once I had the answers

Sure and certain, never fade

Then along came you

And suddenly, I was unmade."

I'd actually enjoyed this track on *Constellations*—which was objectively a good album, if you weren't inclined to hate it on principle, which I was—but Chet had butchered it. And I mean, he'd killed it deader than dead. His voice was decent, and he was definitely talented, but he'd overlaid the simple vocals with a thick, sludgy bass riff that turned the bright melody into a screamo funeral dirge.

"Whaddya think, Jerry? Mind blown?" Chet yelled from the back seat.

Jay and I shared a look. He seemed caught between laughter and outrage. "The, ah, bloodcurdling cries at the end of the chorus really... add something."

"Exactly what I thought!" Chet sat back. "I don't wanna criticize Jayd, but I told him he was kinda singing it wrong. I mean, it's a song about getting frisky, after all. Gotta make it sexy."

"This song's about sex?" Jay's voice sounded strained.

"Duh. *Unmade.* Like a bed with the covers all messed up because he'd been in it doing the sideways Macarena?" Chet made a hole out of his left thumb and forefinger, then fucked it with his right middle finger, while making the high-pitched screechy noise of springs squeaking. "Ya get me?"

"Sadly, yes," I said.

Chet grinned. "Don't blame you for being confused, though. The lyrics *are* a little obscure."

Jay scrunched his whole face up for a second like he was trying to stop himself from speaking.

It didn't work.

"Are they, though?" he blurted in a rush. "Because I think the lyrics are pretty clearly about someone who thought he had all the answers until he met someone who made him question himself. His mind was made up, and then it was *unmade.*"

Chet burst out laughing. "That's a real cute interpretation, Jerry! Wait'll I tell Jayd."

"Yeah, why don't you do that?" Jay challenged. "Text him right now."

"Jerry," I said in a warning voice, and Jay relented with a sigh. He folded his arms over his chest sulkily... which lasted for precisely ten seconds before something out the window caught his attention and his wry smile was back.

God, he fascinated me. I wanted to climb inside his head. See the world through his eyes. Understand him the way I once thought I did.

"Check it out! More signs! 'Only three hundred nineteen miles to the *unmissable* Hole Inn the Wall! Reasonable Rates, call ahead!'" Jay turned to me. "You hear that, Tom? *Unmissable*! And I do love a reasonable rate."

I huffed out a laugh. I knew he was mostly joking... but only mostly. The Hole Inn the Wall seemed like the kind of people-watching spot Jay would have loved before he got famous—the kind of place where he could blend anonymously into a crowd and people watch, which used to inspire his songwriting as much as the salt water and the sunshine on the Key had. I wondered if he ever had the chance to do that sort of thing anymore, and it made me sad to realize that the answer was probably no.

Still...

"We're working on a schedule here, remember?"

"Boring," Jay coughed.

"Responsible," I sang back.

Jay rolled his eyes and pointed out the window again. "But Tom! 'Seventeen *distinct* eateries.' Do you think they mean distinct from each other? Or was that supposed to be *distinctive*? What do you think, Chet?"

"W-well..." Chet began.

"Oh, shit." The man's teeth were chattering. "Lemme turn down the A/C." I reached for the dial on the dash.

"D-d-don't mind me! J-just a little damp from the rain. There's a sweatshirt on the floor back here. Y'all mind if I borrow it?"

I looked at Jay, who glanced back at the hoodie he'd taken off earlier. He hesitated a second, then shrugged. "Nah. Go ahead."

"Oh my Lord! Is this genuine Jayd Rollins *Constellations* merch?" Chet asked after he'd pulled the shirt over his head. "I didn't think this was even on the website yet! You must be a bigger Jayd fan than I thought."

Jay hummed noncommittally and snuck another glance at the back seat, like he was waiting for Chet to put three and three together and get I'm-riding-in-a-van-with-a-celebrity. Fortunately, this level of math seemed to be beyond him, and I could practically see Jay's muscles unbunch in relief.

"Whoa, this is high quality," Chet breathed, running a hand over the sleeve, and Jay gave me a smirky little look that was really fucking charming, damn it.

The song changed over to "Magic Hook," which was not one of my faves. "You know, I think I've heard this one. *You got that magic hook*," I singsonged along with the opening line, which had Jay rolling his eyes at me again and fighting a smile. "What's this one about, Chet?"

"Ohhh, this one here's about Jayd being at a bar with his wingman," he said importantly.

Jay *thunked* his head against the headrest and groaned.

"And it's like, Jayd's wingman could pull anyone in the place," Chet continued, "but Jayd can't get anyone to even toss him a pity fuck. Seems kinda crazy to me, 'cause I told you Chrissea says he's fifty-four flavors of fine, but who knows what the dating scene is like in New York, you know? Anyway, this song is Jayd complaining about his friend. He's saying, 'Why do you have that big dick energy and I don't? Why do you have the magic hook?'"

Jay and I exchanged a look, and I had to really work hard to hide my smile.

"Or," Jay grumbled, like the words were being pulled from him. "*Orrr.* What if it's about someone who draws you in—who *hooks* you—and makes you fall for them, even though they're not the person you were looking for, and they complicate the hell out of your life?"

"Huh." Chet ran his tongue over his back teeth. "That's not bad, Jerry. I mean, don't quit your day job to take up song-writing full-time or nothin.'"

Jay shook his head and looked like he was going to say something, but I pointed out the window. "Late-night karaoke and the best mountain views in Dry Hump." I caught Chet's eye in the mirror. "Is that *your* Dry Hump?"

He nodded. "The one and only. My Chrissea works at the All Ears Corn Cafe. Fanciest restaurant in the whole place," he said proudly. "I used to tend bar at Fantasies Over the Emporium myself once upon a time."

"Oh, yeah? What happened?" Jay asked.

"The call of the open road happened, Jerry." Chet heaved a melancholy sigh. "It's funny, 'cause I started singing at Fantasies on open mic nights mostly to impress Chrissea. Then I got offered paying gigs here and there, and I wanted the extra money so I could take her out, you know? But it turned out that I kinda liked singing. I like making music for people. And I like being something bigger than Chester Hatcher from Dry Hump. When I'm touring with the Newsmen, I got potential."

"Yeah." Jay sighed the word raggedly. "Yeah, I get that. But what about Chrissea?"

He shrugged. "That's the thing, ain't it? I love Chrissea. I think we could be happy for the long haul. But if I stay with her, won't I always wonder what else is out there for me?"

"Maybe," Jay said slowly, like the word was being dragged out of him. "But if you go, you'll always wonder what you might have had if you'd stayed."

I looked at him sharply. So did Chet. But Jay stared down at the CD case in his hand like the mysteries of the universe were written on it and ignored us both.

"Maybe also—" Jay cleared his throat and darted a lightning-fast look at me. "Consider that there could be a solution where you have both? I mean, I'm personally shit at balance, but I've heard rumors that people can have a career *and* a relationship. I... kinda wish I'd tried it."

Say what? With who? Was he talking about Olivia Merry? He couldn't be. Was there someone else?

"Huh." Chet sounded thoughtful. "What would that look like, having both?"

"God, who knows? I guess you two would need to figure that out. Customize it for yourself. Just don't give up on her." Another half-look in my direction. "Relationships are important."

This from the guy who'd stopped talking to me for years? I scowled. What was he playing at?

But Chet was drinking the Kool-Aid. "You're like Dr. Phil, you know that, Jerry?"

It was *my* turn to roll my eyes, and even Jay laughed self-deprecatingly.

"Uh, no. My sister told me just today that my communication skills suck. I'm more of a cautionary tale than a role model, Chet. Don't be like me."

"Wait, you talked to your sister today?" I demanded. "Speaking of shitty communication skills?"

Jay bit his lip apologetically. "Yeah, she called while you were in the restroom, and I meant to mention it, but I, ah... forgot? She's okay, though. *Really* okay."

"Yeah?" I smiled tentatively in relief, and he smiled back.

"She sounded exhausted, but she's as sassy as ever. Said she needs to talk to both of us and explain some things. Apologize?" He shrugged, then glanced back at Chet and said quickly, "She also said you should tell me everything about... you know. Everything."

"Everything about everything, huh?" I snorted. "Sure she did."

But I was surprised to find that I wanted to just tell him. None of the reasons I'd kept Aimee's secrets made sense anymore, anyway. It had all been for Jay, in the beginning. To help my best friend.

And now—I shot a glance at Jay's handsome profile—well, now I was using the secret to shore up the wall between us, with the handy excuse of respecting Aimee's wishes, when I honestly wasn't sure keeping her secret was in anyone's best interest anymore.

And the wall that kept me from wanting Jay back in my life was crumbling with every minute we spent hurtling down the highway in the kidnap van.

"Hey, listen to this, Tom!" Chet leaned into the front seat to turn up the music. "Pretty Girl's my favorite song on the album. I added on a killer intro."

"Yeah?" My voice came out gravelly with emotion, more like Jay's than my own. Trying to lighten my mood, I teased, "Lemme guess. This one's about a guy who falls in love with a girl who's not just *pretty*, she's also really nice and a decent actress, even in those *Scarlet and the Moon* movies?"

"*Scarlet and the Moon*? Oh, you mean Olivia Merry?" Chet's whole face wrinkled up when he frowned. "Good Lord, no. This song's about how the whole world tells Jayd he should be with a pretty girl like Olivia and have the pretty future they want him to have, but he can't do it. He *'can't love a pretty girl.'* You know," he said loftily, "nobody who really listened to this track was all that surprised when it came out in the tabloids a couple weeks ago that Jayd's bi or gay or whatever, 'cause it was right there in the song all along."

"Oh, yeah? Right there in the song?"

I cut my eyes toward Jay, expecting to share more hidden laughter over this wacky interpretation, but Jay wasn't looking at me anymore. In fact, he was staring straight ahead, face flushed and fists clenched tight, looking nearly as stunned and terrified as I'd felt an hour ago when I'd inadvertently admitted I'd been attracted to…

Uh.

Wait.

My breathing went shallow. Jay's eyes cut to mine for half a second. Just long enough for me to read heat and longing and utter, utter vulnerability there.

Oh sweet fucking God.

Chet chattered on and on about the intro and the various guitar chords, but it sounded like white noise. I forced myself to pay attention to the road, but my brain buzzed and my stomach swooped as I remembered Jay's words from earlier.

"It's like you decided that I changed, and you started interpreting everything through that lens. But maybe I haven't changed as much as you think."

I quickly replayed the lyrics to "Pretty Girl" in my head, and when I got to the part about "legends and liars," it was like I'd unlocked a cage around my lungs and I could finally breathe deeply for the first time in years, because I would bet money he was singing legends and *lyres*, as in the name of the constellation we used to look for, and…

Oh. Oh, shit. Oh, *God*.

I was a fool. The biggest fool! The fucking *emperor* of fools.

He'd named his album *Constellations* even though stargazing had never been Jay's thing, because it had been *mine*.

Because he'd written those songs—those *love* songs—about us.

And now that I recognized the truth for what it was, I could have kicked my own ass for being so willfully ignorant. The truth had been sitting right fucking there all along, the most obvious item in all of Obviousville, waiting for me to get over myself and see it, but I hadn't.

All. This. Time.

Well, *fuck.*

I flexed my fingers on the steering wheel as awareness stretched between me and Jay, taut as steel cable. Chet might as well have been riding on the roof because Jay and I were the only two people in the car from that moment on.

All the anger I'd harbored for years morphed like a butterfly in a chrysalis into hot, exquisitely painful pins-and-needles anticipation, like a rush of blood to a vital part of myself that had gone numb years ago.

He said *love* in the song. Had he really loved me? Did he still?

I needed to know.

I kept my eyes focused on the blacktop stretching out in front of us, but inside I was reborn as my seventeen-year-old self, feeling like summer had truly started because the

Rollinses had arrived on the island. I wanted to be alone with my favorite person. To reassure myself that we still understood each other the same way.

When the first notes of Chet singing Jay's words came out of the speakers, I shut off the radio entirely. I didn't want to hear Chet's cover of this song. I wanted to hear it the way Jay wrote it.

The way he wrote it *for me.*

"Let's listen to something else for a bit," I suggested.

I had so damn many things I wanted to say to Jay in that minute that I low-key wanted to pull over and give Chet cab fare. Or buy him a damn car.

Except I was also now weirdly invested in getting him back to his girlfriend. In making sure that they got a chance to *talk* the way Jay and I had been too immature—and then too damn stubborn—to do.

The way Jay and I were damn sure going to.

Today.

Right after I kissed the shit out of him.

"Or actually." Jay's voice was huskier than usual. Softer, too. Arousing as fuck. Like he was thinking the exact same thing I was. "Maybe we should figure out something nice that you can do for Chrissea, Chet. For your six-month anniversary. Maybe plan something really special."

"Yeah, okay. She *does* keep saying 'Actions speak louder than words, Chester.'" Chet pursed his lips. "And she knows I hate it when she calls me Chester. So... maybe flowers?"

"Does she like flowers?"

"Doesn't everybody?"

"No." Jay tapped his lip with one long finger. "And if you want her to take a chance on a future with you, I think you need to show her that you know her. *Really* know her. Like, what's her favorite thing, aside from you? What does she do to make you feel important? Maybe give that feeling back to her somehow."

Chet scratched his scruffy cheek and thought about this so hard I expected to smell smoke rising from the back seat. "Chrissea... she likes picnics. First time I told her I wanted to be her man was on a picnic."

"Okay, then," Jay enthused. "Picnics! So you can—"

"And she likes owls."

Jay blinked and grimaced. "Er, okay. I'm not sure that anything bird-related conveys affection. I personally wouldn't bestow a bird on my worst enemy. But if you're sure she's into that kind of thing..."

"Oh, she is!"

Jay turned to me expectantly. Like I knew the first thing about owls *or* relationships?

"Jeez, I dunno. Get her a stuffed owl?" I ventured. "Write her a song about an owl? Take her to visit an owl? Learn how to say 'I love you' in hoots?"

Jay covered his mouth with one hand and looked away, clearly fighting laughter. "Well," he said finally. "I think it's clear who the *real* Dr. Phil around here is."

The urge to kiss him hit me like a tidal wave, a hundred and ten times harder than anything I'd felt for him even as a horny teen, like maybe because I'd been damming it back so long, the need had built up. My eyes raked over his gorgeous face, his broad shoulders, those muscled thighs…

The rumble of the wake-up strip on the side of the highway shook me out of my reverie, and I put all of my attention back on the road.

Beside me, Jay opened his mouth to say something.

"Not a damn word," I muttered.

From the corner of my eye, I saw him grin, and something inside my chest settled. Things between us were still all out of whack… but I could fix that.

Assuming I didn't land us in a ditch.

I coughed. "So, Chet, I'm thinking maybe we should take you all the way to the, uh… Pleasure Emporium… after all. Make sure you get back to your Chrissea."

"Whoa!" Chet sat forward again. "You'd do that?"

"There's not a lot I wouldn't do to give a couple of star-crossed lovers a second chance," I said solemnly.

"Really?" Chet clasped a hand over his heart.

Jay's head jerked toward me so fast, it must've been painful. His green eyes shone. "Really?" he asked softly.

"Really," I answered them both.

A couple of hours later, we pulled into the parking lot of a carnival on steroids. Interconnected buildings formed a huge horseshoe festooned with lights, and music played so loudly I could hear it through the closed windows.

"Y'all can park right over there," Chet advised, pointing to a spot between the entrance to the Hole Inn the Wall and the Dry Hump Reptile Habitat.

We unfolded ourselves from the car, and Chet offered to hand our luggage off to the baggage guy at the door for us before he went to find Chrissea.

"Least I can do," he said. "After all y'all have done for me."

Jay jammed his baseball hat on his head as we headed into the hotel, and now that I wasn't distracted by driving or by Chet, my fingers literally ached to touch him.

"You sure you're okay staying here tonight? It's not really your scene."

"Yeah, but it's yours." I shrugged.

His green eyes met mine, full of heat and unspoken truths, and I hip-checked him gently before looking away. I was barely hanging on to my control as it was, and if he didn't stop looking at me like that, I was going to drop to my knees for him in the damn hotel lobby and *really* give the tabloids a story.

The lobby of the inn was built around a giant fountain that filled the air with the sound of rushing water and the smell of chlorine. It was packed with people passing through to the bar that was the next building on the right, or the reptile place to the left, but the clerk behind the desk waved us forward.

"Hey, um, we need…" I hesitated. One room or two? I looked at Jay, but Jay's eyes were darting around the lobby like he was a lone gazelle surrounded by predators. "Two rooms," I decided, handing over my credit card.

Just because *I* was feeling some kind of way didn't mean Jay was feeling it, too. And I was done making assumptions where he was concerned.

"Hey!" a voice called from behind us as I handed Jay one of the key cards.

Jay flinched, but it was just the guy from the door pulling a luggage cart with our bags and Jay's guitar.

"If you give me your room number, I'll bring your luggage up to you in just a minute," he said.

Jay let out a relieved breath, and I gave the doorman our information.

"I know you think I'm crazy," Jay said when I stepped back to him. "Somehow Chet had a whole conversation with me *about me* and didn't make the connection, and Shelly at breakfast didn't either. But I swear, I get recognized all the time in New York and other places."

I took a step closer and breathed in the sweet scent of him. "Maybe people see what they want to see. What they expect to see."

I sure had.

"Or maybe your rock-hard abs just look different in magazines," I teased.

Jay's eyes kindled, and he licked his lips. "We need to talk."

"Yeah," I agreed, my entire attention focused on that tongue. "Do you want to—?" I gestured vaguely over my shoulder to the bank of elevators that led to our rooms.

"Let's get a drink," he blurted, then winced. "I, um, have heard that I talk better under the influence of tequila, and we have a lot of things to say."

I nodded, and we headed to the bar, where we managed to snag a little table outside in a shadowed corner close to the parking lot. Jay kept his hat pulled low at first, but he relaxed when the waitress didn't recognize him either.

I waited patiently until she'd brought us each a tequila flight and a beer, but Jay still wasn't talking. "So... Aimee's good, you said?" I prompted.

"Yeah. I think so." Jay downed a shot of tequila, then another in quick succession. "She had a sore throat and was out of breath, a little, but she sounded like herself. And she said she's getting better. And she said..." He shook his head. "Well. She said a *lot* of things. But mostly she said I was an idiot for walking away from you, and—"

My head went back. "Aimee said *you* were an idiot for walking away when she did the same thing herself?" I sipped at my own tequila. "Hmm."

"She was right, though," Jay said in that dreamy, husky voice of his. He tilted his head back to the sky. "You know, I remember you telling me that myth about the guy and his wife—"

"Orpheus and Eurydice," I whispered.

"Yeah. They were finally gonna be reunited, as long as he trusted and believed that she'd stick with him. But he didn't trust enough. And he lost her for good. You don't know how many times I've looked up at the sky and thought of you and summer stargazing. Thought of that myth. But I was too blind to see myself in it."

He took another drink, then set the shot glass down on the table with a clack. His eyes met mine, and he blurted, "I'm sorry, Rafe. I'm sorry I stopped returning your calls. I'm sorry I wasn't at your wedding. I'm sorry I wasn't there for you when you needed me. But it was never because I didn't have room in my life for you. It was because I thought you didn't have room in your life for *me*. I told myself you wouldn't need me as your friend anymore once you had Aimee. You... our friendship... it was so important to me. And I was jealous, so I let myself believe—"

"Lies?" I gave him a wry smile. "Same. Like you were never as invested in our friendship as I was."

"I was way invested! I was *super* invested!"

Without thinking, I laid my hand over his on the table. "And you need to know, you could *never* not be important to me. Hell, you were the *most* important person. You were the reason I—" I swallowed. "See, Aimee and I—"

I broke off and downed a shot of my own, because Jay was right. Pulling back half a lifetime of misunderstandings to get to the truth was *not* easy, and I had a feeling this wasn't gonna go well.

But then Jay twisted his hand under mine, twining our fingers together, and looked at me with so much heat and affection in his eyes that I realized that the alternative, the one in which I might lose him again, wasn't even worth contemplating.

So I'd talk.

And I'd keep talking.

"Three years ago," I began, "Aimee came to the Key, and—"

"Hey! Watch where you're driving, man!"

In the parking lot just a few feet away, a horn blared and someone yelled out some choice obscenities that had both Jay and me turning our heads. As we watched, a white passenger van swerved around a little convertible and peeled out of the lot, blasting a heavy metal version of Jayd's "Broken River."

I blinked and tightened my fingers on Jay's. "This is gonna sound crazy, but..." I forced a laugh. "Did the guy driving that van look like...?"

"No! It didn't look a single thing like Chet. *Pfft*. I mean. What are the chances?"

Our eyes widened simultaneously, and we both bolted for the parking lot because on *this* road trip?

The chances of something bizarre and life-changing happening were way too high.

"Thanks again, Mr. Rollins!" a way too earnest sheriff's deputy with way too many freckles wearing a way too big belt buckle told Jay, tucking away a napkin Jay had autographed for him. Then he slid a fresh, blank napkin across the bar table. "Could I maybe get one more for my little sister? She's a huge fan—"

"And maybe one for me?" one of the people who'd circled the table called out.

"I want a selfie, like the cheek kiss you did with Mabel!" an elderly woman with a walker piped up. "But if I give you five bucks, can you slip me some tongue?"

Jay hardly sighed at all as he pulled the deputy's napkin toward him. "What's your sister's—"

"No. Absolutely not." I pushed the napkin away, crumpled it up, and gave a severe look to the assembled lookie-loos *and* to Deputy Freckles. "This is ridiculous. No more autographs. And *definitely* no *tongue*." I gave the octogenarian seductress a reproving glance. "Mr. Rollins has already signed twenty-three napkins, taken fourteen selfies, and recorded a happy birthday message for the sheriff's wife. The next thing that gets signed over here is going to be a formal complaint to your department. Now, how about you tell me where our freakin' van is!"

"I already explained to you, sir, we're doing the best we can," the deputy said. "Martie-Anne's son's visiting this week, so she's taken a few days off, and it just so happened that Nick Froese got the stomach bug at the same time Nick Van Hooten fell off the ladder while trimming his birch trees and fractured his ankle." He threw up his hands, like he didn't know how I could expect him to work competently under these conditions. "There's only me and a couple uniforms to investigate. The good news is, Dry Hump's a small town, and I know Chester pretty well. My brother August went to school with his oldest sister's oldest boy, Paul. Or was it Peter—?"

"I literally don't think it would be possible for me to care less about this story," I interrupted. "How hard can it be to find a van? Doesn't the rental company have some kind of tracking thing? Can't you—?"

"Rafe." Jay put a hand on my arm and pushed me back down into my seat... which was when I realized that I'd started to stand. And possibly *loom*. "Deputy Horowitz is doing the best he can."

"Sorry, sorry." I blew out a breath. "I just can't believe this whole situation." I'd started to *like* Chet, damn it.

"Well, like I was saying..." Deputy Freckles scratched his temple. "Is it possible there's been a mistake? 'Cause I know for a fact that Chet Hatcher's no hardened criminal. Neither is Chrissea Drake, even if she did run off and leave the restaurant in the middle of her shift, which was real irresponsible when she knows Barbara's short-staffed now that Talia Van Hooten—"

"Please don't tell me *she* fell while trimming the birch trees, too."

"Of course not. She's seven months pregnant!"

"Eight," someone in the crowd corrected.

"Huh. You might be right, Rose," Deputy Freckles allowed. "I remember Nick saying they conceived the night of the bonfire, which I suppose was—"

"Is this in *any* way relevant to this situation?" I interrupted. "Or *any* situation *any*where?"

The deputy huffed. "Well, only in the sense that when Talia saw Nick take a tumble, she thought she was going into labor, which is why Barbara was short-staffed over at the All Ears Cafe, which is why it was so irresponsible of Chrissea to just run off like she did, even if it *is* her six-monthiversary."

I pushed a hand through my hair and stifled a groan. All I wanted, *all* I wanted, was to be alone with Jay with no interruptions. Just him and me, with no lies and misunderstandings, just the seemingly endless stockpile of *want* I'd been storing up for the last decade. But to get to that part, I needed to *not* punch the police dude. Or any of the fucking spectators.

"I have no idea how it could be a mistake," I said between clenched teeth, trying to get back to the topic at hand. "Chet didn't have the key, and if he had to break into the van, then hot-wire it, I don't think he could've stumbled into it by acci—"

"Your boyfriend said it was one of those keyless jobbies," Deputy Freckles interrupted.

"He's not my boyfriend." Jay's voice was firmer about this than it had been about anything since we'd run out to the parking lot and found an empty space where the van had been parked.

I raised an eyebrow. I mean, I *wasn't* his boyfriend, and I understood that he had enough trouble with the tabloids already, but I still didn't like it. It reminded me too much of all the things that wanted to tear us apart when I hadn't even fully wrapped my mind around the possibility of us being together. I wanted to grab Jay's hand and growl at anyone who got close to him.

Down, Goodman, I reminded myself.

"Sorry, your partner, then," Freckles corrected.

"He's not my partner either." Jay was not friendly now; he was deadly serious. "He's an old friend, not that it's any of your business. And yes, it's a keyless starter."

"Show it to him," I suggested.

Jay's eyes flicked to mine. "Show what?"

"The key fob."

Jay frowned. "I don't have it. You were the last one driving."

"*Yeah*, but you were the one with the keys."

Jay shook his head slowly. "I haven't seen the key fob since the diner when I put it in the front pouch of…" He squeezed his eyes shut and groaned.

"Of your sweatshirt, which Chet borrowed," I concluded for Freckles's benefit.

"Aha. Yep, that makes more sense." Freckles nodded sagely. "So it's more like he borrowed it without explicit permission." He shrugged. "If you think about it."

"Assuming he brings it back," I muttered.

The deputy nodded. "If he doesn't, we'll contact the state police in the morning, and the rental car place will get you a new one. Can you think of anything unusual about the van, just in case we need to identify it and can't get in touch with the rental company?"

"Not really." I leaned back and folded my arms over my chest. "The tires had triple treads."

"And the inside smelled like Shalimar. You know, that grandma perfume?" Jay sounded a little nostalgic, and I raised an eyebrow at him. "What? It grew on me."

"I'm very sorry for your loss," the deputy said solemnly. He grabbed another napkin from the stack on the table. "But since life goes on, my sister's name is—"

"Hey, Jim!" A woman with cat-eye glasses and a no-nonsense black bob pulled up a chair beside the deputy. "Maggie called and said to tell you she got the kids in bed, and she had to sing the Olaf song *twice*, so you'd best have gotten her an autograph."

"Thanks, Normandie," Deputy Freckles said. He patted the pocket where his first set of napkins had disappeared. "All taken care of."

She stuck out a hand for Jay to shake. "Normandie Baker. I'm the manager of the inn. Welcome!" She made a sweeping gesture with her hand like a game show hostess.

"Thanks," Jay said shortly.

"I was wondering, Jayd—can I call you Jayd? It's crazy, but I feel like I know you, in a way—if you'd maybe sing a song or two for us over in Karaoke Alley? We're all big, *big* fans." Normandie smiled winningly.

I could almost *see* Jay erecting a wall around himself brick by brick, and I finally really understood what he'd been talking about. These folks felt like they knew him because they knew his name and his music, because he smiled at them from the front of magazines... but they had no idea who he really was or what struggles he was dealing with beneath the surface. They didn't know how worried he was for his sister, or how hard he was trying to hold on to his privacy.

Everyone loved *Jayd*, but how many people cared about Jay? How many even knew there was a difference?

I did, though. And it felt kind of like a privilege.

Jay hesitated, trying to figure out how to say no without seeming like a jerk. "Well, the thing is, I—"

"Will have to take a rain check," I interrupted smoothly. "He's saving his voice for a big concert next week. You may have heard the rumors that he's had to cancel his tour for the past few weeks? That's why. Advanced, um... vocal fatigue. Too much practicing."

Jay gave me a grateful smile and went along with it. "Yeah. Yep. I overdid it. Rookie mistake."

He shrugged sheepishly, and the people around us ate it up, responding to the genuine warmth and kindness in him that shone through even when he was playing the role of a famous rock star.

It hit me again how wrong I'd been about everything with Jay, and how it felt like I'd been given a second chance. I didn't want to wait another minute to show the man how freakin' special he was to me on every single level. Long before he was a rock star, he was the single brightest star in my sky. He always would be.

I remembered Jay telling Chet to figure out what Chrissea did to make him feel important and to mirror that back to her somehow... and I came up with the world's schmoopiest, cheesiest idea. It was the kind of thing Beale would do for Toby or Fenn would do for Mason—the kind of thing I would *never* let them live down—which told me I was on the right track.

I turned to Normandie, who was still seated at the table. "You know, if you're looking for someone to sing karaoke... I could do it."

10

———————

JAY

"What the fuck are you doing?" I demanded as I trailed Rafe, who trailed Normandie, from the bar to someplace called Karaoke Alley. "You don't sing! You hate singing."

And although I would never say it aloud, especially now that we were trying to be friends—or (please, sweet baby Jesus) lovers—it was kind of a good thing Rafe didn't like singing because he was truly *terrible* at it.

"I'm making an exception," Rafe said over his shoulder. "It's an exceptional kinda day."

And, yeah, okay, that was definitely true. In fact, I was pretty sure I'd slipped and hit my head on the sink back at the gas station, because I couldn't *believe* all that had happened since that moment: Chet, and tequila, and revelations, and more freakin' Chet, and then that scene at the bar that made me feel like we were heading toward... something involving significantly less clothing than karaoke.

I tried again. "We could just go upstairs now, you know. I'm tired. *You're* tired. And we still have a lot to say to each other." Not to mention, fingers crossed, *do* to each other.

Rafe hung back a step, just enough to let me catch up. "Oh, I plan to finish our conversation," he said firmly, with a kind of purr to his voice that made my dick chub up against the front of my jeans. "But first we're doing this."

"I'm also fairly sure that Deputy DoRight has more questions for us—"

"I've been calling him Deputy Freckles." He smiled an honest, gorgeous smile that made my knees weak. "And he can wait. His other questions probably have to do with making you sign his *ass* so he can get your autograph tattooed there permanently."

"Hmm." I rolled my lips. "Maggie and the kids might not appreciate that."

Rafe snorted. "Or maybe they *would*. And every single person in town would not only know about it, they'd have a framed picture of his ass tattoo on their mantle. It'd be the Freckles family Christmas card picture."

I laughed out loud. "I dunno, I think the town's kinda cute. It sorta reminds me of the Key."

Rafe frowned. "No way. The Key is its own brand of ridiculous, but not *this*."

"You're telling me Deputy Horowitz doesn't give off a strong Littlejohn vibe? Or that the lady who wanted to french me didn't remind you of Lorenna McKetcham?"

He hesitated. "But the people on the Key don't feel like sharks in a feeding frenzy, though. Do they?"

"No. But only because we care about them and they care about us. They're a bunch of seriously odd ducks, but they're *our* odd ducks." I hadn't been back in five years, but Whispering Key still felt like home in a way that Alabama and Manhattan never had. Claiming them as mine felt right.

"I suppose that's true."

We stepped into a darker room lit only by multicolored neon signs. At a stage to one side, a woman crooned a spectacularly terrible rendition of "I Will Always Love You" while the words flashed like a warning on the giant screen behind her.

"Speaking of odd ducks and the things they do..." I motioned to the stage. "Is you karaoke-ing a cry for help? Because I'm here for you, Rafe. You don't need to do this."

Rafe's lips curved. "Yeah, I do." He pointed to an empty table close to the door. "Sit there. Then we can make a fast escape when the time comes."

"A fast escape?" My eyes widened. "Singing's maybe not your best skill, but I don't think it's bad enough to incite mob violence." Even the Whitney-wannabe was generating polite applause. "What's going on?"

He stepped closer to me and ran a single finger over my knuckles, too fast for anyone to catch. My whole body shivered at the simple contact. "You'll see."

"Wait!" I grabbed his elbow when he turned toward the stage. "What are you even going to sing?"

He gave me a lopsided smile and a wink that felt like a caress, then headed for the stage.

I took the table he'd pointed out and settled in, somehow ten times more nervous than I got when I was doing my own shows. Normandie must've pulled strings, because Rafe cut the line and got onstage immediately, and my stomach turned inside out when he stood in front of the mic with the spotlight on him.

"Hey." Rafe scratched the back of his neck. "So, I apologize to all of you in advance for my singing, but I'm making a point here—"

"You lose a bet?" someone in the crowd hooted.

Rafe grinned. "More like I'm hoping to win something." His eyes cut to where I sat, though I wasn't sure he could see me through the glare. "Y'all might have to help me out if I get stuck, okay?"

I thought maybe he'd never looked more heartbreakingly adorable...And then the intro to "Pretty Girl" came over the speakers, and I stopped thinking entirely.

Rafael Goodman, the first and only man I'd ever loved, was standing in front of a crowd of people, singing the song I'd written him—singing every damn word without having to look at the lyrics on the screen even once—and he was singing it to *me*.

By the time he got to the second verse, I considered pinching my own wrist just to make sure this was really happening, but then I stopped. If this was a dream, I never wanted to wake up.

Daydreams and legends and lyres

Drowning in sunshine like fire

And the truth of you and me became apparent

When winter came, I figured out what love meant.

And it wasn't any pretty girl.

Hearing him sing those words in a voice that was rough and pitchy and utterly sincere, knowing he knew the true meaning behind them, felt like the best part of Christmas morning—the part when someone opens the present you made them, and you know you've gotten it just right, and you're not sure which of you is more delighted.

(*Me.* It was definitely me.)

He made it to the last verse, to the line that went "*I got myself the world, but I still wanted stars,*" and he got a little choked up. Fortunately, the crowd was already singing along by that point, and they took over the chorus for him.

Rafe walked off the stage before the last note faded, and I got what he meant about us needing to make a quick exit, because when he paused in front of me, I wanted to kiss him so badly, it was hard to remember all the many, many reasons why Jayd Rollins couldn't do that in public without causing a riot.

"Come on," Rafe said gruffly. "Before Normandie wants an encore."

"You saying you couldn't give her one?" I kept pace with him as we strode past the gift shop and the bar toward the lobby. "You knew every word of that song," I whisper-accused. "I bet you know the whole damn album by heart!"

"Maybe."

"You claimed you hated it."

Rafe turned toward me so quickly I nearly walked into him, and then he pulled me behind one of the enormous fake ficus trees near the lobby fountain and stood so close my breath became his breath.

"I did hate it, because I thought you'd written it for someone else. I was angry as fuck that you'd felt that way for someone who didn't deserve it. For someone who wasn't *me*."

I swallowed hard. His mouth was literal inches from mine. In all the time I'd known him, we'd never been this close, and we'd never had this honesty between us.

"You think you deserve it?" I whispered back.

"I think there's not a person in this world who cares about you more than me... so yes."

"Even when you hated me?"

"Even when I told myself I hated you."

I licked my lips. I knew exactly, *exactly* what he meant because I felt the same. "We need to be upstairs. Immediately."

"Yeah?" He smoothed the backs of his fingers over my stomach, and my knees shook. "You sure you don't need any more tequila to finish our talk?"

I shook my head. "I'm feeling really talkative already. For example, would you like me to tell you what I want to do to you upstairs?"

Rafe drew a shaky breath, and his eyes went half-lidded. "How do you feel about public indecency?" He reached down to adjust himself. "*Fuck*."

I pulled him out from behind the tree and pointed him toward the elevators. "Oh, we will," I promised. Then I gave him a gentle shove to get him moving.

When we got upstairs, though, and the door to Rafe's room slammed shut behind us, some of my confidence faded. Not that I wanted him any less, but God, it felt so monumental. Fated or something. And I badly didn't want to mess it up.

"So, did you want to talk about Aimee more? Or about why I—"

Rafe answered my question by pushing me up against the door and crowding me with his body like he had downstairs. Except this time, he didn't stop until he was flush against me, and I could feel the hard length of his cock rubbing against mine.

Both of us gasped.

Rafe sifted his fingers into the hair at the back of my neck and tugged gently, forcing my head back.

"If you want to talk," he ground out, "we can talk. But right now, I'd rather—"

I surged forward, pushing his back against the door to the closet, and kissed him.

This was a thing I'd thought about a lot. As in, it had been my predominant sexual fantasy—the *start* of the fantasy, anyway—from the time I was a teenager, and I'd imagined this happening a hundred times in a hundred different ways. In the secret cove on the beach in Whispering Key, in Rafe's bedroom, on his inflatable Sea Eagle, on his dad's boat. Later, in my apartment in New York. Or—in a taboo favorite from my personal spank bank—in front of the entire town of Whispering Key, once I'd come home with my billions of Grammys, bought the biggest house on the island, and shown Rafe the error of his ways.

But now that it was actually happening, I realized that none of those scenarios had been close to correct, because in all of them, kissing had been the prelude—the warm-up scales before I started singing, the opening act at a concert. In reality, though, kissing Rafe Goodman was main stage, sellout crowd. It was holding a note and feeling the perfection of it resonate in my chest.

In short, it was everything.

I lifted both hands and threaded them through the hair over Rafe's ears, holding him in place just in case he was thinking of moving anytime this century, and Rafe made a rough rumbling noise from the back of his throat—something that managed to be forceful and needy all at once. He licked into my mouth, owning it, and I gave myself over to it.

"Fuck," he growled, spinning me around so I was against the wall again, before pulling back to pant against my neck. "You taste like honey and tequila."

"Is that good?" I asked, mostly to keep him talking. To say I liked the twin feelings of his voice vibrating under my hands and his breath flaring hot against my skin was to greatly understate the truth.

He bit down gently on my earlobe. "It's fucking delicious. Makes me want to taste you fucking *everywhere*."

"By all means, you should, ah... do that," I said in a voice that sounded a hundred times gravellier than my usual voice. "Now-ish-ly."

Rafe pulled his face back a couple of inches to look at me. "It's been how many years, Jay Don, and suddenly you're in a rush?"

I looked into those teasing eyes and told the absolute unvarnished truth. "Yes."

His eyes darkened, and I felt his dick go even harder in his jeans, which was so freakin' exciting, my own cock started leaking precum.

He reached for the hem of his shirt and drew it off, tossing it on the floor, and I did the same. Then he flipped open the top button of my jeans as he sank to his knees.

Oh my God.

Nervousness and anticipation and tequila warred in my stomach, and the only conscious thought that crossed my mind was that I wished I could take a picture of this moment because *holy fucking shit.*

Yes, Teenage Jay, dreams really do come true. It sometimes just takes decades longer than you wanted it to.

"You know, there's a whole comfy bed-type-thing over there." I nodded nervously at the mostly dark room. "We could try that out."

His eyes flashed up at me. "Oh, we will." He leaned forward to run his nose over my belly button, then mouthed the tip of my dick through the fabric of my underwear. "At least once."

Gah. I was a guy who'd always enjoyed sex, even during the years when it had been a little dirty and a little dangerous and a little transactional. Heck, sometimes *because* it had been dirty and dangerous and transactional. But I'd never wanted anyone as much as I wanted Rafe in that moment. My body was literally shaking with it, a fucking tuning fork humming at precisely Rafe's pitch. I didn't know what to do with my hands, so I splayed them against the cool wall behind me. I felt like the most virginal virgin.

"Please," I whimpered. "Please put your mouth on me."

Another brush of lips over my cock head through my underwear, along with a rush of warm, damp air.

"Make. Me."

And then suddenly I knew exactly where my hands belonged. I grabbed two fistfuls of Rafe's hair and yanked firmly.

"Take me out and suck me off," I commanded—as much as anyone *could* command when their voice was all breathy and wrecked.

"Fuck, yes," Rafe growled.

He pulled my jeans down to my thighs, then unlaced one boot so I could shimmy one leg out, which might have felt awkward if he hadn't been staring at my bobbing cock the whole time like it was an ice-cold drink and he'd been wandering in the desert for months.

I traced the shape of his mouth with my fingertips—the full lower lip, the graceful arch, all the things I'd seen in my dreams for years. "I want you, Rafe Goodman. I want you so much."

Rafe's only answer was to grab the base of my cock in one hand and suck me all the way to the back of his throat.

"Yesssss."

This was the kind of thing I imagined blow jobs would be, back when I'd first started imagining them. Not just the heat and the—*holymotherfuckerJesusLord*—suction, but the man staring up at me. The intimacy and trust. Rafe's eyes watered and his cheeks were flushed, but he didn't look away. He wanted to see me come apart... because he wanted *me*.

I made a whimpering noise and held his head more firmly, moving my hips against him helplessly.

He let go of my cock and brought both hands behind me to knead my ass and encourage me to fuck his mouth. *Unhngh.*

Once again for the mental scrapbook: my Rafe was on his knees for me. My Rafe wanted me to fuck his mouth.

I didn't know exactly what we were doing together—everything between us, positive and negative, seemed focused on the past, and I couldn't foresee a happy future for us together any more than I ever could—but I was determined to enjoy it while it lasted.

So I focused on how damn good he felt—his hands clutching my ass hard enough to leave finger bruises, his tongue swirling over the mushroom head of my cock on the upstroke before sucking me back into the snug perfection of his throat, the way his groan begged me without words for more and more and more.

I came so hard I was pretty sure my vital organs shifted and my equilibrium got all fucked-up, and if I hadn't been holding on to Rafe's head—clutching him like a life preserver—I would have fallen over before he'd finished swallowing me down.

"Christ, you taste good. Better than I ever dreamed."

He'd dreamed of me?

"Come up," I demanded, pulling at his shoulders with hands as weak as overcooked spaghetti. "Come here."

He surged to his feet, and I kissed him, hard and filthy, moaning as I tasted myself on his tongue.

I wanted to taste him, too. To finally *know*.

I pushed him further into the room and then down onto the giant bed. The light from the entryway cast half his face in shadow, and the colored lights from outside made shifting patterns on the ceiling, neither of which was the precise vibe I would have chosen, but I could work with this. I lifted my leg to straddle him...

And my fucking foot caught in the jeans that were still trapped around my ankle, so I ended up crashing to the bed on top of him.

Because God forbid I'd ever be able to act suave and sexy around him, right?

Rafe caught me in his strong arms and pulled me against him. "You okay?" he demanded, like *he* hadn't been the one getting squashed by my clumsy self. "If you're feeling that tequila, we can—"

I shut him up by pressing a quick kiss to his lips, and this time I *did* manage to straddle him, still wearing my one boot because I was classy that way and because I wanted him more than I cared about being suave.

"I. Have. Never. Been. More. Okay." I made my way down his body, punctuating each word with kisses to his stubbled jaw, his collarbone, his gorgeous, gorgeous pecs. I yanked at his armpits, trying to pull him further up the bed, and he seemed to understand what I wanted, because he shifted up so I could press more kisses to his flat stomach and his navel before dipping my tongue below the button of his jeans. "In the history of okay, I don't think anyone has ever been this okay."

He laughed out loud and tried to prop himself up on his elbows. "Oh, shit, you're drunk. You have some kind of delayed tequila reaction. It's kind of adorable. Makes me wonder why we never tried tequila when we were teenagers."

I shook my head. "It's not tequila." I took a second to remove the rest of his clothes—and the rest of mine—then climbed on the bed to straddle him once more. "It's *you*," I informed him. "I'm having a delayed Rafe reaction."

"Really?" he sounded doubtful.

I nodded solemnly. "You're potent."

His eyes flared, and he wrapped his hand around the back of my neck, pulling my mouth down to his.

"Fucking honey drops," he growled again. "*Please*. Fuck. I need…" He pushed on my shoulder, directing me down toward his waist, which was really convenient since that was exactly where I wanted to be. I wiggled down between his spread legs and caught his eye before I slowly, slowly sucked the hot, hard, wildly impressive length of him into my mouth.

God, he tasted good.

This was hardly my first—or twenty-first—time giving head, and I generally liked it just fine. I'd received it even more often than that, and I'd liked that even better. But tonight I was feeling a little competitive because Rafe had rocked my world, and I was determined to rock his. To make this into something worth waiting half a lifetime for. To ruin him for anyone else who came along.

So I used every trick I could think of. I ran my tongue over the crown of his dick while I rubbed his balls. I stroked his thighs as I swirled my tongue up the length of him. I brought him to the edge, to the point where he was thrusting helplessly into my mouth and fisting the bedspread, over and over again only to back off and explore a new, fascinating part of him: the texture of the scar on the side of his knee, the unique flavor of the skin at the join of his hip, the sound he made when I sucked up a bruise below his navel, just above the line where the sun-kissed gold of his chest met the pale, tender skin below his waist.

I'd known Rafe for more than half my life, but all of this felt like uncharted territory. I'd never gotten to touch his body this way before or unabashedly breathe in the tangy, salt-water scent of him. I'd never learned how to make him tremble.

Now that I had, I was more than a little addicted. I wanted to spend *hours* making him lose his mind, letting him know he was the hottest man in the entire solar system because *he was*. I wanted the perfect timbre of his groans ringing in my ear forever.

The power was fucking heady, and I found myself pressing my own dick into the bed as it started to harden once more.

"Next time," I vowed, staring up at his gorgeous flushed cheeks and glassy eyes, praying there'd *be* a next time, "I'm going to do so many things to you. I'm going to rim you until you forget your own name. I'm going to fuck you so hard and so good, you will *never* confuse another guy for me during sex again, because your ass will know who owns it."

Rafe arched his back, pushing his head into the mattress. "God, yes," he moaned. "That fucking dreammaker voice."

I had no idea what he was talking about, except that my voice was hoarse as fuck from taking his cock... and maybe he liked that as much as I did.

"Mmm. I'm gonna need more candies," I whispered.

"Next time," Rafe said, lifting his head so his fever-bright eyes locked on mine as he said those two magic words that said he wanted the next time as much as I did. "I'm not going to go easy on you like I did earlier."

That had been *easy*? My cock gave a hopeful twitch, and I pressed myself down more aggressively.

"*Next time*," he continued. "I'm gonna lick every damn inch of you. I'm gonna take you slow and gentle and give you every fucking thing you've always wanted but never thought you could ask for."

The thing I'd always wanted but never thought to ask for was Rafe. That was all. As much of him as I could get, for as long as I could have him.

I held his hips down firmly and took him deep into my mouth, trying to convey all that without words. And when he finally shot into my mouth, moaning my name like a filthy curse, I was pretty sure I'd accomplished my goal.

"You just made me see stars," he groaned when I collapsed beside him on the comforter a second later.

The flashing lights from outside made firework patterns on the ceiling, and I snorted.

"Not entirely sure that was the blow job."

The air conditioner was *cranking* cold air, so I turned toward him and snuggled my face into his armpit with my arm thrown over his stomach, *because I could*, and I was gonna revel in it.

"So... I take it you liked my singing, then?" Rafe said sleepily a few minutes later.

I squeezed him tighter. "I'm a fan, Rafe Goodman. A true fan."

I woke up to find orangey-gold tendrils of light beaming through the sheer curtains at the window directly into my sleepy eye holes, and it was a sign of how well fucked I was that I didn't even care.

Rafe sprawled on his stomach in bed with his arm over my chest and his face turned toward me, in a near-perfect mirror of my own position, on my back with my face turned toward him. He had a little pucker between his eyebrows, like he was concentrating really hard on sleeping, and I wanted to reach out and smooth it away, but I also didn't want him to wake up because I had no idea what would happen when he did.

We'd woken briefly in the night to use the bathroom, which had led to me, with the kind of single-minded, stubborn need I only ever felt at three o'clock in the morning, to realize I *needed* my toothbrush. Cue the two of us—yes, *us*, because we were partners in crime again, for now anyway—stumbling next door, giggling and half-naked, to open the connecting door and retrieve our luggage, shushing each other the whole time like a couple of teens with a pilfered bottle of Boone's Farm.

I *had* felt drunk. I still did. And like I'd told Rafe earlier, it had nothing to do with tequila.

Later, we'd brushed our teeth side by side, and I'd grinned uncontrollably. Giddily. *Rafe was beside me, brushing his teeth.*

Last-week-me never would have believed I'd be living that kind of ordinary miracle, and Rafe's eyes said he was experiencing the same wondrous phenomenon.

So we'd shucked off our jeans again and commemorated the moment in the best possible way—by kissing with deep, slow, minty reverence and frotting with our eyes wide open so we didn't miss a second.

After it was over, Rafe had shifted off me just far enough that I could breathe comfortably, and we'd agreed we were gonna get up "in a minute" to clean off and shut the curtains. Judging by the dried mess on my stomach and the laser beams shooting into my skull, neither of us had stayed awake that long, but I couldn't be mad about it.

How often did I get a chance to watch the sunlight turn Rafe's skin to molten gold? How often did I get to just breathe and feel in my heart that there was no place else on earth I'd rather be?

I'd traveled all over and gotten to experience things lots of people could only dream about, but this moment right here was one I knew I'd want to remember forever and replay over and over.

I lifted Rafe's arm gently, placing a kiss to his knuckles, and scooted off the bed to find my notebook, to capture the feeling the best way I could.

By the time Rafe woke up an hour later, I was sitting on the bed cross-legged in my underwear with most of a new song down.

"Hey." Rafe's voice was sandy-rough, and he reached out a hand to rub my knee. "How long have you been awake?"

He rolled onto his back with a groan, exposing all sorts of new parts of him to the sunshine, which was so very distracting, it took me a full minute to formulate an answer.

"Hours and hours." I shut my notebook with my pen inside and tossed it to the foot of the bed so I could stretch out beside him. "While you were getting your beauty rest, I was working. I thought about grabbing Vega, but I didn't want to wake you."

"Vega?" He grinned stupidly. "No *s*?"

"Nope." I trailed my fingers over the curve and dip of his bicep. "You know, it's been a long time since I wrote a song I thought had potential, and now I've written a couple things in just the last few days, which is... unbelievable."

"Maybe the murder van inspired you." He pulled me in closer so his arm was around me and my head rested flat on his chest. "Too bad it was stolen."

"I still can't believe Chet did that," I muttered. "The one time I try to have faith in someone."

He teased the hair at the back of my neck, making me shiver. "You just had to pick the guy with dubious personal hygiene and a weird thing for triple-tread tires to put your faith in, huh?"

"It seemed like a good idea at the time," I said with as much dignity as I could muster. "But I guess I should get up so I can call the insurance company and the deputy sheriff. Get us some new wheels."

I made absolutely zero effort to move, though, which was fine since Rafe tightened his arm around me to keep me in place.

"Not so fast," he said. "We still have stuff to talk about now that we have a moment with no distractions."

I blew out a breath. He was right. He was *totally* correct. And yet I found myself weirdly reluctant. Deep, difficult conversations involving my sister had seemed so important when I was feeling shitty about everything, and so much less appealing when I was cuddled against Rafe's chest.

"I wouldn't say *no* distractions." I walked my fingers up the hard plane of his stomach to pinch one brown nipple.

He clapped his free hand over mine, holding me in place. "Jay." He tugged at my hair until I met his eyes, then raised one eyebrow at me.

"Fine, yes, okay." I waved a hand in the air. "Talking time. I'm ready. You go first."

I reminded myself that Aimee said there was no romance involved… but did that mean it had been purely physical? A one-night stand that made them mistake lust for love?

A night not unlike the night Rafe and I had just shared?

Oh, fuck. I might vomit.

Rafe snorted. "I wasn't aware that the human body could become as tense as yours is right now." He shook my frozen arm. "How bad do you think this story is gonna be?"

"Well. I think it's gonna involve my first lo—*crush* marrying my baby sister," I said softly. "And I already know it's gonna result in years of misunderstanding, during which I spent night after night singing a song I'd written about a guy I wasn't sure I'd ever see again."

Rafe was quiet for a minute. "Yeah, okay, that's fair. But that's not actually how the story starts. I'm not sure how much Aimee told you yesterday—"

"Basically nothing. I know nothing," I admitted.

He sighed and squeezed me tighter for a second, like he knew how much that admission cost. "Okay, then. Three years ago last spring, Aimee started having trouble catching her breath. She figured it was just a bad spring asthma flare, but every time she thought it was under control—"

"It kept coming back," I supplied. "I remember this. And old Dr. Corlia back in Rock Gulch kept finding new things she was allergic to. Pollen and mold spores and dander and whatever…"

"Yeah. Exactly. But then she collapsed one day while she was at work, and they took her to the ER—"

I lifted my head, incredulous. "What? And *no one* told me this?"

"I know. Look, it turned out okay," he reminded me. His big hand caressed my back, but this time I refused to be soothed. I pushed myself up to sit cross-legged near his hip, and he reluctantly let me. "It was actually a really good thing that it happened, because she was taken to the ER, and the doctors ran some tests Aimee's old doctor never ran, and..." He took a deep breath. "It turned out Aimee has a heart condition."

I blinked, feeling like I'd stepped sideways into another world. I knew he wasn't lying but also knew it couldn't possibly be true.

"They said it was probably something she was born with that went undetected for years," Rafe continued, "because the symptoms seemed to mimic asthma—"

"How could she not tell me the second she found out?" I whispered, hurt beyond belief. "How could *you*? Is she seeing specialists? Is she..." I grabbed two fistfuls of my hair to stop myself from jumping off the bed and running to Wyoming so I could demand answers from Aimee or her doctor or... God, I didn't even know.

Rafe, meanwhile, remained annoyingly calm. "Jay. You talked to her yesterday. You said she was okay."

I blew out a breath. "Yeah, I know, but that was before I knew—"

"I know," he interrupted. "I know, but she's been managing this condition for years. She has a cardiologist... or at least she did when she lived on the Key. And her condition can be managed with medication and regular medical care." He reached out a hand like he wanted to touch my leg but thought better of it. "Do you want me to go on?"

"My God, there's more?"

This time, he didn't hesitate. He rolled toward me and slid his palm up my thigh, splaying his tan fingers on my paler leg. I wasn't sure whether he was trying to calm me down or hold me in place, but either way, it was effective.

"Yeah, babe. There's the whole marriage part."

That, right there, was a roller coaster of a sentence, beginning with the casual *babe* and ending in a reminder that he'd once made vows to my sister. Was it possible to get motion sickness while sitting on a stationary surface?

"After she was diagnosed, Aimee was... not in a great place mentally. Emotionally. The new doctors told her she needed to avoid getting pregnant and should maybe reconsider a career working with kids in favor of one that required less exertion." He grimaced. "She thought her life was over. She was depressed as fuck. Jealous of her friends who didn't have this shit to worry about. Angry at your dad, I think, for trusting the doctor. She came to the Key for a visit because she didn't know where else to go—"

"To me! To her brother! That's where she should have—"

"Jay." Rafe sat up and crossed his legs to mirror mine. He lifted my chin and forced me to look at him. "Let me finish, okay? I want you to understand all of it."

There was a strain in the creases of his eyes and the line of his jaw, and I realized Rafe wasn't enjoying this conversation any more than I was, but he was forcing himself through it because he wanted to get to the other side. With me.

I set my jaw so tightly my molars squeaked, but I managed a small nod.

"She didn't want to go to you." He stroked a thumb over my jaw, like that might take the sting away... for both of us. "Think back. Debbie had just organized your very first tour. You were over the moon excited. You'd worked *so* hard for *so* long to get that."

"But—"

"You living your dream was the most positive thing in her life at that time." He smiled a lopsided smile. "Mine, too, if I'm being honest. I'm not saying it was right, Jay. I'm not justifying her choice. Or my choice. I'm explaining it. Okay?"

I nodded again.

"Okay. So. By the time she got to the island, she'd quit her job on her new doctor's advice. She was penniless, avoiding your parents like the plague, and sick as a dog. I was worried about her. I told her I'd help her. And she suggested—" He licked his lips, and I waited with bated breath.

Was he gonna say "*sex*"? He was totally gonna say sex. I locked down all my muscles...

"—that we get married so she could be on my health insurance. A marriage of convenience, she called it."

"Does that mean you and she...? Did you...?" I cleared my throat, trying to find a euphemistic way to ask a question I was 90 percent sure I didn't want the answer to. In the end, I gave up and blurted, "What's a marriage of convenience?"

Rafe shrugged. "I have no idea why they call it that, 'cause it was anything but convenient. It just means we got married at a justice of the peace, and she moved her stuff into the spare room at my house—which is to say, my dad's house, where Beale lived and Gage lived, too, part of the time—and we just... existed?"

He frowned. "I mean... it was nice. She watched *Wheel of Fortune* with my dad every night, which you might recall is the most popular show on the Key. I couldn't do it—drives me batshit when he yells at the contestants like they can hear him—but she found it funny. Oh, and she took turns cooking meals, like the rest of us. Sometimes I'd take her to her appointments. We tried to spend a lot of time hanging out in the same room, especially at first, to keep up appearances, and we talked about you a lot. Where you were on your tour, what you might be doing... why you were probably too busy to call."

I squeezed my eyes shut against the guilt.

"Remember when I told you I thought Aimee was happy until she left? I mean, she never told me she wasn't, so I figured she was. But also... she was probably pretty lonely. She was like a very sweet, unassuming roommate."

"So..." I blinked more. "So you're saying you *never*... You and she didn't..."

"Didn't...? *Oh!* Oh, no. *Nooooo.* Nope. Never," he confirmed. "We never consummated the marriage. We never did more than peck each other on the cheek, even at the wedding. I was never tempted to."

"But you thought she was pretty. You told me! With her green eyes and her hair, and—"

"I meant *you*, Jay." He shook his head. "I always meant *you*."

"Oh my *God*," I groaned, cradling my head in my hands as relief rushed through me, followed quickly by anger. "This is even worse than I thought!"

Rafe pulled my hands away from my face. "Worse? How? I thought you'd be glad, sort of. I mean, to know Aimee and I never…"

"Because I've been *torturing* myself thinking of the two of you!" I exploded. "Can you even imagine what it was like for me, thinking you and Aimee were…? *God.* Even if you were gonna do something as stupid and shortsighted as getting married for health insurance, why wouldn't you let me in on the secret?"

Rafe huffed out a breath. "I already told you part of the reason. Aimee didn't want you to know. She didn't want you to cancel your tour to come sit and stare at her—"

"I wouldn't!"

He lifted one eyebrow.

"Fine, I might have. But it would have been my choice!"

"But she would've felt guilty over it."

"And now *I* feel guilty that I didn't know!" I very badly wanted to scream. "What was the other part of the reason? Go on. Tell me everything."

Rafe rubbed his palms along his hairy thighs. "The other reason is… I wanted to take care of this for you. *Me*." He shrugged sheepishly. "I felt like we were drifting apart. You were going on that first tour, and you weren't gonna have time to come back to the Key that summer, not really—which made sense because the place was so run-down, and you were meant for bigger things—but I... I panicked, I guess. I was jealous of your new life and your new friends. I figured you'd find some woman and fall in love eventually, even though she'd never love you as much as I did. Marrying Aimee meant I'd get to keep you in my life. Which, ah..." He cleared his throat. "Worked well. Clearly."

"I want to hit you again," I bit out. "You wanna talk about jealousy? This whole thing is *gross*. You lied and lied..."

"I know." Rafe grabbed my face in both his hands, cradling my jaw. "I'm truly sorry I hurt you, Jay," he said softly. "That was the very last thing I wanted. But I didn't think it *could* hurt you. I never dreamed there could be a you and me. You were straight, right?" He smiled wryly. "And also... I dunno. I guess I can't be sorry for everything, even if I should be. Because if you'd known about Aimee, you wouldn't have realized your dream. There'd be no *Constellations* out in the world. And like Chet said, you always would have wondered."

Ugh. Part of me—the part that wanted to protect myself from getting hurt again—was fighting to stay angry, but Rafe's voice rang with sincerity and affection that made anger really fucking slippery.

He'd been utterly, completely wrong, but his intentions had been good, and that *mattered*, especially considering how my own jealousy and insecurity had made me push him away.

It was at least as much my fault as his... and I kinda felt like we'd both been punished enough for being idiots.

Still, I felt compelled to point out, "If you hadn't lied, we wouldn't have been so angry at each other all these years."

"True. But then maybe we wouldn't know how awful that felt either."

Warmth spread through my chest. "It was awful for you, too, huh?"

"Like ripping out my own lungs. Sometimes I could hardly breathe. Still, though, maybe things were supposed to happen that way."

I frowned. "No. Bad things are never 'meant to happen.' That's Beale's mystical woo-woo Kool-Aid. It's something people say to explain away a giant fuckup."

Rafe's lips twitched. "Fine, then. How about we both needed to learn our lessons. To wise up. To mature. To know just how far we're willing to go to prevent something like that from happening again." His fingers tightened on my jaw, and he pressed a fierce kiss to my lips. "I know you're hurt, Jay. I know you're angry. I wish I could take that away, and I'll do whatever I can to make it up to you. But I'm not making the same mistake twice, okay? I'm not letting us walk out of each other's lives again. Not if I can help it. I'm gonna sit right here and let you be mad at me."

He spoke confidently, but his eyes were pleading. *Don't walk away, Jay.*

Pfft. Like I ever would have in the first place, if I hadn't convinced myself that's what he wanted deep down.

"I suppose this is what Aimee was talking about yesterday," I grumbled. "She said if I wanted to convince you to talk about this, I should remind you why you promised to keep quiet in the first place." I pulled a face. "Which was because you *cared*."

"I did. I still do." Rafe smiled tentatively. "She really said I should tell you everything?"

"What, did you think I was lying?" I lifted one eyebrow imperiously, even as my insides did a crazy jig. *He'd told me even though he thought Aimee hadn't given permission?* I was petty enough to find this mattered and honest enough to admit it to myself.

"Not lying. But I thought maybe you were using... What did you call it when you phoned Aimee's hospital pretending to be me? Unorthodox methods?" He wiggled his eyebrows.

"No." I shoved his shoulder. *Fuck*, I loved when he smiled. It did crazy things to my insides.

I kinda wanted to ask him what he meant when he said he wanted us to be in each other's lives. How would that even work when I lived in New York and he was in Florida?

But he was here with me now, his eyes hot on mine in a way I'd never seen outside of my dreams until last night, so I pulled away from his hand just long enough to stretch out on the bed with one arm bent back to support my head, and I trailed my other hand down my naked chest to toy with the waistband of my briefs.

"Why don't we back up for a second?" My voice nearly vibrated with want. "Pretty sure somewhere in there I heard a promise to make it up to me?"

His eyes flared even hotter. "I did say that, didn't I?"

"You did." I ran my thumb over his full bottom lip, and when his tongue darted out to lick the tip and draw it into his mouth, I sucked in a breath.

"Maybe we should talk about how, *exactly*, I could do that." He trailed a hand up my thigh to trace the outline of my dick through the cotton of my underwear with one blunt fingertip.

I went hard instantly.

"In the immortal words of Chet's Chrissea," I said, grabbing the back of Rafe's neck to pull him down for a kiss. "Actions speak louder than words, Rafael."

11

———————

RAFE

"Singer Jayd Rollins, perpetually age twenty-five, found dead in Pleasure Emporium bathroom," Jay whispered sometime later. "Investigators say it was death by orgasm."

I snorted, which used up all the remaining energy in my body. I wasn't entirely positive that my feet were still attached to the rest of me, and checking would have involved opening my eyes, which... was kind of a lot to expect from a person who'd had more sex in the past twelve hours than in the three years before.

The only sensation I had below the waist was a pleasant tingling hum—which might have been a symptom of my own impending death by orgasm, or maybe was because I'd collapsed on a pile of towels on the bathroom floor after our last round of blow jobs in the shower and Jay had laid himself out on top of me, cutting off all my circulation.

If this was how it all ended, though, I was perfectly okay with that.

It was kinda funny to remember how I'd fantasized about Jay blowing me two nights ago in that hotel room back in Tennessee. I almost pitied that Rafe, poor asshole. He'd *no* idea how good it actually could be.

"That's tragic," I managed. "Jayd gave so much to the world. I mean, not as much as Ari Friedrich, obviously, but..."

Jay lifted his head just far enough to turn his narrowed green stare on me. His hair had dried in spikes and cowlicks, thanks to me gripping it so hard at various points throughout the morning, and it looked like he'd electrocuted himself. It was fucking adorable.

"Sources say the main suspect is his former best friend, Rafe Goodman."

I tugged on a lock of damp hair, creating another spike right up front. "Former, huh?"

"Mmm. I'd been *considering* reinstating your title," he said haughtily, "since you made things up to me so thoroughly. Buuuut then you invoked Ari's name. Demerits were taken. Significant demerits. It's sad, really."

"Oh, I see," I said gravely. "It's a point-based system. Well, I ordered you pancakes *with topping* between round three and round four, and they'll be here in time to revive us for round five," I reminded him. "That's the kind of forward thinking you can't really put a points value on."

Jay stared at my mouth like he wanted to kiss me. "This is true."

"In fact." I skated my finger down the smooth skin of his flank, making him shiver. "I'm thinking I deserve a promotion."

"A promotion!" he hooted. "To what? Head best friend? In charge of my entourage of best friends?"

"I was thinking more like…" I had to pause to swallow and remind myself that I was committed to being 100 percent honest with Jay moving forward, and that meant putting myself out there, even when I was scared shitless. "More like boyfriend."

Jay's eyes widened, and his face froze in a weird mask of vulnerability. "You want that?" His gaze ping-ponged from my right eye to my left eye like he thought I might be kidding. "With me?"

I pushed his spiky hair back off his face. "I have *always* wanted that with you. It's come to my attention only recently that I might be able to have it."

It was on the tip of my tongue to remind him of the songs he'd written. He'd said *love*, but had he meant it? Was there a possibility he could mean it still?

I'd wanted to ask him yesterday, but I'd let it go. And at that moment, with Jay on top of me, I reminded myself that I didn't have to push. That I could be patient. That what we had right now was more than enough to start with.

The smile that came over his face was like a sunrise, lighting him up from inside. "Well, it just so happens I have an opening for the position. And I *have* been very impressed with your work ethic." He hesitated. "But how exactly would that—?"

There was a knock at the hotel room door, and Jay and I stared at each other wide-eyed.

"I thought you said it would be forty minutes for room service," he whispered, scrambling to his feet.

"Well, we weren't timing it, were we? It could've been forty minutes already." Heck, we could have been lying there for four *hours*. I stood up also and slapped his bare ass lightly. "I ordered, so you go let the guy in."

Jay groaned and grabbed a towel to wrap around his waist, then caught a glimpse of himself in the mirror and gasped in horror. "What the *fuck* is this?"

I wrapped my arms around him from behind, running possessive hands over his abs. "That's sex hair."

"I look ridiculous!"

"No, what's ridiculous is how sexy I'm finding it, since I was the one who gave it to you."

His eyes met mine in the mirror, and he melted against me... until the second knock came.

"Fuck," I muttered, grabbing the towel from Jay's hands. "Fine, *I'll* go hunt and gather your pancakes."

"So very caveman," he purred approvingly. "Meanwhile, I'm jumping back in the shower. I'm not famous enough to pull off this look."

I laughed as I knotted the terry cloth around my waist and was still grinning when I opened the door. "Hey, you can put the tr— Oh. Shit."

My smile fell away as I saw it wasn't the room service person with the cart—or not *just* her—it was a whole freakin' parade of people I did *not* want to deal with, including Deputy Freckles, the hotel manager, a curvy and heavily tattooed brunette with pinup-girl hair, a short dude in a shiny brown suit, and one song-butchering, van-stealing criminal.

"Chet," I ground out. "So the law caught up to you?"

"Heck yeah, he did! Right downstairs in the lobby!" He grinned. "What a to-do!"

"I bet." I narrowed my eyes at Freckles. "Is it protocol around here to bring the perpetrator to the victims' hotel roo—?"

"S'cuse me," the server interrupted. "I've got like twelve other deliveries, so... d'you mind if I set this up?" She motioned toward the little table in front of the window.

I nodded curtly and stood aside to let her through... which the whole rest of the posse took as an invitation to come right in also, while I stood holding the door like an idiot.

"Hey! Nice view!" Chet said, making for the window. "Deputy, I can see your house from here!"

"Excuse me!" I began. "I need you all to—"

Of course Jay chose that precise moment to emerge from the bathroom wearing nothing but a towel and a smile.

"I'm ready for my *topping*," he announced.

"Jerry!" Chet cried happily.

"Mr. Rollins!" The deputy sounded faintly scandalized.

"*Jayd*," Normandie purred.

"Sweet Jesus," I muttered.

"Mother. Fucker." Jay's eyes widened, and his frightened gaze darted helplessly from me to the interlopers.

"Well, well. And what's your name?" The man in brown held his phone in front of my face like he wanted to record my answer.

That seemed to knock Jay out of his trance. "He's no one you need to worry about." Jay smacked the man's hand away from me and gave Normandie such a vicious glare, her fawning smile disappeared like a startled meerkat, and she quaked in her pantsuit. "I assumed there was a certain expectation of privacy at this hotel."

Normandie blushed and stammered. "W-w-well, of course! But Deputy Horowitz, here, wanted to bring Chester up to explain everything, and I offered to accompany him as a matter of hotel protocol."

"Really. Without calling up? Without verifying that I wanted to meet with anyone? Deputy Horowitz isn't investigating *me*, so this strikes me as highly irregular."

She licked her lips. "I was hoping to talk to you about a teeny, tiny little endorsement for, um..." She wilted under his glower.

"And who the hell are you?" I asked the man in brown. "Did they pick you up in the elevator?"

"I'm Mike Kenney from the *Dry Hump Observer*. I figured Mr. Rollins would like to make a statement expressing his gratitude to the fine Dry Hump law enforcement professionals who brought the case of his missing van to such a satisfactory conclusion." He looked from my naked chest to Jay's. "Though, obviously, if there's any *other* kind of statement Mr. Rollins would like to make—"

"Fuck no," Jay said firmly. "The only story here is that the water pressure in my shower next door was *shit*." He hooked a thumb toward the connecting door between our two rooms, which stood open. He turned toward me but almost seemed to look right *through* me, like he barely knew me and hadn't had my dick in his mouth twenty minutes before. "Thank you so much for letting me use your shower, friend. Much appreciated."

"Yeah. Anytime," I said woodenly, my stomach sinking. "Pal."

Normandie gasped. "Oh, no! I'll get someone from maintenance up here right now—"

"Don't bother." Jay lifted his chin in the air, fully cloaked in dignity despite being almost entirely naked. "We're checking out this morning, and we'd like to enjoy our breakfast in peace." He gave a cold nod at the little table where the server finished arranging our breakfast. The personality shift from Jay to *Jayd* was absolute, and it hit me like cold rain.

On the one hand, I understood it—I did. After last night, watching "fans" circle around him like vultures pecking over the scraps of his attention, I understood the need to keep people at a distance. And I also firmly believed that he deserved to keep his private life private. Choosing not to explain our relationship to a bunch of strangers had nothing to do with the way he felt about me, whatever that was.

But no lie, watching him treat me like a polite stranger sucked. It reminded me that getting things right between me and Jay was only part of the battle, and the larger issues of me and *Jayd* were still looming over us.

I had the insane desire to tattoo my name on Jay's chest. Or declare, "He's my boyfriend," at the top of my lungs and push his nearly naked body behind mine. Or go back in time and give him a hickey in the shower—one big enough to be visible from outer space.

Obnoxious? Yes.

Terrifying? Heck yes.

True? Also very much yes.

"I *am* very grateful to the law enforcement people," Jay told the reporter in the same haughty voice. "I plan to make a sizable donation to their retirement fund. And as to any potential endorsement of the hotel..." He pursed his lips and fixed Normandie with a look that spoke volumes. "That's really going to depend on what kind of coverage I see in the media about my stay here. I'm sincerely hoping for *none*."

Normandie blinked for half a second, but she caught on fast. "Come on, Mike." She linked elbows with the reporter and drew him toward the door. "Let's talk downstairs."

"But—" the man protested, "I haven't even asked about—"

"I'll contact you next week with a statement, Ms. Baker," Jay called as Normandie left. When the door clicked shut, he turned to the remaining people in the room.

"Keys, please," he demanded of Chet.

"I already gave 'em to Deputy Horowitz." Chet frowned at Jay uncertainly, like he wasn't sure where his pal had gone.

"Look, Jerr—uh, *Jayd*, this has all been a giant misunderstanding."

"It hasn't." Jay crossed his arms over his chest and raised an imperious eyebrow. "You stole our van. The lure of the triple treads was too much for you."

Chet looked horrified. "I never stole a thing in my life! I just borrowed it. I figured you'd want me to! I mean, you know I left my car back outside St. Louis, and you told me to take my Chrissea on a picnic..."

"A nighttime picnic?" Jay scoffed.

Chet wrapped an arm around the waist of the rockabilly princess beside him. "You said to take her to see *owls*. Can't see owls in the daytime, can you?"

"Occasionally you can, baby," Chrissea said, snuggling into Chet's side and sighing deeply. "But it wouldn't have been the same. Not nearly as romantic."

Jay and I exchanged a look, and I saw his resolve weaken. "Well..."

"Y'all should be the first to know, you were right. About everything." Chet beamed. "And Chrissea said *yes*."

"*Yes*?" I repeated, frowning. "To what?"

"Show 'em, baby," Chet said, and the woman held up her left hand to display a knobby, yellow-brown band on her ring finger.

"Is that—?" Jay began.

"A genuine corncob and resin ring from the gift shop downstairs?" she finished. "Yeah, it is! My Chet knows exactly what I like." She fluttered her eyelashes up at Chet. "And now that we're getting married, I'll never take it off."

"You're *engaged*," I said dumbly. "That's... wow. Congratulations."

Chet smiled even harder, so wide I thought his face might crack. "We talked about everything, just like you two suggested. And we decided we're going on the road together!"

Chrissea nodded. "I don't want Chet to give up his musical ambitions."

"And I can't give up my muse," Chet said proudly.

"Aw." Jay hitched his towel tighter, and his haughty expression gave way to softness. "I... I *guess* there was no harm done." He looked at me for confirmation.

I pushed my lips together to hide the wide smile that threatened to burst out. That, right there, was the guy I'd been half in love with since I was a teenager. Generous, big-hearted, optimistic to the core, no matter how many protective layers he tried to put around himself.

Even if he never declared our relationship to the world, I could be happy knowing I was lucky enough to see this tender, true part of him all the time.

"So, I expect you won't be pressing charges, then?" Deputy Freckles hooked his thumbs in his big gun belt.

Jay shook his head. "As long as the van's in one piece."

"Not a scratch on it," Chet vowed. "We even put the seats back up after we... erm."

Jay and I exchanged a laughing glance. Deputy Freckles coughed and looked at the ceiling.

"Come on, Chester. Chrissea." Deputy Freckles rocked on the balls of his feet. "Let's leave the nice folks to eat their breakfast in peace."

Chet, though, hung back and kept Chrissea with him.

"You coulda knocked me over with a feather when Jim told us my friend Jerry was actually *the* Jayd Rollins," he told Jay. "Nobody's ever gonna believe you were traveling through Missouri incognito, picked me up at a gas station, gave me a ride, sorted out my relationship, *and* listened to my album—I mean, my cover of *your* album—and liked it so dang much!"

Liked was a strong word, but other than a little smirk, Jay didn't argue with Chet's interpretation.

"You know, if you ever need an opening act, I'm your man. Or if you might ever consider writing a song for me..." Chet continued, blushing fiercely. "I'd love that. I don't know if you do that sort of thing, but some folks do. Maybe it could be something with a heavy techno beat? But also country?"

Jay frowned but nodded slowly. "I can honestly promise that if I'm ever inspired to write a techno-country song, you will be the very first person I call."

Chet sighed happily and squeezed Chrissea tighter to his side. "Past twenty-four hours have been the weirdest, bestest day of my life."

I knew exactly what he meant.

Chrissea stepped forward and pressed a kiss to Jay's cheek. "I've been a huge fan of your music, but I had no idea you were so *nice*. You're still my favorite singer... after my Chet here, of course."

"She's my biggest fan," Chet said proudly.

"As I should be," she agreed. "Since you're my main squeeze."

"That's sweet," Jay said gently. "And thank you."

"Baby, we need to get downstairs to give Barbara my two-week notice." Chrissea nudged Chet's arm.

"Ah, that's right. Anyway, nice seeing you again, Tom." Chet offered me a hand to shake, and I realized no one had bothered sharing *my* real name, which was probably for the best.

"Same, Chet. Best of luck to you crazy kids."

Chrissea headed for the door, but Chet dragged his toe over the patterned carpet. "I wanted to apologize. I maybe exaggerated a li'l bit yesterday when I said Jayd Rollins was my close personal friend."

Jay smiled his genuine smile, the one that made my heart kick up a crazy rhythm. "You didn't lie, Chet. You just didn't know we were friends yet." He clapped Chet on the arm, and Chet looked so happy he might cry.

"Wow," he breathed. "Yeah. Okay." He sniffled just a little. "Best of luck to *y'all*, too," he offered. "You're real fun together."

Jay blinked, indecision plain on his face. He shot me a look that said he didn't want to admit to anything... but he also didn't want to hurt me.

"Together?" I huffed out a laugh. "Me and this guy? Nah. Now, if Ari Friedrich were around…"

Jay shot me a look that promised me an infinite number of demerits if I finished that sentence, so I didn't.

"Jay and I are friends," I told Chet instead, knowing I was speaking the truth, even if it wasn't the whole truth. "Best friends."

12

JAY

The next day, Rafe pulled the van into a shaded parking spot outside St. Vincent's Hospital. I groaned tiredly and tilted my head back against the passenger's seat.

The eight-hour drive through Nebraska had been both uneventful and tiring as fuck, sort of in the way that sitting in an airport terminal for long periods was tiring. Like the force of will required to hold yourself still leached the energy from your bones.

We'd ended up spending an extra night in Dry Hump the night before. As it turned out, Deputy Horowitz had needed us to sign some paperwork withdrawing our complaint, Chet had wanted to "gas up the van for my boys," and Normandie had insisted that we get dinner and an upgraded room "*on the house*, so you can experience the true beauty and majesty of the Pleasure Emporium!"

This had been fine by me because the evening *had* been majestic and beautiful... in ways that had nothing to do with the room.

In fact, last night had been so great that if I didn't know Rafe was fielding a dozen texts an hour from the Extravaganza Committee and his dad, wondering when the hell we'd be home, I'd have begged for more nights. Entire months of nights. Years and years of nights. Our stay in Dry Hump felt like a step out of time for us. A fairy tale set in a random midwestern Las Vegas, where trivial things like my career, the tabloids, my sister, my visceral reaction to "Jay and I are friends. Best friends," and the looming question mark above our relationship felt like fiction... while important things like me and Rafe huddled in bed together with our arms around each other, dreaming up ways Rafe could see the world without getting on an airplane, felt like solid truth.

Fortunately-unfortunately, Rafe was way too responsible to let us stay there forever or even let us dilly-dally that morning. So there we were, already in Larindosa, while late-afternoon sunshine filtered through the sheltering tree branches overhead.

"You ready for this?" he asked softly.

"Very. And also... not at all."

He brushed a hand lightly down my arm and toyed with my fingers. "You'll probably feel better once you get it over with."

"Yeah." I sighed.

"Or, if you'd rather not do this, we can just go back to the hotel. Or to Florida."

I cracked open one eye. "Just leave, huh? And have all this kidnapping be for nothing? Don't you wanna see for yourself that Aimee's fine?"

He shrugged. "I want to see *you* fine even more. If this isn't gonna get you there, then we'll reassess." He threaded our fingers together briefly and squeezed. "And just to say, the kidnapping wasn't for nothing. Best kidnapping I've ever experienced. Ten out of ten. I've even learned to love the smell of Shalimar."

I laughed helplessly.

God. There were times when I just *liked* the man so damn much, it was hard to believe it was real.

The steadfastness in his eyes made my stomach settle and my heart leap at the same time—which made a strange sort of sense, when I thought about it, because in a life like mine, nothing was as exciting as stability.

"I'm being a giant baby about this," I confessed, like he wasn't already aware. "Aimee's okay, I know she is. And you already told me the whole story."

He dipped his head, a confirmation. "As much as I know of it."

"So it's really just hearing about what's going on with her right now and why she never told me the truth about any of this, even after she left Florida."

Just that. *Pfft.* Why my sister didn't trust me with important facts of her life. Incidental stuff, really.

Rafe's mouth quirked up on one side, like he'd heard everything I didn't say. "You need this to get your relationship with her back on track, and I know that's important to you. Look how well talking things out has worked for us."

"True. And speaking of which... I, uh, think we should prob-ably tell her that you and I are... you know." I motioned between us. "Together?"

I watched Rafe's face closely. He'd been the one to broach the idea of more-than-friends the day before, but he hadn't said anything about it since then. Nothing except, *"Jay and I are friends. Best friends"* with a look in his eyes that said it had cost him something to deny us to the world. No lie, I felt terrible about it—and as everyone knew, terrible-without-a-clue-how-to-rectify-it was the worst kind of terrible.

"Since Aimee practically threw me at you the other day on the phone, I don't think she's gonna disapprove or anything," I babbled on. "And maybe—"

"I wouldn't give a single fuck if she did," Rafe said without hesitation. "I don't care what anyone thinks. This is between me and you." He cupped my cheek in one strong palm. "I love Aimee a lot. You know that. But making sure *you're* okay is my priority here."

I sucked in a breath. Had anyone ever said something like that to me? I didn't think so. I kissed him, hard and fast, tasting his surprise and his instant response, and then I leaned against him, temple to temple.

"You know, about yesterday morning back at the inn. About us being, uh... best friends? I—" I swallowed. "I'm not sure if I made it really clear that you'd gotten that promotion you suggested. To boyfriend."

I felt his grin against my cheek, and his warm breath curled in my ear. "Oh, that's a relief. 'Cause I promoted you also."

"Yeah?" I'd tried to sound amused, but it was probably probable that I'd overshot the mark and landed squarely on *desperate*. "Also to boyfriend? Because that would be convenient."

"I was thinking about elevating you to *second* favorite singer *ever*," he said in a reverent voice. "Right after..."

I spluttered out a laugh and clapped a hand to his mouth. "Don't you dare speak his name."

Rafe's eyes danced, and he tugged my hand away so he could kiss me quickly. "The sooner we're done here, the sooner we can find a hotel," he reminded me. "It won't be the Dry Hump Pleasure Emporium, but—"

"But it could be our own pleasure emporium. If we try hard enough." I waggled my eyebrows, and he groaned.

And that was more than enough to have me unwrapping a honey drop, getting out of the car, and striding briskly toward the hospital with Rafe's hand in mine.

"We'd like to see a patient of yours. Aimee Rollins," I announced to the receptionist—a bored younger guy this time, rather than the elderly woman who'd been there a few days before. I pointed at Rafe. "Rafael Goodman is here to see her. He's on her NV-whatever list."

"Sure thing." The guy, whose name tag said Cedar, typed something into the computer, and his friendly look disappeared. "Hmm. I'll need to see your ID, Mr. Goodman."

"Of course," Rafe said. But he rolled his eyes at me as he extracted his license, and I could practically hear his voice in my head saying, "Unorthodox methods."

It was a sign of how sappy I was feeling that I let this go.

Cedar frowned down at Rafe's ID. "I'm sorry, this is the wrong address. Wrong date of birth, also—"

"Ha!" I shouted triumphantly. "See? I told you they had your birthday wrong! I totally knew your birthday!" To Cedar, I added, "I totally know his birthday."

Rafe shot me a sideways smile.

"Nifty," Cedar said. "But that doesn't get you on the authorized list, Mr...." His voice trailed off as he looked up at me —*really* looked. "Wait, *Rollins*? As in *Jayd Rollins*? Holy shit."

I tried to duck under the brim of my baseball hat, but I'd forgotten the damn thing again. I wasn't sure why I kept doing that when I'd spent years almost surgically attached to the thing.

Anyway, it was clearly too late to hide because Cedar was already out of his chair, hurrying around the little desk to grab my hand and shake it firmly. "Oh my God. This is crazy. I can't believe you're here! I loved 'Pretty Girl.' You... You *are* him, right? Jayd?"

I looked at Rafe. *So much for under the radar.*

Rafe shrugged. *Your call.*

"Yes, I'm Jayd Rollins. I'm here to visit my sister, but I want to respect her privacy, so if you could not put this on Instagram —" I looked around the nearly empty lobby and silently begged him to keep his voice down.

"Oh! God, no wonder you guys were trying to get through with the wrong ID. No, no, it's cool," he whisper-insisted, all wide-eyed and earnest. "There's, like, all sorts of HIPAA requirements, so I won't let anyone know you're here, but I wouldn't anyway!" He let go of my hand and cradled his own to his chest protectively. "I can't believe I got to shake your hand! You have no idea how much that song meant to me. When I was coming out to my parents, I played them that song, and... like, it's just so great to have queer representation out there, you know?" His eyes widened impossibly further. "I mean, not to claim that for you or whatever. I know you haven't come out yet. Or at all! But just to say..." He swallowed convulsively and repeated solemnly, "Just to say."

He was adorable and so sweetly sincere, I found *myself* tongue-tied in the face of it. How could I look him in the face and say I wasn't gay? But Jesus, confirming it for a perfect stranger would be... would be...

"Jay's had a long week, worrying about his sister," Rafe interjected, saving my ass. "If we could see her?"

"Yeah, no, of course!" Cedar scrambled back around the desk and hit a few keys on the keyboard. A tiny printer spat out a pair of Visitor stickers. "Just put these on. Elevator's right there. Third floor. There's an atrium off the lobby where they do visitor things. I'll call up and let them know you're coming so they can kinda shut it down for you, okay?"

And just that easily, we were in the elevator, on our way to see Aimee, despite being absolutely not authorized to do so. Rafe stood beside me, a silent sentinel who'd openly declared that *I* was his priority.

I took a deep breath. "You realize what this means, right? That I probably could have gotten in here at any time if the receptionist the other day had known I was *the* Jayd Rollins?

That I wouldn't have had to hit you, or kidnap you, or drag you along on this whole expedition if I'd just been open about who I was?"

Rafe grunted, and the backs of his fingers brushed mine.

"What was that other receptionist's name?"

I blinked. "Shirleen, I think? Why?"

"Because I'm sending her flowers, that's why."

The doors opened, and Rafe stepped out into a little lobby, but all I could do was stand and stare at the back of him until the doors started to close with me still in the elevator.

I stepped out quickly. "You don't just get to say sweet things like that," I whispered. "Not in a public place. Not when I can't kiss the shit out of you."

He winked, and the look in his eyes had me *thisclose* to panting right there on the antiseptic-scented floor tiles. "Actually, I do. My promotion says so. It's part of my job description now. Deal with it, Rollins."

Well, damn.

He gestured me to the right, following the signs for the visitor atrium, and when we stepped inside the sunny, greenhouse-like space filled with deep chairs and comfortable sofas, Aimee was already sitting there.

I nearly wept at the sight of her. Her long, sandy-blonde hair had been cut into a short pixie, which was beautiful but also highlighted her fragile face and the hollows of her cheeks. She was way thinner than she'd been the last time I saw her, and I wanted to kick my own ass for failing her so badly.

"Oh my God! Jay! You're actually here!" Aimee's green eyes lit with happiness and affection as she pushed herself to her feet.

"Stop! Don't stand up for us!" I scolded, hurrying to her side like she might need my help to sit back down. "Aimee, you've got to rest—"

"Actually, it's good for her to stand and move around," a mild voice said, which was the first time I noticed the other occupant of the room.

"I beg your pardon?" I slipped into Belinda's Southern church-lady voice.

The man had enormous glasses and a receding hairline which suggested he was a little older than Rafe and me— maybe his mid-thirties—but still way too young to be wearing that lab coat, tie, and hospital ID badge as anything but a Halloween costume. And though he sat in his own chair adjacent to Aimee, he looked at her in a proprietary sort of way that made my hackles rise.

Was this the guy who'd called her *babe*?

I opened my mouth to call him out, but Aimee laid her hand on my arm.

"Jay, this is Dave Clemmons. *Doctor* David Clemmons. He's a miracle worker. Dave, this is my brother, Jay, and my friend Rafe Goodman."

The doctor shook hands with Rafe first, since he was closer, and Aimee hugged me gingerly. "I'm so glad to see you! But stop with the face," she warned under her breath.

"Rafe." She smiled at Rafe, and he embraced her gently, too. "I'm sorry. For everything."

He stepped back. "It's not all on you. We both should have done things differently."

It was all so cordial. Like a happy family reunion. *Kumbaya.*

"Jay." Dr. Babe held out a hand to me. "Aimee's told me lots about you."

I shook his hand briefly. "Yeah, well. That information seems to have only flowed in one direction. I was in the dark about you... which is kind of a running theme."

Fuck. I really hadn't intended to do that.

Aimee made a distressed noise.

Rafe moved to stand closer to me, still in sentinel mode, which made me want to curl up against him.

"Sorry," I mumbled.

Interestingly, Dr. Babe made the same instinctive move toward my sister, but he didn't rush to comfort her or shoot me an angry look or anything. Instead, he ducked his head to meet Aimee's eyes and asked, "Y'okay?"

She nodded. "Yeah. Um. Can we all sit down?"

"Sure." I took a seat on the end of a sofa close to her chair, and Rafe sat on the sofa beside me, close but not touching. Dr. Babe seated himself in a chair on the other side of Aimee's.

"First, tell me again that you're okay," I blurted. Because she looked fucking *awful.*

"I'm okay," she promised. "I'm really good. As good as a person who had heart surgery four days ago could possibly be, right?" She gave Dr. Babe a look, and he nodded in confirmation.

"I'm honestly closer to perfect than I've been in years. I just, um... I didn't sleep very well, knowing you guys were coming today. So." She lifted one delicate hand to touch her hair. "I have so much to say, I don't know where to start."

"The beginning would be good," Dr. Babe suggested.

His simple comment drew my ire like a lightning rod.

"Actually, I'd kinda like to know who *you* are first," I interrupted. "Are you Aimee's doctor?" I was pretty sure there were laws about calling patients *babe*. If not, I was gonna make sure some got written.

"Nope!" Dr. Babe said brightly. "She's technically my brother's patient. I'm just here to answer any medical questions you might have. And for Aimee's moral support." He sat forward and lifted Aimee's hand from her armrest to cradle it in his own.

I narrowed my eyes. I didn't like the way he looked at her, but Aimee clearly did. She freakin' *glowed* as she looked at him.

So, okay. I would back off. If Rafe and I could cut through so much of the bullshit between us, surely Aimee and I could do the same, and the first step was to stop being so damn prickly.

"The beginning *would* be good," Rafe said, jumping in to save me once again. He'd always been good at that. "I already told Jay everything about your diagnosis and how we ended up making our deal—"

"You mean us getting married," Aimee clarified with a wince. "Yeah." She took a breath like she was bracing herself. "Okay. This is good. So you know Dr. Corlia misdiagnosed me for years—?"

I nodded. "And Dad wouldn't want it to get around that he'd ever taken you to a specialist, since that might make it seem like he didn't trust his golf buddy. I could kick him for that."

"Right. Same. And all the while, I had a hole in my heart that meant that my blood wasn't supplying enough oxygen to my body, and nobody knew—" She broke off with a head shake. "Until I collapsed."

"I know this part, too," I said softly. "You were sick and had to quit your job. You didn't have health insurance or money. And you kept me out of the loop because you didn't want to disrupt my career." I couldn't hide a glimmer of bitterness, and I shot Rafe a glance that he met unflinchingly. "I understand why you did that, even if I completely disagree with it."

"I was feeling weak, Jay. Telling you... Having you come home... I would have felt even weaker."

Weaker? I thought we'd always made each other stronger.

"So, yeah. I asked Rafe to do me that favor. To marry me and get me on his health insurance. Because I knew he wanted to protect your career as much as I did. And I swear, I never for a second thought my super-straight brother would have a problem with it." Her mouth twisted to one side, and I winced at the reminder of how my own secrets had caused all this, too.

"I moved to the Key with Rafe and the Goodmans." She gave Rafe a small smile. "And my Florida cardiologist prescribed medication that helped me... sort of. But it had side effects. Pretty debilitating ones. I couldn't work. And I..." Aimee pushed her lips together and took a breath through her nose. "I wasn't going to be able to have kids either. It hit me hard. Really hard. You know I always wanted that—kids of my own, a career working with them, all of it. But the meds I was on weren't safe during pregnancy, and my heart wouldn't have withstood the strain without them. I felt like shit, you know? Physically, yeah, but emotionally, too. Rafe was doing his best. Beale was being his usual awesome self. The people on the Key were... you know. The usual."

"Amazing and helpful?" I ventured.

She snorted. "I was gonna say annoying but sweet. And all that only made me feel worse, because I knew I should feel grateful, and all I felt was pissed off. I didn't *want* people making sacrifices for me. I just... I wanted my life back. The life I thought I was supposed to have." She knotted her fingers together in her lap. "I know now, after being here for a while and getting some therapy, that I was grieving. But at the time? I just got more and more resentful. Which was why I started researching alternative therapies online. Remember, Rafe? I told you about some of them."

Rafe nodded slowly, cautiously.

Aimee darted another look at Dr. Babe, who watched her with an expression of loving encouragement that was... Okay, it was kinda sweet.

It also kinda made me wish I could hold Rafe's hand, too. I mean, this wasn't exactly *public*, right? I felt pretty confident he'd let me... if I tried.

"Through my research, I found this clinic here," Aimee continued. "Dave and his brother, Justin, run the heart center at St. Vincent's, and they're doing amazing research into conditions like mine."

"We lost our cousin Trace when we were teenagers because of a congenital issue pretty similar to Aimee's." Dr. Babe—Dave—rubbed his thumb over the back of Aimee's fingers. "You might say pioneering new therapies has been our mission since medical school. But it's not like we're rolling in funds, you know? So we set up here in Wyoming. It's a nice place, and the overhead is low."

"I talked to them, sent them copies of my medical records, and they offered me a chance at a *cure*," Aimee said fervently, leaning toward me and Rafe like she was willing us to understand. "A surgery, not medicine. Not just a way to stay alive, but a way to have the life I *wanted*. But the insurance company wouldn't pay."

"And I blew you off," Rafe said ruefully. "I said it was too dangerous."

She nodded. "But I contacted them again anyway—"

"She means she stalked me," Dave said with a grin. "Phone calls, emails, sliding into my Instagram DMs. I've never been so popular. But it turned out she only wanted me for my experimental heart treatments. Story of my life."

"Yeah, yeah. I fell in love with you after I'd already been enrolled, buddy. *So there.*"

Dave lifted her hand to press a kiss to her knuckle, and Aimee rolled her eyes, clearly pleased.

"Anyway. Dave told me that if I could get to Wyoming, they'd enroll me in a trial that involved a whole battery of tests over a twelve-month period. EKGs, stress tests, the works. They'd monitor me the whole time. And they'd give me a job working in the outpatient clinic in exchange for room and board, too. I just... needed a way out of Florida and a place to stay for a month or so until the trial started."

"And that's why you needed *me*," I said. "To get you to Wyoming."

I felt like an idiot.

"Yeah." She bit her lip. "I know I'm the *worst*. I should never have let you pay for that apartment for me when I knew I'd only be there a couple weeks—"

"It's not about the money, Aim. I have plenty of *money*. Why didn't you tell me?"

"Well." Aimee licked her lips. "For one thing, I never dreamed you'd show up in Denver and find out that way. But for another... I knew you'd worry. And I wanted to save you from that. And I wanted to save *me* from that, too."

"Save yourself from *me* worrying? What's that even mean?"

"It means... I didn't want you staring at me, thinking this might be the end. I didn't want to see you all upset. I didn't want to deal with your guilt or helplessness or overprotectiveness. I just... I didn't want to have to process your emotions at all. Which I guess is selfish, but..." She shrugged. "It's honest. And also, I didn't want you to try to talk me out of it. I didn't want anyone to judge me if it didn't work. I just... I wanted to handle *my* medical decisions *myself*. I didn't want to be a burden to anyone. I didn't want to be anyone else's responsibility."

Rafe flinched, then sighed.

Aimee stared down at her hands, knitting and unknitting her fingers once more. "I should have come forward about all of this a long time ago. I know that, too. But... once I started lying, I didn't know how to come clean. I didn't know how to speak up. I... I know you probably can't understand that—"

I thought of Debbie, who'd left me another two messages last night, probably begging me to go on *Dateline LA* or *Good Morning USA* or wherever people were supposed to air their private business these days. I hadn't returned her calls because I had no idea what I should say. I didn't even know what I *wanted* to say anymore.

"That part's more understandable than you think," I said softly.

"I kept telling myself that after the surgery, I'd come find you, Jay. Wherever you were in the world. And we'd talk it out. I'd explain everything about me and Rafe." Aimee sniffed. "I mean, Big Rafe made me promise I would, eventually. But then you guys found out while I was still in recovery... and here we are."

"Wait, wait. My dad made you promise?" Rafe said, startled. "What? How'd he know anything about this?"

"I told him. He, ah... found me crying one day on the beach in the secret cove on the Key. You know the one I mean?"

Both Rafe and I nodded. We'd spent many hours there stargazing.

"I didn't know what to do with myself. I wanted to come to Wyoming, but I didn't know if I could take the risk. He talked me through it. He's a great listener."

"*My dad*?" Rafe said again. "Barrel chest, attitude the size of a small country, full of shit opinions. That guy?"

She smiled. "The very one. He said he knew the truth about you and me. Had sorta guessed there was something up from the day we got married—"

"Wait, sorry," Rafe interjected. "Just one more time. This is my *father* you're speaking of. Big Rafe, mayor of Whispering Key?"

Aimee laughed. "Yup. He said he'd always figured Jay was *it* for you, your one and only, and that Jay felt the same. He didn't see how he could've gotten that wrong, so it must've been *you* who did something wrong, by marrying the wrong Rollins—"

"Ahhh." Rafe nodded. "Now it sounds like the same guy."

"So he told me whenever I was ready to leave, I should make a clean break. But he offered to help me with anything I needed, too... which is why I made him my emergency contact."

So many birth date–related details suddenly fell into place. But I was still so confused.

I turned to Rafe. "Your *dad* knew about you and me?" I demanded. "Jesus, *we* didn't even know." Christ, the man had guessed I was gay when literally no one else had?

"What *is* going on between you two?" Aimee demanded excitedly, looking back and forth between us.

Rafe stretched his arm out along the back of the sofa, and his hand accidentally-deliberately brushed the back of my neck. Reminding me he was there. Reminding me that he'd back my play, however I chose to play this.

I grabbed his hand and wove our fingers together. "Big Rafe was right, as it happens. That there was always something more between me and Rafe, even though neither of us admitted it to each other."

"Or even to ourselves, really."

I nodded and squeezed his fingers apologetically. "And now we're... together."

"I knew it." Aimee let out a relieved sigh. "That was the worst part of this, you know. Thinking maybe I fucked things up for the two of you by asking Rafe to help me out and keep my secret. Dave and I have talked about this, and he helped me see how I was isolating myself by keeping all this inside. Hiding, like I'd done something to be ashamed of, because I didn't know how to talk about my condition openly and own it."

"From what it sounds like, you've all been keeping secrets trying to make each other happy, and you've actually made each other miserable instead," Dave said. "So maybe stop lying to each other? That would be my professional suggestion."

"Yeah. I'm thinking honesty is the key from now on," Rafe agreed.

"You know, this whole conversation reminds me of a song called 'Trust,'" Dave said wistfully, "by an artist called Ari Friedr—"

"No!" I shouted, jumping to my feet in instinctive response. "Absolutely not. You shut your whore mouth right this instant and do not ruin this moment for me!"

Rafe grabbed the waistband of my pants, pulled me back down to sit next to him, and clapped a hand over my mouth. "Excuse him. He's a massive Ari fan. *Huge*."

Dave smiled complacently.

"You know, Dave," Rafe said, "I think you and I are gonna get along *just* fine."

I made a retching noise behind his hand and glared at Rafe hard enough to burn the word *demerits* into his brain, but he just smiled hugely like he wasn't worried one bit.

13

RAFE

"Holy shit." Jay threw himself on the king-sized hotel bed so hard he bounced, then stretched out his arms and legs like a very sexy starfish. "I feel so light right now! *Damn.* You know how they say you don't know how good things are until they go bad? Well, the reverse is true, too, because I didn't know how much all this stuff was holding me down."

I leaned against the dresser and watched him. He *did* seem lighter. So light he might fly away, when I really wanted him to stay with me.

I'd tried to be as honest as I knew how to be about what I wanted from him in the future, but it sure would be nice to get an idea of how he saw things working out long term.

If he saw them working out long term.

The end of summer and the Extravaganza were coming. And for all our talk of "boyfriends," I couldn't help feeling like my seventeen-year-old self, counting down my remaining days with Jay.

He toed off his boots and rolled on his side to face me, where I stood against the dresser.

"You're awfully quiet, Rafael." He patted the mattress beside him and gave me a playful grin. "And awfully far away."

I loved playful Jay. It was easily one of my top five favorite Jays, along with melty-hearted Jay, and intense-sex-face Jay, emoting-with-his-eyes-closed Jay, and the lemon-sucking Jay who appeared when I mentioned Ari Friedrich.

I took off my own boots and moved toward him, bracing myself above him with a hand on either side of his face. "This better?"

"Mmm. Somewhat."

I leaned down further to kiss him.

"Uh-huh. That's the stuff." He sighed exultantly and laced his hands behind my neck. "I feel high on honesty right now. It's even better than tequila. Go ahead, ask me anything."

"*Anything*?" I lifted one eyebrow and crawled onto the bed to straddle him, the temptation too strong to resist. "Okay, then. What does us being boyfriends look like to you, ideally?"

Jay's expression sobered. "Wow. Buzzkill." But he didn't let go of me. And, in fact, his thumbs tapped out a rhythm on my shoulders as he thought, the way he sometimes tapped the steering wheel while driving. "Well. I want to be with you as much as possible. I mean, I think that's first and foremost."

I nodded.

"I want to keep you in my life, and I'm willing to do whatever it takes to make that happen."

"Same." I smiled down at him. It had taken us years to overcomplicate shit, and only... what? Three days to get us on the right course again?

"Okay, so in your mind, what happens next for us?"

"Now... we kiss?" Jay asked hopefully.

I flopped down on the bed next to him and pushed his long hair off his gorgeous face. "I *meant*, what happens after we leave Wyoming? Or do you think we should just stay in this hotel room forever and ever?"

"Tempting. You and me, creating our own pleasure emporium." He sighed. "But that's not very responsible."

I shook my head regretfully.

"So we're going to Florida. *Duh*. I have a concert to play."

"And when we get there, are we gonna tell my family about us?"

"I mean." Jay hesitated, then nodded nervously. "I'd like to, I think. Your dad knew there was something there, even when we didn't. But..."

"Look, I'm not trying to push you for answers, I swear." I brushed my thumb over his cheekbone, grounding myself by touching him. "I just want to be clear about how things are now, what we each want, because we haven't been clear in the past, and it fucked us up. Total honesty, right? Isn't that what we said? It's okay if the answer is 'I don't know.'"

"But I do know. About this, anyway." Jay licked his lips and swallowed hard, maybe more nervous than I'd ever seen him. "I want to tell your family. I want your dad and your brothers to know. And ideally, I want us to... to have something real. An *us*. Like we used to be, but better. A gritty, not-fairy-tale thing where we share bank accounts and a house, and I force you to confine your Ari Friedrich shrine to the garage, and you get annoyed because you want to plan every part of our vacations and I refuse. I want a relationship where, even when we fight, we know it'll never break us up because we're it for each other, like your dad said."

I couldn't hold back my grin, even though I was confident I looked like a total sap. "I want that also. But Jesus, you just had to throw my dad in there, huh?" I fake-grumbled. "I still can't believe the man knew all along and never said."

I wanted to be mad about that fact, but I was too happy to be.

Yes, *me*, Rafe Goodman, the onetime angriest man on Whispering Key, too happy to work up a grudge. I was shocked, too.

But I knew as surely as day follows night that if my dad had told me where Aimee was a year ago, my know-it-all self would have ignored everything Aimee had said in her letter and gone to her, just to make sure she was okay. White-knight mode *activated*. And I probably would have fucked things up even more royally for everyone involved.

"The only problem with that picture," Jay whispered, taking my mind off my dad and returning it to the way more pleasant man on the bed with me, "is I have no idea what that kind of relationship between us would look like, practically speaking, while I'm still a… a public figure."

I felt my smile slip.

Jay's phone rang from someplace on the floor where he must have knocked it with his earlier starfishing, but he ignored it, his attention focused on me.

"Alright," I agreed. "That's okay. We can figure out what it would look like."

Jay heaved a sigh that ghosted over my skin.

"I've never told anyone else this, but the truth is, after I got famous, I decided I'd never come out publicly. And it's not because I don't accept myself, or because I have internalized homophobia or anything like that. I know my dad thinks me coming out is career sabotage, and Belinda's small group at church is praying for me, but I'm *proud* of who I am. It's there in the songs I write, you know? And I think fans would be just fine with it, too. It's just…"

"Just?" I prompted, stroking a hand down his back.

"I want my relationship to be mine. *Ours*. Private. I don't want strangers on the internet asking sly questions about whether I like to top or bottom. Oh, and I hate—I mean *hate* —the assumption that every person who stands next to me for two minutes in a grocery line must be hooking up with me. It's almost as annoying as the unsolicited boob pics."

Jay rolled so he was half on top of me and propped his fists on my chest so he could rest his chin on them. "You know how the Olivia Merry rumor started? We went to a spin class at a gym at the same time and walked out together. That's it. We'd been introduced before, but we'd never even had a conversation. Except this particular day, she said she liked my newest song, and I *smiled.* Next day, a tabloid runs a headline that we've been secretly dating for years, I wrote my album for her, and we may or may not be eloping. And all of which gets recycled pretty regularly depending on how slow BlazeNewz's celebrity feed is at any given moment... Or at least it *did*, until the whole 'getting outed at a bar' thing, so who knows what shit they'll print next? And I get so, *so* mad at the lies. I want to argue, you know? To sue them. The injustice of it kills me. But Debbie tells me constantly that you can't prove a negative, and trying to stop those stories is like trying to turn back the tide. She says all publicity is good publicity."

He sighed heavily and toyed with the crewneck of my T-shirt.

"But if it was that annoying having lies spread about me and someone I barely knew, how bad would it be if they printed lies about me and someone I actually cared about?" He shook his head. "No way would I let the crappy part of my career bleed over onto someone that way, *especially* if it's you."

"I could handle it."

"You think? Imagine, tomorrow morning, waking up to an article about Olivia and her 'unnamed rocker boyfriend' getting busy in some rooftop hotel pool in Los Angeles. Even if I'm literally sitting next to you, and you *know* it's not true, the rest of the world will believe it. All your college friends will secretly wonder. Your weird aunt in North Carolina will be all smug about it."

I grimaced. "I wouldn't like it. In fact, I'd probably hate it. But I'd deal with it." It'd be worth it.

"Would you, though? For how long? What about when they drag up your marriage to Aimee? What about when they find Vinnie the Monster Truck Emoter outside a tractor pull somewhere and get him to tell his embellished story of your torrid affair, and your friends and family have to read that shit? Any sane person would run for the hills, Rafe."

He sounded so certain and so sad, and I hated that for him. I hated it for *us*.

But, I reminded myself, this relationship thing was about ten minutes old. In time, he'd see that I meant what I said. That I was *in* this, a hundred percent.

Right now, all I wanted was that chance.

And I wanted my playful Jay back.

I hooked my leg behind his and rolled us so he was underneath me. "So, wait, just so I get it right in my future tell-all interviews... *are* you a top or a bottom?" I blinked innocently.

Jay grabbed a pillow from the stack behind us on the bed and smacked me on the head. "I'm vers. I thought we'd kind of established that."

"Pfft. No. Not *conclusively*. But what a coincidence, for I, too, am versatile."

"Fascinating." Jay attempted to look pissy, but his hands tugged at my hair the way they seemed to do when he was turned on. "That is *not* the point of this conversation."

"Maybe not for you."

"*Rafe*," he mock scolded.

"*Jaaaay*," I scolded right back. "Kiss me, babe. Kiss me because it's been a whole day since you've really kissed me, and longer than that since I got to hold you."

He shook his head up at me, exasperated. "Arguing with you is going to be impossible, isn't it?"

I nodded. "Because I'm always right, and that will be your cross to bear. *Kiss me*," I repeated.

He held my head in his hands and lifted up to take my mouth, licking into me so slow and dreamlike it felt like we were moving underwater. As always, the touch of his lips to mine was like heaven.

"You know," I said when he'd pulled back for breath, "when you and I were out on the boat, I used to imagine you—"

Jay's phone rang again, and I glanced over my shoulder toward the floor. "You wanna get that? Could be important."

Jay shook his head. "Hells no. Four people in the whole world have my number. You're here, Debbie can wait, Aimee was fine half an hour ago and she'd call you if it were an emergency, and Oak would too since he has your number now. I'm pretty sure he likes you."

"Hmph." I wasn't sure how I felt about that.

Jay kissed me again, hard and fast this time. "Look, if Chet's sold our story to the tabloids, or the footage of you karaoke-ing 'Pretty Girl' has gone viral, we can wait until we're done to hear about it. Thirty minutes won't make much difference."

"Half an hour?" I wrinkled my nose. "As if."

"Fifteen minutes?" His green eyes danced.

I raised an eyebrow.

"Fine, fine. I meant we'll be at this for hours and hours, for you no doubt have impressive stamina." He coughed lightly. "Despite all evidence to the contrary in rounds one through five."

"*Excuse* you?" I demanded. "Was this a competition and I was unaware?"

God, I'd forgotten this. How much I loved when he teased me and got competitive. How it lit me up inside.

"It's *always* a competition. And we always both win." Jay bit the corner of his lip. "Now, what were you imagining, back on the boat?"

I shifted to his side so I could run my hand down his chest to the hem of his thin T-shirt, then back up, bunching the material over my hand. I tweaked his nipple with a finger, and he gasped.

"All those days in the sunshine, you and me half-naked. I imagined being able to touch you like this. To just reach over and kiss you. Run my hands over your warm skin."

Jay's pupils dilated, and his abs contracted under my hand. "Aw," he breathed. "That's so sweet."

"Sweet?" I tweaked his nipple harder. "*Sweet*?"

He nodded. "I had fantasies of you, too, you know. But mine were *way* filthier."

"Yeah?" My heart banged out a crazy rhythm as I moved my hand down further so I could outline the hard length jutting against the front of his jeans. More competition? I was down. "How filthy?"

Jay's hips rocked up toward my fingers. "I... *hngh*. I had you bent over the captain's chair on the *Mary Anna*."

Oh, fuck. "*I* was bent over, huh?"

My cock went from half-hard to fully erect in the span of a breath at the idea.

"In that one you were," Jay said in that rough, beautiful voice. "There was another one where you took me out to that tiny island where Beale used to count the plovers—"

"Menucha." I pressed the heel of my hand against Jay's dick, and he bucked his hips.

"Yeah," he groaned, squeezing his eyes shut. "And there were birds all around, taunting us with their beaks and their little bird eyes, and you refused to let me leave unless I sucked your dick right there on the dock." He shivered happily and cracked one eye open. "That one came a bit later. One of my dubcon, post-Fifty-Shades-era Rafe fantasies."

"Your fantasies about me are divided into eras?"

"Yours aren't?"

"Nope. They're kind of perennial favorites. Classics, if you will." I unbuttoned his jeans and clasped him through his boxers, which were already damp with precum. Christ, he was easy. And fuck did I love it. "Can't go wrong with a classic."

"Mmmmph." He pushed his jeans and underwear all the way off so he was bare from the waist down. "I'm developing a new fondness for the classics." He grabbed my palm and licked it, getting it good and wet before settling it directly on his cock and wrapping my fingers around him. When I jacked him lightly, he moaned like a porn star.

I'd never been so amused and so aroused at the same time. The way the simplest touch amped him up was the most erotic thing I'd ever experienced.

"I wanted to fuck you on the beach," I whispered. "On one of those nights when we lit campfires."

"Right there on the beach?" He spread his legs wide.

"Mmmm. In the cove. But we'd have to be really quiet because anyone could hear us." I dipped a hand down to cup his balls, weighing them in my hand.

Jay panted his approval. But the competitive fucker wouldn't give up. "I maybe also pondered what it would be like to be stuck inside that old bunker in the backyard that your dad uses as his man cave. Just the two of us, comforting each other because the world was ending. One last patriotic fuck."

How could he make me want to laugh out loud while also making me quake from the need to hold him down, fuck him into the mattress, and cover him in my cum?

It was a mystery, alright.

But Jay Rollins's dreammaker voice had a special kind of magic to it. One that wove fantasies into realities and turned everyday reality into a kind of fantasy, too.

I leaned into him, kissing him hard and deep, sucking on his tongue to taste the honey essence while I worked him with my hand.

"Since we don't have a beach or a bomb shelter handy," I gritted out sometime later, "maybe you need to tell me a little bit more about this captain's chair fantasy so we can make that happen."

Jay's eyes popped open, glassy and unfocused. "Wait, for real? Now? Here?"

"Where else but here in our very own pleasure emporium?"

"Are you sure?"

I attempted to look severe instead of severely aroused. "Was questioning me part of the script? Are you getting off on it?"

Jay's laugh turned into a groan, and he stilled my hand. "There was no questioning anything. For either of us. And no script either. *That* was the fantasy."

I was so on board with that.

"Tell me where you want me... Captain."

"Fuck." Jay grabbed the base of his cock and rolled off the bed. He stared down at me assessingly, pinching his lip between his thumb and forefinger. "You're wearing way too many clothes, sailor."

I bit my lip and stood up also, shucking my clothes. My poor cock was so relieved, it bobbed against my stomach.

"Mother of God," he breathed.

"He's saluting you," I told Jay solemnly.

Jay licked his lips as he drank me in, and I felt about ten feet tall. No one had ever looked at me that way. *No one.*

"Get over to the window," he croaked.

I hesitated. The sun was close to setting, but it was still very much daylight, and I was very, very naked. We were on the second floor of the hotel, sure, but if anyone looked up…

My cock throbbed, clearly on board with the idea.

"You disobeying me already?"

I grinned. "No, sir." I crossed the room to the window and threw open the curtains. Outside, there was a half-full parking lot and a stand of trees. To say I'd never done anything remotely like this was to understate the case greatly.

"What if someone sees you?" I demanded.

Jay came up behind me and smoothed his palm down my spine. His breathing was already rough, which cranked my excitement up exponentially. "The sun's glinting off the windows. Probably."

"Probably?"

"Well… Definitely too much for them to see *me.*"

I shivered.

Jay leaned down and whispered in my ear. "Would you say this was more or less adventurous than the monster truck rally?"

There was no comparison, simply because it was *him,* and his satisfied tone said he knew it. Like maybe he felt the same about me.

"Not quite the Gulf of Mexico out there, but the fantasy was always more about who than where." He fisted my hair in his hand and brought me in for a kiss, then whispered, "Bend over a little, babe. Palms on the glass."

I complied quickly, squeezing my eyes in helpless arousal. When was the last time I'd let someone direct me like this, especially during sex?

Never. The answer was never. And it made me feel curiously vulnerable and so turned on I could scream.

Long seconds passed, and nothing happened. I knew Jay was right behind me—his honey scent surrounded me, and the heat of his gaze was nearly palpable—but if the man didn't touch me soon, I was going to explode.

"Is there more to this, *Captain*?" I demanded hoarsely. "Because I'm not super into it, gotta be honest."

Jay flattened himself against me, the heat of his smooth chest fucking delicious against my back, and I realized he'd gotten rid of his shirt at some point. He ran one hand over the curve of my ass, then around to cup my cock, which was rock hard even though nothing had touched it but cool air and sunshine.

"I think you're lying," he gritted out. "I think you like having my eyes on you."

"*Fuck*, Jay, don't stop," I pleaded. "I like having any part of you on any part of me, but I've gotta say, I like your hands better than your eyes."

"Yeah? Like this?" Jay caressed the length of me from root to tip, and I writhed.

"More," I commanded. "Harder. Tighter. Just *more*."

But apparently driving me demented was part of the fantasy for him, because he took his sweet damn time, jacking me lightly while he dragged his mouth over each vertebra of my spine from my nape to my ass, licking and sucking and murmuring soft nonsense into my skin.

"I want to make you feel phenomenal, Rafe Goodman. I want to give you as much pleasure as you can handle... and then I want to give you more. I want to fuck you so deep, I'll become part of your DNA, and you'll start to see yourself the way I see you. Strong. Steadfast. *Mine*."

I shuddered and shivered, both from the breath blowing over my sensitive skin and from the words he was saying. I felt them sinking into me, becoming part of me. God, I wanted him so badly.

"Jay—" I began.

When he reached the small of my back, he sank to his knees, pulling my cheeks apart to lick at my seam, and I forgot what I was going to say.

Then his tongue flattened over my hole, teasing the hyper-sensitive skin there and lighting up every nerve ending in my entire body, and I forgot how words worked entirely.

"*Ohmahazmagad!*"

He chuckled lightly and licked over me again, with just the tip this time, tracing the ring with tiny strokes that shot an electric current straight to my cock, making it legit *pulse* against my stomach in ecstasy and leak all over the place, too.

I'd never felt anything that good in my life, and it startled the fuck out of me. My biceps turned to jelly, and I ended up collapsing against the window with my cheek pressed to the glass, making rough, needy, animalistic noises I hadn't known I could make.

I thrust my ass back against his face helplessly, begging him for more. More sensation, more fullness, more *him*.

"Please, Jay?" I begged. "Fuck me."

"Yeah." He squeezed my ass roughly. "You want that?"

"Fuck yeah. There's *nothing* I don't want with you."

I reached behind me blindly, my fingers sliding off his smooth skin until I hooked my fingers around his hip and tugged him against me so his dick could ride the crease of my ass.

"*Fuck*," I groaned.

Jay rutted against me, then pulled back shakily.

"Okay, shit. Strategic error. I forgot supplies. Just... just stay right there, sailor." He leaned over to kiss me, hard and messy, and then he disappeared in a whirl.

I almost laughed because I loved him so damn much, it felt like it was bubbling out of me. I hadn't felt this free in a really long time.

"There's lube in my bag. It's right on top of the suitcase," I called over my shoulder.

"Okay." He reappeared so fast I was pretty sure he'd broken land speed records and dumped the contents of my toiletry bag on the small table by the window. His hands shook, which I swear just made me feel crazier.

"Lube!" he said triumphantly, holding up a tube. "But... condoms?"

I blinked. Shook my head. "I wasn't expecting to need any."

His eyes met mine in a panic. "Oh, God. Me neither."

I leaned over to grab his wrist. "Do we need them? I..." I swallowed. "I haven't been with anyone in a *long* time, and I've been tested."

"I... I've been on PreP, and I'm tested regularly, too. I just..." He stared down at my cock and licked his lips. "I've never."

"Yeah? Me neither." We stared at each other for a long beat as the weight of that fell between us like a concussion grenade, stunning us both. I wanted that first with him, that *commitment* with him, so damn badly.

But when he closed his eyes and sucked in a breath, I made myself let go of his wrist, because—*shit*—there was no way I was going to force this either. That would defeat the purpose.

I smiled genuinely. "Pretty sure they warned us in Health class that you're never supposed to decide this shit in the heat of the moment. So how about we table this for now and—"

"Jesus fuck, Rafael. You think I don't want to?" Jay's eyes opened and blazed with arousal. His fingers clenched around the lube in his hand. "I had to stop to think about chord progressions for a second there or I was gonna lose it before I got inside you." He leaned into me. "Turn around."

I snorted but let him manhandle me with his insistent hands until my face was pressed against the glass. I heard the *snick* of the lube cap, and then cold fingers toyed at my entrance, pushing inside me with almost no resistance since he'd worked me so thoroughly already.

"Oh, fuck yes," he said. "This ass. This ass is what dreams are made of."

I laughed... then groaned when he added a second finger and moved deeper, tagging my prostate.

"Do you have any idea how hot you are right now, Rafe Goodman?"

I didn't. All I could feel was the heat of the man behind me. A fire I wanted to throw myself into with abandon.

"Hurry," I whispered, my breath fogging the glass. "Fuck, baby, just do it."

Jay was clearly in a mood to be accommodating, because after another flick of the lube cap, his blunt head prodded my entrance, and I reached back to grab him and guide him inside of me.

"Jesus," we both sighed in simultaneous satisfaction as he moved against me, filling me, so that even the burn of his entrance felt like fucking perfection.

"I love this," he muttered. "Fuck, I love being inside you. I... this..." He gripped my hips harder, thrust deeper. "All my words are gone. *Fuck*."

He reached around to grasp my cock with his long, calloused fingers, and my palms went damp, sliding against the smooth glass.

The only coherent thought in my brain was "Damn, I really wish I could see his face."

And then, like he could read my mind, Jay pulled out and spun me around, kissed me hard, and shoved me onto the bed. He pushed a pillow under my hips, then crawled in between my legs, pushed my knee to my chest. The whole process took half a minute, and I opened my mouth to remark on how sexy his efficiency was...

But then he pushed inside me again, hard and huge, until he bottomed out, and my fucking toes curled because it felt that good.

"Holy mother of fuck," I breathed.

Jay muttered something as he pumped into me, but I was not paying attention. My brain had officially shorted out, and if Lorenna McKetcham had appeared in the corner of the room to offer tips, I wouldn't have noticed or cared. The entire focus of my being was on the cock filling me and the green eyes staring down at me.

My orgasm barreled into me, yanking all the gravity from the room. The bed was gone, the room was gone, and my entire body floated for an instant, tethered to nothing but Jay.

Which was exactly how I wanted it.

Ideally forever.

Jay shook and threw his head back, calling my name when he came, and when it was over, he stared down at me intently, chest heaving like a bellows, our bodies still connected.

He dragged a hand through the sweaty hair on my forehead, pushing it off my face.

"What's that look mean?" I wheezed.

He shook his head. "Nothing. Just... appreciating the moment."

"The fulfillment of your fantasy?"

"All my fantasies," he whispered tenderly. "*Better* than my fantasies."

"Yeah." Then a thought occurred to me, and I grinned smugly.

Jay narrowed his eyes. "What's *that* look mean?"

"It means I told you I could last more than half an hour. And I did."

14

———

JAY

"I'm just saying, waffles remain the superior food." Rafe's voice drifted out of the bathroom, along with the sound of running water as he shaved. "They're crispy. They're airy. They have crevices to hold butter. Pancakes are fine. They're great. But I'd think you'd have learned the truth about waffles by now."

"And *I'm* just saying you're as hopelessly misguided now as you ever were, because there's *still* no realm where soft, pillowy, butter-and-syrup-absorbent pancakes are ranked under waffles," I called back, dragging my suitcase onto the hotel bed so I could dig out a fresh pair of jeans. "And I'll fight you on that."

"Have you ever heard of chicken and pancakes? No you haven't. But chicken and *waffles*? That's a staple food. Think about it."

"Oh, I'm thinking!" I shouted back, grinning like an idiot. "I'm thinking you just proved my point, because I bet the Venn diagram of people who think waffles are superior and the people who eat fried chicken with maple syrup is a *circle*."

Rafe stepped out of the bathroom, razor in one hand, face still mostly covered in shaving cream, bare chest gleaming in the light, towel wrapped around his waist, pure sex exuding from every freakin' pore. "I'm gonna make you eat those words."

"Mmm. I invite you to try," I countered, but the words came out a little too warm and raspy, more invitation than challenge, and Rafe's answering smile as he turned back to the sink said he heard it loud and clear.

I smiled, too. I really loved our silly conversations almost as much as I loved our competitiveness over absolutely everything. We'd just eaten breakfast, and it was amazing how pancakes three days in a row could improve a man's outlook on life. The sun was shining. Birds were chirping. I was ready to write a love song sappier than any hair metal band ever recorded called "Rafe Goodman Is My Fucking Boyfriend, Fuck Yeah," and life was really, *really* good.

Which, of course, was when my phone started vibrating on the dresser with text message alerts.

"Is that Debbie again?" Rafe called—damn his eagle ears. "You've gotta answer one of these days and find out what she wants, babe. Whatever it is, we'll deal with it. I mean, what's the worst that could happen?"

I blew out a breath. "Her saying she's dropping me as a client because I refuse to do a big media thing. My recording career might be over. I might be forced to give up my apartment, change my name, live off my savings until I'm penniless, and spend the next forty years of my life camped out on a park bench, all alone, talking to myself about how I used to be famous."

"Aw, honey. You know that last part will never happen," Rafe chided gently from the bathroom.

I pressed a hand to my heart. "You mean, I won't be alone 'cause you'll be camping out with me? That's so sw—"

"God, no." He appeared in the doorway again. "I meant, you'd never last forty years on a park bench with all those pigeons around."

I laugh-sputtered and threw a pair of balled-up socks at him, but he ducked back inside to avoid them. "Asshole."

"But I'm *your* asshole, baby," he called back.

I snorted. "I think that line sounded better in your head!" I grabbed the phone off the dresser and punched in my passcode, grinning like a fool now that Rafe was in the bathroom and couldn't see me.

But when I opened the message app to see what Debbie wanted, my smile fell away because I saw that the messages weren't from Debbie.

And, in fact... this wasn't my phone.

Rafe came out of the bathroom wearing one towel and drying his face with another. "What's the message say?"

"It's Littlejohn. He's all upset because Mariah Berger passed away, whoever the heck that is." I glanced up at him and shook the phone in my hand. "This is *yours*."

"Oh." He shrugged, but then his eyebrows winged up. "Wait, how'd you open it?"

"I just… typed my code!"

His eyes widened. "Wait, my birthday is your password?"

I felt my face go hot.

"Oh, shit! Is this what Gage meant when he said we should play 'Guess My Password'?"

"He said that?" I demanded. The boy was dead meat.

"You are so freakin' cute when you blush." Rafe pressed a hard kiss to my lips and took his phone from my hand. "Don't be embarrassed, Jay. That's the sweetest thing ever."

"Pfft. I wasn't blushing because your birthday is *my* passcode! I was blushing because your birthday is *your* passcode. Don't you know social engineering is by far the greatest threat to cybersecurity?" I quoted Gage with no regrets. "You should be ashamed."

"So, so sweet." He grinned smugly and patted my ass before dealing with his texts.

He was lucky his smugness did it for me.

"*Hmph.*" I scooted away to fuss with my suitcase, refolding the clothes there. "Did you still wanna visit Aimee before we leave? What time should we go?"

"Huh?" Rafe looked up from his phone with a scowl still on his face. "Oh, sorry. This Extravaganza stuff." He shook his head in exasperation. "My dad has *three* new food trucks he's already signed contracts with, Dale Jennings threw his back out, and Gage can't find a replacement contractor to fix the stage scaffolding on short notice…"

"And Ms. Berger passed on."

"That too," Rafe agreed. "I keep telling myself that this whole mess is my *dad*'s thing, right? I mean, he came up with the idea, he put the limitations on it, and he's the one who keeps blowing through them. He's the one who should deal with the fallout. But at the same time…"

"It's your responsibility now." I clasped my hands behind his neck. "You want things to go right. You don't wanna let people down. It's your nature."

"Yeah." The word came out like a confession. "It's weird, because I kinda hated this project from the beginning. I wanted nothing to do with it when my dad first put me in charge of it." His thumbs rubbed circles on my hips above my jeans. "Before you crashed into the meeting the other day, I told myself the Extravaganza was the one last thing I was gonna do. My last responsibility on the Key. But…"

"But?"

"How'd you put it the other day? They're odd ducks, but they're our odd ducks?"

I nodded.

"Well, they're ridiculous responsibilities, but they're *my* responsibilities, I guess."

"Mmmhmm. So what you're saying is that it's not so much the Extravaganza that's stressing you out, it's being away from there when there's so much to be done."

Rafe hesitated, then nodded. "You hit the nail on the head."

"So, we leave for Florida right now! Aimee won't mind. We'll gas up the van and take shifts driving through the night. We'll be there tomorrow at noon, and then we'll have a whole afternoon to iron things out before the Extravaganza officially starts on Saturday."

"If we did that, I'd be too exhausted to do much of anything tomorrow night." He shook his head. "I think it's time for me to face my fear of flying. Bum bum *bum*."

"Wait, be serious." I remembered his face in the airport bathroom, even if *he* wanted to make jokes about it. "Are you sure?"

"Yeah, I think so. The therapist I saw after the crash gave me tips on distracting and reassuring myself when I was ready to get on a plane. I just never had a compelling reason to face my fear until now."

I nodded. "The Extravaganza."

Rafe's lips tipped up. "I mean, yeah. But mostly... I've got a boyfriend who goes on tour and stuff. I need to fly if I want to see him play." He stuck his fingers in my belt loops and pulled me closer. "And I do."

That deep sense of rightness I only felt with Rafe settled over me, momentarily blocking out all the other problems in the world.

"I'll hold your hand the whole time," I promised.

"Thank you, baby." He gave me a thoughtful look. "But that might make it tricky to keep our relationship on the down low, huh?"

"Oh." I literally hadn't considered that, not even for a second.

"It's fine," Rafe hurried to reassure me. "I told you that last night. You don't owe anybody *anything*, Jay Don. Not the media, not your fans, not even me. We'll figure it out. One thing at a time."

"Yeah." I chewed my lip. "But it's not fair to ask you to hide—"

"You didn't ask, babe, I'm offering. Because I don't need the world to know, as long as you're cool with telling my family. And as long as there are no more twins from Peoria." His possessive growl made me shiver in the best way.

"I never said they were twins!" I argued.

He shrugged. "I might have added that detail when I was filing the mental image away. Point is, for three years I held Aimee's secret so you wouldn't have to make a hard choice. And I was a dumbass, because life is full of hard choices every single day. There are no perfect options. The best you can do is make choices that line up with your priorities, just like you told Chet. So maybe I'll go on tour and be your muse like Chrissea. Maybe we'll build a recording studio in my yard and you'll live there with me when you're not on tour. We'll figure it out as we go," he repeated.

I frowned. I wanted to believe that he meant that. I mean, I *did* believe he *thought* he meant it. But also, I wasn't sure how long he could be okay with something so unfair to him. I just wasn't sure what I could do to make it better.

"Stop overthinking." He shook me lightly. "Say it with me: we'll figure it out as we go."

I sighed. "We'll figure it out as we go," I repeated obediently.

He winked. "Good." He typed something into his phone one-handed, still holding me tightly with the other. "Ah, shit. No flights until tomorrow at ten. Oh, well. I think we can figure out some creative ways to pass the time between now and then, eh?"

He finished plugging in our ticket information and set the phone on the dresser.

"Now. Where were we?" He wrapped both arms around me again.

"I think we were—"

His phone buzzed again, and he glanced down... then groaned.

"Lorenna asked me to ask you to call your next album *Phalluses*. She ordered three cases of dick balloons, and they're just sitting in her carport."

"Done."

He laughed and leaned in so our foreheads rested together. When I stroked my hand over his hair, he relaxed under my touch.

"You know, I kinda love that you'll stop at nothing to help people you care about," I said. "It's maybe your best feature. Even better than your *big, broad* shoulders."

Rafe whistled. "High praise." After a pause, he added, "You know you're at the top of that list, right? Of people I care about."

"Yeah." I kinda knew it, but hearing him say it was a whole other thing. Entire swarms of butterflies beat at the walls of my stomach. "I'm kind of an overnight success at this relationship business, when you think about it. Today I'm at the top of the list, but I was only promoted to boyfriend yesterday, and three days ago you couldn't stand me."

"No, I couldn't stand feeling so much for you and thinking you didn't feel the same," he corrected softly. "I built up a wall to keep you out, but it didn't work. These feelings were already inside me, getting stronger all this time. Now I feel so much, it's like I'm flooded with it. It overwhelms me."

I knew exactly what he meant. I felt so much it scared me to death when I thought of being without him again. I tugged on his hair to pull him back so I could kiss him, tasting his mint toothpaste and his own warm, comforting sweetness.

When I pulled away, we were both breathing hard. "I think maybe leave the romantic metaphors to me," I teased. "You make your feelings sound like Oak's sewage leak. Eight inches deep and rising fast."

Rafe kissed me again, sliding a hand down the back of my jeans to cup my ass and pull me against him. The hard ridge of his cock pressed against mine, and I moaned exultantly. "Some things are definitely rising fast," he whispered.

"That could be serious," I said solemnly. "We could—"

Rafe's phone vibrated on the dresser at the same time my phone sang out "The Imperial March" from the nightstand.

"Fuck," Rafe groaned. "Okay, I've changed my mind. Responsibility is stupid. We should throw away our phones and just stay here."

"Agreed," I breathed. "Welcome to Jay and Rafe's Private Pleasure Emporium in Nowheresville, Wyoming. Population: us."

But after another deep sigh, Rafe let go of me and pushed me toward the nightstand, then answered his own call.

I took a deep breath and held the phone to my ear. "Debbie! Hey. Sorry I haven't called you back. Look, I know you're not going to like this, but I'm definitely not doing any inter—"

"Jayd, honey, stop!" Debbie trilled. "You're such a card! Like I could ever be mad at my favorite, *favorite* client! How are you, sweetie?"

Sweetie? I pulled the phone away from my ear to check the caller ID, half-convinced I was being punked. "Uh. Good. You?"

"I am *exultant*, Jayd! Proud, thrilled, satisfied."

"Oh." She hadn't been this excited when my album went gold. "Cool."

"And I'm about to make *you* excited, too. You ready?"

I unwrapped a honey candy and put it in my mouth. "Okay? But seriously, Debbie, no inter—"

"You, Jayd Rollins, are going to Iron Pipes!" she announced like a radio DJ telling me I'd won a prize.

I nearly choked on the honey drop. "You got us tickets? Oh, wow! Wait, but doesn't it start tomorrow?"

Rafe threw himself down on the bed with a groan and started massaging his temples. His towel loosened in the process, and the sight was extremely distracting.

"Jayd? Jayd!"

"Hmm? Oh! Uh. Yeah, no, I can't go to Iron Pipes. Thanks anyway. I'm heading to Florida tomorrow. I'm playing a concert there Saturday."

Rafe lifted his head to stare at me. "Iron Pipes?" he whispered.

"Tickets? Good Lord, Jayd! We're not gonna watch the show. No, honey, they want you to *play*. A side stage performance tomorrow at seven, and the main stage Saturday!"

"I... I..." I stared at Rafe helplessly.

"*What*?" he mouthed. "*Tell me!*"

"They want *me*," I whispered, twisting the phone away from my mouth. I was half panic and half pure delight. "Iron Pipes. They want me to *play* Friday *and* Saturday. Holy shit."

"Holy shit is right! You've been dreaming of this since we were kids!" Rafe sat up and swung his legs over the side of the bed closest to me. "Ari Friedrich is gonna be there! Hurry up and say yes!"

I got excited for precisely half a second before reality set in.

"Jayd!" Debbie called impatiently.

"Yes, I'm here. I'm so sorry, Debbie, but I can't go."

She laughed. "You're hilarious, sweetheart, but stop before someone thinks you're serious! So. Your sound check is tonight at eight. No time to fly commercial, so I'm getting you a private plane. I already called in the band, and I'm getting you a room at the—"

"Yeah, but—"

"Fine, a *suite*, then, but only because you're my favorite," she said indulgently.

"No, I mean, I'm already—"

Rafe snagged the phone from my hand. "Debbie?" he rasped out in a *terrible* impression of me. "Debbie! Oh, gosh, this connection is awful. Gimme a minute. I'll call yo—" He shut the phone off abruptly, and our eyes collided. "Have you lost your mind?"

"No, I have not. I have a previous commitment. I promised your dad, Rafe. I promised *you*—"

"I'm hereby letting you out of your promise," he said quickly, leaning up to smack me lightly on the forehead with the heel of his hand. "There. You've been un-promis-ified. Go to Iron Pipes, babe."

"It doesn't work like that!" I scowled. "Your dad's been selling tickets for a show featuring *me*. Besides, I'm not leaving you to fly to Florida by yourself! I'm not the irresponsible person you thought I was."

"Jay," he chided. "I don't believe that. I never really did. You've got dreams. It inspires the crap out of me to see you fulfill 'em. So go *do it*. That's what fill-in acts are for."

Oh, right. The Cheez-Bergers in Paradise.

"Look at my nose," he added. "Not a single twitch. I truly, truly mean it."

"But I don't know how to deal with the fallout from those tabloid pictures. I still haven't made a statement, and—"

"Don't make a statement if you don't want to! Be mysterious, babe."

I rolled my eyes. "And what about you and me?" I began as my phone started ringing on the bed.

"You and I are not about the Extravaganza, just like we're not about your sister, or the kidnap van. It was always gonna be us, Jay. Those things were just the catalyst for bringing us back into the right orbit. Now we're here, and we're sticking together." He tilted his head from side to side ruefully. "Even if we're technically apart."

I bit my lip. How could I make this work, having my body in South Dakota at Iron Pipes and my heart with Rafe? But I supposed I'd have to figure it out sometime, wouldn't I, if I was ever going to go on tour without him? And maybe... maybe being without him now wouldn't feel like it had before, all hopeless yearning, because I'd know that we were okay.

"I'm just bummed I won't get to be there for the concert to see this guy I have a crush on play his heart out." Rafe flashed his killer smile.

I narrowed my eyes. "You'd better be talking about *me*, not Ari Friedrich."

"Ari Friedrich?" He blinked guilelessly. "Never heard of him."

"Correct answer," I approved. I moved between his spread knees. Then, "I'll see if I can get him to FaceTime you with me."

"Yeah?" He grinned and licked his lips. "Wow. I'd be... incredibly appreciative. I bet I could brainstorm ways to show you that appreciation."

I threaded both hands through his hair, swamped with affection.

"How many can you come up with before Debbie calls back?" I wondered.

He sank to his knees, losing his towel in the process, and smiled up at me. "Let's find out."

In the end, Debbie called two more times before I finally answered, but when I finally managed to croak out my acceptance, lying in Rafe's arms, I knew things were gonna be just fine.

Correction: Things were fucking *terrible*.

I was pacing the backstage area at Iron Pipes—which was to say, I was standing within the ring of tour busses and RVs parked in a grassy field behind the ramp to the main stage— listening to the Smoke Jumpers play to a surprisingly huge Friday afternoon crowd. The sky was pink and orange, the air smelled like grass and patchouli, and it seemed like every two minutes, a musician I admired came up and greeted me by name and told me how much they'd enjoyed my songs.

This wasn't just *a* moment; it was *the* moment. The one I'd been working for my whole life. The one I was supposed to tell my grandkids about someday.

But when I closed my eyes, all I saw were white sand beaches and swaying palm trees, busybody residents toting spaghetti casseroles, and the broad, capable shoulders of the man I loved.

I was here at this show living the dream... except hadn't Chet taught me that everyone had their own weird dreams?

And I figured out, a day too late, that this one wasn't mine. Not really. Not anymore.

Also, my cute, naive idea that it would be *easier* to be away from Rafe now that we were together? Utter bullshit. I'd realized this about the time Debbie's car service had arrived at the hotel to take me to a private airfield outside Denver. Kissing Rafe goodbye had been brutal.

All I could think was that it was too soon or something. That the ink on our relationship had barely dried. That for all that we'd talked over, and all we felt for each other, and as much as I trusted him when he said he didn't mind, Rafe couldn't possibly be happy long term if we were only together in secret. That he deserved to be my highest priority, and for me to *act* like he was my highest priority.

I'd wanted to call him last night and tell him all this, but it had been way too late by the time I got back to the hotel, even given the time difference.

I'd called him this morning instead, as soon as I woke up, but he hadn't answered.

I'd tortured myself all day, when Debbie didn't have me scheduled for a haircut, or a meeting with a stylist, or a practice session with the band, imagining my boyfriend freaking out and bowing to the porcelain gods in the Wyoming airport... and then again in the Denver airport, and then once more in New Orleans, since of course there was no such thing as a direct flight from Laramie to Sarasota.

Rafe had texted me back a couple of times to see how *I* was, but every time he texted, I was doing some stupid, less-important thing for Debbie. He'd sent a picture he'd taken above the cloud deck with the caption "Scenic Colorado," so

I knew he was en route, but when I'd asked how he was, he'd cracked jokes about Ari and avoided the question.

I really should have been with him.

My phone rang, and I hit Accept without looking at the screen.

"Rafe?"

"Dude, you've *got* to stop doing this."

I winced. "Shit. Um. Heyyy, Oak."

"Don't you dare 'Um. Heyyy' me, Jay Don Rollins," Oak said severely. "I just saw something on the freakin' internet that you're at Iron Pipes. This is how we are now? I get updates on my best friend from BlazeNewz?"

"Sorry! Sorry. It just happened yesterday." I walked out beyond the far edge of an RV, trying to find an isolated spot. "I've literally had no time to chat."

"Sure, sure. That's what they all say. You might recall that I predicted this whole thing," he reminded me. "'Cause I'm talented like that. I'm gonna start one of those 1-900 hotlines, but for gay dudes. 'I can see your future, and he's ripped and horny! If you want details, it'll be $5.99 for the first minute.'"

"Wait, is this a psychic hotline? Or a sex line?"

"Jay, why limit myself?"

I snickered... and then I sighed.

"Hey!" he complained. "Pardon me, Cinderella, but why don't you sound like a guy who just got asked to the ball?"

I scuffed my foot over a tuft of grass. "You know that expression about doing the same thing over and over again and expecting different results?"

"The definition of insanity?"

"That's the one," I agreed. "Well, here I am in fucking South Dakota, concentrating real hard on being a rock star, while the love of my life is currently flying to Florida without me. Facing his greatest fear. Alone."

Oak was silent for half a second. "Dude, I talked to you a week ago. Who...? Oh, no! Tell me you haven't fallen for Mr. Summer Lovin'. Not again."

I laughed. "Not *again*, more like... *still*. And I finally did something about it. *We* did something about it."

I filled him in briefly—very briefly—and Oak fell silent for a long moment.

"Wow," he finally said. "I'm starting to think I really *am* psychic. So what are you guys planning long term? Are you moving to Florida? Are you gonna come out publicly?"

"No. Maybe?" I rubbed my forehead. Figured *now* Oak cut directly to the point, when he was asking questions I couldn't answer. "I don't know," I hedged. "I don't know what we're doing long term. Things got kinda rushed there at the end. He wants to do whatever I want to do..."

"And you don't *know* what you wanna do, is that it?"

"Jayd?" A PA person with a clipboard gave me a friendly smile. "Thirty-minute warning."

"Coming! Oak, I've gotta go. Almost time for my set."

"Jay Don, you want my thirty-second advice?"

I felt like "no" was not an actual option. "Of course. That's why I keep calling the Gay Psychic Friend Sex Hotline," I joked.

But Oak's reply was as serious as I'd ever heard from him. "You've spent your whole career working for the next big achievement, and as soon as you get it, you change the goalposts. Reminds me of your dad, spending all his time figuring out when to buy or sell so he can move on to the next moneymaker. And that's cool for him. It makes him happy in his way. But, you... Deep down, you wanna take your time with your music. You want to build a solid family. You want to be honest and stop hiding. You want to love and be loved. It's easy to lose focus and let other people's praise be the metric for your success and happiness, but that's weak shit. It doesn't sustain. Plant something and watch it grow, Jay. Live in the moment. Stop trying to convince everyone you're capable of being successful and realize you already are."

"Oak." I gripped the phone tightly. "That was... I don't know what to say."

"Yeah, yeah." He sniffed and cleared his throat. "That'll be $5.99 for the first minute, and casual psychoanalysis isn't even my best kink."

"A total bargain," I agreed, my chest tight and brain buzzing with all the information he'd given me. "Oak, I really love you."

"'Course you do. You're not a total idiot. Just remember I'm here."

When we hung up, I stood in the field for a second, staring at the sky and thinking about what he'd said. Thinking about what I wanted.

Then I shook myself, because whatever my long-term plans were, I had a show to play.

"Jayd!"

I hadn't taken more than two steps back toward the stage when Debbie blocked my path, stepping out of the shadows like a ghoul… if ghouls wore very expensive sheath dresses and heels that must've sunk into the ground with every step.

"Uh, hey, Debbie. They already came to get me. I'm on my way." I lifted my chin toward the stage.

"Lovely! But that's not why I ruined these Louboutins for you. Two words: George Maren."

"One word: Who?"

Her eye roll was visible even in the twilight. "George Maren. The journalist. He wants to meet with you tomorrow to shadow you for a while and do an interview."

"Ah, I see. One more word: No." I stepped around her toward the stage ramp.

"Jayd!" Debbie trailed after me. "George Maren is gay. He's a veteran reporter. He's done articles for *Rolling Stone* and—"

"And I was very clear. I'm not making some big 'I'm Gay' announcement. No way."

"He's willing to let you control the narrative! I don't think you understand what a big deal this is." She tugged at my elbow with her long-taloned hand. "You can spend the whole time talking about your commitment to charity. You can talk about basketball—"

"I don't know the first thing about basketball."

"You can play this any way you want."

I stopped and turned to face her. "I don't want to *play it*. I just want to live my life. Play my music." I hesitated. "I'm in love, Debbie."

"Oh good God. Tell me it's not the guy from the bar!"

"No... though I hear he's actually really nice. I'm in love with my best friend. A guy from this island on the west coast of Florida that's so tiny, it doesn't have a direct bridge to the mainland anymore. A guy who..." Oh, why not be honest? If I ever planned to tell anyone about this, Debbie had to hear it first. "A guy who cared about me so much, he married my sister so she could get on his health insurance so I wouldn't have to quit music to take care of her. The guy who inspired *Constellations*. And that album is the only statement I want to make to the world about him or my sexuality. I don't want to invite anyone to start speculating about me."

"Jayd, darling, you're adorable. You do realize that people already speculate about you, right? Who you date, boxers or briefs, Olivia Merry or not. They misinterpret your lyrics. They make up stories for ratings. You don't *have* to give the media an entree, darling. Rats climb in through the drains."

"Yeah, well, if I did make a statement, they'd come after my boyfriend. I am *not* letting that happen."

"You want to protect him. Because you're a protective sort of person."

"Exactly," I agreed instantly. Then I frowned. This wasn't the same thing as wanting to protect Aimee, though. Aimee hadn't wanted or needed my protection. Rafe, on the other hand...

Uh. Wait. *Was* it the same thing?

I rubbed my forehead. I could feel my sleepless night catching up to me. "I don't owe anyone anything," I said staunchly, reciting Rafe's words from the day before. "I just want to make music."

"No one ever said you owe it to *them*, silly. You owe it to yourself and to your partner to dispel all the wild speculation and tell the truth. You know, it's ironic that you want to hold back with this," she remarked coolly. "You have a rare gift for writing lyrics that are honest and universally understood. In fact, I've had several acts approach me about the possibility of you writing material for them—"

"Seriously?" I wrinkled my forehead and wondered if one of them was Chet and the Newsmen. "Look, I'm not ready to make any decisions right now, okay? I have to think about this. Process it."

"Of course. And find out what your boyfriend thinks."

"No, I'm pretty sure I know what *he* thinks. But he doesn't understand how bad it can get with the media."

Though her forehead was incapable of wrinkling, I could sense Debbie's exasperation. "Jayd, sweetheart, what exactly do you think my job is? I'm not just a pretty face who takes twenty percent. If the media goes after your boyfriend, I'll personally ensure that heads *roll*. I would have clapped back already on *your* behalf, if you hadn't tied my hands."

"Oh." I had done that, hadn't I?

"Tomorrow. George Maren." She nodded firmly and glanced down at her phone. "Okay, fifteen minutes to showtime. You ready?"

"Uh... No?" I laughed weakly. "You go on. I'm gonna hang back for a minute."

I felt raw and way too vulnerable to head backstage yet. Like my thick skin had been exfoliated by other people's feelings or something. I'd been gearing myself up for a battle—to keep my privacy, to protect Rafe and our fledgling relation-ship—only to find that people were really supportive. That they *cared*, way more than I'd ever thought they did, and they wanted me to make my own choices.

It was really anticlimactic.

But missing Rafe was like an aching tooth. I wanted him with me. Holding my hand. Calming me down. Smiling that smile where one side of his mouth hitched up higher than the other, while his dancing eyes teased me without a word. Reminding me that we were a team.

When my phone began vibrating in my hand over and over again, I almost tossed the damn thing away, because I couldn't handle one more *feeling* at that moment. But I glanced down in case Rafe needed me...

And saw my phone had exploded with texts.

GAGE

Welcome to the inaugural meeting of Whispering Key's Jayd Rollins Fan Club!

LITTLEJOHN

Dang it, Gage. We said I was gonna do the
welcome message! We freakin' voted.
Uncool, bro.

LORENNAM

You and Dale voted, LJ. The rest of us were
not informed, otherwise I'd be president.

TOBY

Stick to the point, people! Otherwise Jayd's
gonna remove himself from this convo.
Hello, Jayd, precious! Happy Pype Festival!

GAGE

It's called Iron Pipes, Trey. You're thinking of
the Fyre Festival.

TOBY

It's…not the same thing, then?

GAGE

Let me interpret this for you. Iron Pipes is to
Fyre Festival what Chanel is to secondhand
Primark.

TOBY

Oh dear God!!!!! I'm so sorry!!!!! Happy IRON
PIPES, Jayd!!!!

I laughed out loud, and it was kind of a watery, sniffly
sound. How had all these names gotten added to my phone?
How did they all have my number?

Except I knew. Of course I knew. Only one man could have
done it. Only one man would have thought to do it. And
only one man in the vicinity had had the code.

LITTLEJOHN

He's not replying. Is he there? JAYD, ARE
YOU THERE?

BEALE

Could be that you've written 10 messages in 30 seconds. Chill out. Some of us need a minute to think up an answer.

LITTLEJOHN

Maybe he's meditating before the show. Sting does that.

LORENNAM

I thought he did the tantric sex.

FENN

I don't think Jayd's having tantric sex. Not while Rafe's on a plane for at least two more hours.

MASON

Wait, are they together? Together-together? Officially together?

GAGE

I will bet literally any amount of money they are. Jayd, pls confirm.

LORENNAM

Maybe Jayd's already singing! SING IT, JAYD! What time does he go on? SHAKE YOUR MONEYMAKER, HONEYBUNCH!

GAGE

IDEK. Rafe didn't say, probs bc he doesn't understand how time zones work anyway.

JONQUIL

What's IDEK?

MASON

I don't even know.

JONQUIL

Yes, honey, that's why I was asking Gage.

I snort-giggled. It was like Rafe had known that I'd need this. Precisely this. The ridiculousness. The love.

> **GAGE**
>
> The text just said "Maybe let Jay know you're all thinking of him and you're not mad."
>
> **DONCORLEONE OF WHISPERING KEY**
>
> Mad? Why would we be mad?
>
> **GAGE**
>
> Because Jayd's missing the concert, Dad.
>
> **DONCORLEONE OF WHISPERING KEY**
>
> Only so he can play a bigger concert, bringing even more glory to the island!

I laugh-sniffled again. God. *God.* I loved these people, *my* odd ducks, so much.

But I loved Rafe more. And I hadn't even told him yet.

I'd been so worried about all the other details—the hows and whens of coming out and being with Rafe, the whats and wheres of navigating a career and a relationship simul- taneously—that I'd forgotten that *why* was the most impor- tant component of all.

And then he'd reminded me.

And Oak had reminded me.

And even *Debbie* reminded me.

And nearly every Whispering Keyster had let me know, too.

And at that moment, I finally understood what Rafe had meant when he said we'd figure it out "one thing at a time." Not just that we'd have a conversation and make big decisions about all the things—though that, too—but that we'd keep talking, keep re-evaluating, and keep reminding each other about what was important. That the best way to protect each other's hearts wasn't to make decisions for each other, but to listen.

And to trust.

And to be on the same team.

> **GAGE**
>
> But Jayd might not know you feel that way, hence the texts.
>
> **DONCORLEONE OF WHISPERING KEY**
>
> Oh. Well, Gloria and I send our love, Jayd! We're not angry, son! We just want our boys happy, and that means you. Knock 'em dead.
>
> **JONQUIL**
>
> How lovely!
>
> **FENN**
>
> Wow. Who even are you right now, Uncle Rafe?
>
> **DONCORLEONE OF WHISPERING KEY**
>
> Of course, if Jayd wanted to mention Whispering Key while he was doing his concert, and maybe say it had the prettiest beaches in the world, that wouldn't go amiss!
>
> **GAGE**
>
> Dad!
>
> **BEALE**
>
> God, Dad, really?
>
> **FENN**
>
> Aaaand he's back, folks.

I lifted the collar of my T-shirt to wipe my eyes, caught between tears and laughter, but feeling lighter and freer than I had in a long time. I knew what I wanted. I knew what I wasn't going to compromise on.

LITTLEJOHN

FYI: We're watching the replay of Iron Pipes on Pay-Per-View next week at my place! I'm making vegan spaghetti pie. Everyone's invited.

TOBY

Let's move the party planning over to the Party Planning Chat. We love you, Jayd! Break a leg!

BEALE

And we're not upset! Not even a little.

LITTLEJOHN

Nope! Ain't your fault Quincy Berger told Rafe this morning that he and the rest of the Cheez-Bergers will be sitting shiva for Quincy's mom this week! Rafe'll figure out a new act.

LORENNAM

Sure he will!

JONQUIL

Yes! IDEK!! (Does that mean I agree?)

DONCORLEONE OF WHISPERING KEY

He's already found a new act! A Jayd Rollins cover band that won the Cass County Fair for the last five years! I knew Rafe wouldn't let us down.

My jaw dropped. I only knew of *one* Jayd Rollins cover band, and I was pretty sure Big Rafe meant they'd won *four* of the last five years.

Damn it, Rafe hadn't told me the Cheez-Bergers canceled! But then again, I hadn't talked to him all day. Maybe because he'd been a little busy trying to coordinate *Chet* flying in to save the Key.

To sing my songs.

In front of my friends.

As a favor to my boyfriend.

I ground my teeth together. Yeah, I wasn't too thrilled about that.

But Rafe hadn't been too busy to coordinate a fan club intervention for me, though. Which told me all I needed to know about my boyfriend's priorities…

And helped me finally, *finally* solidify my own.

Now I just needed to go and break the news to Debbie.

ME

I love you guys. Can we do a group call in, say, an hour and a half? After my set? I have a fun idea for the Extravaganza concert. I just need to call in my friend Oak to help us coordinate it.

GAGE

We'll be ready.

ME

Awesome. Hey, um… don't let Rafe know. I want it to be a surprise.

DONCORLEONE OF WHISPERING KEY

Too late, son. I'm right here.

ME

No, I meant the other Rafe. MY Rafe.

GAGE

You mean your BOYFRIEND Rafe?

I took a deep breath and typed...

ME

Yes.

And it was the most freeing thing ever.

I strode up the temporary ramp to the little holding area off the main stage. I was pretty sure the thing doubled as a cow chute when it didn't hold singers, and I was also pretty sure that was supposed to add to the charm of the festival. I spotted Debbie standing near an equipment crate off to one side and made my way through the crowded little area.

"Ow!" I said to the man who'd moonwalked into me.

"Sorry! Shit, was that your foot? Dude, my bad!" Ari Friedrich smiled apologetically. "Just practicing my moves."

"It's fine." It made me bizarrely pleased that Rafe's crush was clumsy as heck. "Excuse me for a sec—"

"Wait, Jayd?" Ari's blue eyes lit with excitement. "Oh, man, how cool! I didn't know you'd be here until they announced the lineup change yesterday! I finished my main-stage set a little while ago."

"Awesome! My, um... my boyfriend is a huge fan of yours," I said casually.

At least I hoped it sounded casual. My stomach was trembling so bad seismologists were probably wondering what the fuck was going on in South Dakota.

God I wished Rafe had been there to hear me say it.

Ari's face split into a grin. "Cool! I was wondering… do you have any free time tomorrow to kick shit around? I'd love to run a couple things by you, maybe get your take on some lyrics? You helped me out a ton with 'Incidental Cruelty.'"

"Actually, I…" I paused midsentence as a thought occurred to me. "Wait, what time are you free tomorrow?"

"The whole day. I've got nothing until the meet and greet Sunday. Why?"

I tapped my phone against my palm, my heart beating a mile a minute as I thought about my promise to FaceTime Rafe and let him talk to Ari. I was pretty sure I knew something he'd like even better than a quick conversation, and I quickly revised my already revised plan.

"Ari, I've got a favor to ask you."

"What kind of favor?"

"The kind where I'll owe you a lot more than helping you tweak some lyrics. Why don't I take you out to lunch tomorrow someplace special and explain?" I wrapped an arm over his shoulders. "My treat."

If this worked out… it was going to be epic. And if it didn't…

Well, as long as Rafe and I were together at the end, it was still going to be epic.

"Thank you so much for flying with SkyJet!" the gate attendant chirped as I dragged my case off the jetway and into Sarasota Bradenton Airport.

I gritted my teeth and forced a smile for her. After all, it wasn't this woman's fault that I'd been so busy nervous-vomiting in the bathroom of Louis Armstrong Airport before the final leg of my flight from New Orleans to Sarasota yesterday afternoon that I'd lost track of time and missed my flight, right?

And it furthermore was not her fault that the entire city had been hit by such severe thunderstorms that all flights had been grounded until this morning, creating a clusterfuck of backups that pushed my ten-o'clock flight's takeoff to six.

And I suppose I also couldn't blame her for the cell network outage in the vicinity of the airport, which had made communication spotty and unreliable.

In fact, the only person I could blame for any of it was *me*.

So much for not letting anyone down.

I stopped by the window halfway down the terminal and typed out a quick text to my dad. Approximately my twentieth message of the day.

ME

What the heck is going on? Did Chet arrive? Is the concert okay? Call me!!!!

I waited an entire minute for the three bouncing dots to appear, but they didn't.

Damn it.

I'd started calling people the minute cell coverage had been restored this morning, but no one had answered. Not my dad. Not my brothers, or Mason, or any of their boyfriends. Not even sweet Gloria, my dad's girlfriend. Not the Extravaganza Committee group chat. Not Chet Hatcher. And not *Jay.*

At this point, I was starting to take it personally.

I might have worried that the rapture had come, except my cousin Fenn wasn't replying either, and there was no way that fucker wouldn't be left behind just like me.

And if this was a preview of what life might be like if I had to stay home while Jay toured... well, I was gonna have to learn to start loving airplanes, even if that meant finding another therapist and getting some better coping strategies or good drugs or something, because I missed Jay like a severed limb.

It was crazy talk. Objectively, I knew that. I mean, we'd been apart for *years* when we weren't speaking, and even before that, we were best friends who only spent summers together. Of the six days we'd spent together this week, at least two of them we'd spent hating each other.

None of those numbers mattered, though. I'd had the tiniest taste of what being with Jay would be like—his long, lean body curled up next to me in the night, his honey scent teasing me all day, his rough voice crashing over me when he said things that made me feel important and seen and cared for...

Yeah, there was nothing I wouldn't do to have that in my life forever.

My phone finally dinged with a text from Jay after I started walking again, but it was only a picture from earlier that had finally come through.

It was Jay and Ari Friedrich, sitting side by side at an outdoor picnic table, sort of like the one where Jay and I had sat at Mitchell's the other day—*Jesus*, had it really only been a little over a week ago?—grinning for the camera.

Jay had captioned it, "Your boyfriend and your favorite singer having lunch. WHICH IS WHICH?"

I grinned.

ME

My favorite singer IS my boyfriend. Who's the dude on the left? I just landed in FL and I'm rushing back to the Key. Call me tonight?

But I also paused for a second to enlarge the picture so I could sigh over Jay's face for a minute.

He looked so damn good. *Happy*. He'd gotten a haircut, but it wasn't that. He just seemed settled in a way he hadn't been a couple of days ago when we'd said goodbye.

Which was good.

Obviously.

Seeing him happy always made me happy.

And I was also not at all worried that he looked happier without me than he had when I left.

I rolled my eyes. I sounded like Jay when he got all dramatic. The truth was, I knew Jay cared about me a *lot*. I knew he wanted us to be together. But I could admit there was, as Jay would say, *maybe possibly* a tiny, uncertain corner of my heart that remembered how I'd had to strong-arm him into agreeing that we'd work things out, and worried that once Jay had gotten back to his regular life on the road, he'd realize having me as a boyfriend was a complication he didn't need.

So I'd just have to show him different, right?

I didn't need the world to know I was his boyfriend. I didn't care if we called me his tour manager, or his guitar handler, or his honey drop supplier, as long as I got to be with him.

The phone rang while I was holding it, and when I saw it was Jay, I answered immediately.

"Jay? Babe, can you hear me?"

"Yeah, hey! Just barely. I'm backstage. I'm playing a show in half an hour."

I squeezed my eyes shut. I'd forgotten he had a show today, too.

"I just wanted to inform you that the dude on the left is going to kick your *ass* for excessive Ari Friedrich jokes if you keep it up, Goodman. You hear me?"

I love you, I wanted to say. *I will never love anyone but you.*

"My feelings for Ari Friedrich are not a joke," I teased instead. But I couldn't help adding, "I can't wait to hear all about your show. Both your shows. Call me later?"

"Yeah. Always. I just, um… I was a little nervous, and I never get nervous. I wanted to hear your voice. Ask how your flight was. Thank you for hijacking my phone and adding every single citizen of Whispering Key to my contacts. That kind of thing."

"I figured, since I knew your passcode…"

"Yeah. And 'cause you know *me*."

I absolutely did *not* clasp the phone to my chest like a Victorian woman with a love letter. No matter what airport security footage showed.

"I miss you," I blurted. "So much. And you're gonna do awesome today."

"I hope so. I'm trying out a new song today. Something I just wrote. So it's really important."

"Uh-huh." And *fuck*, I was so pissed I was going to miss it. "You gonna sing the song for me later?"

"You know I will."

"Is it about me?"

"They all are, babe."

I sucked in a breath that burned my nostrils. Had he ever called *me* "babe"? I was pretty sure he hadn't. I could also definitely get used to hearing it.

"Gotta go, Rafe! I'm the middle act in the lineup tonight, and the opener already started."

I had a lot of other things I wanted to say. Like, "When you're done with this show, get your ass to the island or tell me where to meet you." But the man had a show to play, so I figured I could save that for later.

"Later, then?"

"Definitely. I have a surprise for you."

And just like that, I was almost whistling as I went down the escalator, despite the fact that not a single damn Keyster had called me back.

When my phone rang again from a Sarasota number, I answered it.

"Rafe Goodman?"

"Yeah, speaking."

"This is Officer Hood from Sarasota PD. I'm calling to offer you a ride—"

I started laughing, right there at the foot of the escalator. "Oh, my God. Did Jay put you up to this? Was this the surprise he was talking about?"

"Pardon?"

"Oak, for real. You're a great friend to Jay, but you could get in trouble if you keep doing this. Besides, things are good between us now. No kidnapping required."

"Who's Oak? Sir, I'm afraid there's been a misunderstanding. I'm Officer Rob Hood, and I was asked to give you a police escort to—"

I snorted. "You just won't quit, huh? Is Rob short for Robin?"

"I..." He paused. "Yes."

I laughed out loud again. "Officer Robin Hood? Really? Okay, three out of ten points for names this go 'round. The candle fragrance was a better schtick. But to be fair, you were never gonna fool me a second time no matter what name you used. Be honest, did you come up with the Robin Hood thing, or did Jay?"

"My Grandmother Jennings came up with it, Lord rest her soul! And my parents allowed it."

He sounded so genuinely put out, I almost hesitated... but no. Oak was just really good. "Grandmother Jennings, huh? Was she Maid Marian? Or..."

"As it happens, she *was* named Marian, yes." He sniffed impatiently. "Sir. I was calling to offer you a police escort so you could get to Whispering Key faster—"

"Again?" I hooted. "No, no. You've gotta change it up. You can't kidnap me again! Especially since the kidnap van is in Wyoming, and the guy who kidnapped me is in South Dakota. Two out of ten for originality."

"Mr. Goodman, are you... are you reporting a felony abduction? Are you in a safe place right now?"

I frowned. The dude was really convincing. "Solid ten out of ten for genuine emotion. You almost really sound worried. Listen, Robin Hood, thanks for calling, but I really am in a hurry to get to the Key, so—" I pushed through the sliding doors and out onto the humid sidewalk.

"Cousin Littlejohn and Cousin Dale are going to hear about this," the guy grumbled. "For wasting my time."

I stopped dead. "Wait, Dale and Littlejohn? Littlejohn... Jennings?"

"How many Littlejohns do you know, Mr. Goodman?"

He had me there.

"Our grandmother happened to have an appreciation for the Robin Hood stories," he said indignantly. "Cousin Little-john and I paid the price, while Cousin Alan-a-Dale and Cousin Sherwood got off easy."

Alan-a-Dale? Was that Dale's real name?

No one could make up a story like that. *No one.*

"So..." I cleared my throat. "So when you say you're a police officer, you mean..."

"I mean that I'm employed by the City of Sarasota as an officer of the law. With a badge. And a weapon. And the power to arrest criminals. Yes."

Fuuuuck.

"So, um. About that ride...?"

What followed was an extremely uncomfortable but very quick trip to the Key, during which Officer Hood had me sit in the back of his squad car, behind the cage.

I couldn't entirely blame him. I'd probably have done the same.

He drove down Godfrey Pass toward the center of town, and for the last mile and a half, both sides of the street were lined with so many cars, I had to wonder whether the island could support them all without just sinking into the Gulf. I'd never seen that many vehicles on the Key in my lifetime, and it made my heart swell.

The place was coming back to life.

Officer Hood got as close as he could to the center of town, where the street barricades began, then pulled over to let me out. He had the sirens off but the lights on, which gave the whole thing a definite perp-walk feel.

"There you go, Mr. Goodman," he said, as he opened the back door to let me and my suitcase out. "Take care of yourself."

"Thank you. I just want to say again how *truly* sorry I am for the confusion, Officer Hood—"

"Save it." The man tucked his thumbs into his belt, reminding me a lot of Deputy Freckles... not that I was ever, ever going to say anything like that. "You Whispering Keysters have a unique sense of humor. And strange taste in casseroles."

I nodded slowly. He wasn't wrong.

"Tell my cousins they owe me. And good luck with your little festival."

But as he drove off, I grinned because *no one* could mistake this for a little festival.

The whole town center was covered in stars. Twinkling lights zigzagged across the street, and people strolled beneath them, laughing and dancing to the music that spilled out of the arcade. Silver paper stars hung in streamers from lampposts.

Lety and Bubba had turned the parking lot near the Concha into a patio area, where people clustered around tables, clinking their glasses in the soft yellow glow from the paper lanterns strung around. Even the food trucks parked near the wharf were each topped with a light-up star.

It was everything I'd specifically told Gage not to do.

Thank God he hadn't listened.

Whispering Key had never looked like this in my lifetime, but I knew without question that this was how it was supposed to look all along. How it would look from now on. Cheerful. Festive. *Alive.*

And the funny thing was, nothing much had changed—the fundamental elements of the island and the people were exactly as they'd always been—but *everything* had changed, because now the place felt hopeful. Filled with possibilities. And the possibilities made it beautiful.

Which was kind of how I felt about my own life now...

And *oh my God*, I'd caught whatever sappy disease Fenn and Beale had fallen victim to. They'd never let me hear the end of it. But Jay wouldn't mind. In fact, I kinda thought he'd love it.

"Rafe! Good Lord, son! You are a sight for sore eyes!" My dad came lumbering over with little Gloria practically trotting along beside him to keep up.

He'd never looked so happy to see me in his entire life. I was immediately suspicious.

"You didn't return my texts," I said as Gloria threw her arms around me. "Or my calls."

"I know!" Dad said gleefully. "But some things you just have to see for yourself, huh?" He turned in a circle, admiring the decorations, beaming with pride. "So, tell me all about Wyoming! How was Aimee?"

"She's fine. As you probably knew."

"Well, more or less," he allowed. "But it's still good to hear. I worried about her. I'm glad she's happy."

His voice rang with truth, and the kick of it was... I believed him. He loved us, *all* of us, even though he had really bizarre ways of showing it, and he tried hard to do right by us which resulted in him fucking up in all kinds of large and small ways.

A crowd of people roared and clapped from the park, just beyond the carousel, and a voice yelled out, "Thank you so much, Whispering Key! I've got one last song for you!"

"Chet?" I asked my dad. "He's already almost done?"

Dad grinned like a cat who'd eaten a canary and gotten away with it. It was mildly terrifying.

"What did you do?" I demanded.

"I got a fill-in act for your fill-in act!" Dad rocked back and forth on his feet. "Ha! Who says I can't get things done, Gloria?"

"No one, Mr. Mayor!" Gloria said, gazing up at him worshipfully.

"That's right. And now that I've not only found the Whispering Key treasure, raised enough money to restore the bridge to the mainland, *and* successfully planned and executed this Extravaganza, I think I'm ready to take on my next challenge."

I groaned. "Raising the Lost City of Atlantis, perhaps? Inventing your own language? Raising turkeys?"

"Nope. Grandchildren!" Dad said happily, and I choked on the warm night air. "But first I'm going to make Gloria here my bride. And we're going to go on a little cruise."

"Around the *world*," Gloria added.

"You're going on a cruise around the world?" I repeated. "But you're mayor of the town for another year. How the hell is that going to work?"

"Well—"

"Rafe! Hurry up! Chet's almost finished." Beale jogged over, panting slightly. "Dad," he chided, "you were supposed to bring him right over to the stage!"

Dad pursed his lips. "Honestly, Beale! I was doing a *reveal* over here, and you've completely ruined it! I swear, not a *single one* of my sons was born with a sense of timing."

Gloria patted his arm.

Beale rolled his eyes and grinned at me. "Chet's finishing up his last song. Fortunately, it's his electric-jazz version of 'Stairway to Heaven,' so it's gonna be a minute, but you've gotta come now." He pulled at my shoulder. "Toby's waiting over there."

"We'll stow your bag!" Gloria called as I jogged away.

The town green by the carousel was packed with listeners reclining on blankets, chatting and laughing, while a few little kids ran around playing tag.

Beale forged us a path through without any trouble, though, which was the definite upside of having a younger brother who was half again as broad as me.

"What's the big rush?" I demanded as he rocked to a stop by the left side of the pavilion stage. "Chet's set's almost over, and everything went well, it sounds like." I paused. "I mean, as well as an electric-jazz version of Stairway played by a man whose brand is techno-country *can* sound."

"Oh, no! Everything's great. I just... like hanging out with you," Beale said lamely. He pulled out his phone and shot off a text before leading me up the stairs to the left side of the stage. "I wanted to spend time with my favorite brother."

"Since when am I your favorite?" I lifted one eyebrow. "Did you and Gage have a falling-out?"

Beale smiled a genuine smile. "Don't be silly. I love Gage, but you know you're the one we both look up to." He clapped me on the shoulder. "I'm *so* glad things worked out with you and Jay."

I frowned. "How'd you know that?"

Beale's eyes widened. "I mean. It was obvious. Wasn't it? When you asked us to text him and say we weren't upset?"

I stared at him harder, and predictably, Beale swallowed and began to stammer. "Or Jay may have... said so? On the chat?"

My lips parted in shock. "He told the whole chat? Not just you and Toby, and Gage, and Fenn and Mase, but..."

"But all of us," Beale confirmed. "Dad. Uh... Jonquil? Littlejohn. Lorenna."

"Lorenna! No, no, no! She's the biggest gossip on the Key!"

"Yeah, I know," he agreed. "Everyone knows it."

My heart started to pound. "Did Jay mention that everyone should keep their mouths shut? Did he swear them to secrecy?"

Beale frowned. "I don't think so."

"You don't *think*?" I demanded. "Let me see this text chain. Jay was obviously distracted and forgot. He doesn't want anyone to know about us. Shit. If a reporter ever heard about this, it could fuck everything up, Beale!"

"Rafe, chill. Deep breath. It's gonna be fine, I promise." But he handed his phone over anyway, opened to the chat. "The reporter dude is nice."

"Reporter dude?" Had my dad hired someone? Had he heard the news? The blood in my veins turned to ice. How was I going to explain this to Jay? How could I make this right?

"The reporter dude the next act brought with him," Beale specified. "Just look and see."

I ignored him.

"*Look and see*," he repeated, nudging my arm.

I scowled. "I could *not* care less about the next act, Beale."

I'd gotten to the part of the text chain where Jay asked for a meeting, when Beale grabbed the phone from my hand.

"Rafe," he said, nudging me again, tilting his chin toward the stage. *"Look and see."*

I looked up alright, solely to tell him off… but then saw Jay step out of the right wing onto the bright lights of the stage.

He was all lean muscles and low-slung jeans, bright green eyes and a wicked smile. The secret dream of my teenage heart and the only man I'd ever love. When he looked over at me and winked, I swear my heart stopped.

"How?" I whispered.

Jay couldn't possibly have heard me, but maybe he read my lips because after he grabbed the mic from Chet and they exchanged one-arm hugs, he told the audience, *"Surprise, Whispering Key! I was a little late, and I worried I might not get here, but I called in a favor from a friend who knows a pilot, and I finally made it."* He turned his head directly toward me and touched a hand to his chest right over his heart. "I'm home."

The crowd went wild. The slice of them I could see from my side of the stage jumped to their feet, lawn blankets abandoned in their excitement.

And me? I died and came back to life. Right there.

I had no idea what his words meant, exactly, and I was for sure going to care about that later. But at that moment? The only thing I knew was that Jay was right there in front of me, two running steps and a flying tackle away.

Beale yelled something in my ear, but I didn't hear him. My phone vibrated in my pocket, but I couldn't bring myself to care about that either.

Jay was *right there*. Looking a little tired but really fucking satisfied with life and staring at me like he had a secret.

The *good* kind.

"You guys are amazing! Why would a guy ever want to play anywhere else, huh? Let's have another round of applause for my close, personal friend Chet, who flew in to pinch hit for me *without* the rest of his band! Chet, you're a star, man. And if you guys are fans of Chet's innovative sound, and I think we all are after that awesome set, he's got a whole bunch of music you can check out on YouTube!"

The audience screamed, and I imagined it was the most gratifying sound of Chet's whole career.

"Let's start off with one of my favorites, 'Pretty Girl.' It's come to my attention that some of my lyrics are a little obscure, so I want to make it clear: this is a song about me falling for a *guy*. One particular amazing guy."

I looked around in a panic to gauge reactions. What the hecking *heck* was Jay doing? Had he lost his mind?

"I've been hiding some things about me for a long time, you guys. Important things. Not because I don't love you all, but because I wanted to keep my private life private. Still... a secret is a secret, isn't it? And a bunch of people I'm really lucky to have in my life helped me see that secrets only make you weaker, no matter how good your intentions started out. One of them reminded me representation matters, too. So, Cedar in Larindosa, Wyoming? Massive thanks to you, my friend, if you ever catch this on the internet. Cedar told me 'Pretty Girl' gave him the courage to talk about some hard things, and I wanna thank him right back for giving that same courage to me." He took a deep breath. "I'm gay... and I can't ever love a pretty girl."

Holy. Shit. My breathing went funny as warmth spread out from my chest. He'd done it. He'd fucking done it.

The audience went crazy again—like, dizzying heights of crazy—but when Jay wrapped his guitar around his neck and strummed out the first chord, they fell quiet. In fact, an expectant hush seemed to fall over the whole island, from the graves where Resolute Goodman and his best friend, Jacob Godfrey, lay, past the beaches and the boats where Jay and I spent our summers, all the way up to this stage, like the entire world had been waiting for this moment.

When Jay's powerful voice rang out, he captivated all of us... but me most of all. At the end, he stopped playing and stood there with his eyes closed, two hands clenched around the mic, *emoting*, and every line of the song sounded like a pledge. It sounded like "I love you."

And if the sun setting in your eyes could lock me out of heaven,

I knew I didn't want that heaven.

'Cause you and I were heaven.

Jay turned his head to look directly at me and added...

You and I are still *heaven.*

Then he looked back to the crowd and grinned wildly as he launched into the last chorus...

And I still don't want a pretty girl!

When the last note hung in the heavy air, pandemonium hit. People screamed and cheered. In the front row, I saw Littlejohn openly crying while Caroline Mitchell patted his back fondly, and my dad swaying to the music with his arms wrapped around Gloria from behind.

Jay's eyes popped open, and he laughed out loud at the chaos he'd caused.

"Okay, so." He dragged a little stool forward from the back of the stage. "Let's get serious for a second. *More* serious. Show of hands, how many of you have ever made your crush a playlist? Uh-huh. That's quite a few. And how many of you were scared to death to share it? Yes! Same. See, I had a crush when I was in high school. And after that. And... well, he's still my crush to this day, honestly. So I wrote the man an album. And do you know what happened?"

Jay settled himself on the stool and put the mic back in its holder. He tossed me a grin over his shoulder. A grin that said this would be payback for every Ari joke I'd ever made.

Competitive fucker.

My competitive fucker.

Every cell of my body wanted to rush the damn stage and carry him off.

"He *hated* it," Jay told them dramatically. "He loathed it."

The crowd gasped and booed.

I folded my arms over my chest.

"You loathed it?" Beale demanded, shoulder-checking me. "So rude."

"But," Jay told the audience, motioning for them to settle down. "But! That was mostly because he didn't know it was about him. So I wrote the guy a new song. And this time, I want to play it for him directly. So there's no confusion."

He stood up and beckoned toward me, then patted the seat of the stool, inviting me to share the stage with him.

Holy shit. He was burning it *all* down. Not just coming out as gay, but coming out as mine. I knew he had to be scared as hell, which officially made him the bravest man I knew.

And I knew there'd never be anyone other than him for me until I died.

I didn't hesitate. I took a step forward.

But a hand wrapped around my elbow and yanked me back into the wing with surprising strength.

"Rafe, precious... you need to... pause for... just one second while I fix you," Toby panted, like he'd run a great distance to save me from a fashion emergency. He adjusted the collar of my T-shirt, straightened the hem, then lifted up on his toes to sift his fingers through my hair. "Love may be rose-colored, but telescopic lenses are forever! Have you looked at yourself even once since you left wherever the heck you took off from this morning? Answer: no." He stepped back and assessed me with a critical eye. "*Ugh*. Why do you and your brother look so good in big boots and scruff? The universe is so inherently unfair." He winked and patted my chest, then stood back to lay his head on Beale's arm. "There. My work is done. Go get your man."

"Handsome," Jay said softly as I approached, his eyes

dancing as he appreciated Toby's efforts. "You ready for this?"

"Are *you*?" My eyes searched his. "What happened to waiting? Shit, what happened to Iron Pipes?"

"It came to my attention that if you want to grow something, you can't keep it in the shadows. And you and I are meant for sunshine, Rafe Goodman." He grinned. "And that being the case, I decided the main stage at Iron Pipes can wait. The organizers understood that family comes first, so they let me out of today's show. Now. Any more questions, or are you gonna sit down and let me sing for you?"

That didn't even justify an answer.

I straddled the stool and sat without another word, and as soon as my ass touched the wood, as if by some understood signal, the crowd cheered. I didn't look at them, partly because I thought they'd freak me out but mostly because they didn't matter. They were literally background noise.

Jay took a second to adjust his mic, and then he took a breath and launched into a new song, letting the melody unfurl and twine around me.

He sang about choices. About how the world only wanted to pick and choose certain parts of him but how he was choosing to be whole.

He was choosing *me*.

At first I tried to commit the lyrics to memory, but I gave up pretty fast. I could make him sing it later, over and over and over again. What I wanted to commit to eternal memory was the look in those green eyes as he sang to me in front of an audience containing most of our family and friends.

What I wanted to remember and never, ever doubt again was how good he made me feel.

When he got close to the end, he stopped playing mid-verse and swung his guitar behind him. With the mic in one hand, he reached up and pushed back my hair with the other, then sang to me in a voice aching with emotion.

I choose the love and light of you

The stars shining through the night of you

The always and forever right of you…

His smile flashed as the song ended, and I surged forward, wrapping my arms around him at shoulders and hips. Then I kissed the hell out of him, tasting his honey-citrus sweetness right there on the stage in front of my family and friends and thousands of strangers.

If Jay had wanted a boyfriend who could sit calmly and resist him, he needed to pick a different guy or to stop singing such fucking amazing songs… neither of which was gonna happen if I had any say in the matter.

Jay dropped the mic to thread his hands through my hair and kiss me back, and the feedback whine was swallowed by the stomping and shouting of the crowd as they cheered us on.

"Not too overproduced?" Jay croaked when he finally pulled back.

"I love you," I told him. "I have loved you forever. The day you kidnapped me was the luckiest, happiest day of my life. And I'm gonna tell you so every day from now on, for as long as you'll let me."

Jay's answering grin was brighter than a thousand stars. "Well, damn," he whispered. "I thought it might take a little more convincing to get those words out of you, so I brought you a present. Don't I feel foolish?"

"What?"

Jay let go of me and picked up the mic. "You guys are the best! Thank you so much for indulging me. Right now, I have a special surprise. A guy I know a lot of you are familiar with, a guy I've heard called 'a *real* singer' and 'phenomenal' and someone who 'paints pictures with words.' Give it up for Ari Friedrich!"

"You did fucking *not*," I said, even as Ari jogged out from stage right, lifting a hand to greet the crowd.

"Oh, babe. I super fucking did."

For most of my life, I'd thought nothing in the world could be better than the feeling of being onstage: connecting with an audience through lyrics I'd written or melodies I'd plucked out, making them laugh or smile. It had always been the thing I was best at.

But standing over by the Whispering Key gazebo in the circle of Rafe Goodman's arms, swaying to Ari's final song of the evening, I knew I'd found my true place, because I'd never felt safer or more loved than I was right then. And I knew whatever the future had in store for us, it was going to be exponentially better now that we were together.

"So I was thinking..." I began.

"Mmm?"

"What if I wanted to make this whole thing permanent?"

Rafe's hands tightened on my waist. "Define 'whole thing.' Because if you're talking about Ari Friedrich singing for me on the regular—"

"Do not make me kick you in the shin, Rafael."

He scraped his teeth over my chin, making me shiver. "Seriously. Tell me. You can have anything you want from me, Jay Rollins. What do you want to be permanent?"

"All of it. You. Me. This beautiful island. Playing concerts on the Key. The recording studio in the backyard, and all those other *someday* things we talked about. Basically, if you took the product of every summer day we spent together, added in all the other days of the year plus nightly sleepovers and daily coffee, and multiplied it by the power of probably excessive levels of sex, that's what I'm proposing."

Rafe's eyes searched mine in the moonlight. "Where do I sign?" he whispered. "And when you go on tour—"

"About that," I interrupted. "What if I... didn't?"

"If you didn't," he repeated blankly. "Tour?"

"Uh-huh. Not as much, anyway. If Iron Pipes invites me again, I would totally go, obviously! Also Bonnaroo. And Outside Lands. Coachella. And, um, Shaky Knees."

"Babe, those are just weekend festivals."

"Right."

He shook his head. "If you're thinking of not touring because of us, because of *me*, think again. Don't you dare shrink your dreams down to fit our relationship. I'm your biggest fan, and I'm with you a hundred percent, so believe me when I tell you, *we* will grow to fit however huge your career becomes, okay? And maybe we charter planes from now on, since we have the money... and since I feel like blow jobs during takeoff and landing would really alleviate my anxiety."

"That's not it!" I laughed. "Just listen, okay? And keep an open mind."

Rafe held me tighter. "I'm listening. I promise."

"Okay, so... for the longest time, I focused on one dream, thinking if I just got to the next level of success, I'd finally be happy. But the truth is..." I bit my lip but smiled around it anyway. "The truth is, I was more genuinely happy spending three days with you and a hitchhiking auto thief in a kidnap van that reeked of Shalimar than I was the night I found out I had a gold record. Because that night, I didn't have the man I love to share it with. I was like a chord missing a note. Just the tiniest bit off-key. Because you weren't there."

"Babe—"

"Still listening time!" I said severely. "So now I have a new dream. It's brand-new—it kinda all took shape in my mind in the last couple days—but I know it's soul-deep *right*, the way things sometimes are. I want to play here on the Key. I want to write music here."

"Really?"

I nodded. "And I maybe want to invite other artists to come here, too, so we can work on stuff together and I can help produce their tracks. I want to keep all the parts of my career that I want and get rid of all the parts I don't enjoy but thought I had to do in order to be successful. I want to put a new spin on what success means."

His smile crept over his face like sunrise. "Yeah?"

"Yeah. And like… what if I maybe possibly also wanted to do a summer program for LGBTQ youth in the arts? George gave me that idea on the plane here—"

"George?"

"The reporter Debbie introduced me to so I could make a statement. And before you ask, I agreed to it. Don't get me wrong, I'm still scared shitless that people are going to have a lot of negative things to say. I'm still worried they're going to hurt you, and I'm gonna attack them like a honey badger. But I decided I can't live with my walls up forever. I don't want you to have to either. And I thought about Cedar, from the hospital, and all the other kids like him. Like me. Like *us*. And how they deserve to know what's possible." I shrugged sheepishly. "Anyway, George is really nice. He's, um, giving me edit power over the story. He said it's too important that I have my own say, and he doesn't wanna put words in my mouth, which is pretty awesome. I think you'll like him. I mean," I disclaimered quickly, "if you choose to be part of the story. Which, uh, I guess I kinda drafted you into, but you don't have to if you—"

"I'm with you, Jay," he interrupted softly. "Always. I told you that."

I nodded. I'd known that. I'd *trusted* that. And it meant everything to know I could.

"Uh. Also, George said *Pride Magazine* would pay me a hundred thousand dollars for my story."

"Whoa. They do that?"

"Apparently the money flows differently when you agree to an exclusive interview and don't have a photographer catching you unaware at a club," I said with an eye roll. "Anyway, I'm gonna create a charity with the money. Kick some money over to Dr. Dave in Wyoming, since he's probably going to be my brother-in-law eventually. And maybe start something to help uninsured and underinsured young people get the care they deserve, too. You might say that's relevant to my interests." I looked up at him flirtatiously. "I just wish I had a partner who was really *thorough* and responsible who could help me out with that."

"You already have one," he assured me. "In everything. You and me, partners in crime. Saving the world from all manner of birds."

The fact that he remembered the offer I'd made him the other day at Mitchell's almost word for word made me sigh. "I love you, Rafe. In case that wasn't obvious."

Rafe took my face in both his hands and kissed me like I was the most precious thing in his world. "I will never not want to hear it." He ran his thumbs over my cheekbones and lowered his lips toward mine again. "And I'm glad we're a team ag—"

"Kiss him, Goodman!" a teasing voice called from way too close by. "Kiss him good! Put some phalluses back into this Extravaganza!"

I heard Beale's deep, amused chuckle as he pulled his boyfriend away.

"That was Toby," Rafe began, and then his lips parted in shock. "Oh, fuck. I think there might be one more secret I was accidentally, incidentally keeping..."

"You mean the fact that Beale's boyfriend was the guy from the paparazzi photos? That somehow the two guys in that picture ended up in the same place, of *allllll* the places in the known universe, and dating brothers to boot?"

"Yeah, that," Rafe said. "I, uh, take it you two met?"

"Lorenna McKetcham was delighted to introduce us," I confirmed. "And you know something? I was not as surprised as I'd've thought I would be." I laughed out loud. "*Nothing* about this island surprises me much anymore. It's pure magic, and you just have to go along with it. Though, just FYI, if Lorenna suggests that Toby and I do an act together for the Christmas talent pageant..."

"An act toge— Oh, fuck, no!" Rafe said, shuddering. He started to pull away, but I wouldn't let him. I clung to him instead and kissed him while I laughed.

"Are you *sure* you want this?" he asked in a whisper sometime later. "These ridiculous people? This particular place? 'Cause I've heard amazing things about Vegas. We could have waffles daily."

I laughed. "You mean *pancakes*, and no. This *is* the dream, babe. I don't want a million fans singing along to my songs —I just want one guy who listens to my music and knows the truth behind it. A guy who knows I can't drive for shit and understands my metabolism is not to be trifled with. A man who loves me and wants me to love him back."

"All that in one guy?" Rafe whistled. "That's a tall order."

"Is it?"

"Mmm. As far as I know, there's only one man who can do

the job the way you deserve. But... I'm thinking he's gonna need a promotion, Rollins. *Maybe possibly* to husband."

I threw my head back and laughed, staring up at the stars and loving the man in my arms so much I felt drunk on it. "Consider it done."

EPILOGUE

JAY

Almost one year later

"Falling in love's not falling behind
When the man I want to be
Is in the mirror staring back at me.

And 'enough's enough' is more than enough
When love's not just a thing I sing about,
And I've got someone I can't live without.

So let them talk all day, say what they like,
And turn my life to chatter.
Like ordinary miracles don't matter.

They're objects in the rearview,
much smaller than they seem,
when I know for sure I'm living my dream."

The last notes of the song I'd finished just that afternoon vibrated out of my guitar, drifted in the humid air for a beat, then drifted up past the paper lanterns hung around the patio and disappeared into the constellations that lit the night sky over Whispering Key.

For half a second, there was utter silence, and I wondered, "Did I get it right? Did I fuck it up? Did they understand?"

Then Fisher's Wreck erupted into enthusiastic applause, and my own personal friends-and-family cheering squad in the front of the bar whistled and catcalled loud enough to be heard all the way over on Cooter Key.

"You guys are amazing. Thank you so much for coming out!" I grinned in relief and excitement. "Now I'm gonna take a little break—"

"Jay Rollins! You made me cry, but I freakin' love you!" Mason shouted with the sloppy enthusiasm of a beloved (and slightly overworked) island doctor who'd *finally* hired a second physician for Whispering Key Medical just a few months before and could now partake of craft beers with his boyfriend every other weekend.

"Yeah, get your ass over here so we can buy you a drink!" Fenn called. His eyes were suspiciously shiny as he pressed a tender kiss to the side of Mason's head and draped a possessive hand over his man's shoulder.

A teary-eyed Fenn was a rare sight. It wasn't often that my lyrics snuck beneath his sarcastic hide and hit the tender spot in his heart where Mason lived, but it looked like this song had managed it... which was all the confirmation I needed that it was good.

Toby, who'd stood up halfway through the second verse to sway on his Gucci sandals while holding the LED candle from the table centerpiece in the air like a lighter at a rock show, now cupped his hands around his mouth, leaned over the table, and yelled way too loudly, "Have babies with me and Beale, Jay! Hypnotically talented, ridiculously competent, tree-sized, stylish babies!"

Beale smiled softly as he dragged his slightly-more-than-slightly inebriated boyfriend down into his lap, and then he whispered something in Toby's ear—possibly explaining how babies were actually made... or, given the way his whisper made un-blush-able Toby turn the color of tonight's sunset, maybe an invitation to go home and practice baby-making anyway, biology be damned.

My grin widened. I loved these guys so damn much. They were the family I'd always wanted, and I was thankful for them every single day.

No lie, though, I was especially thankful for them every other Saturday when I played a couple of sets at Fisher's Wreck. Bobo Fisher poured drinks notoriously heavy for us locals, and my friends were not shy about partaking or about expressing their enthusiastic support for me while they did.

They were the best audience I'd ever played for.

From the next table over, Aimee, who'd flown in just that morning for her fifth visit this year, informed everyone, "That's my brother up there!" with as much pride as if I were headlining Madison Square Garden instead of a tiny bar on a Florida island. She'd been my first fan and remained my truest.

Beside her at their table, Dr. Babe watched her with the same warm, loving look he'd worn the first day I met him—

the one that said Aimee was infinitely important to him, which made *him* important to *me*. So important that when he'd decided to propose to her this past June, Rafe and I had flown in an actual airplane to Denver, road-tripped to Yellowstone National Park (because road-tripping was our thing now), then hiked seven miles *uphill* to the top of Mt. Washburn, just so we could surprise them with a song and some biodegradable confetti. The fact that Aimee was the only one of us four who wasn't breathless or tired after the hike had told me everything I needed to know about her health progress, and the way she'd beamed with happiness the whole way down told me more than I needed to know about how solid her relationship with Dr. Ba—I mean, *Dave* —was.

It was hard not to appreciate a man who made my sister feel safe by making her feel *empowered*, rather than rolling her up in bubble wrap.

In fact, I was really hoping Dave would decide to move his research facility to Florida at some point, maybe even before the wedding. I mean, the cost of living on the Key might not be quite as low as in Wyoming, but I knew for a fact that the two biggest donors to his clinic would be more than willing to help defray his relocation costs. (Or at least *I* was, and I was reasonably certain I could convince the other guy, too, since there wasn't a lot Rafe wouldn't agree to if I straddled him in bed and refused to ride his dick until he said *yes*.) I also happened to know the new preschool on the island was looking for a director with a master's in early childhood education, which my sister was only a semester away from obtaining.

Not to mention, the island had something Aimee and Dave would never be able to find anywhere else—free babysitting for my niece, who was on track to make her appearance in January.

All I could do was present these true facts, though. I would *not* push the issue in a big-brother-knows-best (or favorite-uncle-knows-best) sort of way, because Aimee was smart enough to make good choices, and I was smart enough to let her.

Mostly.

Ahem.

"Get your butt down here and gimme a hug, Rollins!" Aimee commanded.

I unhooked my guitar and started to comply, but first I reflexively searched the crowd for one other face—the most important face, the one I sought in every crowd—even though I knew I wouldn't find it until sometime during my second set. Rafe never missed my bimonthly shows at the Wreck, but that evening, he'd had a schmoozy dinner meeting with some guys from the state about rebuilding the Whispering Key Bridge, and he wouldn't make it until later.

Such were the sacrifices required of town mayors and their boyfriends—which was what Rafe and I had somehow become.

When Big Rafe had announced a couple of days after the Extravaganza last year that he and Gloria were going to sail over to Cozumel in the winter so he could spend time searching for the sunken treasures he'd spent half his life daydreaming about, I'd sort of thought he was kidding.

Whispering Key without Big Rafe didn't seem like a thing that should be possible.

As it turned out, he'd been dead serious.

"I'm abdicating the mayor's seat to you, son," he'd told Rafe. "Rule in good health and do me proud."

Gage had made a mildly outraged noise. "Dad, you do realize Whispering Key isn't actually a monarchy, right? You can't pass the title down to Rafe. If he wants it, he's gonna have to declare his candidacy and run? And the island will vote? And they might choose someone else? Because... democracy?"

"Thank you, Gage," Big Rafe had snorted. "I know how it works. I also know there's not a soul on this island who doesn't believe Young Rafe's the best man for the job, *ergo*, he's a shoo-in. The island's in his blood, for one thing. And for another, I've been training him for this role for years, much the way Mr. Miyagi trained Daniel in those movies back in the day." His chest had puffed out proudly. "And it worked."

"Oh, sweet Jesus," Rafe had choked out. "So you're saying me handling the Extravaganza... and working all those hours on the boat..."

"Wax on, wax off, Rafael," he'd said solemnly.

I had tried very hard not to laugh at the absolute horror on my true love's face, because I was a good boyfriend like that.

But Big Rafe had smiled angelically and patted him on the shoulder. "I figure if you can deal with *me*, you can deal with anything the mayor's crown might have in store for you."

In the end, Big Rafe had been right—which was an annoying tendency he had. Even Rafe's sole opponent, Harvey Culpepper, had only declared his candidacy because Lorenna McKetcham convinced him it'd be wrong to deprive the town of an election, but he'd ended up voting for Rafe, too.

And over the past eight months, Rafe had proven himself to be an even better mayor than his dad, because no one was as competent as my man and no one cared about the people on this island half as much. Nothing I'd personally accomplished had made me prouder than watching him settle into his new role and getting to be a part of it myself. Rafe had lived on the island his whole life, but now he'd finally accepted his place on it.

And so had I.

This life—my life with Rafe—didn't look at all like the future I'd planned for myself as a teenager. My last album had been released in March, but I'd shocked the heckity out of Debbie by not touring to support it. Instead, I'd played a select number of festivals all spring and summer, along with limited dates at smaller venues in cities Rafe and I wanted to explore, making sure that my schedule lined up with Rafe's as much as possible.

I'd also built a recording studio in the backyard, just like Rafe had suggested. It had cost a small fortune, but *the* Ari Friedrich himself had said that the view outside was worth every penny, which was why he'd stayed on the Key for a whole *month* last spring so he and I could collaborate on a couple of tracks... and so he and his new BFF, Rafe Goodman, could devise—I kid you not—the ultimate turkey burger recipe.

I'd realized, watching the two of them joke around while drinking margaritas with Toby and Gloria, that while having money and career accolades was wonderful, they'd only ever been a means to an end, and the end I'd always wanted was precisely what I'd found on the Key—friendship, and collaboration, and having a purpose, and watching my lover eat hamburgers with his idol. It was a scary thing to admit that you were happy, to push back against society's drive for *more*. But it was worth it.

So anytime I was tagged in a post about how I'd lost my drive to succeed because I'd gone from playing big shows to smaller venues, I thought about nights like tonight, moments when I held my tiny audience in the palm of my hand and felt the music connecting us, and I thought, *"Nope. This right here is success."*

And every time BlazeNewz speculated on "Jayd Rollins: Where is he now?" I posted a picture on my Instagram of me, sun-kissed and bone-deep happy, on a beach or a boat or cuddled up in bed with a sleeping Rafe, because I knew exactly where I was and what I really wanted, and that made all the difference.

"If you don't come down, I'm coming up!" Aimee threatened, levering her pregnant self out of her chair.

I obediently jumped down from the little stage Bobo had constructed on a corner of the patio last winter, when "Hey, Jayd, could you play a few songs at open mic night?" had become regular shows that drew tons of tourists all year long, and wrapped my arms tight around Aimee's tiny form.

"Your niece is kicking," she told me, beaming as she set my

hand on her belly. "I think she likes hearing her Uncle Jay sing. Think our family could handle two musicians?"

My chest squeezed tight. "I think our family can handle anything."

"Yoo-hoo! Jayd! Jayd Rollins! "

Aimee and I turned to find Lorenna McKetcham bearing down on us. She wrapped an arm around Aimee from the other side.

"Hey, Ms. McKetcham. How's mahjong night going?" Aimee asked.

"Excellent! I'm winning, and Victoria Archbold is crying into her jalapeño poppers." She turned to me. "But we got to talking about our other hobbies, and I was wondering... how's that nice friend of yours doing?"

"Er. You mean Chet? He and Chrissea are doing just fine, last I heard. He's recording his first studio album." An album for which I'd contributed not one but two original songs. "They'll both be back for the Extravaganza next weekend."

"Chet's a hoot, but I don't mean him. I mean the beefcake who visited you over the Fourth of July. The one with the neck tattoo who's built like Beale Goodman's naughty twin brother." Her smile was broad enough to show off all her dentures.

I choked on my saliva. "I guess you mean Oak."

"Ahhh, that's right. *Oak*." She gave an exaggerated shiver. "It's like his mama just *knew* he'd be hard and woody. Is he taken?"

"Taken? I..." I shook my head helplessly as Aimee bit her lip to stifle her laughter. "Not last I heard."

"Excellent! How does he feel about free love and older women?" She wiggled her eyebrows.

I did *not* want to know why she was asking.

"Erm. Pretty favorably about the free love as far as I know? Not much for women of any age. Why?"

(Okay, I lied. I really wanted to know.)

Lorenna sighed gustily. "I thought now that we're getting the bridge back and people are flocking to the island, there'd be more new *men* around."

"There are tons of men," I protested. "Look around! This place is packed with hot guys."

"Bah. Those are tourists." Lorenna waved a hand. "They come for a week or two. That's hardly enough time to let my imagination run wild, let alone break a man in."

I opened my mouth, then shut it again. This time, I *really* didn't want to know.

"There's Beale's Toby," Aimee reminded her. "And the cute new doctor."

Lorenna snorted. "Can't fantasize about men who're that happily shacked up," she said morosely. "And Gage'll be next, just watch and see."

"I'll be next at what?" Gage sauntered up and handed me a glass of mead, which Bobo had begun stocking when he heard how much I loved the taste of honey drops. "Please say the answer is kidnapped by a hot, blue alien to be the most favored concubine in his off-world harem of incredibly handsome, virile men, like in one of Mom's old romances."

"Nah." Lorenna wrinkled her nose. "I just meant shacked up here on the island."

Gage laughed so hard he snorted beer. "Oh, Jesus no. The blue alien is *way* more likely. I have many a wild oat left to sow, Lorenna. Whole *fields* of oats. *Acres* of oats. And when I'm done with the oats, imma sow some carrots and wheat for good measure. *Variety*, you know?"

"Exactly! Gage is still way too young to consider getting serious with anyone," Aimee reminded Lorenna. "Right, Gage?"

"I'm twenty-four, Aim. The only people who think I'm too young are the people on this island." Gage rolled his eyes like it was all a joke, but his voice carried a hint of bitterness. "At least my employment prospects are looking up, though, so there's that. I accepted a job today."

"That's awesome news! Which one?" I demanded excitedly. "The data security company in Miami? Or did you find something in New York? Or—"

Gage held up a hand. "Unless you were gonna say automating an apple orchard, quit guessing."

"Wait, the job up north? You were mocking that offer last week. You said big city or nothing. You said it was a job for a sixteen-year-old—"

He shrugged. "They agreed to the salary I wanted, and I'm starting a week from Monday."

"Wow." I shook my head in confusion. Money wasn't something Gage had to worry about anymore, I would have thought, since his share of the treasure was more than enough to carry him even if he didn't work for a decade, but it was none of my business. "Congrats! We're gonna miss you around here, though. What made you change your mind?"

"Eh. It's short-term, it's easy money, and it's only a few hours from New York City, so it's within driving distance for interviews. It'll pop my 'real job' cherry and make my resume look less like a blank page." He shrugged again. "Plus, the whole state is covered by trees, and everyone knows where there are trees, there are lumberjacks." He wiggled his eyebrows. "I have an affinity for lumberjacks."

"Samesies," Lorenna agreed wistfully.

"Have you told Rafe yet?" I asked.

"Nope. I'm gonna tell everyone tomorrow at Dad's barbecue. But Rafe'll be fine. He's chilled out a lot in the last year." He nudged my arm and smiled in a way that made it impossible not to smile back. "He's still boring as fuck though."

"Don't know if I like you being hundreds of miles from the Key, Gagey," Lorenna lamented. "What am I gonna do if my e-reader freezes while I'm reading again?"

"Um. Call customer service and arrange for them to fix it?" Gage suggested.

"But they're gonna be way more judgmental than you are about my Winchester brothers fanfic habits."

"Nonsense! They couldn't possibly be, Miss Lorenna!" Gage said with such an innocent expression that Lorenna patted his hand indulgently and let the meaning of his words sail right over her head.

He winked at me, and I coughed to cover a laugh. Gage was easy to underestimate. I just hoped the apple orchard lumberjacks were ready for him.

But my concern for our northern neighbors and Gage's career and... well, basically *everything*... evaporated when I glimpsed a familiar dark head threading its way through the crowd.

Despite the year we'd spent "shacking up," as Lorenna called it, despite all the years I'd loved him before that, my stomach still flipped over every time Rafael Goodman was in my vicinity. I was pretty sure it always would.

"Hey there, handsome," I said. "I thought you were gonna be late to—"

I cut off as Rafe's two hands came up to cradle my jaw and tenderly hold me in place for a kiss that sent a jolt of electricity to my bloodstream. When he pulled away a long moment later, I swayed toward him with my hand on his waist to get another taste, completely forgetting where we were, who was around us, and where my half-drunk mead had gone.

I wasn't entirely sure what my name was either.

"Gratuitous PDA is gratuitous." Gage sighed. "Aim, let's go chat with Dr. Dave. He looks lonely."

"Hey, baby," Rafe greeted me belatedly once we were alone. He ran his thumb over my bottom lip. "Loved that last song."

"Yeah?" I blinked dazedly, trying to remember the last song. Or any song. "Oh, yeah!" I felt my smile grow all syrupy sweet of its own volition but couldn't bring myself to care. "Something new I've been playing around with. Can you guess what it was about?"

"Mmm. I don't have to guess—I *know*. My close personal friend Jayd Rollins wrote that one about a frustrated tour boat operator who finally pulled his head out of his ass and told the man he loved how he really felt. Fun fact: that song was originally meant to be sung in rounds with an electric accordion solo."

Laughter welled up inside me, the kind that came from knowing without a shadow of a doubt that my worst day with this man was better than my best day without him. I'd gotten kinda used to that feeling.

"Is that so? Because I thought it was about a singer who realizes he'd rather pull *his* head out of his ass and spend his time with the man of his dreams than just sing songs about it." I bit my lip. "I envisioned it as all acoustic guitar, no accordion."

"Pfft." Rafe snorted. "That's just crazy talk. And not to say you're singing it wrong or whatever, but the song is *way* too peppy without the gravitas of the accordion." He hooked his thumbs through the back loops of my jeans.

"You're a genius. What would I do without you?" I asked, only mostly kidding.

"You won't have to find out, 'cause you're stuck with me for good," Rafe said, not kidding at all. "Now kiss me again."

I started to lift my hand up to cup Rafe's neck... and blinked in confusion when I realized I was still holding my guitar. *Jesus*. I was gone for this man, and that wasn't in doubt, but this was *too* far gone, even for me.

And of course, Rafe witnessed the whole thing. His shoulders shook with laughter as he pressed his forehead to mine.

I grabbed his hand and towed him past the table filled with our friends and family so I could settle my guitar in the case I'd left on the stage.

"I thought you were gonna be late tonight," I said, glossing over the whole loss-of-all-situational-awareness thing.

"I was, but we finished our meeting early. I told them tonight was special." Rafe boosted himself up to sit on the edge of the stage with his legs dangling off the edge.

"Tonight is?" I laid Vega in its case and turned back to him. "What's tonight?"

It was late August, and as far as I knew, we didn't have a single thing on the calendar except a cookout at his dad's house the next day... and the Extravaganza the following weekend, obviously.

Rafe fake-gasped. "It's our anniversary, boyfriend."

I had a minute of low-key panic before realizing he was mistaken. "Uh. It's super not. The Extravaganza is next weekend. That's our anniversary."

I knew this because I had huge plans for Saturday night when I played the Extravaganza's headline show. As in, monumental, down-on-one-knee, ring-in-a-box plans, which I'd only managed to keep from Rafe by not telling a single soul on the island about them.

"But we didn't get together at the Extravaganza," Rafe informed me. "We got together long before that. In Dry Hump, remember? You might recall that a song was karaoke-d? Blow jobs were exchanged?"

My fingers tingled hot and cold, and my dick perked up at the memory.

"I seem to vaguely recall that." I cleared my throat. "But we weren't together-together then. That wasn't our anniversary, it was our... our *sexiversary*."

"So you're saying you weren't all in from the first minute?"

I opened my mouth, then closed it and pretended to be very busy buffing the body of my guitar with the hem of my T-shirt. He was not wrong. But I also would not tell him he was right. Sappy as we were, we were still competitive. Arguably even more so nowadays.

And yet, if celebratory anniversary blow jobs were on the table... well, a man could be flexible.

"Whatever. How were you, um... thinking we should observe this sexiversary? Because there's an employee dressing room backstage, and I have a key—"

"Ah, romance." Rafe clapped a hand to his heart and gave me a soulful look. "Every day with lyrical legend Jayd Rollins is hearts and rainbows—"

I scowled. "*Sexiversary*, remember? The romance is next week, baby."

"Is it?" He lifted one eyebrow. "Do tell."

"What? No! I don't know. Hypothetically," I lied quickly. "Back to your sexiversary plans."

He grabbed my wrist and pulled me between his knees. "We're not calling it that," he warned severely.

"Calling our sexiversary a sexiversary? Oh, I think we are. In fact, I'll write a song all about it, and that'll make it official. What rhymes with 'mighty cock'?"

Rafe grunted. "This better be a song you only sing for me."

"Hmm," I teased. "I *suppose* I could be induced to give you a private concert. If you're nice to me."

The banked heat in his eyes flared hotter, and he jumped down from the stage. "Come on."

"Come on where?" I laughed. "I was kidding about the back room."

Mostly.

"I know." He tugged on my hand.

"And I have a second set to play," I reminded him, tugging back. "Not to mention my sister and your brothers are here" —I gestured to their tables—"and…"

"*And,* I may have informed Bobo that you could only do one set tonight."

My jaw dropped. "You did? What for?"

"And also informed your sister and my family that we'd be leaving early. As in now."

"Wait, really?"

"Yup. We'll see them tomorrow." He shrugged. "And tonight's not just our anniv—"

"Sexiversary," I insisted. And I would die on this hill, because otherwise I'd timed my proposal for the wrong day, and that would be unacceptable.

Rafe rolled his eyes and tugged me against him. "It's also a clear night with no moon. The perfect time for a boat ride under the stars."

"Oh," I breathed. "Damn it, you're going to make our sexiversary more romantic than our anniversary."

He rolled his lips together, laughter in his eyes. "Mmmm. Wait and see. It occurred to me that we still have a whole bunch of your fantasies to work on."

My heart beat triple time. I had about as many fantasies of me and Rafe as I had song lyrics floating through my brain, which was to say a truly distracting number these days. And whenever I even *inhaled* near tequila, I spilled them all to Rafe.

I couldn't imagine which one he was talking about for tonight, but it truly didn't matter. I really was all in. Just as I had been a year ago.

"Beale and Toby are giving Aimee and Dave a ride back to our place," Rafe whispered in my ear. His breath made me shiver. "Boat's waiting at the dock. I packed a picnic."

"You're such a planner," I accused.

"You know it."

I did. And I loved it. A lot.

"So what do you say?" he asked. "You, me, private concert under the stars? We can do anything you want."

As I stared up into his eyes, I remembered the two of us in another summer, in another whole lifetime.

Jay, if you could have anything in the world, what would it be?

I looped my hands around his neck, anchoring myself in the warm reality of him, and I knew I already had what I wanted, and it was messy and off-key and perfectly right.

"I say... I'll go anywhere with you, Rafe Goodman." I leaned in closer and whispered in his ear, "And twenty bucks says I can get to the boat faster than you can."

Want to see how sweet, snarky Gage finally gets his HEA? Grab <u>Pick Me</u>*, book one in the Sunday Brother series, here:* https://readerlinks.com/l/3037778

And if you're looking for another opposites attract, small town road trip romance (plus if you want to see more of Oak!), preorder The Pretenders of Copper County *here: https://mybook.to/ThePretendersMayArcher*

ABOUT MAY ARCHER

May is an M/M author who lives in Boston. She spends her days planning vacations, mainlining diet soda, avoiding the gym, reading M/M romance, and when all other forms of procrastination fail, writing it.

Visit her website at mayarcher.com to sign up for her newsletter to hear about sales and upcoming releases, freebies and behind the scenes info and more! Or join her Facebook group, Club May!

facebook.com/may.archer.author

instagram.com/mayarcherauthor

amazon.com/May-Archer/e/B075JQVGLX

patreon.com/MayArcherRomance

bookbub.com/authors/may-archer

ALSO BY MAY ARCHER

Get my <u>New Release Alerts</u>

Join me on Patreon

Follow me Everywhere Else

<u>Love in O'Leary Series</u>

<u>Whispering Key Series</u>

<u>The Sunday Brothers Series</u>

<u>Copper County Series</u>

<u>The Way Home Series</u>

<u>Licking Thicket Series</u>

(cowritten with Lucy Lennox)

<u>Champion Security Series</u>

(cowritten with Lucy Lennox)

<u>Honeybridge Series</u>

(cowritten with Lucy Lennox)

For a comprehensive list of titles, audio samples, freebies, suggested reading order, and more, visit my website at www. MayArcher.com!

www.ingramcontent.com/pod-product-compliance
Lightning Source LLC
Chambersburg PA
CBHW020347010826
48973CB00005B/1312